Also by Bud Fussell
From Indigo Sea Press

Destiny

Mixed Emotions

Redemption

Scoundrel

Serenity

Shepherds

That One Night

Towers

Whirlwind

indigoseapress.com

A Second Chance

By

Bud Fussell

Deep Indigo Books
Published by Indigo Sea Press
Winston-Salem

Deep Indigo Books
Indigo Sea Press
PO Box 26701
Winston-Salem, NC 27114

For information regarding bulk purchases of this book,
digital purchase and special discounts, please contact the publisher
at indigoseapress@gmail.com

Cover design by Pan Morelli
Manufactured in the United States of America
ISBN 978-1-63066-501-2

Chapter One

The late afternoon was warm, and a gentle breeze rustled the leaves on the trees, and the upcoming sunset over Read's Lake looked as if it was a beautiful painting. A nice bass jumped about thirty feet in front of the bench where Amy and Max were sitting, and Max squeezed her hand, and said, "That was a good one."

She said, "Maybe you ought to come out here after school tomorrow and try to catch it."

"I may just do that."

Amy asked, "Are you about ready to go?"

"Yeah, I guess so. When are we going to talk about what we've been talking about?"

"About getting married?"

He asked, "What did you think I was asking about?"

She said, "Are you really sure you want to do it?"

"Are you not sure?"

"Yeah. I'm sure. I love you, Max, and I want to be your wife. I just think it's gonna be hard, since we're both still in high school."

"Anything worthwhile is usually hard. Why don't we meet out here tomorrow afternoon and talk about it?"

"Okay. Ready to go?"

They held hands and walked up to the road where they were parked and lightly kissed before getting into their cars and going home; Amy to her house and Max to his.

At lunch the next day, Max told Amy, "We can't meet this evening. I saw Coach Perkins, and he said we're going to have a late football practice this afternoon because of the game tomorrow night with Bradley, and they're our biggest rival."

"That's alright. I've got Cheerleading practice, too."

They didn't see each other anymore that day, but they

1

talked on the phone that night. The next day, being game day, they were kept apart again all day.

The game was a real nail-biter. Bradley led for most of the game and was ahead twenty-four to twenty-one with three minutes to go in the fourth quarter. Bradley had the ball with second down and six yards to go when Neal Marler knocked the ball loose and Northpoint recovered on Bradley's thirty-four-yard-line.

On first down, the quarterback, Dub Findlay, gave the ball to Max, and he was tackled for a yard loss. On second down, Dub threw a short pass in the flat to Sonny Parsons for four yards, making it third and seven. On third down, he threw the identical pass to the left flat, and Wes Parker grabbed it for three yards, making it fourth down and four yards to go.

In the huddle, Max told Dub, "Their right tackle is playing off his spot, and I think I can get by him if you'll give me the ball." This was not the play the coach called but Dub was confident that if Max said he could get by him, then he felt that he could do it.

With only a minute and a half left in the game, they weren't about to punt, so they lined up to either run or pass on fourth down. That one play might decide the game.

Max lined up at right end, and when Dub raised his foot to signal to the center to snap the ball, he pulled from right end and Dub handed him the ball as he passed by him on the way to visit Bradley's right tackle. Sure enough, the tackle was out of position just enough for Max to get by him, and after a real cool move on the defensive back, he ran the ball into the end zone for a touchdown.

The extra point was good, and Northpoint was ahead twenty-eight to twenty-four. There was still one minute to play, and Bradley had to have a touchdown to win; a field goal wouldn't do it.

Bradley made a valiant effort to score in that last minute, but the clock was against them, and they fell to Northpoint, twenty-eight to twenty-four.

Max was the hero of the game because of that last touchdown, and everybody tried to shake his hand after the game to congratulate him. Finally, he was able to get to the locker room with his teammates where the celebration continued for quite a while.

After he had changed into his civilian clothes, he left the locker room and saw Amy waiting for him at the gate. When he reached her, she hugged him and told him what a good game she thought he played.

He asked her, "You wanna go to the El Rancho and get something to eat?"

"Yeah, that sounds good."

"I think some of the guys are going over there."

"Good. Is Dub going?"

"I think so. I think he has a date with Charlotte."

"Really? I've been hoping that they would get together."

"Well, you got your wish."

"I thought he played a good game tonight, didn't you?"

"Yeah, he did okay."

Six team members were at the El Rancho after the game. Four had dates, but they included the two dateless members as though they had dates. Since there were ten of them, and since the restaurant didn't have any ten-place tables, three or four of the guys rearranged some of the tables and chairs to where they could all sit together.

That kind of after game get together was common, but that particular night was special because of who they beat. Bradley had defeated Northpoint every year for the past four years, and victory over them that night was especially sweet because none of the Northpoint players had ever beat Bradley until that game.

Everyone seemed to have a good time at the El Rancho, and the party broke up a little after eleven, and they all went their special ways. Max took Amy back to the parking lot at the football field to get her car, and they promised they would see each other the next day.

Before she got out of the car, Max said, "I hope we can continue our talk tomorrow. Where do you want to meet?"

"Why don't you come out to the house, and we'll decide what we want to do after you get there."

"Okay. About noon?"

"That's good."

"Okay. I'm gonna head home. I'm pretty tired. That was a pretty tough game."

"Well, it was a good one, and you were especially good tonight. I wonder if any college scouts were there."

"Coach Perkins said there were."

"Maybe your play tonight locked up a scholarship for you."

"I wish that would be the case. Gotta go. I love you." They kissed goodnight, and he left for home.

When Max got to Amy's the next day, her parents and little brother were all at home. They welcomed him, and her Mom and little brother were extra hospitable, but her Dad was a little more reserved. He acted as if he liked Max okay, but he never acted as though he was a big fan. That was the way it was from the very beginning of his and Amy's relationship; he was polite, but he was not overly friendly, and Max wondered if they would ever find something in common.

Her Mother, on the other hand, was just the opposite. She acted as though Max were her own son, and she made him feel that way.

Then, there was Stevie, her little brother. He was fourteen, and played on the Junior high football team, and according to Max, he was a good player, and he worshipped Max. Max could do no wrong in Stevie's eyes.

After Max had been there for a few minutes, he asked Amy, "Did you eat any breakfast?"

"A little. I had an English muffin."

"Are you hungry?"

"I'm starving."

"How about if we go to Signal Garden and get one of their good milkshakes?"

"Sounds good to me," at which time Stevie said, "I love their milkshakes."

Max smiled and said, "Are you ready?"

Stevie replied, "I'm ready."

"Well, go tell your Mom that you're going with us, and tell her where we're going, okay?"

"Okay. Be right back."

Signal Garden was an unusual place. It was built over Valdeau Creek, and the water flowed under the restaurant, making for a good conversation starter for new customers as well as a nice atmosphere for veteran patrons.

When they sat down, Max asked, "What are you going to get, Honey?"

"I think I'm going to get some fries and a chocolate milkshake."

"No Burger or anything with the fries?"

"No. Just fries and a shake."

At that time a waitress came and asked for their order. Max said, "My friend here just wants an order of French fries and a chocolate milkshake. Stevie, what do you want?"

Stevie said, "I just want a milkshake."

Max said, "Okay," and told the waitress, "I want a cheeseburger and a Coke, please."

While they were waiting for their food, and later, while they ate, they talked non-stop. Stevie was so into football and was in the company of arguably the best player at Northpoint, all he wanted to talk about was football. Max accommodated him with inside stories of the game the night before as well as some of the information they had found about the college scouts that were at the game; some of whom he hoped would be in touch with him about a scholarship to some good school.

After an hour or an hour-and-a-half, Amy said, "Why don't we go?"

"Where do you want to go?" Max asked.

"Well, if we're going to go out tonight, I would like to spend some time with Mom this afternoon. Do you mind?"

"I don't mind at all. I probably need to spend some time with my parents. Good idea, Amy. What are we going to do tonight? Any ideas?"

She looked to see if Stevie was paying any attention to her, and when she thought he wasn't, she said, "I thought you were wanting to talk about things."

"Right. I do. Where? Reads Lake?"

"If that suits you. It's beautiful out there; and romantic."

"Why don't I pick you up around seven o'clock? Will you have eaten by then?"

"I think so. If I haven't, you can come in and eat with us."

"Yeah. I'm sure your Daddy would like that."

"He would. He likes you."

"Yeah. Right."

"He does like you. Ask Stevie."

"I'm not going to put Stevie on the spot. He's my Buddy."

"Okay, but take my word for it. He likes you."

"Alright, I'll take your word for it."

Pretty soon after they got through arguing about whether Amy's Dad liked Max, they reached her house, and she and Stevie got out. She said, "I'll see you tonight," and Stevie said, "Thanks, Max."

"Okay, Sport. I'll see you."

Max's Mom was late with dinner, and Max didn't want to leave without eating, so when she put the food on the table he filled a plate and gulped it down. In a flash, he got up, kissed his Mother and said, "It was delicious, Mother. I've got to go. I'm going to be late," and he ran out the front door.

He didn't get to Amy's house until seven fifteen, and she was just finishing helping her Mother with the dishes. When she saw him, she put her rag down and said, "Mother, Max is here. I need to go, okay?"

"Okay, Honey. You all have a good time."

They got into Max's Jeep, and Max confirmed what they had said earlier by asking, "Are we going to Read's Lake?"

"That's what we said; yeah."

It was only a few minutes ride to the lake, and as they had hoped, there wasn't anybody else there. They got out of the car and walked down to the bench where they usually sat when they came to the lake.

Holding hands, they sat down, and before they could begin their conversation, Amy asked, "Max, do you think we're doing the right thing?"

"Do you not think we are?"

"I'm not sure. I laid awake all night last night thinking about it. What bothers me is that we are both still in high school, neither one of us has a job, and we don't have a place to live. Does that not bother you?"

"It does, but I feel that we can work around those things if we try."

"How?"

"I'm not sure right now. All I know is that we both want to go beyond just kissing, and earlier in our relationship, we agreed that we wouldn't go beyond that until we got married, and we've honored that. Do you want to break that rule?"

"No, I don't. I believe God will punish us if we do. Do you want to break it?"

"No. All I know is that my hormones are raging."

"Mine too."

Max said, "I've been thinking of some ways we might can make it work. Do you want to hear them?"

"Yeah. I hope it's something good."

"Okay, see what you think about this. I know it's far from perfect, but it would be a way we could be together some. What would you think about getting married and keeping it a

7

secret until we graduate? Then, we can tell our parents. We will see each other at school every day, and on weekends we can be together. Do you think that would work?"

"I don't know. What if somebody finds out about it?"

"We'll just have to be extra careful."

"But what if they do?"

"I don't know. We'll just have to ask them not to tell our parents, but if they do, we'll just have to deal with it. You know, there are two other couples in our school that are already married."

"I know, and I'm wondering how they work it."

"I think Jim and Charlyn live with Charlyn's parents, and I don't know about the other couple."

Amy asked, "Would your parents let us live with them? I don't think mine would."

"I don't know. They might, but I think the secret way is the best way right now."

"What do you think? Do you want to get married?"

"Yeah, I do. When and where are you thinking about?"

"Well, week after next is an open date for us in football, and I think that would be a good time. We could go down to Ringgold, and after we're married, we could go down to Atlanta for the rest of the weekend. Do you think you can get Sissy to be your alibi for the weekend?"

"I'm sure I can. Don't we need some people to go with us as witnesses?"

"We should, but I'm afraid if we do, then they'll know we're married and might unintentionally let it slip sometime. The Justice of the Peace should have some people that he uses for that."

Amy ask him, "When are you thinking; Friday night?"

"Yeah, and that way we can have Friday night and Saturday night and half a day Sunday to be together. We can come home Sunday afternoon and resume our normal lives, and we'll probably both be smiling."

She asked, "You think?"

He said, "Yeah, I think. I know I will, and I'll bet you will, too."

"I probably will. I can't wait."

"Oh, another thing, Amy; since we're going to keep our marriage a secret, I can't get you a ring. Does that matter to you?

"No, I'll have you. I don't need a ring."

"Okay, now I know what you're wanting to do about college. I know you want to be a Veterinarian, and you want to go to the University of Illinois. What if I get a scholarship? It's unlikely it would be at Illinois. What will we do?"

"I haven't thought about that. I don't know what we'll do. I guess if you get a scholarship, then I'll just have to go to a school close to you that has a Veterinary school. I really do want to be a vet."

"You would do that for me?"

"I'd do anything for you. Don't you know that?"

From that point on, that night, they stayed at the lake for a long time, just talking and occasionally smooching a little. Since they had made their plans to wed, both of them were kind of nervous, and they weren't in the mood to do much of anything. Amy's curfew wasn't until eleven thirty, but they decided to go home early, and Max took her home a little after ten, much to the delight of her parents.

They didn't see each other Sunday because Amy's parents had promised her Grandmother that they would go to Manchester to see her, and her Dad wanted Amy to go with them.

Everything was normal at school the next week. Amy and Max had classes seven periods each day, then after school, Max had football practice, and Amy had cheerleading practice. That is; he had football Monday through Thursday, and she had practice the same days. Then, the football game was on Friday night. Date night was on Friday night after the game and then on Saturday and Sunday afternoon.

The week after that, things seemed to be normal on Monday and Tuesday. Then on Wednesday, Max told Amy they should start laying the groundwork for what they were going to do from Friday night until Sunday.

It was easy for him. All he had to do was to tell his parents he was going to Atlanta to the fair, and he would be staying at one of his friend's house until Sunday. It was harder for Amy, but not as hard as it would have been had her parents not trusted her.

She asked Sissy to go home with her after school Wednesday afternoon, and she told her Mother that Sissy wanted her to go to Atlanta with her and her parents Friday after school. She said they would be back Sunday afternoon.

She had to confide in Sissy about going to Atlanta with Max, but she didn't tell her that they were going to get married. She trusted Sissy and didn't think she would say anything, but it was like Max said; anyone who knows about the marriage could inadvertently say something and not realize what they had done.

Chapter Two

Thursday and Friday passed without Amy even realizing she was living in them. It wasn't until lunchtime Friday when Max sat down with her and asked, "Are you ready for the big night?"

It was then that she realized that time was nearly up for her teenage life as she knew it, and in a matter of hours she would be a married woman. She asked herself, *can I do this? What will my parents say if they find out? Do I love Max enough? Can I spend the rest of my life with him? Will this affect my becoming a Veterinarian? Are we doing the right thing?* Those, and a hundred other things went through her mind before she realized that marrying Max was the most important thing in her life right then, and she snapped out of the trance she was in and transformed from a sense of doubt to a sense of excitement.

She and Sissy had English together right after lunch, and when they got to their room, Amy told her that she would be ready to leave around four thirty if she could pick her up at that time. Max had a white Jeep that was easily recognized, so they decided that Sissy would take Amy to meet him south of town to avoid the possibility of her Dad or some friend close to them seeing them.

Sissy picked Amy up at four thirty like Amy said and took her to meet Max, just off Interstate seventy-five, in the parking lot of the Best Western Motel in East Ridge. They transferred Amy's things to Max's Jeep and were on their way in a matter of three to five minutes.

When they got back on the Interstate, Amy asked Max, "Do you know where to go?"

"No, but I thought I'd stop at a gas station at the next exit and try to find a phone book to give us the address of a Justice of the Peace. We'll be in Georgia, then, and they should have a Ringgold phone directory."

11

There were two J.P.'s listed in the phone directory, and Max wrote both of them down. Then he went into the gas station and asked directions to both of them. One was just a short distance from the Interstate, so he chose that one and, in about five minutes, they were there.

When he went around to open the door for Amy, he noticed that her face was white as a sheet, and he asked her, "Do you still want to do this? If you don't, we can wait until another time."

"No, I want to do it now. I guess I'm just a little nervous."

"Okay. Let's go inside and get the man to tell us that we're now one. "

She asked, "Are you scared?"

He answered, "Maybe a little."

They held hands and walked up the sidewalk to the door. Inside, the receptionist was getting ready to leave for the day. She was supposed to get off at five o'clock, and it was then almost five thirty, but she asked if she could help them.

Max said, "We would like to see the Justice of the Peace, if he's here."

"He's here. Can I tell him what you want to see him for?"

"We want to get married."

The receptionist smiled and pointed to some chairs and said, "Have a seat right here, and I'll see if he can do it."

In a minute, she came back out with Justice Freeman, and he said, "My name is Harold Freeman," and Max said, "I'm Max Norwood, and this is Amy Hatcher."

Justice Freeman asked, "Do you have a license?"

"Yes sir," Max said, and he handed him the marriage license.

The Justice asked, "You didn't bring anyone to stand up for you?"

Max answered, "No sir. It's kind of a secret."

"Oh, I see," and he asked the receptionist, "Marilyn, do you have time to stay and witness the marriage of this couple?"

"Yes sir. I can stay."

Then he asked Marilyn, "Has Ed left yet?"

"I don't think so."

"Would you please go in the back and tell him to come up here?"

"Yes sir. I'll be right back."

In a minute, the pair came into where Amy, Max, and the J.P. were.

Then, Justice Freeman said, "Okay, Amy and Max; you stand right here," and he pointed to where he wanted them to stand. Then, he said, "Marilyn, I don't have to tell you and Ed where to stand. You've done this so much, the floor probably has imprints of your feet where you've stood so many times."

When everyone was in their places, Justice Freeman began to read the marriage vows. When he came to the places where he asked Max and Amy if they would take the other to be their lawfully wedded bride and groom, they both said, "I do."

Justice Freeman asked Max if he wanted to kiss his bride, and Max said, "Yes sir," and he and Amy did a short kiss.

When Marilyn told them how much the charge was, Max was embarrassed to say, he had forgot to bring his checkbook, but Amy said, "That's okay," and she asked Marilyn if they took credit cards. When she said they did, she gave her her card, and Marilyn swiped it.

As Amy was signing the receipt, Justice Freeman came over and congratulated her and Max and wished them good luck. He called Amy Mrs. Norwood for the first time. She turned around and shook hands with him, and then she shook hands with Marilyn and Ed, and due to the excitement, she forgot to pick up her credit card.

On the way to Atlanta, they acted silly like a couple of kids would and couldn't wait to get into a motel where they could truly express their love for each other. Amy asked, "Do you know where we're going to stay?"

"No. We'll just have to stop at a nice place and get a room. It shouldn't be a problem."

"What if the place we stop is full?"

"Then we'll go to another one."

After stopping at three motels and being told that there were no vacancies, they were finally able to find a fairly nice place that had a vacant room. Max registered, and they went up to room three nineteen. After they decided it was a nice room, and they would stay there for two nights, they went back downstairs and unloaded the Jeep. When they got back to the room, Max asked Amy if she was hungry.

"I'm starved. Do you have any idea where we can eat?"

"I saw some signs on the Interstate as we were getting off to come here that showed several places right around here. Why don't we go see what we can find?"

"Okay. I haven't had anything to eat all day."

"Why didn't you eat?"

"I was too nervous."

Max turned right out of the parking lot and right away they were passing restaurants. He said, "When you see something you like, tell me, and we'll stop."

In about one minute, she said, "There's a Mexican restaurant. Let's go there."

The parking lot was pretty full, but they found a spot and parked. They went in and as in most Mexican restaurants, someone put down a bowl of chips and two dishes of salsa for them to munch on while they decided what they were going to eat. Both of them liked chimichangas, and that's what they ordered. The plates consisted of two chimichangas with salad and rice and refried beans. That was just what the doctor ordered. They ate 'til they were full, and Max had to help Amy finish hers, since there was so much food.

They paid at the cash register and went to the Jeep. Since it was such a short distance to the motel, it didn't take but a minute or two to get there. Max found a parking place closer to the entrance than they had before they went to dinner, so he parked there.

They didn't see the elevator when they first got there and used the stairs each time they went up or down, but that time, Amy spotted the elevator, and they rode it up to the third floor.

When they got to their room, they both needed to use the bathroom, and Amy went first. Max went when she came out, and then, they both sat on the side of the bed and talked. Since that was the first time for both of them, the air was filled with tension, but finally, Max made a move. He put his arms around her and kissed her like never before. She responded, and they laid back on the bed in a passionate lock.

He began to undo her clothes, and she raised up and pulled the sheet and spread over them. She began to undo his, and pretty soon they were both undressed under the covers, and it wasn't long until the marriage was fully consummated.

After a while, Amy got up and said she wanted to put on her gown. She went to the bathroom and brushed her teeth before putting her gown on, and then she came back to bed with Max after turning off the lights and tv.

"You've absolutely worn me out," she told Max. "I think we need to get some sleep. We can start over in the morning."

"Are you sure?"

"Yes. I am. Come on. Let's get some sleep."

"Okay, Party Pooper."

"I'm not a Party Pooper. I'm just tired."

"I know you're not. I'm tired, too. Let me go to the bathroom, and we'll snuggle up while we sleep. You want to?"

"I definitely do. Hurry up."

He went back to bed and they went to sleep in each other's arms. Both of them must have been really tired because neither one woke up all night. About six o'clock, Max woke up and went to the bathroom. He went back to bed and woke Amy up. She got up and went to the bathroom and brushed her teeth before going back to bed.

When she laid back down, Max said, "Hi, Mrs. Norwood. You want to fool around?"

"I'll try. You like to have ruined me last night."

"How did I do that?"

"You've got to remember; I've never done that before, and we did it so much, I'm sore this morning."

"I'm sorry. Does that mean we're not going to do anything all day?"

"No. I just need to take it easy for a little bit. I'll be ready again after a while."

"They have a continental breakfast downstairs. Are you hungry?"

"A little. Are you?"

"Yeah. I am. Why don't we go down and get something?"

The motel had a pretty good breakfast, and Max ate like a football player. Amy, on the other hand only had orange juice and a blueberry muffin.

While they were at breakfast, Max asked Amy, "I'll bet you didn't bring your swimsuit, did you?"

"No. I didn't know I would need one."

"I didn't bring one either, but it's so pretty and warm, it would be nice to go in the pool."

"Why don't we go out by the pool and just get some sun?"

"We can do that if you want to."

"Let's do. I don't want to just sit in the room all day. We can get some sun, and maybe this afternoon, if you want to, we can go to a mall."

He said, "We'll do what you want to, but I didn't know we came down here to go to the mall. I thought we came to make love to each other."

"We did, but we've got to take a break sometime."

Saturday finished out with Max pressing Amy to go to bed, and Amy resisting most of his attempts, but giving in to some of them. Before they checked out, Sunday, they spent the last hour or so loving. Before they left for home, they went downstairs and had some breakfast, and then they got in the Jeep and headed north.

On the way, Max asked, "Did you have a good time?"

"I did, Did you?"

"Yeah. I probably had a better time than you did." About that time, they saw a sign that said their home, Middleton, was only sixty miles away, and Max said, "I sure hate to see this weekend end, don't you?"

"I really do."

He said, "I guess I have to take you to Sissy's, don't I?"

"Yeah. She'll have to take me home. I'll be glad when we have our own home."

"Me too."

Sissy's car was parked in front of the house where she lived with her parents, and Max told Amy, "Before you go in, let's get your things out of the Jeep and put them in her car."

"Good idea," and they did just that.

When they had everything transferred, Max gave Amy a short kiss and told her he loved her, and he would see her the next day at school. He waited until Sissy came to the door before he left, and he waved at her as he got into his Jeep to go to his house.

Sissy took Amy home after Max left, and when she went into her house, there was an atmosphere unlike any she had ever experienced. Her Mother came into the room where she had just come into, and when she said, "Hi, Mother."

Her Mother started crying. Amy put her arms around her Mother's shoulder and asked, "What's wrong, Mother?"

"Your Daddy and I want to talk to you when he gets home. He's playing golf."

"Okay, but what's wrong?"

"We'll wait for your Daddy."

Amy knew in her own mind that they knew about her and Max, but how could they? They didn't tell anybody; not even Sissy, her best friend. It must be something else. In a minute, her younger brother, Stevie, came into the room, and she asked him, "Stevie, what's going on?"

"You got me. They've both been acting strange since yesterday."

She went to her room and put her things up and stayed in there, listening to music, and waiting for the ball to drop when her Daddy got home.

Finally, he came in about four thirty, and her Mother called her into the den where her Daddy was standing. He said, "Hi Amy. Sit down."

She did as he said, and then, he asked, "Where have you been this weekend?"

"Well, Mother and Stevie saw me leave with Sissy. Why do you ask?"

"Where did you go after you left here? Did you go somewhere with Max?"

"I saw him. Why?"

"Amy, we got a call yesterday from a Justice of the Peace's office in Ringgold, and they said you left your credit card down there. Why would they have your credit card? I can only think of one reason to go to a Justice of the Peace in Ringgold, Georgia, and that's to get married. Did you get married, Amy?"

She didn't answer. Instead, she just looked down at the floor.

"I asked you a question, young lady. Did you get married in Ringgold? Answer me."

She summoned up enough courage to blurt out, "Yes. Yes I did, and I'm happy about it. We wanted to keep it a secret until we got out of school, but that's spoiled now. I need to call Max and tell him."

"There's plenty of time for that later. Now, let me tell you what we're going to do."

"What are we going to do?"

"Have you ever heard the word Annul?"

"I think so, but I don't know what it means."

"It means if we're able to get this marriage annulled, then you won't be married anymore."

"How can you do that?"

"If you were older, there might would be a problem, but you're seventeen years old, and at your age, you have to have your parents sign for you to get married. This is for the best, Amy. Maybe later, after you're out of college, you can get married and have a full, satisfying life, but right now I'm not going to let you sacrifice your whole future. Don't you still want to be a vet?"

"Yes sir. I still want to be one."

"Well, it would be nearly impossible for you to become one if you're married before you get out of high school. I'm satisfied that annulment is the way to go on this, and I feel sure that later, you'll feel the same way. Now, I'm going to ask you to not see Max anymore for a while, at least until the annulment is completed."

"Daddy, I love him. I can't be around him at school and at ball games and other things without being with him. Can't we try to work out something other than an annulment?"

"I don't see how, Honey. An annulment will make the marriage disappear as if there never was one, and that is what we need."

She looked at her Mother and said, "Mother, can't you talk to him?"

"Darling, we have talked for two days about this, and I think your Daddy is right. You have a bright future ahead of you, if you'll just take advantage of it. We both like Max, but now is not the right time for you two to be married. If you all will just wait until you get out of college, I know, and I think you know that that will be much better."

Amy asked her Daddy, "Is that all?"

"I guess so."

At that, she ran back to her room and slammed the door behind her. She laid down on the bed and cried her eyes out. For the rest of the afternoon, every time she would pick up the phone to call Max, her Mother or Daddy would be there to watch her. Once, the phone rang, and her Mother answered, and Amy heard her say, "I'm sorry, she's not available right now." After that, she thought she would just have to wait and see him at school the next day to tell him what her parents were going to do.

The next morning, she got to school early in hopes that Max would be early, too. She desperately wanted to talk to him as soon as she could. Her wishes were realized when she saw him drive into the parking lot just minutes after she did. She ran out to meet him as he got out of the Jeep, and he said, "There's my bride. Good morning, Sweetheart."

"We've got to talk."

"Man, I've never seen you like this. What's the matter?"

"My parents know about our getting married and my Daddy says he's going to get it annulled. We can't do anything about it because I'm underage. If we had waited until I turn eighteen, they couldn't do anything about it."

"How did they find out?"

"I forgot to pick up my credit card at the Justice of the Peace's office, and they called my house to tell whoever that they had it. When Daddy heard it was the Justice of the Peace in Ringgold, Georgia, he put two and two together and knew we wouldn't be at a Justice of the Peace office for any other reason."

Max asked, "What are we going to do?"

"I don't know. If Daddy gets the marriage annulled, I guess we'll just have to go back to being boyfriend, girlfriend. Do you have any other suggestions?"

"Not right now, I'll have to think about it. I don't want to lose you, Amy."

"I don't want to lose you, either. I love you."

"Me too. I'll say this; we had a great weekend, didn't we?"

"We sure did."

The Annulment went through, and Amy's parents asked her not to see Max anymore because they thought it would make it harder on her to break away from him. Her Mother began driving her to school and picking her up after cheerleading practice every day. They were putting obstacles in their way to try and see each other every way they could. The only times that they could see each other one on one was during lunch in the school cafeteria each day.

One day, Max, very irritated, asked her, "How long are your parents going to keep this up? You're almost eighteen, and they can't tell you what to do then, can they?"

"I don't know, but while I'm only seventeen, I can't do anything about it."

"You're a senior in high school, but you parents treat you like you are in elementary school."

"I know, Sweetie, but have patience for a little longer. Maybe things will get better."

Northpoint won the football game Friday night, and as usual, when the players had changed in the locker room after the game, there were several people waiting at the gate to tell them what a good game they had played. Some were friends, some were family, and some were the player's dates. Amy was always there, but she was absent that night.

Max looked for her, but she never came, and he was so disappointed. He tried calling several times over the weekend, but Mrs. Hatcher always had a reason for Amy not being able to talk. Once, when he called, Amy's Daddy answered, and when he asked to speak to Amy, he hung up on him.

The usual lunchtime meetings were getting to be not so usual. Amy began to not show up at lunch, or else she would sometimes be sitting with some of her girlfriends instead of Max, and the five times a week lunches were beginning to be one or two times a week.

Max was beginning to get frustrated with the situation because he was very disappointed that Amy wasn't fighting for their right to be together. After all, they did get married, and in his eyes, the annulment was just a piece of paper.

Northpoint lost their football game by one point the next

Friday night, and all the team members were sick about it, especially Max. He caught a pass with just seconds to go, and it looked as though he was going to score, but the safety on the other team tackled him two yards short of the goal line, and time ran out.

After the game, he went to the gate to meet the folks who came to congratulate them, but, once again, Amy wasn't there. Sissy, Amy's friend was there to meet one of Max's teammates, and he went over to talk to her.

"Hi Sissy. How ya doing?"

"Hi Max. I'm fine."

He told her, "I don't know if you know what's going on between Amy and me, but I can't get through to her. Her parents won't let me talk to her on the phone, and after this loss tonight I really needed her, but she's not here. When you talk to her, will you please tell her to call me and tell her I love her. Will you do that for me, Sissy?"

"I will. I know she's having a hard time."

"She's not the only one. If you'll do this for me, Sissy, I'll really appreciate it. Be sure to tell her I love her, okay?"

"I'll tell her."

As he was leaving Sissy, he saw Amy riding away from the stadium with her Daddy, in his car.

Max spent all weekend hoping to hear from her, but she never called. He trusted Sissy to give her his message, and he felt sure she did, so what was he to think. After a torturous Saturday and Sunday, he came to the conclusion that Amy was going to acquiesce to her parents' wishes, leaving him to make a decision.

Sunday night he decided he would write Amy a letter, and if it didn't do any good, then he would try to move on with his life without her. He had never written a letter, so he didn't know how to go about it. All he knew was that he wanted to talk to her and to tell her how he felt, so he got a piece of paper and a pen and began to write. He had seen letters, and he knew what they were supposed to look like, so he began.

Dear Amy,

I always thought that when two people got married that they would stand by each other through thick and thin, but I guess that's not what you think. I've been calling you, and your parents won't let me talk to you. It looks like you would call me if you love me, and I don't know how you could change your feelings in just two weeks. If I don't hear from you after you get this letter, then I guess I'll move on and try to get you out of my mind. I want you to know one thing as I close this— I love you, and I'll never forget that weekend in Atlanta.

Max

He looked in the phone book and got her mailing address. After he addressed the envelope, he went to a mailbox and dropped it in, hoping that she would answer.

Monday was like most of the days the week before, but on Tuesday, he was sitting with some of his buddies at lunch, when Amy went up to him and said, "You want to sit over here with me?"

He immediately got up and followed her to a table that was empty, and they sat down. Before he could say anything, she said, "I got your letter, and I cried. Max, my parents are giving me such a hard time, I'm about to go crazy. I've wanted to talk to you and to see you, but they have been so close every minute, I haven't been able to. You said in your letter that you love me. Well, Sweetheart, I love you, too. I'll be eighteen in two more months, and we'll see what happens then. But in the meantime, I feel like a prisoner in my own house."

Max asked, "What do you think we can do?"

"I don't know of anything right now. It will probably be best if we just kind of wait and see what happens. Honestly, I'm so tired of trying to do things on my own and not being able to because of my parents, I'm to the point of not even trying anymore."

"How did you get my letter?"

"Yesterday, Mother went somewhere and didn't get home before she had to come pick me up. When we got home, she stopped by the mailbox, and I got the mail, and I saw the letter from you and held it out. When Mother saw me get the letter, she wanted to know what it was, and I told her it was for me, and she wanted me to give it to her. She was mad when I wouldn't do it. Oh yeah. You said in your letter that you would never forget our weekend in Atlanta. Well, I want you to know that I'll never forget it either. So far, that's been the highlight of my life, other than marrying you, of course."

He asked her, "Did Sissy give you my message after the ball game Friday night?"

"She told me Saturday. I didn't see her Friday night. She had a date."

Amy's parents kept a tight rein on her, and she was not able to even talk to Max if they had anything to do with it, but her Mother realized that she was a senior, a popular senior in high school, and should not be kept isolated from other kids. She encouraged her to get out and go to parties where she was invited, and even go on dates if some nice boys asked her out, as long as she and her Daddy knew the people and knew where she was going, but Amy wasn't interested.

The rest of the school year went on like that, and Amy and Max were both tired of all the hassle caused by her parents. Their love for each other seemed to fade somewhat, and they knew they had to go on with life and do what would ultimately make them happy.

Memphis State University offered Max a scholarship to play tight end for their football team, and Amy was accepted at the University of Tennessee, where she planned to major in biology and animal sciences. She still wanted to go to the University of Illinois School of Veterinary Medicine after she got her bachelor's degree.

Chapter Three

Max kept in pretty good shape, and after football season was over, he continued to work out. While he was still in school, he was able to use the school's workout machines, and when school let out for the summer, his coach let him continue to come to the gym and work out. As a result, he grew another inch and gained eleven pounds, making him a big six feet three inches and two hundred and twenty-one pounds.

He reported to Memphis State on August first to begin working out for the upcoming football season, and he was excited to become a Memphis Tiger. He was a tight end, and after they had worked out for a couple of days, he found out that he was number six on the list of tight ends. He thought to himself, *I may never get to play with five others in front of me. Maybe I should go somewhere else.*

On the morning of the third day, the Head Coach called for him to come into his office. When he got to his office, the coach said, "Have a seat, Max," and he sat down.

The coach then told him, "Max, we're glad you decided to come to Memphis State. I think you'll have a bright future here. You've grown over the summer, haven't you?

"Yes sir. A little."

I know at first glance, you probably think you're so far down the ladder that you'll be lucky if you ever get to play. Well, here's what we've got planned for you, Max. As you know, there are five or six tight ends in front of you, so we plan to redshirt you this year. Our two starters and our two backups are excellent players, but three of them are seniors and will graduate in the spring. This will leave you and two others to fight for two spots, and I've seen you play, so I feel confident that you will be able to start next year. In the meantime, as a redshirt freshman, you'll be able to learn our system and be ready for next season. Again, I'm glad you chose Memphis State. I think you'll love being a Tiger. Do you have any questions?"

"Yes sir. First, I appreciate you explaining about all the guys ahead of me. When I saw how many there were, I told myself that I'll probably never get to play, so thank you for telling me about that. I feel better now. Will you please explain what a redshirt is? I've heard that a redshirt can still play a few games. Is that right?"

"Yeah, it's possible to play up to four games as a redshirt."

"That's all I wanted to ask you. Thank you, sir."

"Your welcome."

He felt better when he went back to practice. He determined to work so hard that the coaches would have to put him in the four games he would be eligible for.

The Tigers were going to open their season against Murray State on August thirty first, and Max was excited to be a part of the team. Memphis State was not a Tennessee or Alabama, but it was a major college, and everything was altogether different than it was in high school. The professors even called their students Miss or Mister as if they were grown adults, and that took some getting used to. Max didn't think he had ever been called Mr. Norwood before.

He was assigned a room in the athletic dorm with a roommate named Austin Wayne. Since Austin's last name was Wayne, he went by Duke, like the movie star. Duke was a big boy from Meigs County, Tennessee, and his position was defensive tackle. He was six feet, six inches and weighed two hundred and ninety pounds, and he was also a freshman.

The two of them hit it off right away, and it got so that wherever one would go, the other would be right with him. Max was glad to find Duke because it helped with the homesickness he was sure to have, and he still hadn't gotten over Amy completely, even though it had been almost a year since their marriage and annulment.

A Second Chance

***

Amy's parents took her to Knoxville on Saturday, August thirty first and helped her get set up in Orange Hall at the University of Tennessee. She wanted to live in an apartment, but her parents wouldn't pay for one. Instead, they wanted her to live in a dormitory and have a roommate. They still didn't quite trust her after the episode last year with Max, and they weren't sure if she was completely over him

A nice young lady named Joyce Knox was assigned as her roommate, and Amy liked her immediately. Joyce was from Athens.

Amy's Mother and Daddy took her to school on the thirty first so she would have the weekend to get acquainted with her roommate and the University before classes started on September third. She was happy when she found out that Joyce was a biology major like her, and she felt that that would give them another thing in common. When they compared their schedules, they found that they were going to have some classes together, and that would give them a chance to study together, so it looked as if she might not be as unhappy as she thought she would be before she got there.

Of course, football was king, as far as most people in Tennessee were concerned, and Amy and Joyce naturally got caught up in the frenzy surrounding the Vols. The first game was on Saturday, August thirty first in Nashville against Wyoming, and neither Amy or Joyce went to that one, but the next game would be in Knoxville against Houston, and they both bought tickets for that one.

Amy and Joyce settled into school and had three classes together. Their dorm was just a short way from the library, and they spent quite a bit of time in there. Both of them were rushed to join a sorority, but neither of them had any desire to join one.

Joyce was slightly boy-hungry and was pretty receptive to hits by some of the guys. She accepted invitations to date from two or three guys, but Amy didn't go out until one night, Joyce put the pressure on, and she gave in and went out with a guy who was a friend of the one that Joyce was going out with. His name was Tom Marion, and he seemed to be very nice. He lived in Bristol.

The four went to the Rathskeller that night and had pizza. Joyce's date was named Craig, and he and Tom wanted beer, but neither one was twenty-one, so they couldn't buy one, and Amy was glad. She didn't drink and wouldn't have ordered beer anyway, but she was happy that the others weren't able to have it either.

Joyce had been out with Craig before, but Amy had just met Tom, and there were a lot of back and forth questions between the two, such as, "What is your major, Amy?"

"Veterinary Science. What's yours?"

"Business. Veterinary Science, huh? You must be pretty smart."

"I don't know about that. I've wanted t be a vet ever since I was a little girl, and the next eight years will tell whether I'm smart enough to make it, or if I'll have to do something else."

Tom said, "Well, my money is on you. You'll make a great Veterinarian."

"Thank you. I hope you're right."

The evening was surprisingly nice, and they all seemed to have a good time, and when they had finished eating their pizzas, Joyce's date asked, "What would you all like to do?"

Nobody seemed to have any ideas about something to do, so Joyce said, "Would you like to go to a movie?"

The guys weren't too happy about her suggestion, but she asked Amy, "Amy would you like to go to a movie?" She said, "Yeah. I'd like to go."

The guys were trapped. The girls wanted to see a movie, and they didn't, but since they had invited the girls out, and they wanted to see a movie, the guys gave in and drove out to West Hills and went to a theater, and surprisingly, they all enjoyed the picture. The movie was over at eleven o'clock, and both girls said they wanted to go home, so Joyce's date drove them back to the dorm. Joyce let her date kiss her goodnight, but Amy pushed Tom away and said, "Please don't," when he tried to kiss her. He acted surprised, but didn't insist.

Amy and Joyce got out of the car and walked to the entrance of the dorm and up to their room. When they got inside their room, Joyce asked, "Well, what did you think about Tom."

"I thought he was nice."

"Would you want to go out with him again?"

"I don't know. I'm not into dating very much right now. I doubt I would go out again; with anybody."

"Really? Why? Do you have a problem?"

"Yes and No."

"What does that mean?"

"It means that there is nothing wrong with me. Joyce, I'm going to tell you something that I have not even told my best friend at home. Last September, I was going with a boy and had been going with him for over a year. We were in love, and we decided to get married and keep it a secret until we got out of school. He played football, and one weekend, when they had an open date, we went down to Ringgold, Georgia after school on Friday of that week and had a Justice of the Peace marry us. We went to Atlanta and got a room and had the most glorious weekend anybody would ever want.

"Max had forgotten his checkbook, and I paid the Justice with my credit card. There was so much excitement after the ceremony that I forgot to pick up my credit card, and before we got back home Sunday, the J.P.'s office had called my house and told my parents that I had left my card down there. He didn't say I got married, but my Daddy put two and two together and knew there would only be one reason to go to a Justice of the Peace in Ringgold.

"From the minute I got home, my parents closed in on me and I was treated like a prisoner from then on. They took me to school every day and then picked me up. They wouldn't let me use the phone unless one of them was standing there. They wouldn't let Max talk to me when he called, and in general, they made my life a pure hell.

"I was able to see Max a few times in the lunchroom at school during lunch, but that's all I have seen him since we got married. My Daddy had our marriage annulled, so now, officially, I've never been married. I heard that Max got a football scholarship to Memphis State, and I'm up here where we can't see each other. We both still love each other, but we might not be able to get together again until we get out of college. So that's my story, and you're the only one I've ever told it to."

Joyce was in shock. She sat there with her mouth open and said, "Wow. That's awful, Amy. I had no idea. I hope you will be able to get things worked out sooner, rather than later. I feel privileged that you think enough of me to tell me this. Thank you so much."

Amy said, "I feel better now that I've told you my story. I've held it inside me for a year now, and I really needed to tell somebody. I'm glad you're here."

Joyce said, Sweetie, any time you need to talk about something, I'm here for you, and anything you tell me in confidence will stay with me in confidence."

Amy hugged her and said, "Thank you. Now, I think I'm going to go to bed."

"I am, too. I'm tired."

Amy devoted the rest of the school year to her studies, and she decided to go to summer school and to try and graduate in three years, if possible. And then, enroll in the University of Illinois School of Veterinary Sciences for four years.

She and Joyce were able to stay in the same dorm and stay roommates their sophomore year. Joyce didn't attend summer school, so Amy pulled slightly ahead of her in credits. In early September, the fall term began, and both girls really buckled down to their studies, and they both finished the first quarter with A's., then they got A's for the first semester.

When one considers four years for a bachelor's degree and four years for a Doctor of Veterinary medicine after the bachelor's, it takes a year longer to become a veterinarian than it does to become a medical doctor. Of course, a medical doctor has to go through an additional year of residency and another year of internship after their seven years of school, before they can begin their practice.

When Amy thought of eight years of college, she was overwhelmed, so she tried not to think of it that way. She preferred to think of just one year at a time, and that didn't seem to be so long. She had visions lots of times about treating animals after she became a vet, and how much money she would make, and that just made her drive harder.

One time, when school was on semester break, she went to a seminar conducted by some local veterinarians in Knoxville, and it made a huge impact on her. When she got to the dorm that evening, she told Joyce about it, since Joyce didn't go home for the break, and her excitement must have rubbed off because in a day or so, Joyce decided that she wanted to become a vet as well.

Both girls worked really hard the rest of the year, and as a result, they both made the Dean's List for their sophomore year.

Amy decided to go to summer school again, and the first term of summer school ended on July third. There was a five day break between the two terms, so since she wouldn't have to start the second term until July eight, she went home for a couple or three days, and Joyce went with her.

Max was really doing good in football. He had been redshirted as a freshman, but according to the rules, he was allowed to play in four games as a redshirt. He hustled so hard and was such a good player, his coaches let him play in all four games.

He enrolled in the NROTC in his freshman year and when he graduated, he would be a Second Lieutenant in the Marines. Becoming a Marine had been his dream since he was a small boy. His Dad was a Marine, and in Max's eyes, his Dad was America's greatest hero.

Being a member of the NROTC meant that he would have to serve four years of active duty after he graduated, and parts of his summers would be taken up with training, so eight years of his young life were pretty much accounted for. Between, school, football, and NROTC, he had very little free time, but he loved it, and his busy schedule was a great way to keep his mind off of Amy.

At the end of his sophomore year, he spent the last two weeks of May and the first two weeks of June at Marine camp, leaving him nearly six weeks before he had to return to football camp on August first. The coaches expected him in early July for weight training and quickness drills and other kinds of workouts, so his summer vacation would be cut short.

He decided to go back to Memphis on July sixth, and he knew Duke would be going then, too, so he called him and asked him to come to Middleton and spend two or three days and let him ride to Memphis with him.

Duke agreed and arrived at Max's on July third, and after introducing him to his family, Max took him around and showed him some of his old hangouts. It was late in the day when Duke got to Max's, so they stayed at home with his parents that evening.

The next day, July fourth, the two guys hung out at some

of Max's favorite places, but things were different; none of his old buddies were there. That afternoon, Max suggested that they go to El Rancho, everybody's favorite place when he was in school, and he was sure there would be a lot of people there that he knew, but he was wrong. There were a lot of people there, but most of them were younger.

He did see some of his old cronies, and they had a really nice reunion, eating barbeque and French fries and drinking cherry Cokes.

After he had been there for close to an hour, he looked up as the door opened, and he was shocked to see Amy walking in with her friend, Sissy. She didn't see him, and he watched her and Sissy go find a table. He didn't go over to her table right away. Instead, he remained at the table where he and Duke were sitting with two other friends of his.

He positioned his seat to where he could see her and to where she could see him. He continued talking to his buddies and took his eyes off her for a minute, and then, when he looked back around, she was staring at him. When she saw that he saw her, she smiled, and he gave her sort of a nonchalant wave and continued talking to his buddies. The whole time, his heart was nearly beating out of his chest.

When he felt enough time had passed since he first acknowledged her, he looked her way again, and she saw him looking. She motioned for him to come over to her table, and he excused himself from his buddies and went over. When he reached her table, he spoke to her and Sissy, and in the most facetious voice he could muster up, he asked, "Where's your Mother and Daddy?"

He didn't realize how hurtful his question was until he looked into her face and saw the hurt in her eyes. Amy said, "We don't do that anymore."

Max said, "That's a good thing. How have you been?"

"Fine. I'm at U.T. now, studying to hopefully be a veterinarian someday. I heard that you got a scholarship to

Memphis State. How is that working out?"

"Good. They redshirted me my freshman year, but this past year, I was a starter. I'm getting ready to go back day after tomorrow and work out until camp starts on August first. Oh yeah, I almost forgot; I'm in the NROTC too. When I graduate, I'll have to go into the active duty Marines for four years."

"Four years? That's how long I'll be in Veterinary school after I get out of U.T."

"Well, it looks as if we still have something in common."

"It does, doesn't it? Max, are you seeing anyone?"

"No, are you? For some reason I've still tried to be true to you. Silly, isn't it?"

She said, "No, I'm not seeing anyone, and no, you're not silly. I think you're sweet for thinking that way."

In a little more than a whisper, he asked, "Amy, do you ever think of the week when we were married and the weekend we spent in Atlanta?"

"I think about it all the time, and sometimes I cry when I think about it. How about you?"

"I think about it all the time, too. We're not very old, but up until now, that was the best weekend of my life. We could have had a lot more like that if it hadn't been for your Mother and Daddy."

"I know, but they were just doing what they thought was best for me."

When are you going back to Knoxville?"

"Day after tomorrow. I'm going to summer school, and the second term begins on July eighth."

"You're going to summer school?"

"Yeah. I'm trying to graduate in three years."

"Then what? Veterinary school?"

"Yeah, at the University of Illinois School of Veterinary Sciences."

"How long will you have to go there?"

"Four years. I should be out a year before you get out of the Marines."

"Then what?"

"I don't know. I'll probably try to get a job with some Veterinary Clinic, or I may possibly try to open my own practice. I just don't know at this point."

She asked, "What do you think you will do after you get out of the Marines?"

I really don't know. I have been thinking about making a career in the Marines, and then, I think no, I'd like to come home and be a football coach. It's all up in the air right now, and I don't have to rush. It's still six years until my enlistment is up. Let me ask you this, Amy?"

"What?"

"If there could be a way for me to transfer from Memphis to Knoxville, do you think we might could start again?"

"She paused and didn't say anything for several seconds, and then she said, "I don't know, Max. I'm still crazy about you, but it looks like our lives are going in two different directions, and we've been apart for two years now. Do you still have the same feelings that you had two years ago?"

"Boy, Amy, that's a hard one. I can't answer that. I know I still have feelings for you, but I've got to admit, the feelings are not as strong as they were then. Time has made them diminish, I guess. Do you still have the same feelings?"

"I don't think so. Like you, Max, I think time has made them weaker. My feelings are still very strong, but they're not the same."

Max said, "Listen, my roommate is with me. Do you care if I ask him to come over here?"

"That would be great. Did you say your roommate?"

"Yeah. We've been roomies for two years now, and he has become my best friend."

Sissy asked, "Which one is he?"

Max looked over to the table where he had been and asked,

35

"Do you see that big guy sitting next to Ben? That's him. Let me go get him," and he went over and got Duke.

They came back to Amy and Sissy's table, and Max introduced them to Duke, and Duke said, "So you're the famous Amy."

Sissy said, "Duke, you're a big one, and Max, you're bigger than you used to be, aren't you?"

Amy told Max, "You used to weigh a little over two hundred pounds when you were a senior. What do you weigh now?"

Max said, "You didn't say anything about me being taller. I grew an inch the summer after I graduated and gained about ten pounds. After I got to Memphis and started eating at the training table and working out, I gained another fifteen pounds, so now I'm six three and weigh two thirty-five. I'm small compared to my Buddy here. Tell these ladies how big you are, Duke."

"I'm six feet six inches tall, and I weigh two hundred and ninety pounds."

Max smiled and said, "I tell people that he's my bodyguard."

The four talked for a while longer, and then Sissy said, "I need to go. Are you ready, Amy? Max, it was sure good to see you again, and Duke, it was good to have met you."

As the girls were getting up to leave, Max said, "Wait a minute. You can't leave right now."

Sissy said, "Max, I've got to go. I have something I have to do this afternoon."

Max said, "Okay, I understand that. Could we get together tomorrow right here and have lunch together? I'm not through talking yet, and Amy, I need to see you. Sissy, I hope you will come, too. Will you all come back tomorrow?"

The girls looked at each other and asked each other about it, and finally, Amy said, "Okay, Max. I hope Sissy will come with me, but if she can't, I'll see you here at eleven thirty.

Duke, I'll see you then, too."

"Okay, ladies. I hope to see you tomorrow. Bye."

They all stood up, and Max and Amy slid their hands through the other's as a sign of affection.

The guys went back to the table where they had met Max's buddies, and his buddies said they had to go. They all shook hands and left at the same time. In the Jeep, Duke said, "So that's Amy. I can see why you hated to leave her. She's a doll. You know, Sissy's not bad, either."

Max said, "Sometime, I'll tell you a story about Amy and me."

"I can't wait to hear it."

They just sort of messed around the rest of the day and ate burgers and dogs with Max's parents. After supper, when it began to get dark, they went down to the high school and watched the fireworks.

The next morning, Max woke up, semi-excited, over the upcoming meeting with Amy. He got up at seven o'clock, but Duke slept in until almost nine. Max's Mother had made biscuits, and they ate biscuits with jelly; Max, two, and Duke, four. They didn't want to spoil their lunch because they would eat with Amy and Sissy a little later.

They left in plenty of time to meet the girls at the prescribed time, and on the way, Max told Duke, "Duke, I need to talk to Amy a little one on one when we get there. After we eat lunch, would you care to go somewhere with Sissy and leave us alone for a little while. We just need to try to get some things settled between us, and if you'll do that, it'll help me a lot."

"Consider it done, that is, if Sissy will go somewhere with me."

"She will. I think she likes you."

"I don't know about that, but I'll do my best."

"Thanks, Buddy."

Eleven thirty was the set time to meet, and they all got

there right on time. Max and Duke waited for Sissy to park her car, and they walked in together.

When they sat down at a table, they spent a few minutes talking about what the others did the day before, since it was the fourth of July, and then they ordered lunch.

The conversations during lunch were mostly just small talk, and Max tried to steer part of the conversation to some interesting things around town that would interest Duke, if he were to suggest to Sissy that she would take him there.

After lunch, Max picked up the check for all of them, and after they talked a little longer, when he caught Duke looking at him, and nobody else looking, he gave a nod to Duke. Then, Duke said, "Sissy, why don't you take me out to the river to see some of those things that Max talked about."

"Okay, I will, if you want me to. You want to go now?"

"Why don't we?"

Max said, "Amy and I will just wait on you. We have some things to talk about." He looked at Sissy and Duke and asked, "Is that alright with you guys?"

Duke said, "It is with me. That'll give Sissy and me a chance to get to know each other better.

They got up and left Amy and Max sitting at the table. As soon as they were out of earshot, Max said, "I'm sure glad we had this chance to see each other, Amy."

"Me too. I was shocked when I walked in the other day and saw you sitting there, and I didn't appreciate how you asked where Mother and Daddy were. I thought that was mean."

"I know. I've been thinking about that, and I'm sorry. I was just being a smart-ass. I just haven't been able to get over the way they did you and me, but I'm sorry I talked to you that way. You didn't deserve it."

"Okay, you're forgiven."

Max was going to say something that he knew would not work, but he wanted to see Amy's reaction. He said, "Sweetie,

Duke's leaving to go back to Memphis State tomorrow. After he leaves, why don't you and I go down to Atlanta? Would you like to do that?"

"I'd love to, but it's out of the question. I have to go to Knoxville tomorrow. I have classes starting the next day. It's a good thought, though."

"Does that mean that if you didn't have to go to Knoxville, that you and I could go to Atlanta?"

"I don't know, Max. A lot of time has gone by, and a lot has changed. You and I live in different worlds now, and I'm not sure we can ever get them together."

"I don't understand."

"Max, when I went off to college, a whole new world opened up to me, and I don't feel that I have even touched the surface. If I'm able to graduate in three years the way I want to, I'll finish at U.T. next year and move on to the University of Illinois. That will last four years, but it will move me closer to my goal of being a Veterinarian, and that really excites me. I'm not playing down anything I had with you. It's just that we have both moved on, and who knows? Maybe one day, we'll be able to live in the same world."

"Are you trying to get me out of your mind and memory?"

"I don't know, Max. I'm just living each day one at a time."

"Have you dated any since the annulment?"

"No," and then she said, "I'll take that back. My roommate talked me into going out for pizza one night with her date and her date's friend. I went and had a miserable time and wouldn't let him kiss me goodnight. After that, I told Joyce that I didn't want to go out anymore. Have you not dated?"

"No. It's like I told you yesterday or the day before, I haven't dated because I thought I would feel guilty. I guess it's silly, but I can't help it. I still feel like I'm married to you. I know in the eyes of the law, you and I have never been married, but I still feel that way,"

"That's so sweet, but Max, you're just going to have to get over it. If you find someone that interests you, and that you like, you need to ask her out. You don't have to marry her, but that should help you to get over us."

"Are you going to do that?"

"I don't know. Probably, but that situation hasn't come up yet. I've been too busy studying, but if it should come up, I probably will."

"Ouch. Amy, can I write you?"

"You sure can."

"Give me your address, will you?"

"Yeah," and he looked around 'til he found a piece of paper for her to write on.

While she was writing her address for him, he said, "You know, I wrote you several times, but you never did answer me back."

"You wrote me?"

"Yeah, several times."

"I never got one letter from you except that one that you knew about."

"Your parents must have intercepted them."

"I guess they did."

"Do you want my address?" He asked.

"Yeah, you can write it down for me."

He said, "Well, don't act too excited about it."

"I'm sorry. It's just that we will be going in different directions, and I don't know if corresponding with each other will be for the best."

"Okay, but I'm going to write you unless you tell me to stop. It will at least make me feel better. I hope you'll answer me from time to time."

Amy said, "We've been talking mostly about me and me becoming a Veterinarian. What do you plan to do, later?"

"Well, I told you that I have to go in the Marines when I graduate, and that will be four years after I get out of school.

After that, I'm not sure. There's a possibility that I will make the Marines my career, but right now, I don't think I will. If I don't stay in the Marines, I may come back and try coaching high school football. I just don't know. Where do you think you will practice?"

"I don't know, at this point. I guess it will depend on where the best advantage presents itself. It could be around here, or it could be in Illinois or somewhere like that. I'll just have to wait and see."

Max had told Duke before they met the girls that he would like to have about an hour with Amy, and in just about an hour after he and Sissy left, they came back. When Max saw them drive up, he said to Amy, "Well, there's our rides. I hate to see this end, but I think we know where each other stands, don't we?"

"I believe we do. It has been nice seeing you, Max. I wish you a lotta luck with your football, and I wish you a lotta luck in the Marines. Be careful, will you?"

"I will, and good luck to you, too, Amy. I love you."

Amy didn't answer that last remark. She just looked at him, and then Sissy and Duke came up, and Duke asked, "Are you ready to go?"

Max said, "Yeah, I guess so," and they all said goodbye.

On the way home, Amy hardly said a word. Are you alright?" Sissy asked.

Amy didn't answer. She just said, "Max and I ended our relationship. Do you want to know the last thing he said to me?"

"What was it?"

"He said I love you."

"Wow. Do you still love him, Amy?"

"Yeah, but I keep telling myself that I can't love him. We're going into two different worlds now, and neither one of us fits into the other's. I'll be glad to get back in school, so I can get my mind off of him." She started crying and said,

"Sissy, leaving him just now was one of the hardest things I've ever done."

Sissy said, "I noticed that you didn't kiss him goodbye. Didn't you want to?"

"I was dying to." She cried harder and said, "But I knew I shouldn't."

Sissy, trying to get her mind on something else said, "Well, Girlfriend, I know you're not interested in hearing from me right now, but just in case you're wondering, I think Duke and I may connect at some point. I like him a lot, and I think he likes me. He only lives about forty miles from here, so when football's over, and he comes home for the weekend sometime, we said we would get together."

Amy wiped her eyes and said, "That's great news. He seems nice."

Sissy dropped Amy off at her house and then went home.

When Amy went into her house, her Mother said, "Hi, Darling. Where have you been?"

Amy answered, "To the El Rancho with Sissy,"

"Did you have lunch there?"

"Yeah, there were four of us."

"Four of you? Who were the other two?"

"Max and his roommate."

"Max Norwood?"

"Yes, Mother, Max Norwood."

"Well, how did that go?"

Wanting to rub it in a little with her Mother she said, "It went great, with a capital G., and that brings me to something I want to talk to you about, Mother. Max told me that he had written several letters to me, but he never got an answer to any of them. Do you know anything about any letters, Mother?"

Her Mother looked very sheepish and said, "Your Daddy and I thought it would be best if the two of you didn't have any contact, so we didn't send you the letters."

"I know you didn't want me to see Max or to talk to him,

but Mother, you and Daddy didn't have the right to take letters that belonged to me. What did you do? Throw them away?"

"No, I still have them all."

"Did you read them?"

"No, we didn't open any of them."

"Well, where are they?"

"They're in the cedar chest."

"Well, I want them."

Her Mother said, "You don't want them. That part of your life is over. Just forget about them."

"No. I want them. Now, please get them for me."

"Okay, but I hope you're not sorry."

Just as she was bringing the letters to Amy, Amy's Daddy came in. When he saw what was happening, he said, "What's going on here?"

Amy's Mother said, "Amy saw Max, and he told her that he had written her several times, and he wondered why he never got an answer to any of them. I admitted that we held them from her, and she wants them. After all, they're hers."

Her Daddy said, "Are you sure this is what you want to do?"

"Yes, Daddy. You and Mother have ruined my life for the last three years, and now that I'm old enough to do pretty much what I want, I don't intend for you all to keep this up. I know you thought you were doing what was best for me, but Daddy, you can't possibly know just how bad you and Mother hurt me. I loved Max, and I still love him, and you hurt him just as bad as you hurt me, because we felt as though we were one. Then, your precious annulment destroyed our lives as we knew it."

Her Daddy said to her, "Baby, I'm sorry you feel that way, but you were only seventeen years old, and we knew we had to protect you. We had to protect you from yourself, and we only did that because we love you. You're growing into a fine, young woman, and I'm sure you're going to realize that what we did was the best thing for you, and I might add, the best thing for Max."

She said, "I know you love me, Daddy, but you will never know just how bad you hurt Max and me. I love you, too, otherwise I would have left when you threatened me with the annulment. It's three years later, now, and I feel that I probably should have done that."

Chapter Four

Early, the next morning, Amy got ready and left for Knoxville. She had her own car, so she didn't have to depend on anyone else to drive her. After the last two or three days, she was ready to get her mind on her studies and to try and get Max out of her head.

Max and Duke left about ten o'clock for Memphis. It was a hard five-hour drive from Middleton, and before they left, Duke called Sissy to say goodbye, and he promised her that he would write to her, and she promised that she would write to him as well.

Amy arrived in Knoxville at ten o'clock, about the same time that Max and Duke left Max's house. Joyce had not got there yet, so after seeing that there wasn't anything to eat in the fridge, she went to the grocery store to stock up on some things. She was hungry, so she stopped at Mickey Dees and bought a biscuit to take back to the dorm.

After she got back to the dorm, she put the things up that she had bought and sat down to eat her biscuit. While she was eating, Joyce came in, and after the excitement of seeing each other, they told each other what they did during their time off. Joyce was especially interested when Amy told her that she saw Max, and she wanted to know every little detail, which Amy was glad to furnish. It was still only around noon, so they decided they would walk downtown and do some shopping, even though most of it was window shopping.

Around three o'clock they returned to the dorm and decided to take a nap until it was time to go eat dinner. They were both anxious for classes to start the next morning because in Amy's case, especially, they needed to get some new things to concentrate on,

Duke and Max arrived in Memphis around three thirty that

afternoon and went straight to their dorm. Max, like Amy, couldn't wait for the next day to begin, so he could concentrate on something other than her.

The next morning, they both began their routines, and by noon, their minds were on what they were currently doing, and memories of the last few days had virtually disappeared, although, at night, the memories would return.

Max wrote Amy a letter the first day he was back in Memphis because it made him feel like he was in her presence. A couple of days later, he wrote her again, but she didn't answer either one. A few days later, he wrote her again, and that time, she answered.

They corresponded by mail several times over the next few weeks, and pretty soon, the letters slowed down, and then they stopped. Amy and Max both felt a sense of loss, but they realized that their long distance romance wasn't going to last.

Ten Months Later

Amy's hard work and stick-to-it-ivness let her realize her wish to graduate from the University of Tennessee in three years with a degree in Biology. She had already been accepted by the University of Illinois School of Veterinary Medicine, and she was going to enroll in there first session of summer school, in hopes of possibly getting her degree in Veterinary Medicine earlier than four years.

She had two weeks between graduation at Knoxville and the start of classes at UIUC, so at the urging of Joyce, the two of them along with two other friends went to Florida for a few days. From Florida, she went home to Middleton to have her car gone over, just to make sure it wouldn't give her any trouble when she drove to Urbana, Illinois, where her school was located.

Some of her friends wondered why she didn't come home during the summer; instead of staying at school almost twelve months a year, but she confided in her best friend, Sissy, that even though she loved her parents, she still had a hard time forgetting what they did to her and Max, and she would just prefer to not be at home with them during the summer.

Amy was pretty nervous when she drove into Urbana, Illinois on Saturday before classes started on Monday. Champaign, Illinois and Urbana were kind of one big town. They were only nine minutes apart, and the two of them had approximately one hundred and thirty thousand people combined. That was just a tad smaller than Knoxville.

Her new dorm was called Ashton Woods, and it was actually in Champaign, Illinois, but since she was coming in from the south, she came to Urbana first. She hadn't seen the University before, so she thought she would drive around the campus before going to Champaign and her dorm. When she went to Champaign, she had a hard time finding Ashton Woods, so she pulled into a convenience store and asked directions. Luckily, she was just a few blocks from it, and she made it without any trouble.

She really liked the appearance of the dorm when she got there, and she saw a little sign that said 'office', and she went in. She told the lady inside who she was and that she was supposed to move into room two twenty-four. The lady had everything ready for her, and she told her that her roommate was already there, and she thought she was up in their room.

Amy finished the checking in process, and then, before unloading her car, she went up to two twenty-four to see it. Sure enough, her roommate was in there, and they could see immediately that they were going to be good friends. The roomies name was Karen Brock.

They talked for a few minutes, and then Amy said she was going to go unload her car, and Karen said, "I'll help."

Ashton Woods was a three-story building, and there was an elevator about equidistant from both ends. Amy had not taken anything home from Knoxville after she graduated. She went to visit her parents for a couple of days, and then went back to Knoxville and loaded up everything she had and left for Urbana, so there was not only three or four suitcases, there were what seemed like a hundred small bags of miscellaneous stuff. Fortunately, the dorm had some carts that would accommodate hanging clothes as well as suitcases and boxes and things, and Amy and Karen got two of them when they got downstairs. They had both learned how to carefully load a cart to hold the most stuff, and they did a great job loading those two. They got just about all of it in one trip. Amy had to go back out and get two or three sacks of things when they took the carts back, and that completed her move.

When they got back to their room, Karen had already decided which bed she wanted, so Amy looked through her bags until she found sheets and pillowcases and made up the other one. She noticed that Karen didn't have anything to unpack or to put up, and she asked, "How long have you been here?"

"I got here yesterday. My brother is a student here also, and he had to come in yesterday, so I rode with him. That's why all my things are put up."

"Well, I was wondering if you're just real neat, or if I'm a slob."

Karen said, "I've only known you for a few minutes, and I can tell you're anything but a slob."

When Amy finished making up her bed, they sat down and talked and tried to get to know each other better. Amy asked, "Where are you from, Karen?"

"Decatur. It's a town about fifty miles from here."

"Where are you from?"

"Middleton, Tennessee."

"Tennessee! That's a long way. Why did you come all the way to Illinois? Don't they have any good Veterinary schools over there?"

"I'm sure they do, but ever since I was a young girl, I have wanted to be a vet, and I read so much about this place that I knew I wanted to come here. Are you going to be a vet?" Then she said, "I guess you are, or you wouldn't be here."

Karen said, "I was born into it. My Dad is a Vet and has an animal hospital down in Decatur. My brother, Neal and I have worked in the hospital ever since we were little, and there was never any talk about our becoming Vets; it was just understood that that was what we would do. Neal and I will take over the hospital one day; when Dad retires."

"That's great. It sounds as though you and your brother have ready-made careers. I wish I did."

"Well, take my word for it. It won't take you long once you hang your shingle."

"That's what I'm hoping, but in my case, do you think it would be better if I went to work for an established Vet before I went out on my own?"

"Maybe. You'll just have to see how you feel about things when the time gets nearer."

Amy said, "You said your brother is a student here. What year is he in?"

"He's a junior."

"So, is he going to work with your Dad as soon as he graduates, or is he going to work for somebody else for a while?"

"Yeah, he's gonna go work with Dad immediately from here. Dad has two vets in with him, but he's still covered up, and he needs help desperately. We just wish we didn't have to wait so long to help him. We'll go home to help him on weekends with things that can be done that don't require a Veterinarian degree."

"Maybe some weekend, you'll take me with you. I'd like to learn how to do some stuff in an animal hospital."

"Well, if you're serious about that, I'll definitely be asking you."

"Does your Dad work with both large and small animals?"

"No. He's a small animal vet. Occasionally, he'll get a call from a friend that has a sick horse or something, and he'll go help them, but that's rare. He likes to just work on small animals."

Amy said, "Karen, I wonder if we will have any classes together."

"I don't know. Do you have your schedule handy?"

"Yeah. It's in my purse."

She got it, and Karen got hers, and they compared them. Karen asked, "Are you taking anatomy?"

"Yes."

"What period?"

"Eight thirty, Monday.""

"Me too. How about pathology?"

"Yeah, ten thirty, Monday"

"I've got it at one o'clock on Monday."

"Toxicology, eight thirty, Tuesday and Thursday."

"Me too."

They went on down the list of classes and found that they had four of the same subjects. When some of them were two or three days each, the pair had quite a few together.

The next day, Sunday, Karen's brother, Neal, came to see them, and of course she introduced him to Amy.

He was an average size fellow; probably five ten and one seventy-five, and very good looking. Amy was caught off guard, and she found herself staring at him, and a couple of times, she noticed he was staring at her. He, like Karen was very easy to be around, and she hoped he would come around pretty often. He was the first guy since Max that she had even looked at twice. She thought to herself, *I hope I can get to know him better. Since he's Karen's brother. Maybe I'll get to see him quite a bit.*

About ten o'clock, Sunday morning, the phone rang, and Karen answered it. She said, "Hello, yeah, that would be nice. Can you hold for a minute?" She held the phone away from ear, and told Amy, "This is Neal, and he wants to know if we would like to have lunch with him. Would you like to do that?"

"That would be great. Tell him yes."

Karen put the phone back up to her ear and said, "Amy said she would like to. Where are we going?" Neal said something, and Karen asked, "Are you coming by here, or do you want us to meet you?" He answered, and she said, "Great. We'll see you then."

In about an hour, Neal arrived, and came in and sat down. He asked Amy, "Amy, what do you think about this area, so far?"

She said, "I don't know yet. I haven't been anywhere, but if the area is half as nice as my roommate, I'll love it."

He asked, "What if it's as nice as your roommate's brother?"

"Then, there will be no question about it."

He smiled and said, "Karen, I like this girl."

They talked and joked around for a little while, and then at almost noon, Neal asked, "Are you ladies ready to go get something to eat?"

They both said they were ready, and he said, "I thought we would go to a place called Seven Saints. I think you'll both like it."

Amy said, "Okay, lead the way."

They rode with Neal, and they went to a nice restaurant. They got a table and Karen asked Neal, "Have you been here before?"

"Yeah, several times. It's a good place to bring a date because they have such a wide variety of things on their menu."

Amy asked, "Do you have anything special that you recommend?

"I brought a date here one time last school year, and she had the Spring Salmon Salad and a half tuna sandwich and she just went on about how good it was."

"I may get that. I like Salmon and tuna both," Karen said.

Amy said, "I think I will, too. What are you going to get, Neal?"

"I'm gonna have the rib eye sandwich. I've had it before, and it's really good."

"Neal looked at Amy and said, "Karen said you're from Tennessee."

"Yeah. Born and raised."

"What made you decide to come all the way out here? Don't they have Veterinary schools in Tennessee?"

"That's what Karen asked. Oh yeah, they've got 'em, but I've been reading about this place since I was a little girl, and there was never any other school that I wanted to go to."

"Well, I hope it's what you hope it will be. I know I'm happy here, and this is my third year."

When the food came, the conversation slowed down, except for some minor comments. After they finished eating, the talk picked up again, and about a half hour later, Neal said, "Why don't we go? I'm going back to my apartment and watch the ballgame, if I can stay awake long enough. This sandwich will probably put me right out."

Karen was ready, but Amy wasn't, although she didn't feel as though she could say anything, but she thought, *don't go home, Neal. Stay with us this afternoon.*

Neal drove, and he took the girls back to Ashton Woods, where he let them out. Karen said, "Thanks, Bro. I'll see you," and Amy said, "I enjoyed it. Thank you."

Neal said, "Okay. I enjoyed it, too. Good luck, girls, as you start classes tomorrow. I'll see you later."

After Amy and Karen got to their room, Amy said, "That was good, wasn't it?"

Karen answered, "Yeah, it was. Neal knows all the good places since he's been up here for two years, so we can just ask him where someplace is if we want to know."

Amy said, "Karen, I like Neal."

"I think he likes you, too," Karen answered.

"Why do you say that?"

"Because of the way he looked at you."

"That's just your imagination," Amy said.

"No, It's not. I know my brother."

Amy didn't say anything. She just pondered Karen's statement and hoped it was true.

After a lazy afternoon and a snack at dinnertime, both girls worked on getting their clothes ready for school the next morning, and when they had done that, Amy sat down and wrote her good friend, Sissy, a letter.

She didn't have a whole lot to say because she had just talked to Sissy the week before. She mainly wanted to write and tell her about Neal.

She wrote:

"Hi Girlfriend.

This won't take long. I just wanted to tell you that today, I had lunch with the dreamiest hunk. He's the brother of my roommate, and he's gorgeous. His name is Neal. Their Daddy has an animal hospital about fifty miles from here, and they will go down there most weekends to help him, and Karen said they would take me with them some weekends. I'm happy about that because I can be with Neal when I go. It's too early to tell if anything will ever develop, but if he asks me out, I'm not going to say no. This is a far cry from where I was, isn't it? I just wanted to tell you about it since you're my best friend. I'll write later.

Love you. Amy.

The alarm went off at six-thirty the next morning, and both girls hopped out of bed. There was a sense of excitement because it was the first day of classes at a new school for both of them. They had decided to take turns driving, since they were going to the same place, and they didn't see any need to have two cars, so Karen said she would drive the first day.

They settled into their classes quickly, and they found that the different subjects were much more interesting that the ones they were used to in their days of working on their Bachelors degrees.

Each of the girls as well as Neal had their last class of the week at ten a.m. Friday, which meant that they would get out at eleven o'clock, and that helped Karen and Neal get an early start on their trip home to help their Dad for the weekend. Nothing was said to Amy about going that first weekend until Neal came by to pick up Karen.

Amy walked out to the car with Karen mainly because she wanted to get a glimpse of Neal, and when they got to the car, Neal spoke to her and said, "Do you have big plans for the weekend?"

"No, I guess I'll just stick around here."

"Why don't you come and go with Karen and me? We can always use an extra hand."

Amy didn't say anything at first, and then, before she could say something, Karen said, "Come on Amy. I didn't think to ask you, but we'd love to have you. Like Neal said, we can always use more help. Will you go?"

"Well, I'm not ready, and I don't want to hold you guys up."

Karen said, "You won't hold us up. Run up to the room and grab a change of clothes and your toothbrush, and we'll wait on you. Take your time. We're not in any hurry."

Amy said, "Come help me, Karen," and they went to get her things for a working weekend. Neal shut off the car engine while he waited. Soon, they were on their way to Decatur for a new experience for Amy and a nearly life-long experience for Karen and Neal.

They arrived at Brock Animal Hospital around one-thirty and went right to work. Karen introduced her Daddy to Amy, and he told her how happy he was that she came down with Neal and Karen. Of course, Amy had no idea what to do, so they had her go to the outer office and bring the dogs and cats back to the examining rooms when they were ready for them.

Neal was experienced enough to give shots and other things that didn't require a licensed veterinarian, and every chance she had, Amy would stay in the room with him and watch how he treated the animals. Sometimes, when she would bring an animal to him, she would hold the dog or cat until he was ready to treat it, and occasionally, they would touch hands or touch in other ways, and every time, it would thrill her. A couple of times she felt that he was intentionally grabbing her arm or hand, and she made it a point not to pull back. That was just the first week. What would the next thirty-five bring, she wondered.

That evening, at the dinner table, she noticed him staring at her when she would look his way. They stayed at the Brock's Friday night and Saturday night, and on Sunday morning, they left to go back to school.

It wasn't long before nearly everything they did was just routine. Of course, school was number one in importance, but going down to Decatur to help out in the Brock Animal Hospital was number two in importance for Karen and Neal. While that wasn't as important to Amy as it was to Karen and Neal, they invited her to go with them nearly every weekend, and it was starting to become a big deal for her as well.

Neal never did ask her out, and he never did make any advances toward her in a romantic way, but rather, as they continued on with their work at the animal hospital, he treated her more like he did Karen; more like a sister, and that was alright with her. She was just happy to be around him.

Fall break came, and most of the students went home, but Amy didn't want to go, and she stayed in Champaign. Neal and Karen went home and spent nearly their entire break working at their Dad's animal hospital. On the third day of the break, Amy's phone rang, and it was Neal.

"Hi Lady. What are you doing?"

"Just getting ready to wash my hair. What are you doing?"

"I'm helping my Dad spay a cat right now. There's a line out in the lobby waiting to get waited on, and we could sure use some help. Do you have plans?"

"No, I don't have anything."

"Would you be interested in coming down here?"

"To help in the hospital?"

"Yeah. What do you think? Do you think I just want to see you?"

"Well, a girl can hope, can't she?"

He paused for a few seconds and then said, "Yeah, I guess so. I want to see you, but I need your help, too. Can you come down?"

"Well, since you put it in such a romantic way, I guess I can. Give me time to wash my hair, and I'll see you after a while."

"Okay. I can't wait to see you."

"Yeah, right," and she hung up, thinking to herself, *I wonder if he really meant that, or if he was just joshing me because of what I said to him. Oh well. We'll see.*

When she got to Decatur, she fell right into various chores at the animal hospital, and it seemed that the main reason Neal was glad to see her was because of her help. She finished working there for the balance of Fall break and went back to school when Karen and Neal did.

She had worked so much at the hospital; she became like family to the Brocks. She was there nearly every weekend, and Karen's Mother and Daddy grew to love her. She even spent Thanksgiving with them and met other members of their family.

Chapter Five

After Thanksgiving, it wasn't long until school got out for Christmas, and Amy decided to go home. She hadn't been home since before she started at UIUC. She told her Mother when she would be there, and her Mother offered to send her a plane ticket, so she wouldn't have to drive that long distance by herself because it was a little more than five hundred miles, and it took almost eight hours to drive it by car.

On the plane, on the way home, Amy wondered if Max would be home for Christmas, and if she would see him.

The first thing she did after getting home and visiting with her parents for a little while was call Sissy. They had kept in touch by letter, and Amy had called her a few times, but that wasn't like being up close and personal. Sissy said she would come over later, and maybe they could go to the El Rancho and get a burger or something.

That evening, at El Rancho, they went in and ordered a cheeseburger and French fries. There were a few people that they knew and a couple of Max's buddies, but Max wasn't there. After a while, Amy's curiosity got the best of her, and she went over to talk to the guys. While she was over there, one of the guys asked her, "When have you talked to Max?"

She answered, "I haven't talked to him in a long time. Have you heard from him?"

"No. I guess the last time I saw him was the time you and Sissy were here when he was here with his roommate."

She said, "I saw him the next day after that, and I haven't seen or heard from him since. If you see or hear from him, tell him I said Hi."

When she got back to her and Sissy's table, she sat down and said, "I thought maybe Sam had heard from Max, but he said he hadn't. I can't help but wonder about him."

Sissy said, "Why didn't you ask me? I could tell you about him."

Amy looked puzzled and asked, "Why? Do you know about him?"

Sissy asked, "Do you remember Duke, Max's roommate?"

"Yeah, why?"

"Well, Duke and I have kept in touch since he was here with Max, and Memphis State is playing in a bowl game New Year's weekend, and they can't come home. They have football practice."

Amy asked, "Why didn't you tell me? You knew I would want to know."

"Well, all you ever talk about when you write or call is about a guy named Neal, and I thought you were over Max, so I didn't bring him up."

"I think I'm over him, but I'll always be interested in what he's doing."

"What about this Neal guy?"

"Neal is a different thing. He's Karen's brother and now a friend of mine, but he's never shown any interest in carrying our relationship beyond friendship. I care for him a lot, and I don't know if anything will ever develop, so I'll just have to bide my time and see if anything happens."

"Have you told him how you feel?"

"No."

"Why not?"

"Because it's an awkward situation."

"How is it awkward?"

"Well, I've told you about him, and I've told you about Karen being my roommate. Well, nearly every weekend, I've been going with them down to Decatur, Illinois to help them work in their Daddy's animal hospital. I've become close to their parents, also, in fact; I went down and spent Thanksgiving with them. Their parents treat me like their daughter, and Neal acts like he's my big brother. I catch him staring at me from time to time, but there hasn't been any action on his part, and I don't feel that under the circumstances, I can do anything to jeopardize those relationships. What if I tell him how I feel, and he doesn't feel the same way? It might affect my relationship with the whole family."

"Do you think it would affect your relationship with Karen?"

"I don't think so, but I just don't want to take the chance. I'm crazy about her, and I'd hate for something to happen that would cause us to have to live in a strained atmosphere. She and I are a lot like you and me."

Sissy asked, "When's the last time you saw Max?"

"That time when he was here with Duke."

"Have you not talked to him or anything?"

"We wrote a few times, but the letters kept getting fewer and far between, and then they stopped. I guess I stopped writing before he did because I didn't see how a long-distance relationship could work."

"Do you still love him?"

"I don't know. I probably do. I don't want to, but I just don't see how we could ever be together permanently. He has to go into the Marines for four years after he gets out of college, and I have to go to school for four years, too, so I just don't think it will work."

"Do you think you and Neal can work things out?"

"I don't know. I'd like to, but who knows. Enough about my love life or lack of it. Are you and Duke an item?"

"As of now, no. I like him, and I know he likes me, but it's like you and Max. I'm here and he's three hundred and fifty miles away and seldom gets home, so I don't know."

"Are you seeing anyone?"

"No one steady. I'll occasionally go somewhere or to a movie with someone, but I don't see anybody regularly. I'm through. Are you through?"

"Yeah. Are you ready to go."

"Yeah. Listen, I need to run by the mall for just a minute. Do you want to go?"

"I'd like to," so they got up and left El Rancho and went to the mall.

***

It was December twenty-first, and Max and Duke were stuck in Memphis because Memphis State was to play in the Motor City Bowl in Detroit, Michigan on December twenty sixth. They were to leave Christmas morning and fly to Detroit, so there were a lot of families that had Christmas messed up for them because of the game.

Back in November, Max and Duke attended a Fellowship of Christian Athletes meeting, and after the meeting there was a reception, which they attended. The FCA was coed, and several female students attended the meeting as well as the reception. During the reception, Max struck up a conversation with a good-looking volleyball player named Toni Fisher, and from that meeting, they were almost inseparable.

"Why haven't I seen you before?" Max asked.

She said, "I don't know. I guess I'm too busy to be seen," she joked. Then she said, "Seriously, I really don't know. I am busy, and when I get through with my classes, I have Volleyball practice, and then I go home. I live in West Memphis, Arkansas, so when I'm not in class or at practice, I'm usually not on campus."

Max said, "Well, we're going to have to change that. I would like to see you sometime when you're not in class or at practice. Do you think that's a possibility?"

She said, "It's a definite possibility. I've been wanting to meet you ever since I saw you play the last couple of years, but the time or place never seemed to be right. I'd like to see you, too, whenever you want to."

"How about tomorrow night?"

"Okay. When and where?"

"We have a game tomorrow that should be over around five or five thirty. Why don't you come to where we come out of the locker room and meet me there, and maybe we can go somewhere to eat?"

"That sounds great. I was planning to go to the game anyway, so that will work out just fine."

"Great. I'll see you after the game tomorrow."

She said, "I'll be anxious to see you."

"Me too."

From then on, they have been together nearly every day. She invited him to meet her parents a week or so after they began going out, and her parents just fell in love with him. Her Dad was a big football fan, and he knew who Max was before he met him, so he fit right in with her family.

Since it was so close to Christmas, Toni and her parents had to go to some family get-togethers, and it interfered with their dating, but her Mother and Dad invited him over to their house for Christmas Eve, and he gladly accepted their invitation. A little later, after he thought about it, he called Toni and said, "Hi Honey. Listen, I know I told your Mom that I would come to your house on Christmas Eve, but I don't want to leave Duke here by himself, so I think I'll just stay here with him, it being Christmas Eve and all. I'm sorry, but I think I should do that."

She said, "Hold on a minute, Max," and she laid the phone down. In a minute or two, she picked it back up and said, "Max, Mama said for you to get yourself over here Christmas Eve and to bring Duke with you. She and Dad want to meet him."

"Really? That's fantastic. Duke's not here right now, but I'll tell him when he gets here, and I know he'll be happy to come."

Toni asked, "Does he eat as much as you do?"

"Are you kidding? I eat like a bird compared to Duke. Tell your Mom she may have made a mistake inviting him," and he laughed.

"I'll tell her."

Max and Toni saw each other the next three nights, and then it was Christmas Eve. Since they were going to have dinner with Toni's family at their house, the two guys wore nice clothes, and when they got there, Toni's Dad went on over them as much as if they had been NFL stars.

He had them sit down in the den while they waited for dinner to be served, and in the time Max had been dating Toni, he had asked about all the questions he could think of. Now, with Duke there, he had fresh meat, so he could ask him the questions he had already asked Max, and Duke was happy to answer them.

The first one was, "Duke, you're a big one. How tall are you and what do you weigh? The program says that you are six seven and weigh three 0 five. Is that accurate?"

"It's close. Actually, I'm six six, and I weigh about two ninety."

"Well, you're a big boy. I know that. Are you going to try to play pro ball?"

"I don't know. It will depend on whether or not some team wants to draft me. If they do, then I may try it, but if they don't, I'll just get a job. I'm not going to walk on anywhere."

"What would you like to do?"

"I'd like to be a high school teacher and maybe coach a little."

Before Mr. Fisher could ask anything else, Mrs. Fisher called them to dinner. She had gone all out to prepare the meal because she was going to have a huge Christmas dinner the next day for her immediate family and about fourteen more relatives. The Christmas Eve dinner they were having was her way of showing Toni how much she and Toni's Dad approved of Max, and Duke's presence was a bonus.

Dinner was delicious, and Max and Duke both insisted that they be allowed to help clean up in order for Toni's Mom to be able to sit with the rest of them in the den before they had to leave. The team had a ten o'clock curfew that night, and it took thirty to forty-five minutes to get from West Memphis to the University, so they would have to leave between nine o'clock and nine-fifteen.

Around ten 'til nine, Max said they needed to go. It was a little early, but he wanted to spend a few minutes with Toni, telling her goodbye. They both told Mrs. Fisher how good they thought dinner was, and they told both Mr. and Mrs. Fisher how much they enjoyed the whole evening and wished them a Merry Christmas.

Mr. Fisher told the guys, "Good luck, fellows. I hope you put it to those Yankees up in Detroit. I'll be listening to the game. Have a good time."

They both thanked him. Toni walked them out, and she told Duke goodbye and he went on to the car. Max and Toni walked to the corner of the house and stopped and talked. Max said, "When I get back, I want us to talk about some things, okay?"

"What do you want to talk about," she asked naively.

"Guess," he said.

"Oh, that," she said, smiling

"Yeah, that." Then they kissed, and he said, "Love you," and he went to the car.

The downside of the bowl game was that they had to miss being with their families on Christmas, but the good part of it outweighed the bad. They were being rewarded for their hard work during the regular season plus there were other benefits connected with playing in a bowl, such as a lot of money for the school and the conference.

The team flew Delta, the next morning, from Memphis to Detroit, and all the flight attendants had on Santa's Elf's hats. When Max saw them, he thought, *I guess we're not the only ones missing Christmas. Those poor girls have to work today.*" The flight lasted about an hour and a half, and there were two buses at the airport in Detroit to pick them up and take them to their hotel. They arrived at the hotel at eleven forty-five, and everything had been done for them except giving each player his key, and they had to get them at the desk. Each player's roommate was the same as his roommate at school.

There were about ninety-five hungry giants when they got to the hotel, and the Athletic Department had arranged for lunch to be served at twelve-thirty. There were too many to fit into the regular dining room, so they set up one of the conference rooms to serve as a dining room for the team. The hotel set up a buffet in the conference room, so the players could get what they wanted, and as much as they wanted. Normally, with a group that large, there would be a few who wouldn't like what was offered, but on that day, there was not one complaint.

After lunch, they were allowed to go to their rooms and take a nap or whatever they wanted to do. The Head Coach announced at lunch that there would be a team meeting at four o'clock, and everyone was required to attend.

Max and Duke took advantage of the time to take a nap, and they went to their room and crashed for a couple of hours in between watching a ball game. They went down to the four o'clock meeting, and the coaches covered some of the things they would do the next day in the game. The offense was on one side of the room, and the defense on the other side. They met until dinnertime, and then the meeting broke up, but before the coach let them go, he told them that they would have a nine o'clock curfew that night, and anyone missing the curfew would not be allowed to play the next day. He also told them that breakfast would be served the next morning at seven o'clock, and he urged everyone to eat because there would be no lunch due to the ballgame starting at one o'clock.

Duke and Max stayed in that night. They didn't know the town and didn't know anywhere to go, so they were content to stay in their room and watch a movie on TV. At five minutes after nine, someone knocked on their door, and Duke answered it. It was one of the assistant coaches checking everyone's room to make sure they weren't out after curfew. After that, they talked a little football, but not too much because the coach had pretty much covered everything. They turned the lights off around ten o'clock and slept until six fifteen the next morning.

The whole time they were eating breakfast, the coaching staff took turns talking to them. After they finished, they were permitted to go to their rooms to use the bathroom, brush their teeth or whatever else they had to do, and they were told to meet back downstairs at nine o'clock to board the buses that would take them to the stadium.

When they got to Ford Field Stadium, they went to their locker room and changed into their football pants and tee shirts. Some of the guys went out on the field and ran sprints or just walked around, trying to get loose before kickoff. It was only ten o'clock, and kickoff wasn't until one o'clock. There were close to a hundred players on the Memphis State team, and after a while, most of them were on the field. As it got closer to game time, the offensive coordinator and the defensive coordinator gathered their teams together and ran some formations, and about twelve thirty, everyone went into the locker room and put on their pads and got their helmets in anticipation of coming back out to play the game.

Memphis State University was in the American Athletic Conference, and they were playing The University of Akron of the Mid-American Conference, and according to the experts, it was supposed to be a heck of a game.

The experts were right. It was a heck of a game with Memphis State coming out on top, thirty-eight to thirty-one. Max caught four passes; one of them for a touchdown, and

Duke sacked the quarterback twice and recovered a fumble. He was a bear the whole game. During the game, one of the coaches said there were some NFL scouts there to see if there were any good prospects for the upcoming draft in April. The guys who were interested in playing professionally tried to really turn it on, so they would be noticed.

After the game was over, the team gathered at the center of the field where some celebrity former football players, who were now broadcasters spoke with some of the Memphis State players and coaches. When they finished that, the Chairman of the Motor City Bowl presented the head coach with the winner's trophy.

A few Memphis State diehards had come to Detroit to cheer the team on, and after the trophy presentation, the team milled around, talking with those people as well as others who just wanted to meet some football players. Their thinking was that if they met enough players, and some of them were drafted into the NFL and became famous, then they could say they knew them.

Max was afraid they were going to have to go back to Memphis after the game, but when they boarded the buses, they were taken back to the hotel. It had been a long time since breakfast, and promptly at six o'clock, they were fed a huge buffet with things football players like. The head coach announced during dinner that they would be leaving Detroit at ten o'clock the next morning, and they would have breakfast at seven o'clock, the way they did that morning. Then, they were to be downstairs with their luggage at eight thirty, to leave for the airport.

Most of the players who played in the game were either too tired or too sore to try to go anywhere after dinner, so just about all of them stayed in the hotel. Some of the guys who didn't get to play went out, but there weren't many of them. Max and Duke were anxious to get back because school wasn't scheduled to resume from the holiday until the fifteenth, and they would have time to enjoy two weeks before they had to go back to class.

Duke asked Max, "Are you going to stay in Memphis or are you going home?"

"I think I'm going to go home for a few days, and then I'll go back to Memphis for the rest of the time. Are you going home?"

"Yeah. I'm kind of anxious to see my folks, and you know what? I'm kind of anxious to see Sissy."

"You're anxious to see Sissy? Good. I'm glad. She's a good girl. You'll be going through Middleton, won't you?"

"Yeah, Why? Do you want a ride?"

"Yeah, if I can catch a ride home with you, then I'll bring my Jeep back, since I'll be coming back before you do, plus, I need to have some wheels over here if I'm going to keep seeing Toni. When are you going to leave?"

"Early in the morning."

"Good. That'll give me time to see Toni tonight."

The plane landed in Memphis at twelve o'clock, and two buses were at the airport waiting on them. Everybody was ready to get back to school, so they could get ready to go home or wherever they were going. The first thing Max did was call Toni."

Mrs. Fisher answered the phone, and Max said, "Hi, Mrs. Fisher. This is Max. Is Toni home?"

"Yes, she is. Just a minute. Oh, Max, we watched the game and we watched you and Duke especially, and we thought you both played good."

"Thank you, Mrs. Fisher."

"You're welcome. Just a minute, Max, and I'll get Toni."

"Thank you."

Toni picked up and said, "Hello."

Max said, "Hi."

Toni said, "Hi. Where are you?"

"I'm in my dorm."

"Are you coming out here?"

"I'd like to, but I don't have any wheels."

"Would you like for me to come get you?"

"That would be great. Do you mind?"

"No, I don't mind. When do you want to come?"

"Anytime you want to pick me up."

"Okay, I'll be there in a few minutes."

"Great, I'll be looking for you. If I'm not out front, I'll be in the lobby, but I'll watch for you. I can't wait to see you."

After an hour had passed, Toni finally got to the dorm, and Max had gone inside to the lobby to wait. He thought she would be there before then, and he got tired of standing outside. She pulled up in front of the door, and he saw her pull up. He went out and got in the car. He leaned over and gave her a kiss and said, "Hi."

"Hi," she said. She looked at him and asked. "What's that big bruise under your eye?"

"On one play, my helmet got knocked off, and one of those mean Akron guys hit me with his helmet." He smiled and said, "It's really sore, and I was told that the best thing for it is to get a kiss from someone who loves me. Do you know anybody like that?"

"I might can find somebody."

"Well, I sure hope so."

On the way to West Memphis, they passed some fast food places, and as they were coming up on a Mickey Dees, Max said, "Pull in here and let's get a milkshake. Would you like to have one?"

"No, I'm still full from lunch, but we can get you one if you want to."

"Let's do. I haven't had anything since breakfast in Detroit."

He got his shake at the drive thru, and then they headed to Toni's house. Toni's Mom was there, but her Dad was at work, and he wasn't inundated with football questions the way he probably would be later when Mr. Fisher came home.

Mrs. Fisher came in the room where he and Toni were and asked, "Max, would you like to stay for dinner?"

He looked at Toni and asked, "What do you want to do; eat here or go out?"

She said, "Whatever you want to do. Eating here is cheaper than going out, but we'll do whatever you want to do."

He looked at her Mom and said, "Yes ma'am. I'd like to stay for dinner."

"Good. Tim will be thrilled. He watched every second of the game, and I know he'll want to talk about it when he gets home. Did you get that big bruise in the game?"

"Yes ma'am."

When she went back into the kitchen, Toni asked, "Is there anything special that you'd like to do?"

"No. I'm happy just being with you. We can do anything you'd like to do, or we can just stay here, and do nothing. That would be fine with me."

"Are you sure?"

"I'm sure. I'm actually still tired from the game yesterday and the flight home this morning, so staying here will be a treat."

"Okay, if you're sure. I'm sure Daddy will be happy."

At one point, Toni said, "You said that you wanted us to talk about things when you got back. Is now a good time?"

"Not really, I'd rather wait until we have more time and when we're by ourselves. I'll be back in three or four days, and I'll have my Jeep, so I think it will be better if we wait until I come back."

"What exactly do you want to talk about?"

"Our future together."

"Oh," and she didn't say anything else right then. Then, in a few minutes, she said, "Max, let's talk."

"About what?"

"Our future together. I don't want to wait 'till you get back. Let's talk now."

"Okay, if you want to. Have you thought any about what we talked about earlier?"

"Yeah, I've thought about it a good deal, and there are questions in my mind."

"Such as?"

"Such as, are you wanting to get married before, during, or after you get out of the Marines? I don't want to live here for four years while you're gone. What will we do about that?"

"Good question. I'd like to get married pretty soon after I get out of college, and as soon as I know where we'll be stationed. When I get stationed at a base, somewhere, we can get married, and you can come live with me just like normal people."

"What if you have to go overseas?"

"From what people tell me who are already in the Marines, it's unlikely that I'll be deployed."

"But you don't know that for sure, do you?"

"No, I guess not. Let me throw this out for you to think about. I graduate in May, and I'll go into the Marines in June. They'll probably send me to Quantico, Virginia for training before they station me somewhere for a long period, so why don't we get engaged right after I graduate, and wait to set the wedding date when I find out where we'll be? Does that sound like anything you'd go for?"

"Why don't we think about it for a while. It's December now, and you're not going anywhere until June, so we have time before we have to make a decision. What do you think?"

"I think that's a good plan. Let's go with that and see what happens. I've got to tell you, though, I can't wait to marry you."

"Me neither."

There were football bowl games on TV just about every day between Christmas and New Year's, and they watched some of them in between kissing when Toni's Mom would be out of the room, which was most of the time.

A Second Chance

Her Daddy got home a little after five thirty, and he was very happy to see Max. They talked football non-stop until Mrs. Fisher called them in for dinner. When they sat down at the table, football talk didn't stop until Toni's Mom said, "Tim, you need to slow down with football and let Max eat."

"I know. I'm just so excited to see Max after that touchdown he scored. I'm sorry, Max. We'll talk later."

Max said, "Whenever you're ready."

Tim and Max resumed their conversation after dinner, and in a little while, Toni said, "Daddy, I'm going to take Max away from you. Max, are you ready to go?"

Max had no idea where she was going to take him, but he said, "Yeah, I'm ready," and he got up. He asked Toni, "Are we coming back here?"

She said, "I don't think so."

Max said, "Let me tell your Mom bye, and Mr. Fisher, it was sure nice seeing you again. I'm going home tomorrow, but I'll be back in three or four days, and I'll see you when I get back."

"Okay, Padna. Have a good trip."

Toni was tired of sitting at home all afternoon. She loved her parents, but when she had a boyfriend there, she was not comfortable. Since she was driving and lived in West Memphis, Max had no idea where he was, and didn't have any suggestions where they could go, so he had to leave their destination up to Toni.

She didn't ask for any suggestions; she just drove down to the riverfront where there was a huge marina and a parking lot that was even larger. Apparently, Toni had been there before because she knew a spot in the parking lot where they could park, and nobody could see them unless they accidentally happened upon them.

Max could see that she wanted to smooch, and he obliged her. Things started to get out of hand after a few minutes, and Max said, "Honey, I don't want to do this. I think we should

71

go." Toni was aggravated at his suggestion and pulled away from him and started the car. She didn't say anything. She just scratched off and headed back to the bridge spanning the Mississippi River and finally, they arrived at his dorm at Memphis State. She pulled up to the front and stopped.

Max turned to her and tried to put his arm around her, but she just sat there without responding at all. "He said, "I'm sorry I made you mad, but I just don't think we should do that until after we're married."

She said coolly, "You mean if we get married."

He asked, "Now, what do you mean by that?"

She said, "Nothing. I've got to go. Good night."

When she said that, he unbuckled his seat belt and got out of the car. Before he closed the door, he turned and said, "I love you."

She said, "I'll see you later," and drove off.

He went in the dorm and thought about what just happened.

Toni thought about the same thing as she drove back to West Memphis. *I wonder if he'll call me after the way I acted,* she thought. *I hope I didn't mess things up. Maybe I should call him and apologize.*

Max thought about calling her after she had time to get home, but he thought, *I'm not going to do that. I did what was right, and I'm not going to apologize for it. If she wants to talk to me, she can call me. I sure hope she does before I leave in the morning.*

Duke was there when he got home and he could see that Max was not himself, and he asked, "What's wrong?"

"Nothing's wrong."

"Look, I've been your bunkmate for almost four years now, and I can tell when something's wrong. Did you have a fight with Toni?"

"Sort of."

"Well, it'll work itself out. Don't worry."

"I don't know if it will or not. We'll just have to wait and see."

"Don't worry. It will."

"Duke, I've been planning to only be at home for three or four days, but if she doesn't call me before we leave in the morning, I'll probably stay home until we have to be back for school."

Chapter Six

Duke wanted to get an early start the next morning, and Toni didn't call the night before, so they got up and left at seven thirty. It was a little over five hours to Max's and another hour to Duke's. Nothing was said about Toni after the initial statement from Max when he said, "Well, I guess she's not going to call. I hate that, but I'm not going to call her because I'm in the right."

Duke said, "It's like I said last night, "It's work itself out."

"Maybe it will and maybe it won't. Let's go to East Tennessee and forget about it."

They stopped and got some biscuits at a drive thru before they got out of Memphis and ate them while they rode, and then they didn't stop again all the way to Middleton.

When they got to Max's house, Duke went in and spoke to Max's Mother, and she offered to fix him a sandwich. He was hungry because they hadn't had anything since the biscuits they got in Memphis that morning.

While Max's Mother was fixing their lunch, Duke asked Max if he could use the phone, and of course he said he could. He pulled his billfold out of his pocket where he had Sissy's number and dialed it. She was apparently at home because they talked for a few minutes, and then he came in the kitchen and sat down to eat his sandwich and other things Mrs. Norwood had prepared.

The two football players devoured the food Mrs. Norwood fixed for them. It wasn't the training table, but Max's Mom was used to feeding him, and all she had to do was add some to it. In that part of the country, people would say, "We'll just add more water to the gravy." Northerners wouldn't understand that, but all Southerners do.

Duke said, "Max, I'll be back down here tomorrow. I

called Sissy, and she said she would like to see me, and she invited me to come down tomorrow, and I told her I would. Do you want to see if Amy's at home?"

"No, I don't think so. You know what, Duke? I love two women, and I can't see either one of them."

"Maybe you need to look for someone else."

"You may be right." He grinned and said, "Maybe I can find me a lady Marine or a Marine nurse."

Duke grinned, too, and said, "That may be the route to go. Listen, I guess I had better go. I've still got to drive another hour, and I'm anxious to see my parents. I haven't seen them for a long time. Do you know yet when you're going to go back to Memphis?"

"No. I guess it'll depend on Toni. If she calls and apologizes, I'll probably go back in three of four days, but if she doesn't, then I won't go back until around the tenth or twelfth of the month."

"That's when I'll be going back. If you don't go until the tenth or twelfth, do you want to ride back with me?"

"No thanks, Duke. I'll take my Jeep back. Sometimes I need transportation, and I don't want to have to ask you every time."

"Well, I don't mind, but it's up to you. I'll talk to you sometime before we go back. See you."

"See ya. Thanks for the ride home."

Duke left, and Max was left at home by himself and his Mother, and he didn't know what to do with himself. He hung around the house for most of the afternoon, and then he got in his Jeep and went to the El Rancho in hopes of finding some of his buddies, but none of them were there, so he didn't stay. He went to a couple other hangouts, but he couldn't find anybody that he wanted to be with, and he finally went back home and sat with his parents in front of the TV. He enjoyed being with them, but he was lonesome to see some of his friends as well.

He thought, *I was sure some of my buddies would be home from college, and if they are, they're sure not out anywhere. I may as well go back to Memphis, but if I do, Mother and Daddy will be disappointed. I'll just wait 'til tomorrow and see if anybody shows up. Toni may still call. I hope she does, then I can make my plans.*

Just when he thought about Toni, the phone rang, and his Mom answered it. He heard her say, "Yes, he's here. Just a minute."

She held the phone away from her ear and said, "Max, it's for you."

He got up and went to where his Mom held the phone and mouthed silently, "Who is it?"

His Mom mouthed back, "I don't know. Some girl," and handed him the phone.

"Hello."

On the other end, a nice voice said, "Hi. Did you think I wasn't going to call?" It was Toni.

"Hi. I wasn't sure, and I'm glad you did. What are you doing?"

"Just wishing you were here. I'm so sorry about the way I behaved the other night, I was afraid you wouldn't want to talk to me, and that's why I didn't call you when I got home after I let you out. I shouldn't have done that, but I love you so much, I guess I just wanted to have all of you, and I got mad when you wouldn't let me. Will you forgive me?"

"Yeah, you're forgiven. I'm glad you called. I was afraid you wouldn't."

She asked, "When are you coming back to Memphis?"

"I'm not sure. I was going to just be home for three or four days, then, when we had our little hiccup, I decided to stay until time to come back for classes, and that's what I told my parents. If I tell them that I'm not going to stay here that long, it's going to really disappoint them. Let me see what I can work out, okay?"

"Okay. I just hope you'll hurry and get back to me. I miss you like crazy."

"I miss you, too. I'll call and let you know." They talked for a few more minutes, and then they hung up.

When he got back in the den, his Daddy asked, "Who was that?"

"It was a girl that I've been dating."

"She's keeping track of you, huh?"

"Not really. We had a fight before I left Memphis, and she just called to see if we're still okay."

"Well, are you?"

"Yes sir, we are now, but if she hadn't called, we wouldn't be."

His Mom asked, "Honey, are you all serious?"

"I think so, but the Marines are getting in the way. You know, I have to serve four years when I get out of school, and I have no idea where I'll be, or if she can be with me, so we're sort of in a state of limbo right now. We don't want to get married until we know whether or not she can be with me. If we get married, and then I get deployed overseas, it won't be a good thing, so we'll just have to wait and see what happens after I become a Leatherneck."

"Are you going to let us meet her?"

"Yes ma'am. I hope to."

His Daddy asked him, "Now that you all have your spat patched up, does that mean you're going to go back earlier than you said you were?"

"I don't know. I'm going to have to think about that."

"Your Mother and I hope you'll stay until you just have to get back for school. When you go to the Marines, we may not get to see you very much."

"I think I'm going to bed. I'll see you all in the morning."

His Mother said, "Good night, Son."

The next morning, he slept late, and then after lunch, he went to the mall to mess around. He thought he might see somebody he knew, but he didn't. He wondered when Duke would be down to see Sissy, but Duke hadn't said, so he managed to kill the whole afternoon at the mall, and then he went home.

About seven thirty or eight o'clock he decided to go to the El Rancho to see if anybody was there. The first people he saw was Duke and Sissy, and he went over to their table to speak. After a few minutes, Duke asked, "Did you ever get that phone call?"

"Yeah, I got it last night."

"When are you going back?"

"I haven't made up my mind yet. If I leave early, it's going to really disappoint my parents, so I don't know what I'm going to do."

Sissy was taking this all in, and then Duke asked, "Do you know what I'd do?"

"What?"

"I'd stay here until I had to get back to class. That's what I'm doing."

"I know, and I might do that."

Max stayed with Duke and Sissy for a few more minutes, and then he saw a couple of guys he knew, and he went over to see them. He didn't stay with them very long before he left to go back home.

He hadn't been gone five minutes before Amy and Joyce Ann Hartley walked in. They, too, saw Sissy and Duke, and they went over to see them before they got a table of their own. Sissy said, "You just missed Max. He hasn't been gone ten minutes."

Amy said, "Really? Where was he going?"

"I don't know. Home, probably."

"I hate I missed him. Does he look alright?"

"He looks good. Football has agreed with him, and he doesn't just look good; he looks great." She put her hand on Duke's arm and said, "Just like my man, Duke, here."

Amy asked Duke, "Duke, do you know when he's going back?"

"Not really, and I don't think he knows. He was originally only going to be here for three or four days, but he and the girl he's seeing in Memphis had a fight before we left to come home, and he said he was going to stay here until the last minute before he had to get back for class. Then when he was in here a little bit ago, he said he got a call from his girl, and he might go back early."

She said, "Oh. I didn't know he was seeing someone. Is he serious about her?"

He said, "Amy, you'll have to ask Max that, but I'd say he is."

Duke and Sissy went to the nine o'clock movie after they left the El Rancho, and then he took her home. They agreed to get together again in a couple of days. They briefly kissed goodnight, and he left.

About midnight, Sissy's phone rang. She had her own extension, so it didn't wake up her parents. "Hello."

"Did you have a good time with Duke?"

"Yeah. He is truly a gentle giant. I like him, and I think he likes me."

"Well, tell me about Max."

"I don't know anything to tell you, Amy. We saw him for maybe fifteen minutes, and then he left to go talk to some of his buddies, but I'll say this; he really looks good."

"Did he ask about me?"

"No. I'm afraid not. Besides, I thought you were the one who broke off all communications with him."

"Yeah, I guess I did."

Max thought long and hard about going back early, but he decided that since he would be leaving for the Marines in just a few months, he would spend as much time with his parents as he could. Another week of not seeing Toni wouldn't make any difference one way or the other. He saw Duke again during the holidays, and they arranged for Duke to come to Middleton, and they would drive back to Memphis together, but each in his own car.

***

Amy caught a plane back to Champaign the day before Max left, and when she got back to Ashton Woods, Karen hadn't returned yet, so she was all alone.

She called the Brock Animal Hospital in Decatur and asked to speak to either Karen or Neal, and after a long wait, Neal answered. "Hi. It's Amy. I just wanted to let you guys know I'm back."

He said, "Hi, Pretty Lady. I'm glad you're back, and I'm glad to hear your voice. Did you just get in?"

"Yeah, a little while ago. When are you all coming back?"

"We're planning to come back after work tomorrow evening. We should be there by about seven or seven thirty. I'll be anxious to see you."

"Really?"

"Really. Why did you ask that?"

"Oh, no reason."

"There must have been a reason. What was it?"

"I just didn't think you would care one way or the other whether you saw me or not."

"That is totally not true. I've missed you."

"I've missed you too. Have you all been real busy?"

"Like you wouldn't believe, but we're catching up a little bit now."

"Well, I won't keep you. I just wanted to check and see when you're coming back."

"If nothing happens, we'll see you tomorrow night."

"Okay, I'll look for you."

She felt better when she hung up. She was glad that she got to talk to Neal, and she was thrilled that he said he missed her and that he was anxious to see her.

She went to the mall the next day and did anything she could to help pass time until Karen and Neal got there. It got dark a little after five, and she didn't want to be out by herself after dark, so she went home.

She hoped that they would not have stopped to eat on the way back, so she didn't get anything for herself, just in case they would all go out when Neal and Karen got back from Decatur.

Her hopes were realized when they pulled up at seven o'clock, and Neal and Karen both got out, and began unloading her stuff. Amy went out to help, and they all hugged. Karen said, I'm just going to drop this stuff off, and then we're going to go get something to eat. Have you had dinner?"

"No, and I'm starving."

After they got Karen's things unloaded, they went to get some food. In the restaurant, they went to a booth and Neal said to Karen, "Sis, why don't you sit on this side and let me sit next to Amy."

It was hard to tell who was most surprised; Amy or Karen, but that's what they did. Karen sat on one side by herself, and Amy and Neal sat together on the other side. The booth was pretty small, and occasionally, Neal would press his leg up against Amy's, and Amy was just beside herself. He would try to disguise it by saying something to her as he pressed her leg. She hated to leave when they finished eating, but in a little bit, they had to.

They were in Neal's car, and he had to take them back to Ashton Woods. When he pulled up to the front entrance, Amy and Karen got out and thanked him for taking them to eat. As they were walking away, Neal called out to Amy, and when she turned around, he said, "Come here a minute." She walked around to his side of the car, and through the open window he asked, "Amy, I've been thinking a lot about this, and I'm wondering if you would like to go out with me sometime."

She said, "Yeah, I would. When are you thinking about?"

"Well, it should be on a school night because we're always at the clinic on weekends. Why don't we do something this Thursday? Will that work for you?"

"It will. What will we do?"

"I don't know, but we'll figure out something. I just want to be with you, one on one."

"I'd like that. Call me and let me know what time and everything, okay?"

"I can't wait to take you out."

Karen had waited for Amy to leave Neal, and when she caught up to her, she asked, "What did Neal want?"

"Would you believe he asked me out?"

"Really? It's about time. I've been telling him ever since you got here that he should do that."

"Have you really? Why?"

"Because it doesn't take a rocket scientist to see that you two belong together. I won't be surprised if you become my sister-in-law one day."

"You're crazy. We haven't even had one date yet, and already, you're making me your sister-in-law. You're nuts."

"Tell you what. When we get upstairs, you get a piece of paper and write this down with the date and put it somewhere where you can find it, or better still, give it to me, and I'll hold it."

When they got to their room, Karen said, "Okay, get some paper and write down what I said."

"I'm not going to do it. If you want it written, you write it."

"Alright, I will," and she got a piece of paper and a pen and wrote, "I predict that Amy will be my sister-in-law one day." She signed it and dated it and put it in a safe place to keep until her prediction would come true.

The two spent most of the evening telling each other about

what happened with them during the holidays, and after a very busy day, they turned in early.

***

Amy's first full day in Champaign was the day Max and Duke drove back to Memphis. They arrived at their dorm at three thirty, and the first thing Max did was call Toni. When she answered, he said, "Hi. I'm back."

"Good. I've missed you. Are you coming over?"

"If you want me to."

"I want you to. What time can you be here?"

"I'll be there in about an hour. I've got to unload my Jeep, and then I'll head your way."

"Hurry, I want to see you."

"You be puckered up when I get there because I'm going to plant a big one on you."

She laughed and said, "I'm already puckered up. Hurry."

He was pretty close with his ETA. It was almost exactly an hour when he got to her house, and true to his word, he planted a big kiss on her lips.

She said, "It seems like you've been gone for a month. I'm sure glad you're back," and they kissed again before going into the house. Toni's Mother was gone, so they had the house all to themselves.

They hung around the house until Mrs. Fisher came in, and when she got there, she offered to fix supper for Max, but he said, "Thanks a lot, but Toni and I thought we would go out and get some Chinese food. You're welcome to go with us if you'd like."

"No thank you. Tim will be here in a few minutes, and he's not a big fan of Chinese food, so we'll go with you all another time, okay?"

"Let's be sure and do that," Max said.

Before Tim got home, Toni and Max left for the Dragon

China restaurant, since they were both about to starve. Dragon China had a buffet where a person could eat all they wanted, and Max, especially, took advantage of it, and Toni held her own as well.

Five months later

Max finished his senior year and graduated in May, and on the day of his graduation, he received his commission as Second Lieutenant in the United States Marine Corp, and he would have to report to Quantico, Virginia in thirty days for active duty.

He and Toni really wanted to get married, but she wanted to wait until they found out where he would be stationed after his basic training, and he agreed that that was the best thing to do.

Chapter Seven

Amy and Neal had developed into a recognizable couple after they began dating after the Christmas break. Neal was to graduate in May, and Amy would finish her sophomore year. They had talked about marriage, but they weren't able to figure out how to go about it because Neal would be going back to Decatur to work in the family's animal hospital, and he didn't want to leave Amy four days a week, every week.

Not too long before graduation, Neal found out that he would be graduating with Magna Cum Laude honors. That is next to the pinnacle of college honors, and Amy was very proud of him as was his family. His father had graduated Magna Cum Laude, so Neal was following in his footsteps. Since Karen and Amy were studying to be vets, Neal's honor was the standard that they would shoot for.

The University of Illinois School of Veterinary Medicine at Urbana was out for the summer in mid-May, and Amy and Karen finished their sophomore years. Amy was especially glad because she had been going down to Decatur every weekend to see Neal and to work in the animal hospital and then going back to Urbana for school, Monday through Friday.

She was planning to spend all summer in Decatur, but she wanted to go home to see her parents, also, so she scheduled a visit to see them during the week of July fourth. That way, she could see them and more than likely see Sissy, and maybe even some more of her friends. Dr. Brock was paying her a little when she helped at the clinic, and she tried to save all that. She thought she would use part of it to buy a plane ticket to Middleton.

She flew home to Middleton, and the way the Fourth fell that year, she was able to get nine days out of a seven-day week. She thoroughly enjoyed her stay in Middleton, but she missed Neal terribly, and when she got back to Decatur, he was there to meet the plane.

The next day was a workday, and they all were at the clinic early, because they had some early appointments. A couple of them were for surgeries, and while Neal was not going to be the main surgeon, he was going to assist. His surgery was one that he had never done and assisting in it gave him a chance to learn how to do it.

Amy was scheduled to start back to school the third week of August, and the week before, Neal asked her to go to a concert, and she readily accepted. After the concert, it was still early, so Neal drove down to a place he knew on Lake Decatur and parked.

Neal raised the armrests on the seats to make a bench type seat in the car, in order for them to sit closer to each other. After enjoying the beauty of the lights shining on the water and smooching a little, Neal reached into a side-pocket by his seat and turned back to Amy.

"I know we've talked about this, but we've never done more than talk, so now I want to do more." He held up a ring box and opened it to a beautiful diamond solitaire, and said, "Amy, I've loved you from the first moment I saw you when you and Karen first moved into Ashton Woods, and I can't imagine my life without you in it. Will you do me the honor of being my wife?"

By then, Amy was crying, and she said, "You've loved me that long? I've loved you too. Yes, I'd be thrilled to be your wife. They kissed and sat there looking at her ring. In a minute, she asked, "Neal, are you thinking about when we'll get married? I don't want to wait two more years, do you?"

"No, I don't want to wait that long either. I thought I'd talk to you after I gave you the ring to see what you think."

"About what?"

"Well, think about this. Right now, you're in Champaign Monday through Friday, and then you come to Decatur. I'm in

Decatur all that time now, and I get to see you when you come down here. We both work in the clinic, and when the day is over, we go to bed; me in my bedroom and you in the guest room.

"Now, let's say we get married, and we keep the same schedule. You're in Champaign Monday through Friday and come down here after school on Friday. We still work all day, but when we're through, we go to bed. Not me in my bedroom and you in the guest room, but we both go to my bedroom and sleep together.

"We're still working and going to school just like we have been, but there's one major change: We're able to sleep together on weekends. What do you think about that idea?"

"It sounds good to me. Let's talk and think about it some more."

Karen was still up when they got home, and Amy showed her the ring, and said, "You were right."

"I knew I was. When's the big day?"

"We haven't had time to think about it. I still have to go to school, you know."

"I know, but you should be able to work out something."

Amy joked and said, "I guess I could quit school and become just a housewife."

Neal said, "That would be alright with me."

Amy asked, "Are you serious? After me already spending six years in college to become a vet and only having two more? I hope you're kidding."

He frowned and said, "Of course I am. I want you to become the best veterinarian in Illinois and work alongside me until we grow old. We'll figure something out."

Karen said, "The main thing is that you're going to get married. With a little thought, I think all those details can be worked out. Amy, I'm just glad you're going to be my sister-in-law. I couldn't ask for a better one."

Amy hugged her and said, "Thank you, Karen. I'm glad, too. I love you."

The next morning, after Neal's parents had come downstairs, Amy and Neal showed them her ring, and they were thrilled. His Mother and Daddy both hugged him, and then they both hugged Amy. Dr. Brock said, "Amy, it's really going to be good having you as my daughter-in-law. I'm very happy."

"Thank you, sir."

Neal's Mother took Amy's hand and said, "You know, Amy, I felt like you were my daughter when you first began coming down here, and now, I really do. We both love you."

"I love you all, too."

On Sunday night, when Karen and Amy were going back to Champaign, an idea came to Amy. It was like a light coming on. She didn't say anything to Karen, but just as soon as they got back to Ashton Woods, she called Neal.

Neal answered the phone, and she said, "Hi."

"Hi. Is something wrong?"

"No, I just had what I think is a wonderful idea."

"Well, tell me about it."

"What do you think about Monticello? Do you like it?"

"Monticello? You want to know what I think about Monticello? I think it's a nice little town. Why?"

"This idea came to me when we were driving home a little while ago, and I noticed a road sign when we were coming through Monticello that said it was twenty-two miles to Champaign. Well, I did a little figuring in my head and figured that was close to the distance from Decatur to Monticello. Now, here's what I'm thinking. What if we go ahead and get married and get an apartment in Monticello? If we do that, you would only have about twenty or twenty five minutes from the clinic to Monticello, and you're having to drive fifteen or twenty minutes from home to the clinic now, so we're only talking about you driving another ten minutes or so.

"If Champaign is only twenty-two miles from Monticello, then I would only have eighteen to twenty minutes driving time, and I would gladly drive twenty minutes to be with you every day. Would you drive an extra ten minutes to be with me?"

"Wow. You're a sly little fox, aren't you? You know, that idea may just work. Monticello is so small, I just wonder if they have any apartments, but surely they do. If I get some time, I'll drive up there and see if I can find out what they have."

"That might be our answer. I just want to hurry and marry you. I've got a couple of other ideas that I'll tell you about when I see you."

"Tell me about them now."

"No. I'll tell you when I see you. I've gotta go. Love ya. Bye."

Karen had been listening to the conversation, and when she hung up, Amy asked her," Did you hear what I told Neal?"

"Yeah, I heard."

"What do you think?"

"I think you hit on something good. What did Neal say?"

"He said he thought it was a good idea, too. He said when he gets some time, he's going to go up to Monticello and see what he can find in the way of apartments. It's such a small town, we wonder how the apartment situation is."

Karen said, "I'm sure there are apartments down there. Monticello isn't that small. I'll bet you can find a nice place when you start looking."

"I hope you're right. Do you know what bothers me more than anything else, Karen?"

"What?"

"If we get married and move into an apartment, you'll be by yourself, and I don't want to leave you by yourself."

"Don't let that bother you. I'll be just fine."

"Still, it bothers me. You may just have to move in with us."

"Yeah, right. I can see Neal Brock living with his sister

and new bride." They both laughed and said they might just tell him that was what they were going to do to see what he says.

Amy said, "He's such a nice and easy going somebody, I'll bet when we tell him that, that he'll say that's fine with him."

Karen said, "I'll bet he doesn't, but what if he does?"

"Wouldn't that be something?" There was a pause in the conversation, and then Amy said, "You know what, Karen?"

"What?"

"I wouldn't care if you did stay with us. The three of us have always gotten along great, and you'd have your own room, so why not?"

"Girlfriend, I wouldn't think of staying with you two. Now, if you had been married for twenty-five or thirty years, and you asked me to come stay with you for a while, I might would consider it, but not while you're newlyweds. It's sweet of you for thinking about it, though."

As soon as they quit talking, Amy called her Mother to tell her the news. When her Mother answered, Amy said, "Hey, Mother. What are you doing?"

Her Mother told her several things that she was and had been doing, and then she asked, "Are you alright? You don't usually call this often."

"Yes ma'am. I'm great. I wanted to tell you something. Guess what?"

"What?"

"I've told you about Neal, Karen's brother, haven't I?"

"Yes you told me. What about him?"

"Mother, he gave me a ring, and we're going to get married."

"Wow. I wasn't expecting that. When is the wedding, and where will it be?"

"I don't know the answer to any of your questions yet. I just got my ring last night, and I had to leave to come back to school today, but I'll let you know everything when I know it. I just wanted to tell you about my ring."

"Well, I'm happy for you, Darling. Oh, where will the wedding be? Are you coming home to get married?"

"Like I said, I don't know that yet, either, but I'll let you know."

Amy had never had trouble concentrating on her school work, and she had always paid close attention to the professors as they lectured, but now, since she had an engagement ring and knew she would be getting married pretty soon, she caught herself thinking about getting married and not on the lectures. She realized that she was not paying attention, and she knew that it would affect her grades, so she made every effort to correct what she was doing, or in that case, not doing.

Neal called Tuesday night and said, "Hey Sweetie, what's up?"

"Just studying. What's up with you?"

"I took some time off today, and I drove up to Monticello to look around."

"Did you like what you saw?"

"You know what? I did. That's a nice little town, and there are lots of apartments for rent as well as a lot of condominiums, so we shouldn't have any trouble finding something when we need it."

"That's surprising. I wonder why there are so many."

"I went to see a realtor, and I asked him the same thing. He said that Monticello is more or less a bedroom community for Champaign and Decatur. A lot of the population works in both places, and there is a constant turnover in real estate. The more I think about your idea of moving there, at least until you get out of school, the better I like it. Are you planning to come down here this next weekend?"

"I'm planning on it. Why?"

"You've been getting out early on Fridays and getting down here early, and I thought that if you do that this coming

Friday, maybe I can get away from the clinic early and meet you up in Monticello as you're coming down here. I'm sure Karen won't mind stopping. Do you want to do that?"

"Yeah. I'd like to."

"I saw a couple of places that I liked, and I'll try to find them when you get here."

"Great. I'm so excited, I'm having a hard time keeping my mind on my schoolwork, and this is going to add to it."

The next three days were even harder for her to concentrate because of what she and Neal were going to do Friday afternoon. Finally, her last class dismissed early Friday, and she and Karen literally ran from the classroom to Karen's car, which they had driven that morning. Just as soon as they got to their room at Ashton Woods, Amy called Neal. When he answered she said, "Are you ready to leave?"

"Yeah. I can leave in about ten minutes. Why don't I meet you at McDonalds? It's at exit one sixty-four right off I-72. I'll try to be there in thirty minutes."

"Sounds good. See you then. Bye."

They got to McDonalds about five minutes apart, and Neal told Karen to just leave her car there in the parking lot while he took them to see the things he had found. They drove around some very nice residential sections in Monticello, where there were some beautiful homes for sale, and then he drove to three or four nice apartment buildings. At one of the buildings he told Amy, "I went in one of the apartments in this building, and it was very nice.

They continued the tour for another hour or so, and then they went back to McDonalds to get Karen's car. When they pulled up to it, Neal said to Amy, "Why don't you ride with me, and Karen can follow us?"

She hesitated for a minute and then said, "I'll just ride with Karen. I came down here with her, so I need to go on with her, or else it'll be bad luck," and she and Karen got out of his car and got into Karen's. In thirty minutes, they were at the

Brock's home in Decatur.

When they arrived at the Brock house and got out, Neal said, "I timed how long it took from McDonalds to here, and it was thirty minutes. When we passed the exit where the clinic is, we had driven eighteen minutes, and to here was another twelve, so if we get an apartment in Monticello, it'll take me about twenty minutes to get to work as opposed to about fifteen minutes now."

Karen said, "That's pretty good. Actually, it's about six of one and a half dozen of the other. What do you think, Neal?"

"I think we should start planning a wedding. Let's go in the house and sit down. Mom and Dad might want to get in on it."

When they got in the house, Neal and Karen's Mom had dinner ready and told them to come eat. While they were eating, Amy asked, "Neal, did you tell your Mom and Dad what we've been talking about?"

Dr. Brock asked, "Is this a surprise?"

Neal said, "Well, kinda. You know, Amy has another year in school after this one, and we don't want to have to wait two years to get married, so Amy had this great idea. She said we could go ahead and get married, and we could rent an apartment up in Monticello until she graduates. She would have to drive about twenty minutes to school every day, and I would only have to drive about ten minutes longer than I do now. We're still in the talking stages, and we're wondering what you guys think?"

Neal's Dad said, "That sounds pretty good to me. I can't think of any objections. When do you think you all will get married?"

His Mother chimed in before they could answer his Dad's question and asked, "Where will the wedding be?"

Neal said, "Those are two questions we have to talk about. Hopefully, we can resolve them tonight or tomorrow, and we would welcome your input."

His Mom said, "I hope you'll decide to get married here in Decatur. What are you thinking, Amy?"

"I'm having a hard time with that. I know my Mother will want me to get married in my home church, but I've been gone for more than six years, and I really don't feel like it's my home church anymore. What do you think? I know you want us to get married here in Decatur, but if Karen was seven hundred miles from here and had been gone for more than six years and wanted to marry someone who lived where she was, what would you expect her to do?"

Dr. Brock said, "You do have a problem there, don't you, Amy?"

"Yes I do. I like the church we go to here, and I'd like to get married here, but if I do, I'll feel as if I'm turning my back on my Mother, and I don't want to feel that way."

Neal's Mother said, "Darling, why don't you call your Mother and talk to her? Tell her how you feel and see what she says."

"Thanks, Mrs. B. I'll do that. Neal, Honey, before I call my Mother and try to decide where the wedding is going to be, I think you and I need to sit down and decide when it's going to be."

Neal said, "I guess you're right. Why don't we do that tonight?"

After they all finished dinner, the three women busied themselves cleaning up the kitchen and washing dishes while Neal and his Dad went in the den and turned on a ballgame.

When the ladies came into the den, Neal said, "Amy, why don't we go out to the mall? We don't have to go shopping. We can just walk around and talk and maybe make a decision on a wedding date."

"Okay. Whenever you're ready."

"I'm ready now. Are you ready?"

They got up to leave, and as they were leaving, Neal told everybody, "We'll see you in a little while."

Hickory Point Mall was not huge, but it was the perfect place for Amy and Neal to go to spend time talking. Neal asked, "Have you thought about a date?"

"I've thought about a hundred dates, but I can't settle on one, and that's why it's going to take both of us."

Neal said, "Well tell me your thoughts."

"I first thought about getting married during Christmas break at school, but then when I thought about everything that goes on at that time, I decided that that might not be the best time. Then I thought we should wait until school is out for the summer, and that's probably the best time, but it means we'll have to wait that much longer. Have you thought about when would be best?"

"I have. I've thought about two scenarios, and whichever scenario we choose will have to be strictly your decision."

"I don't understand. What do you mean?"

"Okay, the first scenario is that we go to a Justice of the Peace, and we can go whenever you want to. The Second scenario is a church wedding which will take a lot of planning by both our parents and the two of us, and in that case, I think it would have to take place after school is out for the summer. Now, what do want to do?"

"Boy! You have done some thinking haven't you?"

"I think about it all the time."

"Which one would you rather do?"

Neal said, "Whichever one you would rather do, but let me say this. I would personally rather just go to a J.P. and get it done very simply, but I don't know if my parents would ever forgive me if we did. I don't know your parents yet, but I'll bet they would rather you have a church wedding. It doesn't have to be huge, but I think we need to include our family and friends in it. This means we'll have to wait a little longer, but when we do get married, we'll be married for the rest of our lives, and I don't think a delay of just a few months will matter in the grand scheme of things."

Amy said, "You know what? I think you're right about a church wedding and waiting until next summer." She thought about her experience with Max at a J.P.'s earlier and said, "Besides I definitely don't like the idea of going to a Justice of the Peace."

Neal was a little surprised at her definite opinion of a J.P. She had never told him about her high school marriage, so he didn't know why."

He said, "Do we know what we're going to do now?"

"Yeah, I think so. Now, we can start making some plans, and we won't have to rush so much. I'll call Mother tomorrow and talk to her about where, and the location is also going to make some difference in who I ask to be my attendants. I don't feel like I can ask my friends here to go all the way to Middleton, and at the same time, I don't feel that I can ask my friends in Middleton to come out her. First of all, it's too expensive."

Neal asked, "Are we going to have a big wedding?"

"I don't think so, unless you want a big one. I think two or three attendants for each of us will be enough. What do you think?"

"That's fine with me. We'll be just as married in a small wedding as we would be in a huge one. I'm glad you don't want to go so big."

She said, "Why don't we go back to your house so we can tell your folks and see their reaction. I'm anxious to call my Mother now. She and I may argue about the location, but I think I want to get married here, because this has been where my life has been for three years."

Chapter Eight

Max went home after graduation to spend some time with his parents before he had to leave for Quantico, and Duke went home as well.

The two were going to be separated for a long time in just a few days., and they hated the idea. They had become such close friends over the last four years.

Before he left Memphis, Duke was contacted by a Sports Agent, who wanted to represent him in the upcoming NFL Draft. He told Duke that it looked as if he would be drafted no later than the second round, and he was thrilled. He had no idea where he would go, but it didn't matter to him. He was just happy with the idea of playing professional football.

Ever since Max took him to Middleton the first time and he met Sissy, he has been smitten with her. Sissy has had chances to date several very nice young men, but her loyalty to Duke kept her from going out with any of them, and Duke remained true to her, also. Since Max was going to be home for several days, Duke took advantage of that, and spent a lot of time in Middleton; the days with Max and the evenings with Sissy.

Whenever Max was in Sissy's presence, he and Sissy were both careful to not mention Amy or what she was doing, even though the two of them kept in close touch.

Max's thirty days were ending too soon, and he was getting ready to report to Quantico but first, he wanted Toni to come to Middleton to meet his parents, so the week before he was scheduled to leave, he asked her to come for a day or two.

When he told Duke that she was coming, Duke insisted that he and Toni go to dinner with him and Sissy, and Max agreed to do it.

Toni arrived about two o'clock the next afternoon, and

Duke was already there. He had come down from Meigs County that morning. When he had had time to speak to her and to talk for a few minutes, he called Sissy and set up a time and place for their double date that evening.

Max hated for all four of them to ride in his Jeep, so he asked Duke to drive. They picked Sissy up at seven o'clock and went to the Depot, one of Middleton's finer restaurant. Toni was interested to know Max and Sissy's background together, and when they told her that they had grown up together and were kind of like brother and sister, she seemed satisfied.

Sissy was very curious about how Toni and Max had gotten together, and she asked if they were serious. Max acted as the spokesman and he said to Sissy, "You know I'm leaving next week for the Marines, and I have made a commitment to them for four years." He kind of rubbed it in because he knew that whatever he said would be relayed to Amy just as soon as Sissy had a chance to talk to her, and he said, "I was hoping that Toni and I could get married before I left, but she, being the wise one, thought it would be best if we waited until we knew where I would be stationed and for how long, so I guess to answer your question about how serious we are, I'd say we're pretty serious." He picked up Toni's hand that she had on the table and kissed it.

The whole evening was very pleasant. They spent quite a bit of time talking, and it seemed as if the more they talked, the more Max dreaded leaving. He had come to love Duke as a brother because of their four years as roommates and teammates, and he loved Sissy because of their background together. Of course, he loved Toni because she would hopefully, soon be his wife.

The evening ended too soon, and Duke took Max and Toni home before he took Sissy. Not knowing if he would see Sissy again before he left, he asked her to get out of the car, and he gave her a big, long hug when she got out. He told her, "Sissy,

I'm always interested in what goes on around here, so if there's anything you think I would want to know, how about calling my Mom or Daddy and tell them, will you?"

"I will. You be careful, ya hear? If you'll send me your address, I'll write you, if you want me to."

"I'd like that, and if you hear anything about any of our mutual friends, let me know about it." When he said that, he winked at her and said, "Bye, Sissy."

"Bye Max."

Before Duke drove off, Max asked him, "Will I see you before I leave?"

"Yeah. I'll be back down here Friday, and I'll come by."

"Be sure you do, okay?"

"I will. I'll see you Friday."

Toni left to go home the next afternoon, and parting was hard for both of them. He told her, "Honey, I'm not very good at this kind of thing, but I want you to know that I really love you, and I want you to be my partner for the rest of our lives." He pulled out a small box and opened it to a beautiful diamond ring and asked, "Will you marry me, Toni?"

She looked shocked, and after several seconds of silence, she said, "Yes, I'll marry you."

He said, "Whew! With that pause, you had me worried. They kissed, and he told her again that he loved her. He promised that just as soon as he could find out how long he would be at Quantico; if he could, indeed, find that out, he would send for her. With the romantic moment giving her the ring and telling her that he loved her two different times, he didn't notice that she never told him that she loved him.

He spent a lot of time on the phone talking to anybody that would talk to him to try and get information on length of stay, housing, and other things that he wanted to know before he left, but nobody seemed to know anything, so he would just have to wait until he got there to get any kind of information. He found out real quick that in the military, nearly everything is on a *need to know* basis, and apparently they didn't think he needed to know most of the things he asked about, but what he did find out was that for the first six months of active duty, he and all the other newcomers would report to The Basic School (TBS) for six months of all around combat training.

He didn't know how to tell Toni how to get in touch with him before he left home, so one of the first things he did, when he got to Quantico and found out what his address was, was to write her and give her his address. He told her he would write again just as soon as he could, but he didn't know what kind of demands on his time were going to be required.

At TBS, all students qualify on weapons, act in each role of a fire team, practice land navigation, ride in tanks, shoot field artillery, do landings in Ospreys, and whatever else instructors decide is relevant.

After TBS, students are assigned their Military Occupation Specialties (MOS's), which are awarded based on a student's preference and class ranking. After that, Second Lieutenants go on to their next schools, whether for infantry, Field Artillery, Flight School, etc. All USMC Officers attend TBS.

Second Lieutenants are typically assigned a Platoon of forty to fifty Marines, depending on their community. Upon arriving, new Officers must work hard to earn the respect of their Marines. Despite their authority over all the Enlisted ranks, Second Lieutenants require mentoring from their Non-Commissioned Officers in order to learn how to perform their duties and lead Marines in combat. The most successful Second Lieutenants are hardworking, humble, honest, and have a strong backbone when required. Second Lieutenants who refuse to heed the advice of their Platoon Sergeant and Squad Leaders tend to be socially isolated and perform poorly, with little chance of remediation. Second Lieutenants or Butter Bars learn over time how to implement the skills they learned over the course of their training.

The discipline and teamwork Max learned while playing football really helped him when he got to the Marines. He finished TBS at the top of his class, and the Platoon Leaders and Squad Leaders, not only from his Platoon, but from other Platoons as well gave him well deserved respect.

When he was in college, taking ROTC, he heard about all these things, but still, he was shocked when he was actually exposed to them up close and personal. While he was in TBS, he got acquainted with a fellow named Earl Tedder, and Earl became a good Buddy. He had practically the same kind of background that Max had in terms of school and athletics. Earl played football at Georgia State University, and like Max, he started three years. They seemed to have a lot in common, and they became not only Buddies, but close friends.

He wrote to Toni whenever he had a chance during TBS, but he couldn't write as often as he wanted to. She had been faithful with her letters, but they had slowed down a little the last month or so. He tried to call her at least once every week or ten days, but the long-distance romance was bearing on both of them. His last call was to tell her that he would be through with TBS in two weeks from that day, and he was going to get a fourteen-day leave. He told her he was going home, and that he wanted to come to West Memphis for a few days during that time, and she told him she would look forward to it.

The two weeks passed quickly compared to the six months at the TBS, and Max found a deal on one of the regional airlines. He flew into Middleton, and his Mother and Daddy were at the airport to meet him. They were all happy to see each other, and they went home to one of Max's Mother's good home-cooked meals. He called Toni when he got home, and she wanted to know when he was coming to West Memphis. He said, "I'd like to come day after tomorrow. Is that good for you?"

"Yeah. That's fine."

He said, "I'll come for a couple of days and then come home for Christmas, and then come back to your house after Christmas. Is that alright?"

"It is, except we have two road volleyball games the week after Christmas, and I won't be home hardly any that week."

"Darn! Something's always messing us up. I can't come the week after that because I have to go back to Quantico."

"When's your next leave?"

"I don't know. I have MOS School for fifty-two days, and I've heard rumors that we might be deployed after that. I'll have to let you know. I hope we're not deployed because I want you to come be with me."

"Max, are you forgetting that I'm not going to do anything like that until I graduate?"

"No, I haven't forgot. I'm just so anxious for us to be together. Look, I'll see you day after tomorrow."

"Okay. Be careful, and Mother and Daddy want you to stay here. Is that alright?"

"Perfect. I love you."

"See you."

After he hung up, he went into the den and told his parents that he was going to Memphis the day after tomorrow, but he would only be gone two or three days. Then he asked his Mother, "Mother, would you be interested in letting me drive your car to Memphis? The Jeep doesn't ride as smooth as your car, and I hate to be tired out when I get to Toni's. What do you say?"

She asked, "Is your Jeep automatic?"

"Yes Ma'am. It's real easy to drive. It just rides rough on a long trip."

"Okay, you can take my car, but you be very careful."

He left really early for West Memphis and got there at lunchtime. He stopped and got a burger before he went to Toni's and then went to see her. Her Mother acted as though she was tickled to see him, and they spent an enjoyable afternoon together before Tim came in from work.

Max asked Toni, "What do you want to do tonight?"

"I don't know. Do you have any suggestions?"

He said, "You know what? I've been told that the Lafayette Music Room is a great place to go. They are supposed to have fantastic food and great music. I spent four years going to school in Memphis, but I never did go there. Have you ever been there?"

"No. That's one that I've missed. You want to go there?"

"Why don't we?"

"Okay, and I want us to go to the Blues Hall while you're here. They're famous for their music."

"That sounds good. Maybe we can go there tomorrow night. Do they serve food?"

"I think so."

"Good. We'll try it."

The Lafayette Music Room was outstanding that night. The entrees they chose from the wide variety on the menu were delicious, and the live band was excellent, playing just the kind of tunes that Toni and Max liked. They stayed a long time after they finished eating, and while they didn't close the place, if they had stayed another hour, they would have. They were both very good dancers, and they took full advantage of the good music to satisfy their terpsichorean appetites. They didn't dance to some of the faster music, but some they did, and just about all the slow ones brought them to the dance floor.

Max was very much in the mood while dancing to the romantic slow tunes, but Toni didn't seem to share the mood quite as much, and while Max noticed it, he couldn't put his finger on just why.

The same thing happened the next night at the Blues Hall, although the music there was different than at the Lafayette Music Room. He only had that one last night to be with Toni, and he tried his best to be as romantic as he could, but she just didn't respond the way he had hoped she would, and it bothered him. He had to leave the next day, and he didn't want to go with her feeling that way, so before it got too late, he said, "I'd like to spend some more time with you away from all these people. Are you about ready to go?"

She said, "Yeah. I sure am. We'll go whenever you're ready."

"Well, I'm ready. Let's go," and they got up and left while the band was playing Tiger Rag. The beat was so catchy that Max half danced all the way out.

On the way back to Toni's, Max thought about the way she said she was ready to leave when he asked her, and he couldn't figure out what was wrong.

When they got to the house, they sat outside for a little while because it was such a warm night, and Max asked, "Honey, I'll be finished with my training in a couple or three months, and I should know where I'll be stationed if I'm not deployed overseas. You will almost be ready to graduate when I'm through with my training, so after you graduate, when are you going to be ready to marry me?"

She said in an almost inaudible voice, "I don't know."

He was looking for her to say, "I'll be ready immediately," or "As soon as possible," or "I'm not sure, but I can't wait," or something like that, but instead, she said where you could barely hear her, "I don't know."

He just looked at her and asked, "Is something wrong?"

"No, there's nothing wrong. I'm just tired. I didn't sleep very well last night."

"Well, I hope that's all it is."

She didn't say anything when he said that.

He still had the feeling that something was wrong, and he didn't know what it was, so after a few more minutes he said, "I'm tired, too. I think I'll turn in." He went over and kissed her goodnight and headed toward his room.

Toni didn't say "Good night," or anything. She just sat

there when he kissed her goodnight.

Before he got to his room, he thought about that and turned around and went back outside and said, "Look, I don't know what's wrong with you, but you get a good night's sleep tonight and stay in bed late in the morning. I'm going to get up early and leave before the traffic gets heavy, and I'll call you when I get home. I love you," and that time, he made it to his room.

True to his word, he got up at five o'clock the next morning and was on the road at five thirty. By the time he got to Memphis, it was six o'clock, and the fast food places were all open, so he pulled into one of them and got a couple of steak biscuits and a large coffee, and he was back on the highway in a matter of about eight minutes. He was ahead of the rush hour traffic and made good time to Middleton.

He made it home in a little less than five hours, and he had all that afternoon to do whatever he wanted to do. He called Duke, but Duke had been drafted by the Atlanta Falcons and was in Atlanta getting ready for a game on Sunday. His Mom said he was coming in for Christmas, and she would have him call him. Max told her he would be leaving the following Monday, and he really would like to talk to him, or better yet; see him.

After the drive from West Memphis, he was tired, and he laid his head back on his Daddy's recliner to take a nap. No sooner had he got close to dozing off, the phone rang. He answered, "Hello." It was Toni.

As soon as he answered, she said, "Hi."

He said, "Hi. I didn't know if I would hear from you or not."

"I know. I'm sorry I was such poor company. I should have told you what was wrong, but I was embarrassed to."

"What do you mean?"

"I mean it was my time of the month, and I felt awful. I'm so sorry I didn't tell you."

"Toni, look. We're close enough to get married, and that's plenty close enough for you to be able to tell me when you're having your period. Don't you think?"

"Yes. I agree.

"I tried to call Duke a few minutes ago, and his Mother said he was in Atlanta with the Atlanta Falcons. Did you know he got drafted?"

"No, I didn't."

"Well, he must have made the team. Tell your Daddy, will you?"

"I'll be sure to. He'll be happy about that. Listen, I won't keep you. I just wanted to tell you how sorry I am about the way I behaved when you were here. Do you forgive me? Say you do."

He said, "You know I forgive you. I love you."

"I love you, too. I'll talk to you later, okay?"

"Okay. Bye bye."

He felt a lot better when he hung up. *I should have known she wouldn't act like that without something being wrong. I just wish she had been up front with me. If I had known what the problem was, I might would have stayed with her another day. Oh well, too late now.*

The next afternoon, Max was in the den watching ESPN when there was a knock on the door. When he opened the door, none other than Duke Wayne was standing there. He had been huge ever since Max had first met him, but on that day, he looked as if he had gotten even larger. Max opened the storm door and the two friends gave each other a real bear hug. The size of those two guys were actually bigger than a lot of bears. They went in the den and sat down and caught up a little on what each other had been doing since they last saw each other.

After Duke had filled Max in on the happenings with the Atlanta Falcons, and after Max had filled Duke in on the happenings in the Marine Corps, Duke asked, "Are you and Toni still an item?"

"I guess you can call it that even though I've only seen her briefly in six months, and that brief visit was pretty rocky. How about you? Are you still seeing Sissy?"

"Yeah. Every chance I get. We see each other about once a week. We're usually off on Tuesdays, and I drive up to see her. Occasionally, she'll come to Atlanta."

"It sounds as though you guys are serious. Are you?"

"We're pretty serious, in fact; we're talking about getting married next summer."

"Fantastic! Congratulations, Ole Buddy. Sissy's a great girl."

The two friends finished the afternoon talking, and when it got late, Duke said, "Well Padna, I had better go. I'm supposed to eat dinner with Sissy and her parents. They feed us like kings at the Falcon's training table, but it's still good to get a home cooked meal every once in a while."

They hugged again and wished each other good luck, and Duke left.

After Duke left, Max was sort of at loose ends trying to figure out something to do, and he came up with what he thought was a good idea, and he called Toni to ask her a couple of questions.

When she answered he said, "Hey, Pretty Lady. What are you doing?"

"Nothing much. Just cleaning up my room. What are you doing?"

"Trying to figure out a way to see you. Let me ask you something. You said you had two road games the week after Christmas. Where are they?"

"One is in Orlando, Florida, and the other is in Wichita, Kansas. Why?

"Darn! I had thought that I might come see you when you played one of the games, but they're both too far away, so I guess that idea is a bust."

"I'm sorry."

"Me too."

He spent the rest of his leave hanging around home, mostly. Christmas came and went, and he dreaded having to go back to Quantico, even though he was bored at home. He changed his plane ticket to one day earlier than originally booked because he thought Earl might come back earlier as well, and they might be able to do something together before they had to begin MOS School, but Earl didn't come.

Max and Earl began MOS School together, and it was going to be an eye-opening experience. They were going to go through combat skills which included several things, such as unconventional warfare, escape training, air operations, and shooting. All of these things were things included in Green Beret training, except Green Beret training was more in depth and took eighteen months compared to the Marine MOS School which would take fifty-two days.

When school was over each day, no one felt much like doing anything but eating dinner and going to bed. It was a really rough experience, and every day brought a little less exhaustion than the day before.

One day, when they were getting toward the end of MOS School, Earl asked Max, "I wonder where they're going to put us when we finish this?"

"I don't know, but I hope we're still together."

"Me too."

"I just hope they'll give us a place that will be long term. My girl and I want to get married next summer."

Two weeks later, on Friday afternoon, they finished MOS School and felt like the world was lifted off their shoulders. Earl said, "Let's go out tonight and celebrate. You want to?"

"Yeah, what do you want to do?"

"I don't know. Go somewhere and get some beer and pizza. That's what sounds good to me."

"That sounds good to me, too. Pick a place, and we'll do it."

Neither one of them drank very much, but they did enjoy a beer every now and then, especially with pizza, and they were looking forward to going that night. When they got to the pizza place, apparently a lot of the other guys who finished MOS School felt the same way because there was a crowd. Luckily, they found an empty booth and sat down. Before they ordered, two other guys came in and asked, "Are you saving these seats for somebody?"

Earl said, "No, do you all want to sit with us?"

"That would be great. Thank you," and they sat down and introduced themselves as Barry Shupe and Jimmy Snow. As soon as they did that, they all recognized each other; not by name, but as fellow MOS students. They had a very enjoyable evening and talked about everything from football to their girls back home. Max and Earl were glad they ran into Barry and Jimmy because they felt as if they could become buddies the way they were.

They finished their pizzas and each ordered another beer, and they sat and talked for a long time. Finally, they ran out of things to talk about, and they paid their bills and left.

Monday was a memorable day for Max. First of all, there was a bulletin in his mailbox from his Commanding Officer telling him to report to the Marine Assembly Center at three P.M. for an important meeting. Attendance was mandatory.

Second, also in his mailbox was an envelope from Toni. He always enjoyed hearing from her, especially when she told him that she loved him, and she always did that in her letters, but when he opened this one, it was different. Her letters always began with *My Dearest Max*, and that one began with *Dear Max*. He knew what it was going to say before he read it, but he read it anyway.

She said, "This is a very hard letter for me to write, but I felt like I had to. You said that rumors are going around that you are going to be deployed, and if you are, you will be gone another year in addition to the eight months you've already been gone. Max, I think it is best that we break our engagement, and if you'll tell me where you want me to send your ring, I'll mail it to you. You might want me to send it to your parents to keep for you while you're gone. I'm not breaking up with you because of another man, however, I have become a very good friend of a guy on the men's volleyball team at Memphis State, and I don't know where that will go. Good luck if you get deployed and come back safely. Sincerely, Toni.

The letter shook Max all the way down. He read it twice and then put it back in the envelope and put it in his footlocker.

When Earl came in, Max asked him, "Do you remember me telling you that my girl and I want to get married next summer?"

"Yeah, why? Are you moving it up?"

"I'm afraid not. I just got a 'Dear John' letter a while ago."

"You're kidding. Really?"

"Really. It looks as if she likes a volleyball player. Can you believe that? A volleyball player.

"I'm sorry Max, but maybe it's for the best."

"Thanks, Earl."

Max pondered over Toni's letter for a long time, and after a few hours of feeling sorry for himself, he thought, *maybe Earl's right. Maybe our breakup is for the best. Sometime I might find me a girl that truly loves me, and one I truly love. I'd like to find one like Amy, but that's probably impossible. There's no sense in crying over spilt milk, so I'll try to put Toni out of my mind. I just hate that I lost out to a volleyball player. Man!! That sucks.*

Earl got a bulletin just like Max did, and they left their quarters about two forty-five and walked to the meeting place. On the way, they talked, wondering what the meeting was going to be about, and they both thought it might be about getting deployed.

Sure enough, when they got to the assembly hall, there was

a crowd of Marines. Everyone was sitting around, talking, when a voice sounded above the talk. "Attention."

Everyone stood up at attention, and the Commanding Officer came in. He said, "At Ease. Be seated," and everyone sat down.

The C.O. began his remarks by saying that the United States Marine Corps was the greatest and best fighting machine ever known in the history of the world. He continued to praise them, and in a minute, he said, "Men, in keeping with the President's program of fighting terrorism, he has ordered men from all branches of service to be deployed to Iraq. He has ordered a total of five thousand Marines. One Battalion, or twelve hundred men from Quantico Marine Base will be included in that number. They are Able Company, Baker Company, Kilo Company, and Lima Company. If you are in one of these companies, please remain here after we are dismissed."

Max was a Platoon Commander of one of the Platoons in Kilo Company, and Earl was the Commander of one in Lima Company.

They remained in the assembly hall after the others were dismissed and the C.O. said, "Men, our orders are to leave Quantico on October twenty nine, and arrive in the country of Kuwait on October thirty, where we'll prepare to move into Iraq a short time later. Our deployment will be for a period of approximately twelve months. Prior to deployment, on October fifteen, each of you will be given a ten day leave for a return to Quantico on October twenty five.

The date, that day was October eight, and Max and the others had a week before their leave began. The phone lines at the airlines were flooded with calls from Marines wanting to schedule flights to their homes on the fifteenth. Max and Earl thought it would be good if they went to the airport to talk to the airline agent about getting their tickets, and it was a wise decision on their part. They walked into the terminal and up to the ticket agent and got their tickets without any wait at all. They were back at the base while many of the other guys were still trying to get the different airlines on the phone.

Max called his Mother and told her he was coming home on the fifteenth and asked her if she or his Daddy could meet him at the airport. He gave her the time, and he told her why he was coming home again so soon after his previous leave.

The rest of that week was spent mostly by each Company Commander and each Platoon Commander going over nearly every conceivable scenario that they might encounter when they got to the battleground. Since Max was a Lieutenant, abbreviated by the letters LT, and Lieutenant was a long word to have to say every time, his men adopted the name L.T. for him. He liked that and was glad they gave it to him. He didn't much like the formality of his rank.

On the fifteenth, he caught an early flight to Middleton, and his Mother was there to meet him. He kissed her hello, and after he got his bag, they went home. He didn't know what he was going to do for ten days, but doing nothing at home was better than doing nothing at Quantico.

One of the first things he did was call Toni's house to tell her where to send her engagement ring. It was late afternoon when he called, and Toni's Daddy answered the phone. Max said, "Hi Tim, it's Max Norwood. How are you?"

"Hi Max. I'm fine. It's good to hear from you. How are you doing?"

"I'm fine. I'm shipping out week after next for Iraq."

"I hate to hear that. How long will you be gone?"

"They tell us twelve months."

"Man, that sucks. Well, I wish you a lotta luck, Max."

"Thank you, sir. Tim, is Toni there?"

"No, she's not. Can I give her a message for you?"

"Yes sir, you can. I guess she told you that she broke up with me."

"Yeah, she did, and I'm terribly sorry. I like you, Max."

"Thank you. The reason I'm calling is this. Toni wrote me a letter, telling me she was breaking up with me, and she said to let her know where I wanted her to send her engagement ring. Tim, please tell her I'd like for her to send it to my parent's house," and he gave him the address when he got a pen and paper. He said, "Tim, if you'll give this to her, I'll appreciate it. I'm going to be home for nine more days, so if she'll send it right away, I'll probably be here to get it. Tim, I enjoyed getting to know you. Maybe we'll cross paths again someday."

"I enjoyed getting to know you, too, Max. Good luck in Iraq."

Next, he called Duke's Mother. When she answered, he said, "Hi, Mrs. Wayne. This is Max Norwood. How are you doing?"

"I'm fine, Max. How are you?"

"I'm fine. Listen, will Duke be home tomorrow?"

"He's supposed to be. Can I have him call you?"

"Yes Ma'am, you can. I'd like to talk to him. I'm getting ready to go to Iraq, and I'll be gone for a year, and I'd like to hear from him before I go."

"Okay Max. I'll be sure he calls you. You be careful in that Iraq, you hear?"

"Yes Ma'am. I will."

About noon the next day, Duke called. "Whatta ya say, Duke?"

"Whatta ya say Max? Mama said you're fixing to go to Iraq. Is that right?"

"Yeah, I'm afraid so. I just wanted to talk to you before I have to go back and tell you bye."

"Look, I'm coming to Middleton to take Sissy out to eat tonight. Why don't you go with us?"

"Thanks, ole Buddy, but I don't know how that would go over with Sissy."

"Don't be foolish. Sissy looks at you like her brother.

113

She'd love for you to come."

"Okay. If you're sure, but I'll meet you somewhere. That way, I can leave you guys when we get through eating, and I won't mess up your whole date."

"You're not going to mess up anything. I insist you come with us, and if you want to meet us, you can."

"Okay. Where are we going to eat?"

"Anywhere special you'd like to go? This is your farewell dinner, so you should pick the place."

"There's a new place that we might try. It's called Coaches, and it's supposed to be good. You want to try it?"

"That's fine with me. You want to meet us at, say, six thirty?"

"Six-thirty it is."

Max was there right on time, and Sissy and Duke were right on time as well. They went in and ordered and had a great time. Sissy seemed genuinely concerned for Max and asked if she could write to him. They exchanged addresses and promised they would write each other. Max and Duke exchanged addresses also, and Duke asked, "How do you know what your address will be in Iraq?"

"I don't, but if you send it to my address in Quantico, they'll forward it to me."

After the address exchanges. Max said, "Well, I'm going to get out of here and let you guys get on with your evening, and Sissy said, "Take care, Max. I love you," and she got up, hugged him and kissed him on the cheek.

Duke got up and hugged him also and said, "You keep your head down over there, and give those Rag Heads what for, you hear?"

Max said, "I will. I love you guys. You're my very best friends. I'll be in touch. See ya," and he left them and went by the El Rancho to see if he could see any of his old friends, but none of them were there, so he went home.

On Thursday, the ring arrived from Toni, and he took it to

the jeweler where he bought it and explained the situation. When they realized he was a Marine about to be deployed, they felt sorry for him and refunded all the money he had paid for it.

For the next few days, he spent most of his time with his Mother in the daytime and both his parents at night. They went out to eat three or four times, and just enjoyed being together. He thought a lot about what it was going to be like in Iraq, and he prayed quite a bit about it. Finally, the twenty fifth came and he caught the plane back to Quantico to get ready to go to Iraq.

Chapter Nine

Buses, the Greyhound kind, arrived at the departure point to pick up the Marines that were going to Iraq and delivered them to the airport. They were to fly to Kuwait first, and to Max's surprise, they were going to fly to Kuwait on a commercial airliner. Actually, the planes were Lufthansa seven thirty sevens, which were fairly comfortable, and he welcomed that kind of plane because it was going to take a little over fifteen hours to get there, and he thought it would be much better than flying on a C-130 transport plane or one similar to it. They had to land in Munich, Germany to refuel and then on to Kuwait City. Flying time from Quantico to Munich was eight hours, and then, flying time from Munich to Kuwait City was five and a half hours, but the layover in Munich made it over fifteen hours.

There were five planes waiting for them at the airport, and the Marines would be divided into three Platoons or one Company per plane. Since Max and Earl were in different Companies, they flew on separate airplanes. Wheels were up on the first plane at ten o'clock, Monday morning, and with the length of the flight and the time difference of eight hours, it landed at nine a.m. Tuesday. Each plane landed eight minutes after the one in front of it.

There were buses at the airport to take them to their quarters, and everybody was ready to stretch their legs from the long trip. Jet lag was a problem for several of the guys, and their meals weren't eaten at the usual time, so the USMC's first job was to get everyone accustomed to regular mealtimes, and breakfast was first, even though it was after nine a.m. when they served it. On subsequent days, it would be served at six or seven o'clock.

Lt. Col. David Lowe met with the Company Commanders,

and told them to return to a designated area, and to have all the Platoon leaders and their Sergeants report there as well at o three hundred.

At the meeting that afternoon, Lt. Col. Lowe told them, "Men, on Saturday we are going to move to a location just outside the city of Fallujah, where we will more than likely be involved in heavy fighting with Iraqi insurgents, but first, preparations are going to have to be made.

"Before beginning our attack, U.S. and Iraqi forces will establish checkpoints around the city to prevent anyone from entering, and to intercept insurgents attempting to flee."

Colonel Lowe told them, "Overhead imagery was used to prepare maps of the city for our use. Our units are being augmented by Iraqi interpreters to help in the planned fight."

He said, "After weeks of withstanding air strikes and artillery bombardment, the militants in the city appear to be vulnerable to a direct attack. Now, we're not going in there by ourselves. There will be U.S., Iraqi, and British forces, totaling about thirteen thousand five hundred men. The U.S. has assembled some sixty-five hundred Marines and fifteen hundred Army soldiers that will take part in the assault with about twenty-five hundred Navy personnel in operational and support roles."

Colonel Lowe then broke down the combat teams and how they would be made up. There were so many units, he had to read the list. Then he said, "About two thousand Iraqi troops will assist in the assault. All the troops will be supported by the 3D Marine Aircraft Wing fixed and rotary aircraft, Navy, and Air Force fixed wing aircraft and U.S. Army artillery battalions and U.S. SOCOM Sniper Elements, and last, but certainly not least, the eight-hundred and fifty strong Black Watch has been ordered to help U.S. and Iraqi forces with the encirclement of Fallujah. As part of Task Force Black, D squadron of the British SAS prepared to take part in the operation, but British political nervousness about the possible scale of casualties stopped any direct U.K. involvement in the ground battle.

"Men, that's all for now. It looks as though we might be in for a rough few days, but with the preparations that have already been made and the preparations still to be made will hopefully not be as bad as they could be. We're taking the attitude of 'preparing for the worst, but hoping for the best.'

"You men have all been given the best training in the world, and the President has the utmost confidence in you. The next three days will be free, so enjoy yourselves, and we'll meet again next Saturday morning before we leave for Fallujah. You're dismissed."

On the way back to their quarters, Max and his Sergeant, Penny Pendergrass, walked together, and Max asked, "What did you think, Penny?"

"I think we're going to have to keep our heads down."

Max said, "You think? It sounds as if we might be in for it when we get to Fallujah. We're going to have a lot of help, but I'm concerned about how many insurgents there will be. I've heard that you can be with someone who you think is your friend, and then he might try to kill you, so be careful about associating with any Iraqis. You know what, Penny?"

"No sir, what?"

"I feel confident in myself and our military, but I think I'll write some letters home before we go to Fallujah."

"I was just thinking the same thing."

Unlike most U.S. Military bases, that one was very informal, in regard to the separation of officers and enlisted men. Everyone ate together and slept together and many officers became good friends with their enlisted subordinates. After all, they would be fighting together, and everyone would have to depend on everyone else for their own safety.

Pretty soon, after Max and Penny reached their quarters, Earl Tedder and his Sergeant, Homer Setliffe, came in. Earl asked, "Well men, what do you think?"

Max said, "We think we're going to have our hands full. What do you think?"

"I think you're right. Each one of us is going to have to watch each other's back. After we were dismissed a while ago, I heard Col. Lowe talking to some Major, and he said the numbers had doubled on the insurgents. He said that back in April, there were about five hundred hardcore and a thousand 'part time' insurgents, but now, it's estimated that the numbers have doubled to about three thousand, however, he said a number of the insurgent leaders are trying to escape before we attack."

The guys talked for a long time, and then they went to the mess hall and ate supper. After supper, they went to their bunks and wrote letters. Max intended to write to his Mother, to Duke, to Sissy, and to his Pastor., and he began with his Mother's, and then he wrote to Duke, but he fell asleep before he could get Sissy's and his Pastor's written, and when he woke up, he said to himself, *I'll write them in the morning,* and he did. He asked all of them to please pray for him and the rest of the forces that were there to defend their freedom and to ask God to protect them from the bombs and gunfire from the enemy.

It was hard not to think about the upcoming battle, and everyone was writing to get their minds on something else. Earl came by Max's and said, "Put on some long pants and a long sleeve shirt, and let's go to the mall."

"Why do I have to put on long pants? I want to wear shorts."

"No can do. Did you not see the directive on the bulletin board? It says we have to wear long pants, and long sleeve shirts in order to not offend the local cultural customs. Did you bring any long sleeve shirts with you?"

"No, I didn't, but I can wear my fatigue top. It's long sleeve."

They all got dressed, and Max, Earl, Penny, and Homer took off for the mall. It was a huge mall called The Avenues.

119

It had four hundred stores and no telling how many restaurants. A few things were familiar, such as Ikea, McDonalds, and Chilis. They noticed several non-Muslims, who they assumed were American or possibly European. None of them were interested in buying anything, but they did have lunch at McDonalds. After they ate, they spent a little more time at the mall and then went back to the base, where they stayed for the next two days. On Saturday morning, Lt. Colonel Lowe assembled the entire force and talked to them.

"Men, today's the day. We're going into Fallujah to kill terrorists and to make our country safer. You need to know that Fallujah is occupied by virtually every insurgent group in Iraq: al Qaeda in Iraq, known as AQI, Islamic Army of Iraq, the IAI, the Army of Mohammed, AOM, the Army of the Mujahedeen, and the Secret Islamic Army of Iraq. The AQI, the IAI, and the National Islamic Army have their nationwide headquarters in Fallujah.

"The Iraqi insurgents and foreign mujahedeen present in the city have prepared fortified defenses in advance of our anticipated attack. They have dug tunnels, trenches, prepared spider holes, and built and hid a wide variety of IEDs. In some locations they have filled the interior of darkened homes with large numbers of propane bottles, large drums of gasoline, and ordnance, all wired to a remote trigger that could be set off by the insurgents when we enter the building. They have many other tricks and won't hesitate to use them all, so be careful. The insurgents are equipped with a variety of advanced small arms, and they have captured a variety of U.S. armament, including M14s, M16s, body armor, uniforms, and helmets.

"They have booby-trapped buildings and vehicles, including wiring doors and windows to grenades and other ordnance. Anticipating U.S. tactics to seize the roofs of high buildings, they have bricked up stairwells to the roofs of many buildings, creating paths into prepared fields of fire which they hope we will enter.

"Intelligence briefings given just days ago report that coalition forces will encounter Chechen, Filipino, Saudi, Libyan, and Syrian combatants, as well as native Iraqis.

"Men, let's go in and kick their butts and show them that they can't get away with trying to ruin our religious freedom as well as many other things. Before we're dismissed, remove your caps and helmets, and let's ask God to be with us as we go in."

Rather than have one of the Chaplains pray, Col. Lowe led the prayer, himself, and many of the troops were impressed to know that they had a Christian Officer leading them into battle.

Four C-130 transport planes were lined up at the airport, prepared to take them into Iraq, and about twenty more were loaded with Humvees, trucks, and other equipment that would be used by the troops upon their arrival.

With Navy SEAL and Marine recon Snipers providing reconnaissance and target marking on the city perimeter, ground operations began that night.

On the plane, on the way to Fallujah, Max prayed silently. He said, *Father, I don't know exactly how to pray this prayer, other than to just ask you to please take care of us. Please be with me and my men, and please bring us through the battles that they tell us we're going to have to fight. Father, if you'll bring me through and let me go home again, I promise you that I'll try to be the best man I know how to be, and I'll devote my life to doing good for you. Thank you in advance, Lord, and I pray this prayer in Jesus' name.*

As soon as the C-130s landed and the troops disembarked, Max and Earl shook hands, and Max said, "Take care, Earl." Then he told Homer, "Homer, take care of my main man here, okay?"

Homer replied, "Yes sir, I will, and you take care of yourself as well. Penny, good luck," and Penny said, "Thanks. When this is over, we'll go get a beer together."

Max told Penny, "Penny, it looks like we're going to attack

from the west, and Earl and his men are going to attack from the south. Both men's Platoons were joining the Iraqi 36th Commando Battalion with their U.S. Army Special Forces advisors, and about fifteen other units, consisting of other Marines, U.S. Army, Tank Battalions, and Combat Support Battalion 1.

Right away, they captured the Fallujah General Hospital, the Blackwater Bridge, ING building, and villages opposite the Euphrates River along Fallujah's western edge. Kilo Company, along with the U.S. Army III Corps. Then moved to the western approaches to the city and secured the Jurf Kas Sukr Bridge.

Max told Penny, "Good job, however, these attacks were just a diversion intended to distract and confuse the insurgents holding the city.

Max's Kilo Company was also recognized as Regimental Combat Team 1 (RCT-1), and they along with Regimental Combat Team 7 (RCT-7) launched an attack along the northern edge of the city. They did that just after Navy Seabees from MEF Engineer group interrupted and disabled electrical power at two substations located just northeast and northwest of the city.

When his Platoon was passing one of the substations, Penny yelled, "L.T., look out. There's a guy behind that little building over there."

"Where?"

"See that little building down there to the right of those transformers?"

"Yeah, I see it."

"When he saw us, he ducked in behind it."

"Okay, let's get him. You go around to the right, and I'll go to the left. Be careful."

They eased up to the building, and when they got to approximately twenty yards from it, a guy came out from the left, firing at Max and the Platoon. Max saw him first and opened up on him, killing him instantly. The rest of the Platoon gathered around the slain man and congratulated Max.

After the excitement died down, they continued on with their mission, and while Max was a highly trained combat Marine, thinking before he went into combat that he could kill anyone who got in his way, the thought of actually killing someone then bore heavily on his mind. He had to concentrate on keeping track of his men because there were so many other units involved in the battle, and each unit had several men.

There were many insurgents killed that day, but Max only killed the one man at the substation. None of the men in his Platoon killed any that day, but he heard that Earl's Platoon ran into some heavy fighting, and several insurgents were killed. He didn't know if Earl had killed anyone or not.

The day was very busy, with different units doing different things. Some units were tasked to infiltrate the city and destroy any fleeing enemy forces. The British Army's 1st Battalion, The Black Watch patrolled the main highways to the east.

The United States Air Force provided close air support for the ground offensive, employing a variety of kinds of aircraft.

Late that afternoon, Max and the other troops withdrew to a quiet area, where they got some rest. There was a meeting of the Officers to plan out the next day's offensive, and then they were allowed to go to sleep.

Max told Penny, "We're going to start very early in the morning. There will be an intense artillery barrage firing about twenty-five hundred 155s plus an air attack. We're going to follow that with an attack on the main train station, which the insurgents are using as a staging point for follow-on forces."

The attack went as planned, and by that afternoon, the Marines had entered several new districts. The Seabees used armed bulldozers to plow the streets clear of debris from the bombardment that morning.

Most of the fighting had subsided on the fifth day, but the U.S. Marines and Special Operations Forces continued to face determined isolated resistance from insurgents hidden throughout the city.

After nine days of fighting, the Marine command described the action as mopping up pockets of resistance. Sporadic fighting continued for a few more weeks. Two months later, news reports indicated U.S. combat units were leaving the area and were assisting the local population in returning to the now heavily damaged city.

After Fallujah, Max's Company along with other Companies from Quantico, moved over to Camp Arifjan, Kuwait, where they set up temporary quarters. Actually, Marines from other places that helped make up the five thousand that was deployed with the Quantico twelve hundred moved there as well. Camp Arifjan was a large place that could accommodate as many as nine thousand, so there were troops from different branches of service there, also, and it was almost like home to the Americans.

Troops lived in transitional barracks, which were prefabricated concrete buildings. Camp Arifjan is in an area that Congress had deemed a hostile-fire zone, and as such, deployed troops are unaccompanied on their tours of duty.

There are three excellent dining facilities on Camp Arifjan, furthermore, the food courts provide a taste of home: Burger King, Pizza Hut, KFC, Charley's, Taco Bell, and Baskin Robbins are all available.

Camp Arifjan has two AAFES post exchanges, and local vendors sell additional goods.

The Camp has two community centers, and troops are provided with a game room, free snacks, board games, foosball tables, and pool tables. Free movies and music nights are also offered.

Two fitness centers are provided, and for outdoor amenities, there is a swimming pool, but female soldiers cannot wear bikinis. Their swimming costumes must be one-piece only.

The chapel in Zone 1 serves all major religions at different times, including Islam. Additional services are held in Zone 6. Kuwait has a desert climate that is extremely hot and dry. During the summer months, temperatures can reach 124 degrees.

The troops that pass through Camp Arifjan all serve under harsh conditions far from home, but given all the amenities available on post, it is little wonder that Camp Arifjan is affectionately known as 'Camp Cupcake.'

It was blessed relief being in a place where they weren't constantly being shot at or otherwise threatened in other ways, but there was still danger. The fence surrounding the Camp was designed to keep the enemy out, but it was useless against mortars, and there were daily mortar barrages from the insurgents.

Max could tell people something about mortars. Most of the bathrooms at Camp Arifjan were porta-potty's, and one day when he was using the bathroom in one of them, the Camp came under a mortar attack. Since nobody knew where the next mortar was going to hit, he just sat there, praying that it would soon be over. All at once, one hit and exploded just outside the porta-potty that he was in, and a piece of shrapnel came through the side of the little building and lodged in the toilet paper roll about a foot from him, nearly scaring him to death.

From the porta-potty, he left and went back to the room he was sharing with Penny, Earl, and Homer. When he got in, he told them about his experience in the porta-potty, and they all died laughing, especially Penny. He had tears in his eyes.

Each unit was able to segregate themselves from other units, and as such, they were able to meet and get information specific to them, however, one word that kept coming up in all the units was 'Ramadi'.

Every day, it seemed like, there were reports of fighting and reports of Americans being killed in Ramadi, and all the men felt as though it was just a matter of time until they were called to go over there.

Their feelings were justified because at one of their daily briefings Lt. Col Lowe told them that they would be moving into Ramadi in two days.

The troops had been hearing about the unrest in Ramadi for a while, but they didn't know why until Col. Lowe explained it. He told them, "Since the fall of Fallujah, Ramadi has been the center of the insurgency in Iraq. The Islamic State of Iraq, a front group for al-Qaeda in Iraq, has declared the city to be its capital. Ramadi has five hundred thousand people in it. It is located about sixty-eight miles west of Baghdad, and it has been under the control of the insurgency except for a few places where the Marines have set up remote outposts, that were virtually under siege. Law and order has broken down, and street battles are common, and we are being asked to come in and help restore law and order to the city."

When Col. Lowe finished talking to the men, he asked them to stand and remove their caps and pray with him, then, they loaded into trucks and were driven to the Patton Army Airfield on the base. There, they took off to Ramadi, where they would set up to get ready to battle the insurgents. Their temporary home would be at the Khan Al Baghdadi Airport, and they finished the day settling in after the hour and a half flight from Camp Arifjan.

Max prayed every day, but on the days when he was being taken to known trouble spots such as Ramadi, he prayed extra hard for God to deliver him and his men.

He wasn't sure who was responsible for intelligence, but, whoever it was, was right on the money. He and Penny were talking about that when a report came in that insurgents were congregating just outside the city of Ramadi.

Almost immediately after the intelligence report, Kilo Company, Max's Company, was moved out to the Government Center, and Earl's Company, Lima Company, was moved to Observation Post Virginia. No sooner had they got to those posts than all heck broke loose.

A complex and heavy attack was launched by insurgents attacking Observation Post Virginia, the Government Center, the Snake Pit Outpost, and Camp Ramadi, all simultaneously by forces led by Abu Musab al-Zarqawi. OP Virginia was the target of a heavily armed vehicle-born suicide bomber. The suicide bomber drove an armored yellow dump truck loaded with approximately one thousand pounds of explosives through the gate of the outpost and detonated it. Insurgents with small arms and RPGs then moved into the post, and a major firefight ensued. Earl and the other Marines in Lima Company eventually repelled the attack, killing dozens of insurgents with only a few Marine casualties.

Teamwork was important during the attack because more than once, a Marine would be in an insurgent's sights when one of his team members would shoot the insurgent and save him.

Once, when an insurgent was shot down at the feet of Earl, he asked, "Homer, did you get this guy?"

"I did, and it is a good thing that I did. He was about to blow your head off."

"Thanks, Sergeant."

Nearly every man in Lima Company killed multiple insurgents that day, and that was good because if they hadn't, there's no telling how many American Marines would have fallen victim.

Simultaneously, the Government Center defended by Max's Kilo Company had repelled insurgents trying to infiltrate the government compound and kidnap the Governor.

Max said to Penny, "Penny, there is a place that has CDs with videos showing the attack on Observation Post Virginia and of Abu Musab al-Zarqawi planning the attack. This was released, bearing the logo of the organization of the Mujahideen Shura Council, and it's unknown what else they have. Get your first Squad together, and let's go raid it and see what else they have over there."

Counting Max and Penny, there were fourteen of them, and they approached the building carefully. There were two guards there, and they were quickly dispatched. Three or four members of the Squad opened fire on them, so they didn't know whose bullets actually killed them, but it didn't matter. All fourteen were there to do one job, and they did it. Everyone had everyone else's back.

On the fourteenth, U.S. and Iraqi forces over in Baghdad began Operation Together Forward, an operation intended to curb the sectarian killings in the capital.

Earlier that month, the 1st Brigade Combat Team and elements of the 2nd Brigade Combat Team were deployed to the Ramadi area from Tal Afar and Kuwait respectively and began preparations to take on the capital of Al Anbar province, Ramadi. Word of an offensive had already gotten to the half million citizens of the city who feared another Fallujah style attack. But Lt. Colonel Lowe decided to take it slowly and softly, without using heavy close air support, artillery, or tank fire. By the tenth of the month, U.S. Troops had 'cordoned off' the city. U.S. air strikes on residential areas were escalating, and U.S. troops took to the streets with loudspeakers to warn civilians of a fierce impending attack.

The objective of the operation was to cut off resupply and reinforcements to the insurgents in Ramadi by gaining control of the key entry points into the city. The Marines also planned to establish new combat outposts and patrol bases throughout the city, moving off their forward operating bases in order to engage the population and establish relationships with local leaders.

The operation had some initial success, but the effect that the Americans wanted to achieve didn't happen. Very soon the American forces were bogged down in heavy street fighting throughout the city.

The main target throughout the campaign was the Ramadi Government Center which was garrisoned by the U.S. Marines of Kilo Company, including Max and his Platoon.

Roadside bomb attacks and ambushes of patrols happened nearly every day as the Marines went outside the wire. Sniper attacks were also a constant threat to Marines during the battle, and there were also several suicide-bombing attacks on the outposts.

At the beginning of July, Max said to Penny, "I've been told that we're going to go really deep into Ramadi and capture the Ramadi General Hospital. Tell your guys to be careful because it looks like it's going to be a rough ride."

"Okay, L.T., I'll tell them, but I don't see how it can be much rougher than what we've been going through for the past few months, do you?"

"No, but still tell them to be careful."

Max, Penny, and two of their squad members loaded into a Humvee and started out for the General Hospital with a convoy of other Humvees. Max's vehicle was the lead vehicle, and after they had gone about three miles, BOOM. They had run over a roadside bomb. The two squad members in front were killed instantly, and Max and Penny were seriously injured.

Of course, the convoy stopped, and Marines got out of each vehicle and stood guard next to their vehicle to ward off an attack by insurgents. A Marine in the second Humvee radioed that one of their group had been hit by an IED, and it wasn't long until a CASEVAC helicopter arrived to pick up Max and Penny.

The CH47 Helicopter is commonly used as CASEVAC helicopters because of their maneuverability. CASEVAC differs from MEDEVAC as CASEVAC is used for troops in dire need, and they can get to their first aid faster.

Max and Penny were both unconscious as they were loaded into the helicopter, but Max regained consciousness soon after the helicopter took off for the American Military Hospital in Baghdad. The first words he uttered were, "Is everybody alright?"

One of the medical personnel said, "No sir, they're not. You and your Sergeant are both alive, but the other two didn't make it."

Struggling to talk, he asked, "Where are we?"

The Medic said, "We're taking you to the American Military Hospital in Baghdad for initial treatment."

"What happened?"

"It looks as if you ran over an IED. Were you in the back seat?"

"Yeah, Penny and I were."

The Medic said, "I'm guessing that's why you're alive. The two in the front seat weren't so lucky," and as he said that, Max passed out.

The copter landed at the Military Hospital in Baghdad, and Max and Penny were both rushed to the operating rooms. They had to have their clothes cut off because they were hurt so bad, it would have been torture to try and take them off the normal way. A person in each OR carefully emptied their pockets and put their belongings in bags with their names on them and gave them to someone to put in a safe place.

Penny was very critically injured. While he was hurt all over, head injuries seemed to be the most serious. His face was almost unrecognizable. His nose was broken, and his left eye was out of its socket; lying on his cheek. Doctors were going to try to temporarily fix him good enough for him to reach Landstuhl Regional Medical Center in Landstuhl, Germany.

The Humvee ran over the IED with its left side, and while the men were injured all over, the injuries on their left sides were worse than on their right side.

Max had his left arm and left leg injured. The arm was broken, but the doctors didn't think it was beyond repair. Three ribs were broken, and he had internal bleeding. The left leg, however, was a different story. The x-rays indicated major damage, and the doctors predicted that he would lose his leg, but they didn't want to amputate it there. They wanted the doctors at Landstuhl to make that decision. The doctors in Baghdad were going to do surgery to try and help the leg and ribs and the internal injuries that he had, and they recommended that both he and Penny be kept there at least until the next day and then be moved to Germany.

Penny was still unconscious when they operated on him, but Max had come to, and he was talking a little. He asked the doctor about his injuries, and the doctor told him that he was not sure they could save his leg; they would have to decide when he got to Landstuhl or possibly Walter Reed or the Bethesda Naval Hospital in the States.

Max told the doctor, "Doc, do whatever you have to do to save my leg. Patch me up good enough to get me home and maybe somebody over there can save it if you can't."

The doctor said, "Lieutenant, we're not going to amputate it here. We hope it doesn't have to be done, but if it does, it will probably be done when you get back to the States."

When the doctor said that, he told Max, "Lieutenant just relax if you can. You're going to take a little nap," and the Anesthesiologist shot the anesthetic into him, and he immediately went to sleep. The surgery lasted for more than four hours, and then he was transferred to the recovery room for a couple of hours.

After quite a bit of time in recovery, he began to wake up, and while he was lying there, he heard someone talking to another patient, and he heard them say, "Sergeant."

That made him wake up a little more, and he said as loud as he could, "Penny; is that you, Penny?"

Penny said, "L.T., yeah, it's me. It's good to hear your voice, L.T."

A nurse came in, and Max asked her, "Nurse, can you arrange for Sergeant Pendergrass and me to room together?"

"I'm afraid not, Lieutenant. We only have private rooms, but I'll see if we can get you two close to each other."

"Thanks."

When they moved them from the recovery room, they put them in Intensive Care, and they told them that they would be flown to Landstuhl Regional Medical Center the next day, if their condition permitted it.

Max was beginning to get more alert, and as soon as he saw one of the doctors, he asked, "Do you think I could call home?"

The doctor said, "Of course, you can. I'll have someone bring a phone in here to you."

"Thanks, Doc, and I'm sure Sgt. Pendergrass would like to call home, too."

"Okay. I'll take care of it."

"Thanks."

Wounded warriors were treated like kings in the hospital, and it wasn't long until someone brought a phone for both Max and Penny. Being halfway around the world, Max was a little unsure how to make the call, so a nice orderly dialed it for him, and he did the same for Penny. It was a little after four p.m. in Baghdad, which meant it was a little after midnight at home, and while Max hated to wake his parents up, he wanted to talk to them.

The phone rang and on the fourth ring, a sleepy voice on the other end said, "Hello."

"Hi, Daddy. Did I wake you?"

"Max, hi, Son. No, I'm in bed, but I'm not asleep yet. Do you have a problem?"

"Well, kinda. I've suffered a little hiccup, but I'm going to be alright."

His Daddy told his Mother, "It's Max. Go in the den and pick up the phone," and she got up and ran into the den.

As soon as she picked up, his Daddy said, "Okay, Son, tell me about your hiccup, as you called it."

132

"Well, we were on our way to capture the Ramadi General Hospital this morning, when my Humvee ran over an IED, and I got hurt."

His Mother asked, "Darling, where are you hurt, and what's an IED?"

"Let me answer your second question first. An IED stands for Improvised Explosive Device, or in everyday terms, it's a homemade bomb. Penny, my Sergeant and I were in the backseat, so we didn't get hurt as bad as we could have. The two Marines in the front seat were both killed."

She asked again, "Where are you hurt, Max?"

"Mother, I hurt my left arm and left leg, and they tell me I have some broken ribs and some other stuff that I don't know about."

His Daddy asked, "Where are you right now?"

"I'm in Baghdad in the American Military Hospital."

"How long will you be there?"

"I don't know. They said they're taking me to a hospital in Germany tomorrow, and from there, they'll bring me to Washington and put me in the hospital there."

His Daddy said, "With all those hospitals, it sounds pretty serious. How do you feel?"

"I'm sore, but I feel okay. I don't know too much about what's going to happen, so I'll call you again when I have some more information."

His Mother said, "Max, I wish you were at home."

"I'm alright, Mother. Don't worry about me. These Doctors know what they're doing, and they're going to take good care of me. Oh, I nearly forgot; Mother, in my bedside table, Duke's number is written down. Tomorrow or sometime, would you please call him and tell him I got wounded, and I'll call him when I get back to the States?"

"I'll call him. When's the best time to reach him?"

"I'd say at night. He's pretty busy during the day."

"Listen I need to hang up for now. I just wanted to tell you about my little problem in case you heard about it before you talked to me. They said they're taking me to Germany tomorrow, so when I get there, I'll try to call you and bring you up to date. I love you both, and I don't want you to worry."

His Mother said, "We love you too, Darling. I'm going to call the church tomorrow, and have you put on the prayer chain."

His Daddy said, "I love you, Son. Take care."

They all hated to hang up, but there was not much else to say, so Max finally said, "I'll talk to you later," and he hung up.

He was in terrific pain after the anesthetic began to wear off, and he asked for something to ease it up. Between the shot and the left-over anesthetic, he went to sleep pretty soon after they gave him the pain shot, and he slept for quite a while. They kept him sedated most of the rest of the day and just about all night, and the next morning, they prepared him for his flight to Landstuhl. He was in terrible pain.

Early the next morning, the medical staff came in and unhooked Max from some of the monitors and re-hooked him to others. When they got everything done, they rolled him down a hall and onto an elevator that went down to a floor that exited to the back of the hospital. There were six ambulances parked there, waiting on patients to be transported to Boeing C-17s which would take them to Landstuhl. Max couldn't see from his gurney, so he asked one of the medical people if Sgt. Penny Pendergrass was being taken with him, and they said he was.

"How about hooking me up close to Sgt. Pendergrass," he asked one of the men working with the group.

The man was very nice, and he said, "Let me see what I can do. Is Sgt. Pendergrass a friend of yours?"

"Yeah, he's a real close friend, and he's also my Platoon Sergeant. We went through a lot together, and I want to keep him near me."

There were only six soldiers and Marines going to Landstuhl, and when they put them on the huge airplane, Max couldn't help but think, *man, talk about overkill.* The plane took off at O-eight hundred hours and headed non-stop to Landstuhl, Germany, a flight of a little over six hours.

Things were just reversed when they landed. Ambulances were at the airport to meet them, and after loading the six troops, they sped to the Regional Medical Center. Upon arrival at the Medical Center, Medical personnel were all over them.

First, they went over the paperwork that accompanied them from Baghdad, and then each patient was treated according to their needs. In Max's case, they did x-rays, and then took him to a pre-op location, where they prepared him for another surgery. All in all, he was in Landstuhl eight days and had four surgeries. Two days after his fourth surgery, he was transported on a giant C-130 airplane to the Walter Reed National Military Medical Center in Bethesda, Maryland.

The airplane was configured inside to hold around seventy-five stretchers; three high. Many service men were claustrophobic when riding in the airplane because there was little head room between the racks, and they felt as though they were smothering. Max was lucky in that respect because there weren't many patients on the plane, and they didn't have to put them in so tight. He had a middle rack with the top rack removed, and that gave him plenty of room. It was still a hard trip because the flying time was over nine hours.

Finally, they landed in Washington, and ambulances took them to Walter Reed, where Max was told he would be for an indefinite period.

Chapter Ten

On Saturday morning, after Amy and Neal had pretty much decided how things were going to be for their wedding the night before, Amy called her Mother from the animal hospital. She was excited, and her mood was sky high when she called her, but that didn't last long.

When her Mother answered, Amy said, "Mother, hi. What are you doing?"

"Amy, hi. I just got back from the store, and I was putting up groceries. I'm kind of surprised that you called this time of day. Is everything alright?"

"It's better than alright. Mother, Neal and I have figured out how we're going to be able to get married sooner than we thought we could, and I wanted to tell you. I'm so excited."

"Oh my, but you're still in school. You're not going to quit school, are you?"

"No ma'am, I'm not going to quit school, and here's the good part. We've had a hard time figuring everything out so we could get married before I graduate, and we think we now have everything worked out."

"Well, tell me about it."

"Okay. First of all, we're going to get married next summer after school's out, and we think that we'll temporarily live in Monticello, Illinois until I graduate."

"Monticello! Where is that?"

"Monticello is about midway between Champaign and Decatur. It's only a twenty-minute drive from there to school, and it will be the same for Neal to go to work. By temporarily living in Monticello, we can go ahead and get married and not have to wait until I graduate. Of course, Neal has already graduated, and he will be working full time when we get married, so we won't have to worry about money. Doesn't that sound wonderful?"

Her Mother didn't answer that. She asked, "I'm assuming the ceremony will be here at Middleton Community Church, won't it?"

"That's something I need to talk to you about. Mother, we have decided to have the wedding in Decatur at Neal's home church, and the one I've been going to for the last three years. What do you think about that?"

"I think you should get married in your own church. This is where you were raised."

"But Mother, I've been gone from Middleton for over six years, and I feel that Decatur is my home now. I hope you'll accept that."

"Are you saying that you'll be living in Decatur after you're married?"

"I thought you knew that. Neal's Daddy owns a large animal hospital that Neal will own, one day, and as you know, I've been working there on weekends for almost three years, and I'll work there when I get my degree. Besides, I'll have to live where my husband lives. Don't you agree?"

"I guess. Boy, this is a day of surprises."

"I hope you feel that they are good surprises."

Her Mother didn't say anything when she said that. Then, she asked, "Will this be a big wedding?"

"Not too big. I'll probably only have maybe three attendants."

"Will they be from Middleton?"

"Well, I plan to ask Sissy, but the other two will be from this area."

Her Mother said, "It sounds like you have everything planned."

"Yes Ma'am, we think we do, and listen, I want you to be a big part in this wedding. Maybe you and Daddy will come out some, and I'd like to get your input in making some of the plans for the ceremony and the reception."

"It doesn't sound as if you need me or us."

"Don't be like that, Mother. I want you to be happy for me, and I do need you."

"Ever since you were a little girl, I've dreamed that when you get married, you will get married in our church, and you would be surrounded by our family and friends, and I would play a big part in it. Now you're going to get married a thousand miles away, and it's too far for any of our family or friends to attend."

Her Mother's comment went right through her, and she said, "Mother, first of all, Decatur is not a thousand miles, and secondly, we don't have any family left there, and thirdly, nearly all of my friends except Sissy have moved away. Most of them got married, so my getting married in Decatur, Illinois is no big deal. Sissy will probably want to come, and I hope you and Daddy will, but you don't have to if you don't want to. You and Daddy didn't like my first marriage either."

When she said that, Mrs. Hatcher knew she had hit a nerve, and she said, "Honey, I'm sorry. I didn't mean anything by that. It's just that I'm disappointed that you're not going to have your wedding here."

"It's okay, Mother. Maybe one day you'll accept it. You haven't met Neal yet, but when you do, you're going to love him the way I do. He's a good guy, and while I'm thinking about it; he doesn't know about Max, so be sure you don't say anything when you meet him."

The conversation had become somewhat strained, and Amy didn't want to talk anymore, so she told her Mother goodbye and they hung up.

After her conversation with her mother, her 'high' changed to that of a 'low', and she went to where Neal was, in hopes that he could cheer her up.

When he saw her, he said, "You look like you just lost your best friend. What's wrong?"

"Oh nothing. It seems as if it's like this every time I talk to my Mother. I think I'll stop calling her."

"What did she say?"

"I knew she wouldn't like it when I told her that we're getting married out here, and not in Middleton, but I didn't know I'd feel this bad."

"Look. If it means that much to her, maybe we can have the wedding in Middleton. It doesn't matter to me where we get married, as long as get married. I don't care if we have to go to Devil's Island as long as you're with me."

That brought a smile to her face, and she said, "No. We're getting married in Decatur, no matter what. She'll just have to not like it."

They were there to work, so after the brief conversation about Amy's call to her Mother, they got busy, treating animals. Amy had been doing it long enough, part time, to learn how to give shots, as long as she was in the presence of a vet or someone qualified to give shots, take stool specimens, and a host of other things. The Brock Animal Hospital had enough business to keep them both busy as well as the other people who worked there, so she didn't have any trouble keeping her mind occupied.

Once again, school started, and Amy and Karen moved back into their apartment at Ashton Woods. The new school year began like the others, but Amy could feel a difference because when the school year ended, she would be getting married and move into a different place with Neal. She was worried about Karen, however, and still wanted her to move in with them until they graduated. They didn't talk anymore about that, but it stayed on Amy's mind, and she thought that when the time was right, she would make a determined effort to get her to move in with them. After all, it would only be for about nine months. She hadn't said anything to Neal about it, but she would, later.

Fall break came, and then in early December, it was time for finals, and that took a whole lot of studying. Once they were over, it was time for the Christmas break, and Amy didn't want to go home, but she felt as though she should. She wanted to stay in Decatur with Neal, and then, *Neal came up with an idea.

Over the weekend, she was dreading going back to Middleton when Neal said, "Amy, I've got an idea."

"What is it?"

"Why don't I go to Middleton with you? That way, I can meet your parents and stay two or three days and then come back here for Christmas, and you can stay home until Christmas is over. That way, you and I can be together part of the time, and we won't have to be separated the entire time that school's out. What do you think?"

"Wow! You want to go to Middleton with me? That's surprising. Let me call my Mother to see what's going on down there. I'd love for you to go with me, but let me talk to her first, okay?"

Neal was sort of indignant with her attitude, and he said, "Well, don't fall all over yourself with excitement. I certainly don't have to go. Maybe it's best if I don't."

"I'm sorry. I don't mean to sound that way. It's just that things are strained between my parents and me, and I don't know how they will take my bringing a man home with me, even though he's going to be their son-in-law. They have strange ideas, but let me call and see what's going on with them. I want you to go with me, but I don't want you to be put in an awkward situation, and they have a way of doing that. Give me a minute and I'll call her."

She went into the other room and dialed her Mother, and when her Mother answered, Amy said, "Hi Mother. What are you doing?"

"Just cleaning up a little. What are you doing?"

"I just wanted to call to see if anything special is going on while I'm home for Christmas. I'd like to bring Neal with me, if I can."

"Well, nothing special will be happening as far as I know, but we've been invited to Nashville, to your Uncle Raymond's, the week before Christmas, and they want you to come with us, if you can."

"When did you say?"

"The week before Christmas."

"Darn, that's the week I get home. What day do we go to Uncle Raymond's?"

"They want us to come on Tuesday and stay 'til Friday. What day will you be here?"

"Sunday."

"Well, that will work out, but I don't know about Neal. Can he come Christmas week?"

"No, he can't. He wants to spend as much time with his family at Christmas as he can, and that will cut it too short."

"I'm sorry, Honey. Maybe he can come down the week after Christmas."

"That won't work either. I'm coming back up here the week after Christmas. Okay. It was just a thought. I wanted you to meet Neal, and he wants to meet you, too, but I guess you can meet him when you come to the wedding."

"What do you mean when we come to your wedding? Aren't you going to get married here the way we talked about?"

"Mother, when we talked, I told you plainly that I'm getting married here in Decatur, and I thought it was settled. Do you remember that?"

"Yeah, I guess. I was just hoping that you changed your mind."

"I've gotta go. Bye Mother."

"Bye."

She went back into the other room where Neal was and she said, "Well, so much for that."

"Why? What happened?"

"She's okay with you coming, but not the week before

Christmas. They're, or rather we are going to Nashville to my Uncle Raymond's, and we'll be there from Tuesday 'til Friday. She asked if you could come Christmas week, and I told her no. Then she said how about the week after, and I told her I'm coming back here that week."

"Okay, but if you decide to, there are two or three spots in there that we could work out for me to go down. I only want to stay a couple of days, but it'll have to be up to you."

"We'll talk about it, but I don't think you want to go down there."

"Okay. Subject closed."

***

Max had been at Walter Reed for nearly three months, and he just got word that he was about to be presented The Purple Heart. When he found out the date of the ceremony, he immediately called his parents.

His Mother answered when he called, and he said, "Hi Mother, are you busy?"

"I'm never too busy to talk to you. Why are you calling at this time of the day? Is something wrong?"

"No Ma'am. Everything's fine. I have just found out that I'm going to be getting a Purple Heart at a ceremony ten days from tomorrow, and I would sure like for you and Daddy to be here. That's a week from this Friday. They said that there's a good chance the President will be here to make the presentation, and if you all are here, you can probably meet him. Do you think you can come? I know you were just here, but this is pretty important, and if you can come back, I sure would like for you to."

"Of course, we'll be there. We're so proud of you, Darling. I'll talk to your Daddy when he gets home, and we'll call you back."

"Good. Mother, would you please call Duke's Mother and

ask her to tell Duke about it?"

"I'll call her when we hang up."

Max had been receiving therapy since almost immediately after his fourth surgery at the Walter Reed Amy Medical Center, and it had paid off well because he was in such a state of wellbeing that if someone didn't know what he had been through, they couldn't tell that he had had such serious injuries.

He got word that his Company and all the Marines he went to Iraq with were coming home, and he was ecstatic because he had made some awfully good friends since he had been in the Marines. According to the information he had, they would be back the same week he was to receive his Purple Heart, and he hoped that maybe some of his Platoon would be able to come see him, or better still, come to his Purple Heart ceremony.

On Friday night, the night before the Purple Heart ceremony, Max's parents arrived, and when they got to Bethesda, they went straight to his room to see him. He was in sort of a festive mood, and they were as well. He knew he was going to receive a Purple Heart, but he had no idea what else he was going to get, and neither did his parents.

The ceremony was scheduled to begin at ten o'clock, and everyone was there except the President. There were microphones everywhere and TV cameras from all the networks plus a few from independent news agencies. Precisely at ten o'clock the President arrived, and someone said, "TENCH HUT". All the servicemen who could stand, rose to attention, and these who couldn't stand, sat in their wheelchairs trying to sit at attention. The President had a slight smile on his face, and he said, "Relax, men. At ease." Then, the ceremony began.

Seven Marines were there to receive Purple Hearts, and five of them were in Max's Battalion. Battalion Commander, Lt. Colonel David Lowe acted as Emcee, and he said a few words before he introduced the President, and then he introduced him.

The President went to the mike and said a few words about how proud he was of the ones receiving the Purple Heart that day, and what a sacrifice they and their families have made for their country, and then he called the name of the first recipient. They were going to present the medals in alphabetical order, so Max would be third or fourth. Norwood began with N.

As soon as the Purple Heart was presented to each of the recipients, the President asked if they wanted to say anything. The first Marine said, "No Sir," and he was allowed to sit down. The second one said a few words. He said, "I want to thank everyone in the medical field—you kept me alive."

Next was Max's turn. The President called his name, "Second Lieutenant Max Norwood, and he walked over to where the President was standing and snapped to attention. The President presented him with his Purple Heart, and Max saluted and started to walk back to his seat, and the President said, "Just a minute, Lieutenant, there are a couple of other things before you go."

Max looked puzzled, and it must have shown on his face, because the President said, "It looks as though you're surprised at this, but I'm very pleased to award you one of our country's highest awards; the Bronze Star." He held out his hand to shake Max's, and he said, "Congratulations, Lieutenant," and then Max made a move to go to his seat, and the President said, "One more thing, Max. It's my pleasure to inform you that you have now been promoted from Second Lieutenant to First Lieutenant. Congratulations again." Would you like to say something?"

"Yes sir, I would," then he stood at the microphone and thanked everyone; his doctors, nurses, all the medical staff, and his fellow Marines. Then he said, "I want to especially thank my Platoon Sergeant, Sergeant Penny Pendergrass. He's the one sitting over there with the cool eyepatch on. If it wasn't for Penny, on more than one occasion, you would probably have had to award me my Purple Heart and Bronze Star posthumously. Not only was he my Sergeant, but he has become one of my two best friends. Thank you, Penny, and thank you, Mr. President."

The President had two more Purple Hearts to award after Max, and one of them was Penny, who also got a Bronze Star. When it came time for him to say something, he said almost the same things that Max did, except he thanked Max for saving his life on more than one occasion.

When the ceremony was over, the recipients and their families stood around talking and meeting the President and Lt. Col. Lowe. When Lt. Col. Lowe shook Max's hand and congratulated him, and they were talking, Max asked, "Sir, I think I would like to go back to Iraq or maybe Afghanistan, and I wonder if you can tell me how to go about making it happen."

Col. Lowe said, "Marine, I think you're getting ahead of yourself. The first thing you have to do is get released from the hospital, and the second thing is to get a release from the doctors. You had some serious injuries, and we need people in excellent physical condition to fight. When you have done those two things, if you still want to go back, contact my office."

"Thank you, Sir."

"On the contrary, thank you."

The President seemed to enjoy talking with the Norwoods, and while his Mother and Daddy were talking to him, Max went to Penny. Max held out his hand, and Penny said, "Whatta ya say, L.T.? Congrats on your promotion."

"Thanks. Congrats on your Bronze Star. Where do you go from here?"

"Well, the Marines are giving me a medical leave, and I'm going to the V.A. Hospital where they're working to fit me for a prosthetic eye."

"Well that's good, but you know what? I kinda like your patch."

"Yeah, but I'll take the eye. I don't care anything about looking like Blackbeard. Did I hear you talking to Col. Lowe about going back to Iraq?"

"Yeah. Either there or Afghanistan."

"With all we went through, why in the world would you want to go back?"

"You know, it's kind of dumb, isn't it, but I guess I feel that with all that God has given me, I should try to give some back."

"Well, if you go, good luck."

He and Max hugged and told each other bye. Before he left, Penny said, "L.T., I'd like to stay in touch. Here's my address and phone number. Could I get yours?"

"You bet", and he found a piece of paper and wrote down the information and handed it to him.

As soon as everybody had a chance to meet and talk to the President, he left, presumably to go back to the White House.

Max was tired after all the hoopla, and he realized he wasn't ready to go back to Iraq just yet. He visited with his parents in the lobby of Walter Reed for a while, and then they said they needed to leave for home. It took about six hours to drive from the outskirts of D.C. to Middleton, and that didn't count all the traffic between Bethesda and the outskirts of D.C. They all hugged and his Mother and Daddy told him how proud they were of him, and they left. They had just been there about two weeks ago, so they didn't feel it was necessary to stay too long on that trip.

When he got back to his room, he laid down on his bed and immediately went to sleep. It was about one thirty when he went to sleep, and about two thirty, there was a knock on his door. He wasn't sure he heard it because he thought he might still be asleep, so he just laid there. Then they knocked again, and a voice said, "Max, are you in there?"

That time, Max jumped up and went to the door, and it was none other than Duke and one of his friends. Max said, "Duke, what are you doing here, you rascal? Boy, am I glad to see you."

"I'm glad to see you, too. Max, this is Dwayne Moody. Dwayne plays for the Falcons with me."

Max said, "Dwayne, I'm sure glad to meet you. Are you keeping my main man here out of trouble?"

"I'm trying, but sometimes it's hard. I'm glad to meet you too."

"You guys sit down. What are you doing up here?"

Duke said, "We've got a game with the Redskins tomorrow, and Coach was kind enough to let us off long enough this afternoon to come see you. Mom said you were getting the Purple Heart. Did you get it yet?"

"I did. This morning plus I got a coupla surprises."

"What were the surprises?"

"They gave me a Bronze Star, and they promoted me to 1st Lieutenant. I wasn't expecting either one."

Duke said, "You must have done good in Iraq."

"I guess. Boy, it was rough over there, Duke. You should be glad you weren't over there."

Duke joked and said, "I didn't need to be. You were enough to send those rag heads running. You did send them running didn't you?"

"Some of them ran, but some of them stayed and shot at us and buried bombs."

"Is that what got you?"

"Yeah. It was an IED."

"What does that stand for?"

"It stands for improvised explosive device, and they are powerful. The insurgents bury them along roads, and they can't be seen. Then if you're unlucky enough to run over one—BOOM; you're either injured or dead."

"Did you know anybody that got killed by one?"

"Yeah, the two guys in the front seat of my vehicle died when we got hit. Luckily, my Sergeant and I survived. Enough about me. Are you getting to play a lot?"

"Not a lot. I'm playing some. Rookies in the NFL are a lot like Freshmen in College. You have to work yourself up to it, and there are a couple of seasoned veterans in my position that don't want to give up their position, so it may be another year or two before I can get a lot of playing time."

"Dwayne, is that the same with you?"

"Yeah, Duke is at right tackle and I'm at right guard. We're both stuck behind some real good players."

Max asked, "Duke, how about you and Sissy? Are you all still an item?"

"We are. I'm going to give her a ring at Christmas and hope she says yes."

"I'll bet she does. When you see her, give her a hug for me, will you?"

"I will. Do you know when you'll be home?"

"I hope I can talk the doctors into letting me out of here, and then I hope I can get a leave so I can get home for Christmas. If I do, maybe we can see each other."

"Boy, that would be great. Be sure to let me know. I think your Mom and mine have become good buddies with your Mom asking my Mom to pass along messages from you. I think they have started carrying on conversations when your Mom calls now."

Duke and Dwayne stayed a little longer, and then Duke said, "Ole Buddy, I guess we're going to have to go. We don't want to abuse the favor that Coach gave us or else he might not do anything like it again. It was great seeing you, and if you get home for Christmas, we'll have to spend some time together."

"I'll look forward to it."

Max got up when they did and hugged Duke. As they embraced, Duke said, "I love you, Bro. I've prayed for you, and it looks like it worked."

"Thanks for that. I love you too. I'll watch the game tomorrow and hope you guys beat the Skins. Dwayne, it was great meeting you. Maybe we will see each other again sometime."

Dwayne said, "It was my pleasure. I'll look forward to it. You take care."

With all the excitement, earlier, and then, with Duke's visit, Max didn't have any lunch, and he was getting hungry. He had become friends with a few of the patients at the hospital, and he decided to look a couple of them up to see if they wanted to go with him to the cafeteria to grab a bite to eat.

The first guy he asked said, "Yeah. I was just getting ready to go. I'm glad you stopped by."

After they ate, they talked for a while, and then each went back to his room. Max stood in front of the mirror and held his medals up over his chest and said to himself, *impressive.* He turned on the TV and then laid on his bed and ran his fingers over his Purple Heart and reminisced about how he earned it.

The next day was Sunday, and Max attended the non-denominational church service conducted by one of the Marine chaplains. That chaplain used to be a pastor at a Baptist church, and one day he felt like God was calling him to be a minister in the Marine Corps, so he did what he had to do and became a chaplain. He alternated with other chaplains to conduct services at Walter Reed, and it was not just for Marines; it was for all branches of the Military

He was a powerful preacher, and at the end of the service, he issued an alter call, and several servicemen and women went forward and accepted Christ as their Savior.

After church, he went to the cafeteria and ate lunch, and then he went to his room to watch the Falcons play the Redskins. He hoped Duke and Dwayne would get to play, and he wanted to see them. He dozed, on and off during the game, and neither Duke or Dwayne got to play, so when the game was over, he changed into some shorts and t-shirt and went to the gym to work out a little.

His arm was in better shape than his leg, and he had a hard time getting the leg to do what he wanted, but he was persistent and knew that he would have to get it working normally if he had any chance of getting redeployed. The arm was back close to normal, so he had to concentrate of the leg.

After a couple of hours, he was just about worn out, and he gave up for the day. He went back to his room and changed clothes because he didn't want to wear shorts to the cafeteria for supper.

The next day, a Marine brought him an envelope, and when he opened it, it was paperwork for a thirty-day leave. He immediately called the airline and booked a flight to Middleton for the next day, with a return for January 15., and then he called his Mother to tell her he was coming home, and would she please meet him at the airport.

***

Amy was really having a hard time concentrating on her schoolwork. She was a very smart girl and had been making the Dean's List every semester since she was at the University of Tennessee, but now, with her wedding coming up in about six months, her mind was everywhere.

She and Neal decided that he would not try to go to Middleton over the Christmas holidays for a couple of reasons, and she really didn't want to go, but she felt that since her Mother and Daddy were there, she was obligated to go. She was dreading going to her Uncle Raymond's, too, but she reasoned that it would only be for three nights, and her little brother, Stevie, would be there, and he would help with the boredom.

Stevie had grown up. He was no longer the fourteen-year-old *little brother* that he was when she was in high school. Stevie had developed into a handsome young man with a great personality. He had tried to follow in Max's shoes in terms of playing football, and he did pretty well. He never reached the point that Max did, but he was good.

He was a handsome twenty-year-old and a junior at Tennessee Wesleyan University, and he was very popular with all the young ladies. The more Amy thought about it, the better she liked the idea of Stevie being there. Uncle Raymond didn't have any children, so there would be no young people there, and she thought that maybe she and Stevie could do some things together.

Finals were over at last, and Neal helped her book a plane ticket to Middleton for the next morning after the last final. He took her to the airport and kissed her goodbye when she got ready to board the plane, and he waited and watched it take off.

The whole family was at the airport when the plane arrived; Mother, Daddy, and Stevie, and she felt more welcomed than the last time she was there. She didn't know why, but even her Daddy was warmer than usual. She hated to be a skeptic, but she wondered if the warm welcome was a way to maybe lead up to trying to convince her to have her wedding in Middleton instead of Decatur, and she was determined not to let that happen.

It was still a couple of days before they had to leave for Uncle Raymond's, and Amy took advantage of the time by spending a lot of it with Sissy. The day she got home she called Sissy, and Sissy was busy that night, but they set a time for the next day to get together. Amy was actually going to Sissy's, then they were going to the mall.

They had so much catching up to do and had so much to talk about, they had a hard time letting the other talk; each of them was trying to tell the other their own news, and it took a little while for them to settle down and listen to the other. They spent a couple of hours at Sissy's house, and then they left for the mall. They wanted to have lunch there, and it was also a good place to talk; much better than at Sissy's house.

Chick-Fil-A was where they chose, and when they sat down and got their order, Sissy said, "Okay, enough suspense. Tell me about this Neal fellow."

"Sissy, you'll love him when you meet him. He's the nicest, kindest man you'll ever see. I think I told you; his sister is my roommate, and that's how I met him. Her name is Karen Brock. Their Daddy has an animal hospital down in Decatur, Illinois, and Karen and Neal went down there every weekend to help their Daddy in the clinic, and right away, when we became roommates, Karen asked me if I would like to go down with them, and rather than having to stay at school by myself over the weekend, I jumped at the chance to go. From then on, it became an every weekend thing. It already was an every weekend thing for Neal and Karen, and then, it became that for me.

"Neal and I were exposed to each other that way for a long time, and the three of us were just like siblings, then one day I realized I was feeling something for him. That was before he realized he had feelings for me, and then one day, he asked me out. I didn't hesitate; I said yes immediately, and we've been seeing each other that way ever since.

"Sissy, his Mother and Daddy have accepted me like one of their own, and when Neal and I got engaged, they were ecstatic. Neal graduated last year, and he is now Dr. Neal Brock, and he is working full time at the clinic. Karen and I graduate next year, and we'll both be Dr. Brocks. In another year, you'll have Dr. Mike Brock, Dr. Neal Brock, Dr. Karen Brock, and Dr. Amy Brock. Isn't that neat?"

"It is. If somebody comes to the clinic and yells Dr. Brock, the whole company will turn around. I think that's great." They both laughed when she said that.

"Sissy, tell me what's been happening in your life since I last saw you."

"Not much has changed since the last time we were together. When I got out of college, I went to work for the Keese Insurance Agency, and I just love it. They are such nice people that I actually look forward to going to work every day."

"Are you and Duke still seeing each other?"

"Yeah, we are, and Amy, we love each other."

"Do you think you all will get married?"

"We've talked about it, but there's nothing definite at this point."

"He's playing professional football, isn't he?"

"Yeah, he plays for the Atlanta Falcons."

Amy said, "I've heard that professional football players make a lot of money."

"They do. Duke is just a rookie, and he hardly ever gets to play, but they're paying him four hundred and eighty thousand dollars a year. Next year, he'll get quite a bit more if he stays with them."

"Wow! You'd better hold on to him, Sis."

"I'm going to. He's my gentle giant."

"I hesitate to ask you this, but have you heard anything about Max? I heard he was about to get married."

"Yeah, he and Duke keep in touch. Did you hear about him in Iraq?"

"No. I didn't hear."

"Well, you knew he was in the Marines, didn't you?"

"Yeah, I knew that."

"Well, they sent him to Iraq, and he was supposed to be over there for a year, but after he had been there for several months, he got blown up by one of those roadside bombs."

A look of horror came on her face, and she asked, "Is he dead?"

"No, but he was hurt real bad. The explosion broke his arm and leg, several ribs, and I don't know what all internally. He has been at the Walter Reed Hospital in Maryland for several months, and Duke went to see him, and he said that he was doing good, and he wants to go back to Iraq. He thinks he's going to get to come home for Christmas, and if he does, the three of us are going to get together. He and Duke are like brothers. Max and I have exchanged letters a few times, and he sort of keeps me up to date on what he's doing. As for him getting married; he's not. He was engaged to a girl from Memphis, and either before he went to Iraq or shortly after he got over there, she wrote him a Dear John letter and sent his ring back. Her name was Toni. I don't know that he has ever mentioned it to Duke, so it must not have been too earth shattering for him."

Amy asked, "Did you say he might be home for Christmas?"

"That's what Duke said. If he comes in, and Duke and I get together with him, would you like to come along?"

She hesitated for several seconds and then said, "I guess not. I don't think that would be a good idea. What do you think?"

"You may be right. You know what?"

"What?"

"You can't imagine how much I wish you and Max were still together. I love you both, and I thought you two made the perfect couple."

"Sissy, let me ask you something, and if you don't feel like you can, it will be alright, but will you be in my wedding? It will be in Decatur, Illinois, where I'll be living. I know it's a long way, and I hope you will do it, but if you can't, I'll understand. I don't feel that I can ask you to travel that far and stay in a hotel plus buy a dress, so if you can get there, Neal and I will take care of everything else, except your dress, and if you need for me to, I'll help with the dress."

"Is this going to be a fancy wedding?" Sissy asked.

"No. Not really. I'm only going to have three attendants, and in these times, that's considered small."

Sissy said, "Count me in. You and I have been like sisters all our lives, so there's no way I would even think about not being there when you marry the man of your dreams. Just get me all the information when you have it, and I'll mark my calendar."

After a while, they decided to do a little shopping because neither one of them had done any Christmas shopping. Sissy's main one to buy for was Duke, and Amy's was Neal. It was harder for Sissy than it was for Amy, because buying clothes for a three-hundred-pound man wasn't easy. On the other hand, Neal could wear things from just about any store.

They finished out the day, and then they went back to Sissy's where Amy had left her car. They told each other bye, and promised to get together again before Amy had to leave to go back.

Chapter Eleven

Max's plane landed at eleven o'clock Monday morning, and his Mother was there to pick him up. Normally, she would let him drive home from the airport, but she wasn't sure how well his leg was, so she didn't offer to let him drive. She got in the driver's seat and they went home. He never thought he would be so glad to be anywhere as he was that day when he got home. He was there right before he was deployed, then he was in Iraq for just slightly longer than nine months and at Walter Reed for a little over four months, so it had been over a year since he had been there.

Everything at home was the same as it was before he left, but with all he had been through, everything then took on a special meaning to him. He spent the day with his Mother and didn't offer to go anywhere. He did call Duke's Mother to tell her he was at home, and would she please ask Duke to call him when he came home on Tuesday. She said she would, and she told him how happy she was that he was doing okay.

On Tuesday morning, Duke called and said he was coming to Middleton that afternoon, and he said he would come by when he got down there. Naturally, he had a date with Sissy that night, so his time with Max, one on one, was limited. He and Sissy were so good to include Max in whatever they did made him grateful, but at the same time, he felt like a fifth wheel sometimes.

When Duke got there that afternoon, they renewed where they left off the last time they were together. Duke said that he and Sissy were going to go eat and then take in a movie, and he invited Max to go with them. It had been so long since Max had seen Sissy, he didn't argue about going. The only thing he insisted on was driving and meeting them at the restaurant so he could leave when he wanted to and not be with them through their entire date.

They met at a new restaurant that Sissy had wanted to go to, and the atmosphere was very relaxed. They talked and talked, and Max told them about some of the things he experienced in Iraq, and Duke told of some of the things he had experienced in the NFL.

The whole time they were talking, Sissy was debating with herself about whether to tell Max about her having seen Amy, and then, when they finished telling about their experiences, she said, "Well, let me tell you about an experience I had today," and Duke asked, "What was it?"

She said, "Max, this will be especially interesting for you." She said, "I spent most of the day with your friend, Amy."

He said, "Really? How's she doing?"

"I asked her if she would like to come with us if the three of us got together, but she said she didn't think it would be a good idea. Did you know she's getting married?"

He had a terrible, shocked look on his face when she said that, and then he said, "No, I didn't. We haven't been in touch for a long time now. Is she marrying somebody from around here?"

"No, she's marrying a veterinarian in Decatur, Illinois named Dr. Neal Brock. You know she's going to be a vet herself."

"Yeah, I did know that. If you see her again, tell her I said "Hey", and I wish her good luck."

When they finished eating, Max tried to excuse himself, but Sissy and Duke both insisted that he go to the movie with them, so he acquiesced and went with them. He was amused when they got in the theater because Duke was so big, he had a hard time fitting into the seat.

Max joked and said, Duke, if you'll wait here, I'll go see if I can find a couch for you to sit on."

"Ha ha. Very funny," Duke said.

The movie was good and when it was over, and they went

outside, Max said, "Guys, this has been truly a real pleasure. I'm gonna go on home now and let you all get on with whatever you're going to do. Thanks for including me tonight. It was a lot of fun. Duke, I'll be here for a total of thirty days, so whenever you get a chance, let's get together again."

"Okay, Buddy. I enjoyed it. Have a good rest of the week."

"I will. Thanks. Sissy, it was great seeing you. If you have a chance, call me one day, and I'll buy your lunch."

"I may just do that. Thanks. It was good to see you too, and I'm glad you're doing so well. Good night."

Max got into his now aged Jeep and headed home, all the time thinking about what Sissy said about Amy getting married. The mention of her name brought back so many memories, both good and bad.

On Wednesday night, the phone rang at Max's parent's house and it was Duke. "Hey Duke, what's up?"

"Max, would you like to come to the Falcons game Sunday? I can get you a pass."

"Man, that sounds wonderful, but I'm afraid this bum leg won't let me drive that far just yet. I sure wish I could, but thanks anyway, Padna."

Duke asked, "Do you think your Dad would like to come. I can get passes for you both, and he can drive you all down."

"Hold on a minute, Duke. Let me ask him."

He held the phone down and asked his Daddy if he would like to go to the Falcons game Sunday, and his Daddy said he would love to go.

He raised the phone back to his ear and told Duke, "He said he'd love to come. You know, he's a big Falcons fan. Where do we come to?"

Duke gave him all the necessary information, which included one special gate, and he told him for them to wait on him after the game, and he would see them then, if not before. Before Max left Walter Reed, they gave him a *Handicap* placard, and he brought it to Atlanta with him. When they pulled into the parking lot at the Georgia Dome, they looked for two things; the gate number that Duke gave them and the handicap parking places. After driving around for a couple of minutes, they stopped and asked an attendant where both places were, and he directed them to exactly where they wanted to go.

After they had parked, Max put on a baseball cap that had USMC on the front. They got out and walked up to the stadium and the gate where they were supposed to go. There was a booth outside the gate that looked like a guard's station, and Max went up to it, and told the person inside, "Hi. I'm Max Norwood. There are supposed to be two tickets left here for me and my Dad."

The person inside asked, "Did you say Norwood?"

"Yes, Max Norwood."

The man said, "Wait here," and he exited the booth and went into the stadium. In about two or three minutes, he came back out with someone else, and the person with him walked around the booth to where Max and his Dad were standing, and asked, "Max Norwood?"

"Yes, I'm Max."

"Hi Max. I'm Bob Watkins. Did Duke tell you where your seats were?"

"No. He just said to come here, and he would leave passes for us."

"Okay. Follow me", and he led them down and away from the seating area to a place on the field, where there were benches for the players to sit on. "Here are your seats," Bob said. "I suggest you sit on the end, so you won't get run over by some of the players. The team will be out in just a minute, so enjoy yourselves," and he left them.

The team had already warmed up and had gone back into the locker room, and just as Bob said, it wasn't but a minute until they came running out onto the field and over to the benches where Max and his Dad were standing.

In the minute before kickoff, the Falcons Coach went over to Max and said, "Max, I'm Marion Putnam. It's nice to have you here. I hope we can show you a good game this afternoon," and then he ran back over to the team.

It was a real good game, with the score at halftime, Falcons, ten, Carolina, seven. When the gun went off, ending the first half, one of the assistant coaches ran over to Max and his Dad and said, "Would you all like to come in the locker room at halftime? Coach Putnam would like for you to," so they followed him into the locker room.

Before Coach Putnam began his halftime speech, he said, "Men, give me your attention." When they all quietened down, he said, "I want to introduce you to an American Hero," and he called Max to step to the center of the room, "This is First Lieutenant Max Norwood, United States Marine Corp. Max has just recently returned from Iraq where he was seriously wounded, protecting all of us, so we would have the freedom to play this football game today. If you get the chance, you might want to thank him before you leave here."

Max could feel himself blushing, and he knew his face had to be bright red, but at the same time, he really appreciated what the Coach said.

It didn't seem as though it was more than a minute or two until the half was over, and it was time to go back out for the second half. Duke took a minute to speak to Max and his Dad, and said, "Wait for me after the game," and he ran out with the team.

The lead changed three or four times the second half, and with only three seconds to go, the Falcons kicked the game-winning field goal and won by a score of thirty-one to twenty-eight. It was a great game.

Max and his Dad waited for Duke outside by the guard gate where they came in, and after what seemed like forever, Duke came out, followed by Dwayne, the one who came with him to visit him at Walter Reed. "Duke, we really appreciate the passes for the game today, and we especially thank you for the sideline seats. It was really a lot of fun. Thank you."

"Glad to do it. Where are you going from here?"

"Back to Daddy's, I guess."

"Well, be careful. I'll probably be in Middleton Tuesday if you're going to be around."

"I'll be there."

"Okay, good. I'll make it a point to come by."

"Great. I'll look forward to it, and Dwayne, it's nice to see you again."

"It's nice to see you too. Take care."

They planned to wait until most of the traffic cleared out before they even tried to leave, and it was a good thing because a lot of the players came over to Max when they were leaving to say, "Thank you for your service." Atlanta was always a nightmare to drive in during normal times, but when you had more than seventy-five thousand fans trying to get out at the same time, on top of the normal traffic, it was especially stressful. When there were hardly any cars left in the parking lot, they finally started the car and left.

On the way home, they talked non-stop about the game and for Max's Daddy, getting to sit on the bench and meeting a lot of the players was a once in a lifetime experience. He knew that without Max's experience in the Marines, those things would not have happened, and it made him even prouder of him than he already was.

It was suppertime when they finally got home, and Max's Daddy didn't want his Mother to have to cook, so they decided to go out. When they got back home, Max called Sissy.

"Hello."

"Sissy, Max. How ya doin?"

"Hi Max. I'm doing okay. How are you?"

"I'm fine. I just wanted to call and let you know that Duke got passes to the ball game for Daddy and me, and we went down this afternoon, and I saw Duke. He said he would more than likely be coming to Middleton Tuesday."

"That was nice of him, wasn't it?"

"It was, and everybody on the team, including the Coaches made us feel at home, and the Head Coach recognized me in the locker room at half time."

"Really? I'll bet that made you feel good."

"It did, but I think my face turned red. Look, I won't keep you. I just wanted to tell you what Duke did. I'll be here 'til after Christmas, so maybe I'll see you again before I have to go back."

"I hope so. Bye, Max."

"Bye."

It just so happened that Amy was at Sissy's when Max called, and she was very interested in the conversation. She asked Sissy, "Was that Max?"

"Yeah. In living color."

"What did he want?"

Sissy related the whole conversation to her, and she said, "You know, I kind of wish I had gone with you guys the other night."

"Well, Duke's coming Tuesday, and we'll probably go out again, and you can go with us then if you want to."

"I can't. I've got to go to Nashville with my family on Tuesday."

"Maybe next Tuesday."

Amy said, "That's Christmas Eve, isn't it? I'll need to stay home then, and you probably will, too."

"That's right. I probably will. How about the Tuesday after Christmas?"

"I don't know. I'm going back to Decatur that week, and I don't know which day yet. Maybe it'll be best if I don't see him, anyway. It may stir up old feelings, and I'm engaged to Neal, remember?"

"I remember."

"Look, Sissy. I need to go home. I'm not spending very

much time with my family, and I feel guilty for being gone so much. I'll talk to you tomorrow."

"Okay. Call me."

On Monday, Amy spent the day at home with her Mother. They cleaned house, washed clothes, and other things that needed to be done around the house, and then on Tuesday morning, they loaded the van and went to Nashville to see her Uncle Raymond; her Daddy's brother.

Duke went to Middleton on Tuesday, and he went by Max's for a visit, and he didn't mention Max going with him and Sissy that night. He stayed until about five o'clock, and then said, "Well, Ole Buddy, I've got to go. Sissy promised her parents that we would go out to eat with them tonight, and I had better not mess up with my future in-laws.

"You had better not or else you'll be in the doghouse for a long time." They laughed about that, and Duke started out.

Before he left, he said, "Next week is our last game, so I'll be free after that. I'll call you, and maybe we can get together some before you have to go back."

"That would be good. Have a nice time with the in-laws tonight."

Duke smiled and said, "Right. See ya."

Everyone was really busy for the next few days. Christmas was on Wednesday the following week, and there was still some shopping to do, and the women were working hard to make sure their houses were standing tall when company came in.

On Christmas Eve, Duke called Sissy and said, "Sweetheart, I know you all are going to be really busy tonight, but would it be alright if I came down for just a few minutes? I promise I won't stay but a very few minutes."

She thought about how busy things were that day and night, but she didn't want to refuse him, so she said, "Yeah, it'll be alright. When are you coming?"

"Would four o'clock this afternoon be a good time?"

"Yeah, we'll probably be taking a break about then. Come on at four."

"Okay. I'll see you then."

He was there at exactly four o'clock, and when she came to the door, she said, "Come on in."

He went in, and her parents were there, and he couldn't talk privately at all, and what he had to say was best said in private. He said, Sissy, let's take a ride; maybe go to Chick-Fil-A and get an ice cream. You want to?"

She thought he was acting a little strange, but she went along with it and said, "Okay, let's go, but I can't be gone long."

They went to Chick-Fil- A and pulled into the parking lot. Before getting out, Duke said, "Sissy, I wanted to talk to you alone, and this is the only place I could think of."

She looked at him and asked, "Duke Wayne, what are you up to?"

He said, "Sissy, I've loved you from the first time I saw you, and every time we get together, I love you more, and I would like to spend the rest of my life with you." He pulled out a ring box and asked, "Would you do me the honor of being my wife?"

Her eyes were the size of saucers, and she stared at the ring and almost shouted, "Yes, I'd love to be your wife, and at the same time hugged and kissed him."

Duke, always laid back, said, "You probably don't want any ice cream now, do you?"

She said, "No. I'm too excited to eat it. Let's go to my house so I can show my Mother," and he started the car and headed to her house.

When they got there, Sissy ran on ahead of Duke and went in the house yelling for her Mother. When she found her, she said, "Mother, look what Duke gave me. Isn't it beautiful?"

"It really is," and she called her Daddy to come in there. She showed him the ring, and they all went on over it, and the fact that she and Duke were going to get married. The Von Cannons were expecting a crowd at any time for Christmas Eve dinner, so Duke didn't stay. He told Sissy and her parents Merry Christmas and said he would see them sometime the next day, and he headed home, leaving Sissy wishing he didn't have to go.

The Hatchers, Norwoods, Brocks, Waynes, and Von Cannons all had Merry Christmases, and each family had much to look forward to in the coming year, with the possible exception of Max. He wanted to return to Iraq or possibly Afghanistan, but he had to go back to Walter Reed Medical Center for more therapy and treatment before he could go anywhere, even Quantico.

On Christmas afternoon, Duke went back to Sissy's, and they resumed their engagement celebration. Sissy had called Amy to tell her the news and Amy was going to go over there that night to see her ring, but before time for Amy to go, Duke wanted to go to Max's to share the news with him, since he was his best friend.

Max was very happy for them, and they only had a short time to celebrate at Max's before Amy was to go to Sissy's, so they left and went back to Sissy's. Duke told Max he would call him and come by and spend some time with him in the next few days. Since football was over, he would have plenty of time. Sissy and Duke got serious about the wedding just as soon as Christmas was over.

Duke asked her, "Do you know when you want us to get married?"

"I've been thinking about it, and I don't know exactly; probably sometime in May."

"I thought you would want to be a June bride. Why May?"

"Because Amy's getting married in June, and she's asked me to be in her wedding. I don't think I can be in hers and have one of my own in the same month. I hope we can have ours when she can be in it, but I don't know. She gets out of school in May, but she will have finals before that, so it will probably be a miracle if she can be in it."

"Well, do we have to get married in May?"

She thought for a minute and said, "You know, I don't guess we have to. We can get married when we want to, other than football season. When do you think?"

"I think a Spring wedding might be good. Everything is turning green and coming back to life, and I think that might be a good time."

"You may be right. I didn't think about spring. How about July?"

"No. July's out. Football camp starts around the first of July. If we're going to not conflict with football, the wedding will have to be sometime between the first of January and the end of June."

"I wonder if we could schedule it when Amy is on Spring Break."

"When is that?"

"Usually in March sometime."

"Would that be a time that you'd want?"

"I don't know. It's still cold in March, and I'd like for it to be at least a little warm. I'll check with Amy and see if she knows when Spring Break is."

"Let me ask you something, Sissy, and I don't want you to get mad at me, but is it absolutely necessary for Amy to be in the wedding?"

"YES. Amy has been my best friend since we were little, and I would hate to take such an important step in my life without her being involved in it."

"Okay. I understand, but sometimes when you're grown, you have to do some things that you don't want to do. For instance, there's a good chance that Max won't be able to be in it."

"Why?"

"Because he may be going back to Iraq, and if not, Afghanistan."

"After all his injuries, they'd let him go back?"

"He thinks so."

"Okay, we've got some time. Let's think about it and try to come up with a time that's good for both of us."

"Ten four."

"Ten four? What are you; a policeman?"

He smiled and said, "And you thought I just played football."

Sissy's Mother came in and asked Duke, "We're having leftovers tonight. Do you want some?"

"Yes Ma'am. That sounds real good."

"Well, you all come on, and I'll get them out of the fridge."

They ate until they were full, and Duke stayed for a little while longer, and then went home because they were all tired.

Amy had decided to go back to Decatur on Sunday, and that meant she only had three days left at home, and she and Sissy wanted to spend as much time together during that three days as they could. The place where Sissy worked closed all week for Christmas, and that helped.

Duke told her to spend as much time as she wanted with Amy, and he wouldn't interfere, so he took advantage of the time and went to see Max a couple of times. The two friends did some serious talking during that time, and Duke was intrigued with Max's tales of the war. When Max said he wanted to be redeployed, Duke asked, "After what happened to you when you were over there, why, in the name of common sense, would you want to go back"

"Remember when we were at Memphis State and would lose a game? We couldn't wait until next year to play the team that beat us so we could maybe get revenge for their beating us. That's kind of the way I feel about going back. I don't feel as though I finished my job, and I want to finish it."

"Yeah, but we're not talking about football here. We're talking about people wanting to kill you, and you killing them. Did you kill anybody when you were there the first time?"

"Yeah."

"How many?"

"Several. I don't know how many. When there are dozens or hundreds coming at you with guns blazing, you don't have time to count. All you can do is shoot back and hope you don't get hit. When it's over, you count the bodies, but you don't know how many you got because your whole team was firing at them."

"Did you ever feel guilty about killing someone?"

"I did about my first kill. I carried that burden until we got into a big firefight, and I had to shoot, and hope I hit a whole lot of what some people call ragheads."

"Well, I'm going to tell you, Buddy, that I hope they won't send you back."

"They may not. We'll just have to wait and see."

"You said you have to be back the fifteenth, Where do you go from here?"

"I have to go back to Walter Reed."

"How long will you be there, do you know?"

"Until they think I'm ready to get back to being a regular Marine. I hope it won't be long. By the way, Did I show you my Purple Heart?"

"No, but I'd like to see it."

"Wait here a minute." He got up and went into his bedroom and came back with two boxes. He opened the first one and said, "This is the Purple Heart," and then he opened the other one and said, "And this is the Bronze Star."

"Really? I didn't know you got a Bronze Star. Man, you're a hero."

"No. I'm just Max."

"Wait 'til I tell my teammates. Man, a Purple Heart AND a Bronze Star. I feel like I ought to ask you for your autograph."

"You're a nut. Did you know that?"

"Maybe I am, but I'm in awe over this."

"Well, get over it. Nothing's changed between you and me. We're still Duke and Max."

"Before I get off of this, can I ask a favor?"

"What?"

"Would you mind if I brought Sissy over here to see your medals. I'm sure she's heard of a Purple Heart, but I doubt if she's ever seen one, and I'd like for her to see yours. If you'll let me bring her, then I'll get off the subject."

"Of course, you can bring her over. She's like my sister."

He brought her over the next day, and they had a great time visiting. Max and Sissy had known each other since junior high school, and Sissy had no idea that Max was such a hero until Duke emphasized the fact.

Amy and Sissy spent time together on Thursday, Friday, and Amy stayed home with her family on Saturday because she was leaving on Sunday. Both parents and her brother, Stevie, took her to the airport Sunday morning and put her on a plane for Decatur.

It was still almost three weeks until Max had to leave, and he and Duke spent quite a bit of time together during that time. Some nights Max would go out with him and Sissy, and they made the best of what time they had together.

Finally, it was the fourteenth of January, and Max had to be back at Bethesda the next day, so he told Duke and Sissy goodbye on the thirteenth. Sissy and Duke were nervous about him leaving because he had told them that he was going to try to get deployed again, and they were afraid of what might happen if he had to go back.

There were three flights a day from Middleton to Washington, and Max booked his flight on the latest one at four o'clock in the afternoon. Flying time was a little less than two hours, so he could get to Washington and take a limo to Bethesda and still get to Walter Reed in time for dinner.

Upon arrival at Walter Reed, he checked in, and found that he had been moved from his old room to new quarters in a dormitory type setting. It was very nice, and he was glad they moved him.

He resumed physical therapy the following day, and it was easy to tell that he had been away for a while because when the last session was over, he was fatigued. He showered, ate dinner, and went to bed early. On the third day, after therapy, he was resting in his room and there was a knock on his door. He couldn't imagine who would be knocking on his door, and when he went to answer the knock, it was his good Buddy, Earl Tedder.

"Earl, whatta ya say, Buddy? When did you get back?"

"I've been back for a while, in fact; they shipped us back a couple of months after you were hit. That was the end of our twelve months."

"Well, it's great to see you. I see they gave you a silver bar. Are you going to stay in the Corps?"

"For a while, anyway. There's still two years left on my enlistment. I'm thinking about volunteering for another tour."

"I've still got close to two years left on my enlistment, too. I think we came in at about the same time. I want to go back, too. In fact; I mentioned it to Colonel Lowe."

"What did he say?"

"He said I had to get over my injuries, and then we'd talk about it. Have you talked to anybody yet?"

"No, but I may this week."

Max asked him, "What are you doing since your promotion?"

"They made me Executive Officer of Charlie Company."

"I wonder where I'll be when I get out of here."

"You'll probably get some Company," Earl said.

"I wonder how they'll work it if they give both of us a Company and then let us go back overseas. I doubt they'll send the whole company."

"I don't know. I'll let somebody else worry about that. I'd say that they'll pull us and send us over and take some other First Luies and make them Executive Officers. Like I say, I don't know."

Max asked, "Do you know who to talk to about deployment?"

"I have no idea. I'm going to go to the Battalion office and ask them. I'm sure they can tell me."

"How about letting me know when you find out."

"I'll do it. Do you have any idea how much longer you're going to have to be in here?"

"I hope no more than two or three more weeks. I'm getting stronger every day, and my Doctor acts like he's my friend, so I'm going to try to put a little pressure on him to release me."

Earl said he had to go, and he told Max he would be back in touch when he found out about how to get redeployed. They shook hands, and he left.

On Tuesday of the following week, Earl went back to Max's and told him, "I went to Battalion Headquarters last Friday to try and find out what I needed to do to get redeployed and guess what."

"What?"

"They told me that our whole Battalion was going to be redeployed, and I asked them when, and they said sometime within the next month or six weeks, so Ole Buddy, if you can get out of here, you can probably go with us."

"Man, that's good to know. I'll do whatever I need to to get released from the Doctors care. He's supposed to be here tomorrow, and I'll apply the pressure when he gets here."

"Atta Boy. We need to be over there together."

Six weeks later

Everything was the same as when they were deployed the first time, except there were many new faces. Several of the old veterans either retired or their enlistments were up, and they didn't want to go back. The first time was really rough, and nobody blamed them.

Another change that affected Earl and Max were their outfits. On the first deployment, Earl was Platoon Commander in Lima Company, and Max was Commander of a Platoon on

Kilo Company. On this deployment, two new 'Specialty' Platoons were created, and Max and Earl were put in charge of them. Earl called his "Mad Dog" and Max named his "Blue Bird," and that's what they would go by on the radio transmissions.

Once again, they flew commercial to Kuwait, and spent three days at Camp Arifjan before being flown into Iraq by huge C-130 airplanes, landing at Basra.

The area they were going to fight in was known for its snipers, small arms fire, and mortars. As soon as they got there, Max noticed the new guys just milling around and joking with each other, excited to be in a place where they were being shot at and not being at all concerned with taking caution. All at once, Max heard the sound of a mortar, and he yelled at his guys to take cover. Fortunately, the mortar hit away from anybody, but when the young guys saw what happened, they got serious. It made Max realize that those young kids with fresh minds knew nothing about combat. They were like innocent virgins, and there he was on his second tour.

At about the same time as the mortar hit, Max happened to look to his right where there were stacks of crates waiting to be unpacked, and through the space between some of them, he saw two insurgents creeping toward them. He motioned to his men to stay down, and he crept around to the left of the crates, and when he got out in the open, they saw him, but they didn't have a chance to shoot before he mowed them down. His men cautiously came out from where they were taking cover and went out to see the two dead insurgents, and when everyone got out there, he said, "Men, the way you all were so lackadaisical when we first got here, you're lucky that these guys didn't take some of you out. You can't let your guard down for even a minute out here because somebody is probably watching you. Luckily, you won't have to worry about these two."

Some of them went to him and said how glad they were that he saw them first and took them out. Some just stood there and looked at the bodies because they had never seen a dead body before. Max went over to the ones who were staring at the bodies and said, "Guys, does this bother you?"

One man said, "Yes sir, it bothers me. I knew we were coming out here to take care of these guys, but when you see it in person, it's different. I appreciate you saving us from getting killed," and then two or three others made comments.

"Well, Padna, out here everybody watches everybody's back. You might save my life tomorrow or the next day. Just be careful, and make sure your Buddies are careful."

Max hated that he had to kill two men in order to teach his men a lesson, but he knew he had no other choice.

Later, that same day, the Company Commander called him and Earl over to where a temporary headquarters had been set up. He said, "Men, you were told that you are going to command two Specialty Platoons, and this is where it begins. What you have to do is work together but separate. Here's what I mean. There are many residential neighborhoods in the city, and it will be your job to clear the houses of insurgents. Max, your Platoon will take one street, and Earl, yours will take the one next to it. That way, if either of you gets into trouble, the other can get there to help in a short amount of time.

"When one of you gets your street cleared, wait at the end of the street for the other one to finish clearing his, then both of you move over to the next two streets. Tell your men to keep their eyes open, because those houses are very dangerous. You will more than likely encounter small arms fire, snipers, IEDs, and RPGs, so be careful. Talk to your men and make them aware of what they're going to face, and you're to move out in the morning at o five hundred hours. For what it's worth, get a good night's sleep."

At five o'clock the next morning Mad Dog and Blue Bird

Platoons loaded into Humvees and headed to the first neighborhood they were to try and clear. Both Platoons were successful clearing the houses they went in on the first two streets, and only encountered some minor small arms fire, which they took care of with no problem. Then at the fourth house on the third street they went to, all heck broke loose.

Max, and six of his men were getting ready to enter the house when a machine gun opened up, pinning the men down behind a rock wall in the front yard. The fire was so intense, the men couldn't move.

Max studied the situation, and in a couple of minutes, he told Tom, his Platoon Sergeant, "Tom, on my signal, have all the men start firing so I can fall back." He gave the signal, and his men began firing steady while he drew back. While they were firing, the machine gun went silent, and that gave Max a chance to draw back from the rock wall. When he got out of sight of the house where his men were pinned down, he walked down past the houses they had already cleared, and then went to the back of them and started back up toward the house where his men were. He was careful to dart in between each house as he passed it before moving on to the next one, so the insurgents wouldn't see him, and then, when he got to the house where the machine gun was, he paused for a couple of minutes.

He carefully studied the situation, and then, all at once, he took off toward the house and going to an open window he had spotted, he threw a grenade inside. It exploded, and everything was silent. Just to be on the safe side, he threw a second grenade inside, and after it exploded, he went into the house. He walked through it with his gun at ready and found no one alive. There were four dead insurgents. He went to the front door and waved his men to come in.

His Sergeant was a fellow from Rome, Georgia named Tom Rutledge, and Tom was a seasoned veteran. He was on his third tour, and when he saw what Max did, he said, "Good job, L.T. You can be on my team anytime."

"Thanks, Tom."

The six men who were pinned down told Max "Thank you, L.T."

One of the men said, "That's twice you've saved me, L.T. Thank you."

The two Specialty Platoons continued on in the same neighborhood until they finished around four o'clock. Between the two Platoons, sixteen insurgents were killed and twenty-two were captured. The Sergeants for both Platoons radioed their headquarters from time to time to ask for help transporting the prisoners. Each time they asked, transportation and guards showed up pretty quickly and took the prisoners away.

Max didn't know where they took them, and he didn't care. His job was to just capture them, if he didn't have to kill them.

The next morning, the two Platoons were going into a different neighborhood to clear the houses, when as they came close to their destination, one of the Humvees in Mad Dog Platoon was hit by a rocket propelled grenade. It exploded on contact and hurt all five Marines inside it. Luckily, it didn't kill any of them.

Earl's Sergeant radioed for help, and in about a half hour a truck showed up to take the men to the hospital. They didn't send any ambulances because they saved them for the wounded who needed gurneys, and none of the Marines in the Humvee needed a gurney.

When the injured men got back to the bivouac, they were treated for burns; some worse than others, but none were life-threatening, fortunately.

Chapter Twelve

After four months in Iraq, Max's Specialty Platoon had done amazing work, and whenever they would clear a town of Insurgents, Battalion would move them to another town to do the same thing. The work was fairly easy in some of the places, but in others it would be red hot; with casualties on both sides.

Max had become recognized as one fine leader. He looked on his troops as if they were his children. Whenever they would go on a mission, he would be in the lead, willing to take the first action initiated by the enemy, and his reputation grew among the Marines.

After completing their main job of clearing houses in towns where they went, they were put to work setting up automobile check points. His Platoon would take, say the north and east side of a town, and Earl's Platoon would take the other two; the south and west. They worked great together, and they had become very efficient with their missions.

Then, one day, Max was grazed by a bullet. It hurt like crazy, and he wanted to stay with his men, but Tom said, "L.T. I think you should go to the Battalion Aid Station and get some treatment, and then maybe you can come back."

The wound hurt so bad that he told Tom, "I think you're right. Radio for a medivac, and I'll go. Maybe I can come back tomorrow."

Tom said, "Okay, I will," and he radioed for a medivac to come get Max.

As he was waiting on the medivac, he told Tom, "Tom, you're in charge while I'm gone. Watch these young guys. They're maturing fast, but they still have a lot of kid in them, and if you don't keep a tight rein on them, some of them are going to get killed. I don't think I'll be gone too long, so be careful."

"Okay, L.T. have fun."

"Yeah, right."

When Max got to the Battalion Aid Station, his wound was a little more serious than just a graze, but it wasn't too bad. They cleaned it good and put some kind of salve on it and then bandaged it. They told him that he would probably need to stay there for two or three days, and that didn't set too well with him.

Finally, on the fifth day, a Marine drove up to the Aid Station, got out, and went into the front. Someone asked if they could help him, and he said, "I'm here to pick up Lieutenant Max Norwood." The man went through some papers and files and then told someone to go to a certain place and bring Lt. Norwood out.

When Max got to his man, he said, "Man, am I glad to see you, Walker." It was one of the young men in his Platoon, and Walker said, "I'm glad to see you, too, L.T. We've missed you."

"You missed me? Why? Didn't Tom do good?"

"Yes sir, he did good, but he's not you. We all feel safer when you're with us."

"That's good to know, but you're probably safer with him than with me. He's been over here three times and hasn't even got a scratch, and this is my second time, and I've been wounded both times. I'd say you're safer with him."

"Still, we feel better when you're there to lead us."

"Thanks Walker. I'll try not to let you all down."

They went to their bivouac, and when they got there, the Captain told Max to rest the rest of the day, and he could go out with his men the next morning.

He was glad of that because he felt really weak. He didn't realize how much just four days in the hospital could drain your strength, but he remembered what Walker said about feeling safer when he was with them, and he wasn't about to let them go out without him again.

***

Just as soon as Amy had time to get back to Champaign, Sissy called her. "Hi. I don't know why we didn't talk about this when you were here, but Duke and I have decided to get married in March, and we want the wedding to be when you can get here during Spring Break. Do you know those dates?"

"Hold on. Let me check."

She came back to the phone and said, "March seventh through the fourteenth."

"Okay. If we get married on Saturday, the thirteenth, will you be able to come? When you were here, you talked like you would come to be in the wedding."

"If that's during Spring Break week, of course, I'll be there. You know what, Sissy?"

"What?"

"I thought I'd get married before you did, but you're going to beat me by about three months."

"I know, but that's only because of football season. Their training begins in early July, and I can't get married in June because you're doing that, so it looks like March is it."

"Well, that's okay. March is a good time."

"Okay. I won't keep you. I'll be back in touch in a few days and be sure to let me know when yours will be when you all set a date.

"Love you. Bye."

Just as soon as Amy got back to Decatur after the Christmas holidays, she and Neal set the date for their wedding. It was going to be on June sixth, and she wished she had known the date before Sissy called. She'll have to call her back and tell her. They also decided to go ahead and rent an apartment in Monticello as soon as school was out for the summer.

Word had spread among the Brock's friends about Amy

178

and Neal's wedding, and soon after Amy returned to Decatur after Christmas, two or three of their friends began talking about giving her a shower.

Four women went together and gave her one on February nineteenth, and another one was scheduled for April fifteenth, to be given by three others; Karen and two other friends of Amy's.

Amy was committed to making the Dean's List, and she didn't let anything get in the way of that, but it was hard for her. She was so excited about getting married that sometimes she wished she could just quit school, get married, and let Neal do all the work, but then, her better judgement would kick in, and she knew she couldn't do that. She had already spent seven years in college and only had one more to go before she could get her doctorate and become a full-fledged veterinarian.

Since there were only two months before her wedding, Sissy wasn't in panic mode, but she was close to it after thinking about everything that had to be done, but fortunately, her Mother was a pretty cool customer, and she helped her do things in an orderly manner. The first thing they did was make a list of things to do; in order of priority when possible.

The first thing Duke did was to write Max and tell him about the wedding and ask him to be in it. He said, "Everybody will be wearing dark suits, but I'd really like for you to wear your dress blues, if you don't mind." He went on with the details and told him how anxious he was to see him.

By the time the letter got to Quantico and then forwarded to Iraq, it was four days, and then when Max finally got it and read it, he had a hard time finding time to answer it. He did get a break the next afternoon, and he wrote Duke an answer.

"Dear Duke. Congratulations on your wedding, and thanks for inviting me to be in it, however, I'm back in Iraq, and I'm afraid I won't be able to get there. I wish you and Sissy the best, and I'll look forward to seeing you both when I get back.

Maybe you all can practice your culinary skills by fixing me supper one night. (ha ha)."

He wrote several more paragraphs and then closed the letter.

The fighting had sort of leveled off, and while the Marines couldn't let their guard down, things weren't as intense as they had been earlier.

About three months later, he got a package in a brown envelope, and when he opened it, it was a letter from Duke and Sissy, along with several snapshots of their wedding. He really enjoyed looking at them, especially the ones with Amy in them, and he sat down, later, and wrote them a letter, thanking them for the letter and the pictures.

He noticed that in the pictures, there was some guy that seemed to be around Amy in nearly all the pictures of her, and he assumed they were of her fiancé, since he didn't know him. He was a nice-looking guy.

The war went on, and the troops weren't as frazzled as they were when the insurgents were constantly shooting at them, but they were warned daily to not let their guard down because one morning might be quiet, and the afternoon might be red hot.

In early June, Max got a letter from Duke, telling him that he and Sissy were getting ready to go to Decatur, Illinois, where Sissy was going to be in Amy's wedding on the fifteenth. He said they were going back to Middleton on Sunday, the sixteenth because Sissy had to go to work the next day. He said he still had a little over two weeks before he had to begin training camp. He told Max he hoped he would be home before the regular season was over, and he thought he was going to get to play quite a bit.

Neal and Amy had found a great apartment in Monticello, and Amy moved into it as soon as school was out. It was on the first floor, and it had two bedrooms and two baths with a large living room and a nice size kitchen. There was a deck running all the way across both the living room and master bedroom with large sliding, glass doors opening out to the deck from both rooms.

Sissy and Duke were going to arrive at Decatur on Thursday, and they would have time to meet some of Neal's family and get acquainted with Decatur a little before the rehearsal and rehearsal dinner on Friday night.

The wedding went without a hitch on Saturday, and the reception was a blast at the North Side Country Club. Neal and Amy were to fly out on Sunday morning for a honeymoon in the Florida Keys. They spent their wedding night at the Country Club, and since they weren't leaving until the next morning, the reception lasted longer than usual Saturday night.

Neal's Daddy had given him ten days off from the clinic for his honeymoon, and he and Amy were really looking forward to it.

The next morning, Sissy and Duke as well as Amy's Mother and Daddy were booked on the same flight, and Duke was able to get better acquainted with Amy's Daddy. Sissy was on pins and needles the whole time because she was afraid Mr. Hatcher would say something about Max, and she didn't want to get into that. Mr. Hatcher seemed content to hear about Duke's experiences on the football field and with the Falcons, and if the conversation would start involving Amy, Sissy would tell Duke to tell Mr. Hatcher something else about the Falcons. She had cautioned Duke ahead of time to not mention Max.

Neal was intrigued with the Florida Keys. The fact that the Atlantic Ocean was on one side of the highway, and the Gulf of Mexico was on the other fascinated him. That was his first trip down there, and he wanted to experience as many neat things as he could.

He loved seafood, and there was no shortage of that in the Keys. They talked to some people who were old timers when it came to visiting the Keys, and some of those people would tell them about good places to eat or would make suggestions of where to get certain things, such as lobster reubens or scallops or coconut shrimp or some other delicious dish.

On two different nights, they ate at a restaurant that was literally just a few feet from the Atlantic Ocean. The main part of the restaurant faced the west, and diners could watch the sunset as they ate. Someone suggested they go there, and when they did, they liked it so well, they went back a second time. In the Keys, when the sun goes down, it's a custom for many people to blow conch shells.

He was also fascinated with the small deer that are the size of a large dog, called Key Deer, and in the southernmost part of the Keys, chickens roam around wild.

All in all, it was a great honeymoon, and they hated to have to go back to Decatur, but at the same time, they were looking forward to setting up housekeeping, although, it would only be temporary until Amy graduates in another year.

Before they left for their honeymoon, they went to one of the furniture stores in Decatur and bought some furniture. It was to be delivered and set up in their apartment while they were in Florida. They didn't buy enough to furnish a whole house because they would be moving in the spring after Amy graduated, but they did buy enough to get them by until that time. They went ahead and bought a bedroom suite with a king size bed, a sofa and two chairs, and a small table with four chairs to fit in the breakfast nook or whatever meal they wanted to eat there.

Karen and her parents were super excited to welcome them home from Florida, and they were all at the airport to meet the plane. Before Amy and Neal went to their apartment in Monticello, they went to the Brock's and spent most of the afternoon. A big part of that time was devoted to talking about all the things they saw in the Keys. Everyone was interested in hearing about it because none of them had ever been down there, except for Amy.

Later, that afternoon, Neal and Amy went home to their apartment in Monticello, and they were thrilled when they saw the new furniture. When they got to the front door, they did the traditional carrying the bride across the threshold, and then they settled into their new home.

It didn't take long to get back into the swing of things when they went to the clinic the next morning. It was almost like they had never been gone. When patients would come in that had been seeing Amy, they would address her as Amy Hatcher, Miss Hatcher, and sometimes Dr. Hatcher. She would always correct them and tell them that she was not Miss Hatcher anymore; she was Amy Brock, and that excited her. Sometimes, if she had a minute or two without a patient, she would daydream ahead for a year to when she would be Doctor Brock, and that really excited her.

The summer passed quickly, and it was almost time for Amy and Karen to start back to School, and the two would soon find out who's will was the strongest. Ever since Amy had thought about getting an apartment in Monticello, she told Karen that she wanted her to live with her and Neal until graduation, and Karen said, "No."

Amy said, "Girlfriend, we've been roomies ever since the first day of veterinarian school, and I want us to be roomies until the last day, so quit arguing and get your things and move into that spare bedroom, and I mean it."

"Boy, you sure are bossy. What do you think my brother would say if he knew you were inviting me to move in with you all?

"I think he'd be just fine with it, besides, it's not like we'd be sleeping in the same room. We'd be completely separated, and you would have your own bathroom, so I don't want to hear any more about it."

"Tell you what. You talk to Neal about it, and if he's okay with it, I'll consider it, but I definitely won't unless he gives his blessings. Okay?"

"Okay. I'll talk to him tonight, and for your information, I'm not bossy."

That night, Amy aggressively presented her case to Neal about having Karen live with them, and it was unclear whether he wanted to have her or not, but Amy was so forceful, he gave what might be called a *lukewarm* approval.

The next morning, Amy exaggerated and told Karen, "I talked to Neal last night and he said he wants you to move in with us, so you can start bringing your stuff over whenever you want to."

"Are you sure he said I could move in?"

"Yeah. He was excited about it."

"I know better than that. Neal Brock doesn't get excited about anything."

"Well, he was excited about you living with us. Just ask him."

"I may just do that."

"In the meantime, go get your things."

"See how bossy you are."

Amy just laughed.

Karen told her, "Amy, this is what I'm going to do. I'm going to continue to live at home until school starts, and then, I'll move in and live with you guys during the school year. Does that meet with your approval?"

"Yeah, that's fine."

"Oh, another thing. If I lived at Ashton Woods, Daddy would pay the rent there, so I'm going to ask him to take that money and pay you and Neal."

"I'll let you and Neal and your Daddy work that out."

"You mean you're not going to argue about it?"

"No, Miss Smarty Pants. I'm just glad that you're going to be here, and whatever else you all work out is fine with me." She walked over and gave Karen a big hug and said, "You know, I don't have a sister, but if I did, I'd want her to be like you."

Karen smiled and said, "You mean someone pretty like me?"

"No. Someone who will mind me when I tell them to do something."

Karen said, "Ha ha. You're funny."

The two Doctor Brocks and the two Apprentice Brocks worked hard the rest of the summer, and then it was time for school to start again, and Karen brought a lot of her clothes and other things and moved in with Neal and Amy. It was a little touchy the first day she was there, and then everything seemed to relax, and all three of them had a good time.

Amy and Karen thought it was foolish for both of them to drive every day, so they worked out a plan whereby each one would drive every other week. Karen said she would drive the first week, and it seemed good. Their schedules were almost identical; they each started at eight o'clock in the morning and ended at three in the afternoon.

The entire senior year was uneventful for Karen and Amy. Every day was like the day before, and they could hardly wait until May, when they would graduate and get their Doctorates. They both had been working on their dissertations since enrolling in the University of Illinois School of Veterinary Medicine, and they were virtually complete, with only approval from the necessary faculty advisors remaining.

Graduation was scheduled for May seventeenth, and Amy and Karen were both going to graduate Magna Cum Laude, one step below the highest honor awarded to a graduate. Karen's Daddy and Brother had graduated Magna Cum Laude, and now, she and Amy. That would make the Brock Animal Hospital have four Doctor Brocks and all four with Magna Cum Laude honors, which was probably the only animal clinic in the country with such an elite staff, all in the same family.

One night, in late March, Amy and Neal were lying in bed when Amy said, "Honey, I haven't started my period yet, and it's past time."

"Well, maybe it's just due to tension. You know, you've had a lot on you lately, finishing your dissertation and your upcoming graduation. You'll probably start in a day or two."

"I hope so," and nothing more was said for several more days.

Easter was on April twelfth, and the entire Brock Klan got together after church and for some reason, that morning, Amy didn't feel well. Later, in the day, she felt better and participated in all the activities with everyone else, but she didn't eat as much lunch as she normally would. She attributed it to a slight upset stomach, Neal thought that was more than likely the problem as well. He had forgotten about Amy telling him about missing her period.

When she and Neal got to their apartment later that evening, she was still feeling better, but not as well as she would like, and she laid back in the recliner and closed her eyes. She dozed for a few minutes, and then when she woke up, Neal asked, "Honey, I looked at the calendar, and it's only four more weeks until graduation. What do you want to do about the apartment after you graduate? Do you want to stay here?"

"I thought we were going to move to Decatur after I graduate. Why do you ask? Do you want to stay here?"

"No. I would like to go back to Decatur. I was just giving you your choice. This is why I mentioned it now. If you remember, our lease say that we have to give a thirty-day notice before we move out, and if we're going to go to Decatur, we need to give our landlord notice. If we tell him this week and move at the end of May, we will have given forty-five days' notice, so there shouldn't be any complaint.

"Okay. That's fine. Let's turn in the notice. Will you do it?"

"Yeah, I'll go see him tomorrow. Now, next question; Do you want to live in another apartment or try to find a house when we go back to Decatur?"

"I don't know. What would you rather do?"

"I would rather live in a house. I've always lived in one except for this past year and the time I was in college."

"Me too. Let's try to find one we like and can afford."

"I'll look around this week, and we can both look some next weekend."

Amy said, "Neal, before you turn the notice in, you need to ask Karen what she wants to do. She might want to stay here. She likes this apartment."

"Okay, I'll ask her, but I know what she'll say. She'll say she wants to go back home."

The next morning, before they left for school and work, Neal told Karen, "Sis, Amy and I talked last night, and we want to move to Decatur when school's out and maybe buy a house. Do you want to stay here or move back to Decatur? If you want to move, I'm going to turn our notice in to our landlord this morning."

"No question; I want to go home."

"I thought you would."

Amy had not missed a day of school, ever, but she felt so bad the next morning, she almost told Karen to go on without her, but she didn't want to miss, so she sucked it up and got in the car. It was her week to drive, and when she opened the door and started to get in the car, she had to throw up. She said, "Karen, how about coming around here and drive. Will you?"

Karen did. Amy got in the passenger seat, and Karen drove to school for her. On the way, Karen asked, "What do you think is wrong, Amy?"

"I think I know. Did I tell you I missed my period last month?"

"No, you didn't. Do you think you're pregnant?"

"I'm afraid I am."

"Does Neal know you missed your period?"

"Remember when I felt so bad Easter Sunday?"

"Yeah. You said you must have had an upset stomach."

"I know, but that's when I realized I had missed my period, and I told him that night after we went to bed."

"What did he say?"

"He said it was probably tension."

"That idiot. Doesn't Mister, Doctor Brock know that when his wife misses her period and is sick, that it's not tension? Those animals we treat at the clinic know better than that. Are you going to the doctor?"

"I thought I'd wait 'til I miss another period, and then, if I miss, I'll go."

"So, in the meantime, you're just going to stay sick."

"I get better up in the day. I'll be alright 'til I see a Doctor."

"I hope so. When's your next period due?"

"Actually, the first of this week."

"Great. When are you going to call the Doctor?"

"If I haven't started by Friday, I'll call."

"Who are you going to go to?"

"I don't know. Do you know one?"

"No, not personally, but I've heard that Doctor Carleton Earnhart in Decatur is good. Maybe you can call him."

"I'll call him Friday if I haven't started. I don't know when I can see him since I still have to go to school."

"We get out early on Friday, remember? Maybe if you call this afternoon, you can get in late Friday afternoon. If you missed last month, it's unlikely you'll start this month. I'd go ahead and call, and then if you do start, you can always cancel."

"Good idea."

When she got home that afternoon, she called Dr. Earnhart's office, and just as she had hoped, she got an appointment for four thirty, Friday afternoon.

Every morning she was sick, and before she left for school each morning, she would have to go to the bathroom and throw up, and then she would feel a little better. By noon, she would feel much better and then, start all over the next day.

On Friday, she and Karen got out of school at one o'clock, and as usual, they were to go to Decatur to work in the clinic, but that day, Amy had an appointment with Dr. Earnhart, and she wanted to go to her apartment first, to take a shower and put on clean clothes before going to see him.

She wanted Karen to go with her, but Karen said, "I'll be happy to go with you, but don.t you think it would be good if Neal goes with you?"

"Oh, I guess it would, especially since, if I'm pregnant, it's his fault."

Karen drove and fortunately, Dr. Earnhart's office was not too far from the clinic, so she detoured off the route and went to the clinic to get Neal. He didn't know they were coming, so it was a surprise to him. Amy went in to get him, and he was examining a Yorkie. She told him why she was there, and she wanted him to go to Dr. Earnhart's with her, and he immediately called someone else to take over for him. He took off his smock, washed his hands, and said, "Let's go."

Chapter Thirteen

Max was finishing up his second deployment to Iraq, and aside from the wound to his neck that he sustained earlier, he was feeling good about going home soon.

Even though the fighting had slowed down from what it was, there were still times when it would flare up, and when it did, it was intense.

One day, Max and his men were going through the city when they got ambushed from the rear. Max heard a rocket propelled grenade coming in. He zigzagged and heard it so close, it landed right in front of him, coming from his back. It blew up, and he was peppered with shrapnel and burned on his face. He remembered what Walker told him about the men feeling safer when he was with them, so he didn't let anyone know he was hit.

His men were getting hit right and left. They medevac'd them out when they could, and then the fight got really intense. Snipers were firing on them, and they couldn't get artillery or air support. They tried, but they said no because they were in the firing zone. Max said he didn't care. It was getting that bad. He and his men figured bring it on. Some of them would get out. They wound up having to fight their way out.

When they got back to the bivouac, Max thought he would try to pull some of the pieces of shrapnel out himself and was successful with two or three pieces, but he couldn't do anything with the others. As a last resort, he went to the first-aid station, where medics were on duty. He happened to get a Captain to help him, and he told him, "Sir, can you help me get some of this shrapnel out? I tried myself, but some of it I can't get."

The medic looked at his wounds and said, "Marine, you need to go to Battalion Aid. Stay right here, and I'll call medevac."

"Max said, "No sir. I'm not going to Battalion Aid. I'm going to stay with my men. This is not that serious. I can handle the pain if you'll give me something for it. My face is burned, too, and it doesn't seem to be much worse than a bad sunburn, so if you'll just give me some pills, I'll be out of here. I do wish you'd help me get some of this shrapnel out, though."

"You're a hard case, aren't you, Lieutenant? Lay up here on this table and let me see what I can do."

"Thank you, sir."

Some of the pieces of shrapnel were buried fairly deep, and the medic had to give him Nova Caine in order to probe deep enough to remove the metal pieces. After a lengthy time on the first aid table, he was finally able to extract all the pieces of shrapnel from Max, and when he was through, he said, "Lieutenant, you're probably not going to like this, but I'm going to contact your Company Commander and recommend that you be given some time off so your wounds can heal."

Max said, "Sir, I would appreciate it if you wouldn't do that," and he got up off the table, put his clothes back on and was leaving, but before he left the room, the medic Captain said, "Good luck, Lieutenant."

When he got back to his Platoon's area, some of the men who were still left, said, "Hey, L.T., we're glad to see you back. Are you alright?"

He said, "Yeah, I'm alright."

No sooner had he got back to his Platoon area than his Company Commander came by and said, "Max, I just talked to a Medic Captain who told me that he thought you needed to stay out of action for a while, and I'm supposed to do what he says. What do you say?"

"I say he's just overreacting. There's nothing wrong with me. I can't stay out of action; I told my men that I would be with them all the way."

"Well, I have my orders and I'll have to give you one. When your Platoon goes out in the morning, you stay here and let Tom Rutledge take over. Do you understand?"

"I hear what you are saying, but I don't understand. I thought we were over here to fight; not take R and R."

"Don't cross me on this Max. It's not my decision, okay?"

The next morning, Max's Captain went out with another Platoon, and when Max found out that he did, he got all his stuff together and got in the Humvee with Tom."

Tom said, "Good morning, L.T. I didn't think you were coming this morning."

"Well, I'm here. Where are we going?"

"We're going to area four where there has been quite a bit of mortar fire. A sympathizer came in and said the bad guys were using a car to transport their mortar tube, so we're going to set up an impromptu vehicle checkpoint."

Nothing happened, and they didn't see anything suspicious all day, and then, just at dark, a suspicious looking car pulled up. It was red in a place where most cars are bland colors. It was very clean, too, which was unusual. There were three squads involved, including an interpreter. As the car came near, and the Marines were using flashlights looking for a mortar, the driver started yelling at them. He sped off. In reverse, like in a war movie. The Platoon was in a staggered ranger column to prevent any one shooter or bomber from taking everybody out. As he sped off, Max's men opened up on him. Driving in reverse, he pulled a gun out from under the seat. Max's guys on either side had cover, but Max was exposed. Just as he was hitting the deck, pulling his weapon up, he saw a couple of flashes from the bad guy's muzzle. He saw the dirt kick up in front of him, then he felt like he had been kicked by a horse. He blacked out and later said, "It happened fast, but it was in slow motion."

The car crashed as Max's people were shooting at it. Max was given a shot of morphine. It took forty-five minutes for them to come pick him up, and things did not look promising when they got there. He had been shot in the face.

He was bleeding and having seizures. When his guys put him on the Humvee they thought he was dead. He was semiconscious when they got him back to the base. At the base, it was surreal as if everything was going two hundred miles per minute. He saw all those people moving around, but he didn't know what was happening. The bullet broke his jaw and disrupted his nerves. A doctor was probing for the bullet, looking for an exit wound.

Then the Battalion Commander went in and the Battalion Sergeant Major went in too, which wasn't a good sign, telling him they got the bad guys. Max was wondering if he was going to die. He had the presence of mind to want to pray, and he said, silently, *Lord, I've asked you several times to look after me and bring me home, but it looks like I'm in a real mess right now. Are you going to take care of me? I pray that you will.* He had been there two days and all at once a helicopter shows up. "What's that for?" he asked.

They said, "That's for you, knucklehead. We're taking you to Baghdad. They told him the bullet was up in his jaw and they had to find it. They finally found it at the base of his skull, and they decided to leave it there because they thought taking it out would be more dangerous.

On the first day after his surgery in Baghdad, a backpack bomber blew himself up in area four, where Max had been. He was there waiting to be shipped to Germany, and he wondered, *what else can happen?* He was finally sent to Germany where he stayed for two weeks, and then he was sent to Bethesda, Maryland, which, after all the time he had spent there, felt like he was at home.

They never got the bullet out. He was told it would calcify and become part of his body. He considered himself lucky in that it didn't leave much of a scar. When he was in the hospital in Germany, the guy next to him had lost half his face, and he said, "I hate people like you. You got shot in the face and look fine. I got shot in the face, and I look like a monster. Max didn't take his words for granted. He thought, *I have a substantial injury, but not so obvious. It was rougher on him, a lot rougher.*

Soon after he got back to Walter Reed, he called home. His Daddy answered, and Max said, "Hey, Daddy. What are you doing?"

"Max, thank God, you're alright. Where are you?"

"I'm back at Walter Reed."

"How are you doing, Son?"

"I'm doing okay, considering."

"Have they told you how long you'll be there?"

"No. I just got here today. They probably don't know."

"Well, look; your Mother and I will come up there. Do you think it would be alright if we come later this week?"

"I'd say it would, but why don't you let me ask and call you back?"

"Can you call tomorrow?"

"I'll try, but Daddy, it'll be tomorrow before I will be able to find out."

"Okay. Just let us know as soon as you can. We've been worried sick about you and can't wait to see you. Your Mother has been frantic."

"I'm anxious to see you too. Is Mother there?"

"Yeah, hold on a minute."

When she answered, she said, "Max, Darling. It's so good to hear your voice. We've been very worried about you. How do you feel?"

"I feel pretty good, Mother. It looks like I'm going to live."

"Well, we'll thank the Lord for that, won't we?"

"We sure will. I've already thanked Him a lot. Daddy said you all might come up here later this week if they say it's alright, and I'm going to ask tomorrow and call you back. Oh yeah. Mother, would you call Duke's Mother and ask her to have Duke get in touch with me?" He gave her his room and phone number and said Duke could call him when he had a chance.

"I'll call her when we hang up. Duke called last week to see if we had heard from you. He'll be glad to know you're back in the United States, and he can call you.

When the doctor came in the next morning, the first thing Max did was ask him if it would be alright if his parents came up later in the week. The doctor said, "Of course, they can come. You can have anybody you want come, but you might want to tell them that it would be better if they came in the afternoons because you'll be pretty busy in the mornings, at least for a while."

"Thanks, Doc. I told my Mother and Daddy I would call them today and let them know."

While he was talking to the doctor, his phone rang. He excused himself from the doctor and answered it. It was Duke. "Duke, whatta ya say, Buddy? Listen, can I call you back? The doctor is in here right now," and the doctor said, "Go ahead and talk. I'm through for now. They'll come get you in a little while to take you to x-ray, and I'll see you later."

"Duke, are you still there? The doctor told me to go ahead and talk to you, and he'd see me later. How are you doing?"

"I'm doing good. The question is how are you doing? You're Mother said you had been wounded again. Are you alright?"

"I'm doing okay, considering everything that has happened. Actually, I got wounded three times, but who's counting?"

"Are you serious? Your Mother only told me that you got wounded. I didn't know you got hurt three times. Boy! Couldn't you keep your head down?"

"I guess not. Mother didn't tell you about two of the times because I didn't tell her about them. They weren't real serious. I was only out of commission a few days each time."

"What happened those two times?"

"Well, the first time, I got shot in the neck. It was only a little more than a graze, and I was only in the hospital five days. The second time was when a rocket propelled grenade exploded in front of me, and I took shrapnel in several places and got burned on my face. The doctor over there told me not to go back in combat for a while, and I told him I was going so I could be with my men. When I left the aid station, he called my Company Commander and told him not to let me go back out, and my boss gave me orders not to go out the next morning. He said the doctor's order overrode his."

Duke said, "You always were a stubborn rascal. I'll bet you went out anyway, didn't you?"

"Yeah. The next morning, I found out that my boss went out with another Platoon, so when they left, I joined my Platoon and went with them. Duke, my men told me they felt safer when I was with them, so I went with them, and that's the time I got shot in the face. I may be in trouble for disobeying orders. I hope I'm not, but I could be."

"Did you say shot in the face? How are you still alive?"

"God took care of me, Duke. I don't even have any bad scars."

"Well, do you know how long you will be in the hospital?"

"No. Not at this point. The bullet is still in my head; at the base of my skull, and they told me in Germany that they were afraid to try to take it out because it could be worse than leaving it in. I don't know what they are planning here. I hope they try to get it because there's pressure on my nerves."

Duke asked, "On your nerves?"

"Yeah, when the bullet hit me in the face, it damaged some nerves."

"I'll bet that hurt, didn't it?"

"Do you remember the time, when we were seniors at Memphis State and playing Southern Mississippi, when that linebacker hit me and knocked me out?"

"Yeah, I remember that. He really cold-cocked you."

"Well, getting shot didn't hurt as bad as that did."

"You want to hear something funny, Max?"

"Yeah, I need to hear something funny."

"Well, that linebacker that hit you is named Desmond Walker, and he now plays for the Atlanta Falcons. He's a teammate of mine."

"Are you serious? The next time you see him, why don't you remind him of that game?"

"I'll do it. I forgot all about that. Desmond is a good guy."

"That's because he didn't hit you. I haven't forgot about it and probably won't. Enough about my troubles. How is Sissy?"

"She's good. She's gone to the grocery store right now, or I'd let you talk to her."

"Well, tell her I said hey, and I'd like to see her."

"I'll tell her."

Just then two people came in with a gurney, and Max knew he was going to be taken somewhere. He told Duke, "Duke, they're in here to take me somewhere. Can you call me back later?"

"Yeah, I can. When do think would be a good time?"

"The doctor told me this morning that the afternoons are the best time, so let's try this afternoon."

"Okay, Buddy. It's great to talk to you. I don't know if I can call back this afternoon, but I'll get back to you real soon. Love you, Bro."

"Love you too."

They wheeled him down to the x-ray department where they did a lot of x-rays on his face and jaw. He asked the technicians several questions, and as usual, they told him that the doctor would have to answer them. When they brought him back, he called his mother. "Mother, hi. What are you doing?"

"Just folding clothes. Since you're not here, I only have to

197

wash once a week, and today's the day. What are you doing?"

"I'm just laying here, being lazy. I told Daddy that I'd find out if it would be alright for you all to come up here this week, and the doctor said it would be okay. He said the afternoons are better because they will probably keep me pretty busy in the mornings."

"Okay. I'll tell your Daddy. He's anxious to see you, so maybe we can come Friday afternoon and stay 'til Sunday."

"That will be great. I'll look for you."

"I talked to Duke's Mother yesterday, and she said she would give him your number, so he'll probably call you."

"He called this morning. It was sure good to hear from him. Thanks for getting my number to him."

"I can't wait to see you, Darling. If nothing happens, we'll see you Friday."

"Okay, Mother. I love you."

That afternoon, one of the doctors came in and said, "Lieutenant, I want to talk to you about something."

Max said, "Okay."

The doctor said, "Max, you don't mind if I call you Max, do you?"

Max said, "No sir. That's what I prefer."

"Okay. Max, do you feel pressure in your head and jaw?"

"Yes sir, I do, and it's very uncomfortable."

"Well, after going over your x-rays, I conferred with some other physicians, and we all feel that in spite of what you were told in Baghdad and Germany, we can go in and remove the bullet that's lodged at the base of your skull. Would you be agreeable to having surgery to remove it?"

Max said, "They told me that it was too dangerous to remove it; that I might be paralyzed. Are you saying that you can take it out without that risk?"

"That's exactly what I'm saying. When we get it out, you shouldn't have any more pressure, and you'll feel much better."

"Will it leave a big scar?"

"We'll have a plastic surgeon do a procedure on the incision, and you probably won't even know there's a scar there. What do you say?"

"I say if you're sure I won't be paralyzed, go ahead and do it. When will you do it?"

"It looks as if it will have to be next Monday. I checked before I came in, and all the O.R.s are booked until then.

As soon as the doctor left, Max called home. His Daddy answered. "Hi Daddy, whatta ya say?"

"Hey Max. How ya doing today?"

"I'm good. Listen, the reason I called is to tell you that the doctor just left here, and they're going to do surgery on me next Monday. I thought that since you and Mother are going to be here over the weekend, maybe you can stay until Monday or Tuesday."

"What are they going to operate on you for?"

"I don't think I told you, but there's a bullet lodged in my head at the base of my skull, and they seem pretty sure they can get it out without doing any damage, and I told him to go ahead and do it. There's a lot of pressure in my head now, and the doctor said that when they get the bullet out, there should be no more pressure."

"My goodness. I had no idea that you've got a bullet in your head. It looks as if you've got a lot to tell us when we see you."

"I guess I do, Daddy. I'll tell you all everything when you get up here."

Max was sitting in a chair when his parents arrived Friday afternoon, and he was as glad to see them as they were him. He hugged his Mother first and then his Daddy, and there wasn't a dry eye in the room. There were two chairs in the room, and when they finished their hugs, Max sat on the bed while his Mother and Daddy sat in the chairs.

Naturally, his parents had a lot of questions, and he

answered all that they asked. When the question and answer period was pretty much over, he told them about some of the battles he was in as well as the ones he was in when he got wounded.

His Daddy was spellbound with the stories, and his Mother was horrified that her little boy had experienced such horrible things.

His Daddy said, "After hearing your stories, you'll get another Purple Heart, won't you?"

"I don't think so. From what I can find out, you can only get one Purple Heart. If you're wounded after the first one, then they give you an Oak Leaf Cluster, and that's probably what I'll get, if they give me anything."

"Well, they should give you everything they've got," his Mother said.

After the war stories were over, Max wanted to know what was happening in Middleton, and what was happening with a lot of their friends. His Daddy asked, "Son, what's going to happen with you when you leave here?"

"I'm not sure," he said. "I've still got about a year left on my enlistment, and I don't know what they're going to do. I've heard rumors that they may kick me out with a disability discharge. I just don't know."

His Daddy said, "If they give you a disability retirement, they'll give you a pension, won't they?"

"I think so. I'm not sure how that works, but I think I'll get something."

"Well, with what you've been through, they ought to give you a lot," his Daddy said. "Son, if they kick you out, as you call it, will you come back to Middleton, and if you do, what will you do?"

"I'm not sure. I guess I'll have to find a job doing something."

"Any idea what?"

"Not really. I've thought about trying to coach high school

football, but I don't know if I can find a coaching job. I may have to just try to find a job selling something. I think I would be pretty good at selling."

"I think you would be too."

Max and his parents spent the rest of the afternoon together, and at one point, Max drifted off to sleep. He was still weak from all his ordeals, and his parents understood. They debated whether to leave or not, and they finally decided to stay until he woke up. They thought that if they stayed until then, they would leave soon after he awoke, and that way, they could tell him bye and not just leave and have him wake up alone.

He didn't sleep long and woke up in about twenty minutes. As his parents planned, they told him they were going to leave, and they would come back the next morning. They all thought that since the next day was Saturday, the medical people wouldn't be doing much to him, but they were wrong.

When they got to his room about nine o'clock the next morning, he wasn't there. Since he was going to have surgery on Monday, they did most of the pre-op on Saturday. They waited in his room until he was brought back, and soon after he returned to his room, Doctor Montgomery came in and told them that he would be pretty busy until lunchtime, and then not much after lunch.

The Norwoods decided to go back to their hotel and come back after lunch. Before they left, they asked Max if he would like for them to bring him something to eat, and he said, "Yes sir. I'd love to have a Burger King Whopper, some fries, and a chocolate milk shake."

His Daddy said, "Okay, Padna, we'll bring it. You want anything else?"

"No sir. I'll do good to eat that, but thank you, anyway."

The medical staff finished doing things with Max a little before lunchtime Saturday, and his parents got back with his food at just the right time. They didn't do anything with him

Sunday, except the surgeon came in late Sunday afternoon to confirm that surgery would be on Monday morning.

Max's Daddy asked the surgeon, "Doctor, how long do you think the surgery will take?"

"It's hard to say. It all depends on what we run into when we get in there, but I'm guessing about an hour and a half or an hour and forty-five minutes."

Max was told that his surgery would be around seven o'clock the next morning, and his parents were there at six. They visited with him until they came to get him around six thirty. His Mother kissed him, and his Daddy squeezed his hand, and said, "We'll be here when you get back. We talked to God about you, and we're confident you're going to be okay. We love you."

"Love you too,"

His Daddy asked his Mother, "I could use some coffee. Would you like to go downstairs and get some?"

"Yeah, and maybe something to eat."

They knew they had plenty of time because the doctor had told them how long he estimated the surgery would last, so they took their time eating and had a second cup of coffee before going back upstairs to the waiting room.

It had been an hour and a half since they took Max when his parents got back to the waiting room, and they thought it would only be a few more minutes until someone would come out and tell them that the surgery was over. They waited and waited and still no word. Two hours, two and a half hours, three hours, and finally, after three hours and thirty five minutes, the surgeon came out and told them, "The operation went well, and we were able to get the bullet out without damaging the spine. Max will be in recovery for about an hour, and then he will be taken to his room instead of ICU, which is normally what we do."

His Daddy asked the doctor, "Do you know how long he'll be in the hospital?"

"No sir, I don't. Max has some other issues that have to be resolved, but I don't see him having to stay here too much longer. We'll have to talk to Dr. Montgomery, his regular doctor, to see if we can narrow down the time."

Just then, a man came in and said, "Please tell Lt. Norwood that there will be an awards ceremony two weeks from today, and he should be there," and they thanked him.

Chapter Fourteen

Due to the late hour on Friday afternoon, Dr. Earnhart's office was practically empty, and Amy didn't have to wait long before she was called back to see the doctor.

She waited in a small examining room for about ten minutes, and then the doctor knocked on the door and came in. He said, "Hello, Mrs. Brock. I'm Carleton Earnhart. So you think you may be pregnant?"

"Yes sir."

"Why do you think so?"

"Well, I have missed two periods, and I'm terribly sick just about every day."

"I see. Get up on this table, and we'll take a look."

She got on the table, and Dr. Earnhart gave her a full examination. When he finished, he said, "Well, Mrs. Brock, you were right. You are with child. When was your last period?"

She told him, and he did some figuring and said, "Well, based on when you say your last period was, it looks like you should give birth on or about September tenth. What do you do? Do you work?"

"Part time. I'm due to get my Doctorate of Veterinary Medicine degree in May, and then I'll be working full time at Brock Animal Hospital."

Dr. Earnhart said, "Oh, you're part of Mike Brocks family?"

"Yes sir. He's my father-in-law. I'm married to his son, Neal."

"Is Neal a vet as well?"

"Yes sir, and Mike's daughter, Karen, gets her diploma in May also, and she'll go to work there as well, so including me, there will be four Dr. Brocks at the clinic."

"That's wonderful. I would like for there to be another Earnhart or two to come in here when I retire."

When Dr. Earnhart finished, he told her to come back in one month, and he gave her a prescription for some medicine to help her nausea. She walked out into the waiting room with a big smile on her face, and Neal asked, "What did he say?"

"He said you're going to be a Daddy in September."

Neal was elated. When she told him what Dr. Earnhart said, he said, "Really? Let's see; this is March," and he counted on his fingers, "so that makes you three months, right?"

"That's right. I hope I'm not showing at graduation. Neal, I don't want to tell people just yet, okay?"

"Why? I think this is wonderful news. Why don't you want to tell it?"

"Let's just wait 'til after graduation, okay?"

"Okay, if that's what you want."

"That's what I want."

Neal looked at Karen and asked, "Sis, what do you think?"

"I think it's wonderful. I can't wait to be an aunt."

There were hugs all around, and then they left the doctor's office. On the way to the clinic, Neal asked Amy, "Honey, are you going to tell Mother and Daddy?"

"Of course. The family should know. I just don't want to tell other people. I'm going to call my Mother tonight. It will be interesting to see what she says."

Karen said, "I'll bet she'll be thrilled."

Neal said, "Listen, why don't we go over to Mother and Daddy's this afternoon when we get off and tell them both together? Is that alright with you Amy?"

"Yeah. Whatever you want to do. Your Mother has asked us to eat with them tonight, anyway."

"Okay, just try to act normal when we get to the clinic. We won't be there but maybe an hour. It's already nearly five o'clock."

When they walked into the clinic, Neal's Daddy asked, "Where have you been? We've been busy as all get out, and we couldn't find you."

Amy and Karen were afraid their secret was about to be uncovered, so they found a reason to leave the room where they were. Neal told Dr. Brock, "Amy was feeling poorly, and when she came in from school, she told me and I took her to the doctor. You were tied up, and I didn't want to disturb you, so since I didn't think we were that busy, I left. I'm sorry if I messed up."

Dr. Brock asked, "What's wrong with Amy? She's not pregnant, is she?"

Neal gulped and asked his Daddy, "Why would you say that?" And before he could answer, one of their technicians came to the door and said, "Dr. Brock, they need you in room two, stat," so he left Neal and went out of the room almost in a run.

At six o'clock, they closed the clinic for the day, and they all went to Neal and Karen's parent's house, not only for Amy and Neal to make their big announcement, but their Mother had invited them to eat dinner with them.

She had fixed a delicious dinner, and they all ate like they hadn't eaten all day, and then when they were through eating, Neal said, "Mother, Daddy, Amy has something she wants to tell you. Tell them, Amy."

"Mom, Dad, Neal and I are wondering how you would feel about becoming grandparents."

Silence. Then Neal's Mother said, "We would love to become grandparents. When?"

"September tenth."

Everybody began figuring on their fingers and concluded that she was three months then.

They had a good time, visiting, after dinner, and Neal and Karen's Mother and Daddy told several tales about when Neal and Karen were just babies and toddlers. After a while, Neal and Amy left to go to their apartment in Monticello.

On the way to Monticello, Amy said to Neal, "We should start looking for a house or an apartment in Decatur, don't you think?"

"I think you're right. When do you want to start looking?"

"How about tomorrow when we get off work? Tomorrow's just a half day."

"Sounds good to me."

They bought a Decatur newspaper when they got to Monticello and scoured the real estate section in the classifieds. Amy asked, "Did you see anything interesting?"

"No, there's not a very big classified section in this paper. We'll probably just have to get a realtor in Decatur if we want to find something. Which one would you rather have; a house or an apartment?"

"Do you think we can afford a house? If we can, then that's what I would like, but that may have to be down the road. If we can't find a house we can afford, an apartment will be okay, if we can find a nice one. Of course, we can't move into an apartment until I graduate, but we can keep our eyes open for one."

"Your wish is my command, My Lady. We'll start looking immediately. I'm like you. I would rather have a house, so let's concentrate on finding one."

"Thank you."

They looked around, on their own, after the clinic closed the next day, but were unable to find anything. Neal said, "I think we're going to have to get a realtor because a lot of houses that are for sale don't have signs out front. We still have time, and maybe next week, we will get one."

They stopped at a nice restaurant in Decatur and ate dinner before they went to Monticello, and when they got home, they just kicked back and enjoyed the evening.

Amy was deathly sick Sunday morning, and the pills that Dr. Earnhart gave her helped after a while, and she was thankful she had them.

Same thing, Monday morning. It was her turn to drive, but she was so sick she got Karen to drive. She popped one of the pills and was feeling a little better by the time she got to school. As they walked to class, she said, "Karen, I thought when you got to three or four months, your sickness would get better, but mine's sure not. I don't know if I'll have any more children if it makes you this sick."

"Sure you will. When that little boy or girl gets here, you'll forget all about being sick. You'll be ready to have another one."

"I don't know."

Every day was the same. Get up, get dressed, throw up, take a pill, feel better, and then go to school. That went on until about thirteen days later, when she got home, she noticed that she was bleeding; not a lot, but bleeding none the less.

The next morning was Friday again, and there was no blood, and she seemed to feel a little better. She got dressed and left for school, and sometime during the morning, she went into the rest room and found that she was bleeding a lot more than before. She only had one more period until she was out for the day, and as soon as Karen got to the car, Amy said, "Karen, I'm bleeding, bad, and I think I need to go see Dr. Earnhart. Will you drive, please? Don't stop by my apartment; just go straight to Dr. Earnhart's."

The speed limit on I 72 was seventy miles per hour, and they normally drove five over the speed limit, but that day, Karen kept it on eighty or higher all the way to Decatur. They were just lucky that a Highway Patrolman didn't see them.

When they got to Dr. Earnhart's office, they literally ran into the office, and Karen acted as spokesperson. She told the receptionist, "This is my friend Amy Brock, and she's three months pregnant. She's bleeding quite a bit, and she needs to see the doctor real quick."

The receptionist called for a nurse, and when one got there, she told her, "This is Amy Brock. She's three months, and she's bleeding. Have the doctor check her."

"Okay. Follow me, Amy," and she led her to an examining room in the back. It wasn't but a couple of minutes until Dr. Earnhart came in.

He said, "Hi Amy. You say you're bleeding? That's not good. How about getting undressed for me from the waist down," and she did. "Can you get up on the table?"

She answered, "Yes sir, I can."

He began his examination, and during the whole time, he didn't say a word. Toward the end of the exam, he said,"Mmm," but that was the closest he came to saying something. When he finished, he said, "Amy, I hate to tell you, but it looks as though you're not going to be able to continue with your pregnancy."

Amy was shocked, and she hung her head and cried.

Dr. Earnhart told her she could put her clothes back on, and when she was dressed, he put his arm around her shoulder and said, "Amy, this shouldn't stop you from having children in the future. Most of the time, there's a good reason for miscarrying. It could be that if you went full tern, your baby could be severely handicapped, or have some serious medical problem. Do you believe in Jesus, Amy?"

"Yes sir, I do."

"That's good because He controls these things, and He knows what He is doing. Just remember that. You'll have children, and hopefully, they'll all be perfect. Just pray about it, and trust Jesus to do you right."

"Thank you, Doctor. I feel better now."

When she and Karen left Dr. Earnhart's office, they went to the Brock clinic. Karen got out and went in and told Neal, "Neal, you need to go out to the car." He asked "Why?" and she said, "Because Amy's out there and she needs you."

He looked puzzled and asked, "What's going on?" as he walked out to the car. When he reached the car, Amy was crying, and he asked, "What's wrong, Honey?"

She said, "I just miscarried."

"Are you sure? Did you go to the doctor?"

"Yeah, and he told me I wasn't going to be able to finish my pregnancy. I'm so sorry, Neal. I know how much you wanted the baby.

"Dry your tears. Sweetie. It's probably for the best. We can still have children."

"That's what Dr. Earnhart said. "You know, Neal, he's a good man. He asked me if I believed in Jesus, and I told him I did, and he said that Jesus is in control."

"How do you feel right now?"

"I don't feel sick like I have been, but I'm sick in my heart."

"I know you are, but it will be okay."

"Neal, I'm going to get Karen to take me home, and I think I'll stay there tomorrow and Sunday, so I can go back to school Monday."

In a few days, after the heartache got better, Amy and Karen began to get excited thinking about their graduation. In a little over a month, they would both be Doctors of Veterinary Medicine, and how great was that?

Amy was feeling good, and she didn't know how she ever lived through all the morning sickness she went through while she was pregnant. She and Neal were getting serious about finding a house, and they were house hunting practically every minute that they were not working. They hoped to find one and get settled before graduation.

***

The human mind can work in strange ways, and the time Max was in recovery after his surgery, was a good example. While he was still partially under the anesthesia, his mind went to Duke, and he thought, *I'm going to call him and ask him to come up here.*

About that time, an orderly and a nurse came to get him and take him back to his room. His Mother and Daddy were there waiting for him, but he was too sleepy to talk. His face and head were bandaged from his eye to down below his throat and about three fourths around his head. He looked a mess, and his Mother was visibly upset. In a couple of hours, he woke up for a little while and tried to talk, but the anesthetic was still in control, and he kept drifting off to sleep.

The Norwoods decided to go downstairs and get some lunch while he slept, hoping that he would be a little more alert in the afternoon. They wanted to be able to talk to him, but at the same time, they were thankful that he was sleeping because they didn't think he would be in pain when he was asleep. Around two or two thirty he woke up, and he was awake for a good while. He must have remembered what he thought about Duke while he was in the recovery room because he asked his Daddy to please call him.

When he told his Daddy to call Duke, his Daddy said, "Oh, I haven't had a chance to tell you yet, but a guy came in this morning and said they're having an awards ceremony two weeks from today, and he said you should be there."

"Really? Okay, maybe they're going to give me something. Daddy, before you call Duke, let me ask if we can make long distance calls from here. If we can, I can call him, myself. Wouldn't it be neat if he could come up here and see me get an award?"

"It would. He's really proud of you."

After Mr. Norwood said that, there was a moment of silence, and during that brief moment of silence, Max went back to sleep. That time, he slept until almost supper time. His parents were going to leave the next day, and they hated to miss that time with him. After he finally woke up, they talked for a while, and then they left to let him get some rest. His Mother kissed him bye and said they would be back in the morning before they left for Middleton.

211

Max stayed awake for a while after they left, and in a little while a pretty nurse came in, and he asked her if he was permitted to make long distance calls from his room. She smiled and asked, "Who are you going to call? Your squeeze?"

"No, my best friend."

"Darling, you can call anybody you want to call. I'll bet your squeeze would like to hear from you."

"If I had one, I'd call her."

"You mean you don't have a girl back home?"

"I'm afraid not. I had one, but she sent me a Dear John letter."

"Bummer. You probably didn't need her anyway, did you?"

"No. Not really. She left me for a volleyball player."

She laughed. "Are you serious? Did you play sports?"

"Yeah, I played football at Memphis State for four years."

"You mean she actually left you for a volleyball player? Is she a full-fledged woman?"

"I thought she was."

"Well, I'm going to tell you something, Big Boy. If I was your girl, you would not get a Dear John from me."

He asked, "Even if I looked like this?"

"Even if you looked like this. Remember, I saw you before you got the bandages."

"Thank you. Maybe, sometime, when I get these bandages off, we can get a cup of coffee."

"That would be nice. I'll hold you to that."

"You know from my chart that my name is Max. What's yours?"

"I'm Pat. Pat Thomas."

"I'm glad to know you, Pat Thomas."

"I'm glad to know you, too, Max Norwood."

"I've got to go, but I'll see you a little later, okay?"

"Okay."

After dinner, which was a bowl of chicken soup, Max watched TV for a little while and then went to sleep and slept for most of the night, except for the times they came in to check his blood pressure and other things.

Morning finally came, and he woke up feeling surprisingly good for one day after having major surgery. He asked for some real coffee, not the decaf kind, and a nurse soon brought him a cup.

While he was drinking his coffee, Dr. Montgomery came in to see him, and after removing the bandages and looking over the incision, he said, "Max, you're a lucky man. Your healing is all that's left now, and that shouldn't take too long. Then you can get back to normal and live a normal life. By the way, here's the bullet we took out of your head," and Max said, Thank you."

Dr. Montgomery told the nurse who came in with him to get some things, which Max figured were things to bandage him up with, and when she came back with what the doctor sent her for, the doctor put fresh bandages on him, himself. As he left, he said, "Have a good day, and I'll see you later."

Not to long after the doctor was there, his parents came. They were going back to Middleton, and they wanted to see him before they left. They were pleasantly surprised when they saw the new bandages, and they thought he looked much better than he did when they left him the night before.

They visited together for about an hour, and then they said they needed to leave, but they would be back up for the awards ceremony in two weeks. Max sat up on the side of the bed, and they all embraced and said they loved each other. Then his parents left.

After his parents left, Max called Duke, and when he answered the phone, Max said, "Hey, what are you up to this morning?"

"Nothing much. Just got back from a run. What are you up to?"

"Just living the good life. Listen, I want to ask you something. You may or may not want to do it, but I'm going to ask you anyway."

"What is it?"

"In two weeks, there will be an awards ceremony here at Walter Reed, and I think they may give me something, and I would like for you to be here with me. When they gave me my Purple Heart, the President was here to give it to me, and I don't know if he'll be here for this one or not, but if he's not, they'll have some high government official present the awards. If Sissy can get off for a couple of days, I'd like for her to be here, too. Do you think you all can come?"

"Wow! Right now I'll say yes, but give me the rest of today to make sure we don't have anything urgent happening, and I'll have Sissy ask her boss if she can get off. Do you know the exact date?"

"Yeah, it's two weeks from yesterday. I don't know the date, but you can look it up. When you find out, give me a call, will you?"

"I will and thanks for asking us, Partner. I'll try to call you back later today or no later than tomorrow. Oh yeah, how did you do with your surgery?"

"Great. They took the bullet out without damaging anything else, and they say I'll be okay. I look a mess right now, but I should look better in a few days, after some of the bandages are taken off."

"Okay, let me get off of here so I can get to work on our trip to Washington. I'll call you as soon as I know something."

"Okay, Buddy. I'll listen for you."

Duke called back the next morning and said that he and Sissy would both be at the awards ceremony, and that they would arrive on Sunday evening before the ceremony on Monday. Max was really glad they were coming.

Each day got better, and they changed the bandages every day. About every two or three days, the size of the bandages were reduced until they were soon not much larger than a large band-aid.

One day, after they had put on some smaller bandages, Pat came in, and while she was there, she said, "Max, how long has it been since you shaved?"

"I don't know; probably over a month or two. I don't think I've had a shave since before I was shot. Why? Do you want to give me a shave?"

"Yes, if you would like for me to. You don't want to grow a beard, do you?"

"No, I don't like beards. I would like it if you would shave me."

"Okay, I'll be back in a minute."

She left. And in just a very few minutes, she was back and got started. First, she soaked his beard with a hot, wet towel, and after she was satisfied that his beard was tender, she began shaving. He laid back and relaxed and closed his eyes. He didn't remember when anything felt so good. Pat seemed to be enjoying it also, and she took her own good time, being careful to not get too close to the bandages."

When she finished and was wiping off the excess shaving cream, he noticed that she had a very soft touch, and he liked that a lot. He asked her, "Will you be working two weeks from this past Sunday night?"

Always the jokester, she said, "Why, are you going to take me somewhere?"

"I thought we might run away together."

"That sounds good to me. Let me check something."

She looked at the calendar on the wall and did some figuring, and then, she said, "Yep, I'll be here, so I guess running away will have to wait. Why did you ask?"

"Two weeks from yesterday, there's an awards ceremony, and my parents and some good friends are coming up for it, and I thought maybe I could get you to shave me again, so I'll look pretty."

"Darling, you don't need me to shave you for you to look pretty, but I'll be happy to shave you. Sunday night, you say?"

"Yeah, the night before the ceremony."

"I'll write that down. You've got yourself a date, Marine."

"I wish. Thanks, Pat."

All he had to do now was rest and heal and wait on his visitors to come. Now that he wasn't having to worry about somebody shooting at him, he began to think about the future. There was still about a year left on his enlistment, and it was probably not going to be up to him to finish or not finish it. If he stayed in the Marines, what would he be doing. He didn't want a desk job, and he didn't think they'd let him be deployed again with his injuries. If they kicked him out, what would he do? He had thought about coaching high school football, but that was a longshot. He sort of settled into the thought of becoming a salesman for some company; maybe a company connected to the company his Daddy worked for. His Daddy worked for a large hosiery manufacturer, and he thought that maybe he could get a job selling something used in hosiery manufacturing. Maybe his Daddy knew somebody he could talk to. Oh well; he didn't have to worry about that now. He just had to get well.

His surgery was getting better every day. His stitches were removed on day seven, and by Sunday, the day before the awards ceremony, he barely had a bandage on his neck. His parents got there about mid-afternoon, and Duke and Sissy arrived a little before dinner time.

Sissy had known his parents most of her life, and they looked at her almost like one of their own. Of course, they knew Duke from when he and Max were in college, so it was almost like a family reunion when they were all together.

Not long, after Duke and Sissy arrived, Max's dinner was brough in, and not wanting to eat in front of everybody, he let it sit there. Seeing what he was doing, Max's Daddy asked Duke, "Did you all eat before you came?"

"No, we thought we'd get something up here after a while."

"Well, I, for one, am hungry, and I'd like to go get something. Would you all like to go? There's a fast food place down the street, and we wouldn't have to be gone too long. That would help us and give Max a chance to eat his supper. Whatta ya say?"

Duke said, "I'm with you. Let's go."

Max was hungry, and he was glad his Daddy saw what was happening, and he ate every bite on his tray. When the others got back, they had a great visit together, and before they left for the night, Pat, the nurse came in and saw the company and said, "Oh, I'm sorry. I'll come back," and Max said, "Come here a minute," and he introduced her to everybody.

Pat said, "I don't know if Max told you or not, but when he gets well, we're going to run -away together."

His Daddy said, "That's great. I hope you'll let us know where you are. He has already been gone a long time."

She said, "I know, and for that reason, I may not go."

Max said, "Shucks," and everybody laughed.

Pat told everybody how glad she was to meet them, and she told Max she would be back later.

He said, "I'll be looking forward to it," and she left.

Everyone left around nine or nine thirty, and Pat came in shortly afterwards. She asked, "Are you ready to get pretty?"

"I'm ready. Do you think you can do it?"

"I'm sure I can. Lay back and relax, and I'll get to work."

That time was even smoother than the first time she gave him a shave, probably because his beard wasn't as long as it was the first time, and he thoroughly enjoyed it.

"He said, "If I was rich, I'd hire you to be my full-time barber."

She laughed and said, "If you were rich, I'd do it, but in the meantime, I'll do it for free. How about that?"

"That'll work. Just make me pretty for tomorrow, and I'll let you off the hook."

"Okay. That's a deal," and she finished shaving him, and while she was there, she trimmed his hair to make him look a whole lot better. When she finished, she gave him a quick kiss on the cheek and said, "There you are, handsome. You look great, and I'll see you Friday."

"Thanks a lot. You're a lifesaver."

After she left, he watched TV long enough to see the local news and sports, and then he turned the TV off and went to sleep.

He had told his parents and Duke to go straight to the room where the ceremony was to be held, and he would see them in the morning. When he got to the room, they were already there and while they could talk, there was a reverence in the room, and everyone was either quiet or they spoke in soft voices.

Like in Max's last awards ceremony, all the networks had cameras there, plus some independent networks and the Pentagon channel. In a little bit, an officer with a booming voice said, "Everyone, please stand. The President of the United States", and Max and Duke both said later that when they announced the President, the hair stood up on their arms.

The President said a few words and then recognized the recipients. There were nine people getting awards; four soldiers, three Marines, and two Air Force Members. Everyone was getting a Purple Heart or equivalent plus some got other awards.

When the President got to Max, he said, "The word Hero is not adequate enough to describe this next recipient. I presented him with a Purple Heart and Bronze Star with a Combat V several months ago, and he wanted to go back into action. His Company Commander said he was like a security blanket for his men. They didn't feel safe unless he was there leading them. On his second deployment, he was wounded three times. The first time he was shot in the neck. The second time, a rocket propelled grenade exploded in front of him causing burns to his face and multiple pieces of shrapnel going into his body. The third time, an insurgent in an automobile was trying to overrun a checkpoint and while his men had taken cover, he was in the open, firing at the insurgent. His men finally killed the insurgent, but this Marine took a bullet to the face during the firefight.

"I'm very proud to present Lieutenant Max Norwood with the following awards. Our country only awards one Purple Heart to a serviceman or woman, and when they sustain subsequent wounds, they're awarded oak leaf clusters, and I'm please to award Lt. Norwood with three oak leaf clusters."

The people attending the ceremony started to applaud, and the President said, "Wait. That's not all. I'm also proud to present Lieutenant Norwood with the Silver Star, and finally The Navy Cross. In case you're not familiar with what the Navy Cross is, the Navy Cross is the second highest award given to anyone by the United States of America. Lieutenant Norwood, congratulations", and then everyone, including the President, applauded.

After the ceremony everyone milled around, and everybody wanted to meet the President. Since Max was sort of the star of the show that morning, the President paid special attention to him and his parents. The President remembered meeting his parents at the Purple Heart ceremony, and he wanted to tell them again how proud he was of Max.

Max introduced Duke and Sissy to the President as his closest friends, and he told the President that Duke was an NFL player. The President asked, "Who do you play for, Duke?"

"The Atlanta Falcons, Mr. President."

The President said, "Hmm, I wonder if we could get you up here in Washington. The Redskins need some help, and you look as if you could give it to them."

He talked to Duke for a couple more minutes and then shook Mr. and Mrs. Norwood's hands and saluted Max. He said, "Max, I'm very proud of you."

"Thank you, Mr. President."

Then, he left, and everyone milled around for a while longer, and Max and his parents could tell that Duke was overwhelmed with pride for his friend.

The Norwoods and Duke and Sissy had to leave to go home; the Norwoods to Middleton, and Duke and Sissy to Atlanta, where they had moved after Duke was signed by the Falcons. They had enjoyed being together so much, it was hard for them to leave. Duke and Sissy were leaving first, and Max hugged both of them like he would never see them again. "I can't tell you how much I appreciate you guys coming up here. It really means a lot. Thank you so much."

Duke said, "You're not half as glad as I am that we came. I've never been a party to anything like what we saw this morning. I was proud of you when you caught that game winning touchdown pass against Southern Mississippi that time, but that paled in comparison to this. I'm so proud of you, I'll probably never get over it."

"Yeah, you will. Don't get too sappy on me. I hope to be home soon, and maybe we can get together. Sissy, I am so glad that you came. If I had a sister, I couldn't love her anymore than I do you. You all be careful driving home, and now that I know I can make long distance calls from here. I'll be calling you. I'll probably worry you to death."

They left and Max turned to his parents. His Daddy asked, "What's next, Son?"

"I don't know, Daddy. I guess they'll tell me before much longer."

"Okay. We need to go. It's a long six hour drive home. Call us and let us know what's happening. We're very proud of you. I hope you know that."

"I know. I love you both. Maybe they'll give me some leave when I get out of here. I'd like to come home. You all be careful, and I'll talk to you soon."

Soon, after everyone had gone, lunch was brought, and he

ate. When he finished eating, he laid back on his bed and dozed off. He hadn't been asleep very long when someone coming into the room woke him. He opened his eyes, and it was Captain Bob Cox, his Company Commander. He attempted to get up real quick, but Captain Cox told him to relax and be at ease.

He sat in a chair across from Max's bed and asked. "How're you feeling, Max?"

"I'm feeling pretty good. There was quite a bit of excitement around here this morning, and it took a lot of my energy, but all in all, I feel pretty good."

Captain Cox said, "Max, I came by for two reasons; first was to congratulate you on your awards, and second, to ask you what would you think about a thirty-day leave?"

"I would love a thirty-day leave, sir."

"Oh, there's another thing, and I think you'll like this one. I looked over your enlistment and other things, and it looks as if you still have approximately one year left. Here's my suggestion, Max. Instead of kicking you out of the Marines with a disability discharge, now, I suggest you finish out your contract, and by the time the year is up, you should get promoted to Captain, and then take Medical Retirement.

"That way, you can get a nice pension for the rest of your life, along with other perks afforded retired Marines. I can see that you will have an enjoyable job during your final year, and I strongly suggest you do it. Think about it, and we'll talk more later. Your doctor says you can leave here the end of this week, but when your leave is up, you are to return here for procedures by plastic surgeons. I'll have your paperwork brought over here for you, so when you get ready to go home or wherever you're going, you can leave from here."

"Captain, I don't know what to say. That's more than anything I could ever have dreamed about. Thank you so much."

"You've earned it, Lieutenant. Thank you. I hope you

enjoy your time at home or wherever you're going on leave."

"I'm going home, sir. My family and I are pretty close."

Chapter Fifteen

One Friday afternoon in mid-April, when Amy and Karen arrived at the clinic, Neal met Amy at the door and said, "Do you remember Bracky Robinson, the realtor?"

"Yeah, why?"

"He called and said a house has just come on the market that he thinks we might like, and he wants us to come look at it before he puts in on multiple listing. Do you want to go look at it?"

"Right now?"

"Yeah, don't take your jacket off."

Bracky had given Neal the address, so they met him at the house. Neal called him before they left the clinic, and he knew when they would be there. When they pulled up to the front of the house, they were both blown away. It was beautiful.

They all got out and walked up the sidewalk to the front door and went in. The inside was every bit as impressive as the outside, and Amy immediately fell in love with it. As far as she was concerned, she didn't have to look any farther; this was the house for her. Every time she and Neal would look at each other, they were smiling. Neal liked the place just as well as Amy did.

Neal told Bracky to please excuse them for a minute while they talked, and they went into another room, and Neal asked Amy, "What do you think?"

"I love it. What do you think?"

"I love it, too. Do you want to get it?"

"Can we afford it?"

"Yeah. Remember, in another month you'll be bringing in a fulltime salary, and with that, added to mine, I don't see any reason why we can't buy it if we want it."

"I want it."

"Me too. Let' go tell Bracky."

When they found Bracky, Neal said, "Bracky, we think we want this house. What do we do now?"

"That's great. You'll need to sign an offer to purchase agreement and give me a check for some earnest money, and I'll do the rest."

Neal asked, "How much earnest money do you need?"

Bracky told him, and Neal said, "Okay, I'll write you a check, but Bracky, you'll have to give me time to transfer some money, Monday morning, before you cash it."

"No problem. It might be a week or longer before it gets to your bank. Are you going to be at the animal hospital Monday?"

"Yeah, I'll be there all day, and Amy will be there before we close Monday afternoon."

"Great. Suppose I come by around five o'clock, Monday afternoon because you'll both need to sign the Offer to Purchase."

"That will be fine. Honey, do you want to look at anything else?"

"No, I don't think so right now."

"Okay, Bracky, I think we're done. We'll see you Monday."

"Good, I'll see you then. Congratulations. I know you're both going to love this place, and this neighborhood is one of the finest in Decatur. I'm very happy for you."

He shook hands with Neal, and he shook Amy's hand and also gave her a hug. They left and said they would see each other on Monday. Neal and Amy were ultra-excited, and they could hardly wait to tell Karen and Dr. Brock when they got to the clinic.

On the way to the clinic, Neal looked over at Amy and asked. "Are you happy?"

"I'm more than happy. I'm ecstatic. How long do you think it will be before we can get in?"

"It depends. First, all the red tape has to be done, and the loan has to be approved, and then, it will depend on what you want to do to the house in terms of painting, new carpet, or anything else you want to do or have done before we move in. If we move in without doing some of those things, I'd say the paperwork, loan approval, and other red tape will take three or four weeks."

"That will be close to graduation. We're going to be busy.

"I know. You've got to remember, too, that finals come before graduation, and you're really going to be really busy. I think we need to give ourselves plenty of time and set the date for our moving out far enough to where we know everything will have been settled down after you graduate."

"Makes sense. Let's just plan on moving sometime in late May. Does that sound alright to you?"

"Sounds perfect."

When they got to the clinic, and when Karen and her Daddy were together, Neal said, "Amy and I have a surprise for you."

Karen asked, "A surprise for us?"

"Well, not exactly for you, but it's something we want to share with you. Amy and I are buying a house, if all goes well."

His Daddy asked, "Where is it?"

"In Shepherd Hills. The guy who owns it has just been transferred and has to sell it."

Amy chimed in, "It's beautiful. I can't wait for you to see it."

Dr. Brock asked, "How old is it?"

Neal said, "It's six years old; almost new."

"How long has it been on the market?"

"It just has come on. Bracky Robinson called this morning and told me about it, and he thought we might want to see it before it went on Multiple Listing, and he was right. He said that we're the first to look at it, and we're very thankful that he thought to call us when he did."

Dr. Brock said, "Well, I think that's great. I'm anxious to see it."

They all finished out the afternoon, working, and then, when the clinic closed, Neal and Amy went to his parent's house to tell his Mother about buying the house."

The clinic always closed early on Saturday, so when it closed the next day, they all got in Dr. Brock's RV and went by to pick up Neal's Mother, and they rode by to see the house that Amy and Neal were buying.

They all got out and walked around the yard and looked in the windows, and Mrs. Brock said, "My goodness, Neal, this is beautiful, and they must have a full-time yard man, the way it's manicured. I'm anxious to see the inside."

"Maybe we can get Bracky to meet us one day next week, and you all can go inside. It's just as pretty inside as it is out here," Neal said.

On Saturday night, Amy called her Mother and Daddy and when her Mother answered the phone, she said, "Hey, Mother. What are you doing?"

"Hi, Amy. I'm just watching TV with your Daddy. Stevie's coming over in a little bit, and we're just waiting on him."

"Tell him I sent my love. Listen, the reason I called is to tell you that Neal and I are buying a house. Are you and Daddy coming up for graduation?"

"Yeah, we're planning to."

"Good. I want to show you our house."

"Well, I'll be anxious to see it."

FOUR WEEKS LATER

The atmosphere at the University of Illinois Urbana campus was almost carnival-like. Most finals were over and many of the kids were through for the year and on their way home, and most importantly for Amy and Karen, graduation was set for Friday, May fifteenth.

Amy's parents were flying into Decatur on the fourteenth,

and Amy and Neal were meeting them at the airport. Karen was going to go ahead and move back home, and that way, there would be a spare bedroom at the apartment that the Hatchers could sleep in.

Neal bent over backwards to make them feel at home, and Amy really appreciated his efforts. When they got to Decatur, Neal and Amy took them out to eat, and then they went to the apartment to visit until bedtime.

Neal took off work Friday in order to be with the Hatchers and Amy. Since graduation wasn't until five o'clock that afternoon, they had time to go see Amy and Neal's new house. Their loan had been approved and all the paperwork had been finished and they had keys, so they could go in and out as they wanted. Amy's Mother and Daddy thought the house was beautiful, and after they had finished looking at it, they took them to Neal's parents' house, which was also very impressive. They finished out the morning with a quick lunch and then returned to the apartment to get ready for the graduation ceremony.

Neal didn't have to do anything to get ready. He had showered and everything when he got up that morning, and he was going to graduation the way he was. Amy had cleaned up before they left that morning, as did her Mother, so her Daddy was the only one to take a shower when getting ready to leave for Urbana. The Graduates were told to be at the venue at four o'clock, so they left the apartment at three thirty.

Neal and the Brocks and the Hatchers found five seats together, and they all sat together. Pretty soon, a band began playing, and all the graduates marched in in double file; one group on one side and the other group on the other side.

There were the usual boring speeches from people not many had ever heard of, and it seemed like forever before the School of Veterinary Medicine began their graduation. The University of Illinois at Urbana was made up of fifteen colleges and schools, and there were about three or four of them having their graduation ceremonies at the same time as the School of Veterinary Medicine. It seemed as if everything was in alphabetical order, and since veterinary began with 'V', the veterinary School was almost last.

Finally, when it started, all the graduates stood and walked up to the stage by rows. Since Amy and Karen's last name began with 'B', they were located not far from the front of the line, and after a few students were called, they called the name of Amy Lee Hatcher Brock and said she was receiving the Doctor of Veterinary Medicine Magna Cum Laude.

Neal and both sets of parents applauded. Next, they called the name of Karen Lynn Brock and said she was receiving the Doctor of Veterinary Medicine Magna Cum Laude, and once again Neal and the others applauded.

When all the graduates from the veterinary school got their diplomas and returned to their seats, a faculty member stood on the stage and congratulated them for their hard work and told them to move their tassels from the right side to the left side. They all did it and then applauded and yelled. Some threw their caps up in the air.

When it was over, they marched out in the reverse order in which they came in, and graduation was over.

They mingled with many of the other students who they were buddies with or who they had had classes with, and at one point, Karen's Mother told her and Neal and Amy to wait right there and she would be back. In a few minutes, she came back and had a photographer with her. She wanted to get a picture of her husband, her son, her daughter, and her daughter-in-law; four Doctors of Veterinary Medicine and all four with Magna Cum Laude degrees.

The photographer worked at the Champaign newspaper, and he had the picture printed in the paper. He also had it put in the Decatur newspaper, and the Brocks were famous for about a day.

Neal and Karen's Daddy wanted the day to be a special

one, and as part of that, he made reservations at Timpones, one of the best restaurants in the entire area. It was going to be his and his wife's treat, and he told everybody to order whatever they wanted, which they did. Amy's parents weren't used to eating in such a high-end place, and she could tell her Daddy was not comfortable trying to decide what to order. He kept his eye on Neal's Daddy and ordered what he did. Amy coached her Mother on what to order, and everybody was completely satisfied with the dishes they ordered.

Dr. Brock ordered wine before they ate and with that and dinner for six, the bill came to almost two hundred dollars. The Hatchers weren't used to such an upscale dinner, but they truly enjoyed every bite.

In the four years Amy had been involved with the Brocks, and especially after she became involved with Neal, she started calling Dr. Brock, Dad and his wife, Mom. While they were at Timpones, Dr. Brock told Amy, "I'm surprised you aren't going to take a vacation to celebrate your graduation. Why is that, since most of the other graduates are going somewhere next week."

Amy said, "Well, Dad, I've worked hard for seven years in order to get to be a veterinarian, and now that I am one, I'm anxious to apply what I learned. Plus, we have a new home we want to move into. Maybe, after we get settled, Neal and I can go somewhere in late summer or in the fall before it gets cold."

"That sounds like a good plan," he said.

Amy did take off the next day, which was Saturday and spent the day with her parents because they had to leave, Sunday. She took them all around Urbana and Champaign and the University where she had spent the last four years. They had lunch, and then afterwards, she took them down to Decatur, and once again, she took them through her and Neal's new house. That night, she and Neal took her parents out to eat, and then went back to the apartment, where they spent the rest of the evening.

On Sunday morning, she took them to the airport to catch the plane back to Middleton. Her parents had never been very outgoing, but that trip brought out something in them, especially her Daddy, and they acted like two people that she didn't even know by the time they left. They acted as though they actually had a personality, and she was very glad that they came.

Monday was a very busy day at the clinic, and all four Dr. Brocks were there to treat the sick animals that were brought in. After treating the first two or three patients by herself, it dawned on Amy that she was actually a legitimate Doctor of Veterinary Medicine, and nobody could ever take that away from her.

According to her and Neal's plan, they were going to move the following Friday. The moving van was scheduled to come to their apartment on Thursday and pick up their stuff and deliver it to their house on Friday morning. The couple was going to take off from work on Friday and Saturday to get things somewhat straightened out.

They hired a janitor service to clean up the apartment, so they wouldn't have to do that.

The first week after graduation was a good week. Amy and Karen felt as though they were finally more important to the clinic than they had been before, and that feeling was accepted with pride.

There had been another vet working at the clinic, and he was doing a good job, but when he learned that Karen and Amy were coming into the business after they graduated, ho told Dr. Brock that he would leave when they came in. Dr. Brock hated to see him leave and tried to talk him into staying, but he wanted to go up to Champaign and open his own practice. There was enough business for all five of them, but he left anyway.

Dr. Brock thought he would see how well things would run without the other vet, and after a couple or three weeks, he felt that he made the right decision. It took that long for Karen and Amy to gain efficiency, and when they did, it was clear that four vets were enough, and it wouldn't be necessary to hire an additional person.

Things were running very smoothly at the clinic, and the Brock family was enjoying it immensely, and they had all gotten back to their individual routines. Dr. and Mrs. Brock walked three miles every morning, and Karen and Amy ran every morning. They didn't have a set distance; they just ran until they decided to stop, and Neal started back at the gym. He went through an intense workout every time, and he was getting in very good shape.

It had been almost six months since Amy graduated from vet school, and she and Neal were really settled. Almost a year had passed since she lost her baby, and she and Neal thought they would try to get pregnant again, but it wasn't working. Thanksgiving came and went. Christmas and New Years rolled by and then Easter. Still, no pregnancy.

Amy was getting discouraged after a full year of trying to conceive, and both she and Neal pretty much gave up on the idea, and thought if it happens, it happens. Maybe their trying so hard had something to do with it not happening.

One Thursday morning, while she was getting ready to go to work, the phone rang, and she wondered who would be calling that early. She answered and a voice on the other end asked, "Is this Amy Brock?"

"Yes, it is. Who's this?"

"Mrs. Brock, this is Sally at Decatur Health. Neal was working out a little bit ago, and something happened. He fell down, holding his chest, and we called the ambulance. He could possibly have had a heart attack. The ambulance is taking him to St. Mary's."

Amy asked, "Was he conscious?"

Sally said, "He was in and out. I'd hurry to St. Mary's if I were you."

"Thanks for calling."

As soon as she hung up, she called Neal's parents. Dr. Brock answered. "Dad, they just called from the gym, and said Neal may have had a heart attack, and they took him to St. Mary's. I'm leaving now to go over there."

"Okay, Honey. I'll leave right now, too. I'll see you over there."

Neal's parents both went to the hospital and met Amy. They went to the Emergency Room and were told that Neal had been taken to the Cardiac Care Unit and was currently being examined.

They waited and waited for word from somebody in the Cardiac Care Unit, but no one came out, then, after about two and a half or three hours, a doctor came out and asked to see Mrs. Brock.

Amy said, "I'm Mrs. Brock."

The doctor said, "Mrs. Brock, I'm Doctor Dean Hilton. We have been working feverishly on your husband, but I'm very sorry to tell you that he didn't make it. He had what is called a Myocardial Infarction, and there was really nothing we could do. I'm very sorry. How old was your husband?"

"Twenty-eight."

Dr. Brock introduced himself to Dr. Hilton and said, "Hi, Dr. Hilton, I'm Mike Brock, Neal's Dad. How could a healthy, young man like Neal die of a heart attack. It doesn't make sense."

"I know it doesn't, but the ages of heart attack victims are getting younger and younger. The rate for victims under forty is now up to twenty percent."

By then, Amy and Mrs. Brock had their arms around each other, and they were both bawling. The doctor left them, and then Dr. Brock went over and embraced both his wife and Amy. He asked Amy, "Honey, where do you want them to take Neal?"

"I don't know. You know more about that than I do. Where do you suggest?"

"Well, most of our family is buried at Fairlawn, and that's where we will be buried. The Graceland—Fairlawn Funeral Home is connected to it, so they can do everything for you, if that's who you want."

"They will be fine. Can you help me with things?"

"Of course, I will. Let me find somebody and tell them who to call."

Neal's mother said, "Mike, we need to call Karen."

"I know. I'll call her when I finish here."

"Dad, I'm going to go home. I have to call my parents. When should we go to the Funeral home to make arrangements?"

"Probably sometime this afternoon. I'd say whenever you're up to it. In the meantime, I don't want you to be by yourself. How about I have Karen go over to your house and be with you?"

"That would be good. I'd love to have her with me. I'm going to go call my parents, and I'll see you a little later."

"Okay. I'll see you after a while."

Amy left and went straight home and straight to the telephone. She called her Mother's number, and when she answered, she said, "Hey Mother."

Before she could say anything else, her Mother said, "Honey, why are you calling this early. Is something wrong?"

"Mother, Neal had a heart attack this morning and died."

"Oh no. Are you alright?"

"I don't know, Mother. He just died a few minutes ago, so I don't know."

"I guess you don't know when the funeral will be do you?"

"Not for sure, but I'm looking at maybe Saturday."

"Well, I'll call your Daddy, and we'll see if we can get up there sometime tomorrow. Do you think someone could meet us at the airport?"

"I'm sure we can get somebody to meet you. Call and let me know what time, and Mother, you all can stay here with me."

"Okay, and if I can't get you, I'll leave a message on your answering machine, and Honey, I'm sorry about Neal."

"Thanks, Mother."

As soon as Amy hung up from her Mother, Karen got there. When she got to where Amy was, they hugged without saying anything. They just stood there, hugging. Finally, Karen said, "I'm so sorry."

Amy said, "I'm sorry, too."

Karen asked, "What are you getting ready to do?"

"I'm just waiting on your Daddy to call. We're going to the funeral home to do whatever we have to do there, and to decide on the day and time for the funeral."

In a few minutes, Dr. Brock called, and they set a time to meet at the funeral home. Karen was going to drive Amy and help her pick out a casket.

Dr. Brock told Amy she should pick out the clothes she wanted to have Neal dressed in and bring them with her, so she and Karen picked out a nice suit and shirt and tie. Amy said, "I always thought he looked real nice when he wore this suit."

Karen said, "It's a petty suit. Are you ready?"

Amy said she was, so they went out and got in Karen's car for the ride to the funeral home.

Amy, Karen, and Neal's parents all went to the funeral home to pick out a casket and to make all the arrangements for the funeral. Amy and Neal didn't have a burial plot, so it was necessary that she buy a lot while she was there.

When they finished at the funeral home, Amy wanted to go home, so Karen took her and let her out. She told Amy, "Girlfriend, I'm going to go home and get some things and I'll be back in a little while. I'd like to stay with you for a few days, if you don't care."

Amy said, "Thanks, I'd like that. Try not to be gone too long, okay?"

"Okay. Look, why don't you go with me. We won't be

long, but you won't have to be by yourself. You want to?"

"Yeah. I think I do."

They went to the Brock's and while they were there, Mrs. Brock asked Amy, "Honey, do you think you could eat something?"

"No thanks, Mom. I don't have any appetite right now."

Before they left to go back to Amy's Dr. Brock asked Amy if she wanted him to call the Pastor at their church to do the funeral, and Amy said she did.

When Amy and Karen got back to Amy's, there was a message on the machine from Amy's Mother, saying that she and her Daddy and her brother would be in Decatur the next morning, and she hoped someone could meet them at the airport. Karen said, "Don't worry about it. I'll take care of it."

Amy said, "But I don't want you to have to go to the airport. I can go."

Karen came back with, "Hush up. I said I'd take care of it. Neither one of us will have to go. I'll get Mickey, at the clinic, to go pick them up."

"That's a good idea. Thanks."

The next morning, Mickey met Amy's parents and brother at the airport and brought them back to Amy's. Friends from church began bringing food to the house as well as to Neal's parents' house, so they didn't have to worry about eating. There was plenty of food. On Friday night, Amy and the Brocks received friends at the funeral home, and there was a huge crowd. The Brocks had lived in Decatur all their lives, and everybody knew them, and when Amy became part of the family, that number grew.

Neal's funeral was on Saturday afternoon, and there was a crowd there as well. The Pastor delivered a very touching eulogy, and Amy and the Brock family was pleased with the service, overall.

After the burial, the family and friends from out of town returned to the church for a meal made up of food fixed by friends and church members. While it was a sad occasion, spirits were lifted by the fellowship, and Amy and the rest of the Brocks were strengthened by their friend's presence.

Amy's parents and brother had to go back home on Sunday morning, and Amy took them to the airport. There were a few tears, but all in all she was doing very well. After the plane took off, she returned home where Karen was waiting for her, and then, the two of them went over to the Brock's for lunch.

The next morning, Monday, Amy got up, got ready and went to the clinic just like she always did. Karen also went, and some of the employees couldn't understand how they could come back to work so soon, but Amy explained that she thought it would be best because she could get her mind on other things beside Neal, and Karen felt the same away about herself.

Chapter Sixteen

After Max got his medals, they gave him a thirty-day furlough, which he spent at home. He still had issues with his wounds, and when his furlough was over, he had to go back to Walter Reed for more therapy and to have his scars worked on by a plastic surgeon. When they finished with him, the scars were hardly noticeable.

He and Captain Bob Cox had become good friends over the last year or year and a half, and Capt. Cox made him a promise before he went home on his furlough. He said that if he would not try to get out of the Marines right then with a medical discharge, and if he would stay in until his enlistment was up that he would give him an enjoyable job and see that he was promoted to Captain before he got out.

When the plastic surgeon and the other doctors released him for duty, the first thing he did was to go to Captain Cox and tell him he had been released. Bob said, "Max, I told you I would give you an enjoyable job, and I'm a man of my word. Here's what I want you to do. I want you to be in charge of the Marine Corps PFT program here at Quantico."

"What's a PFT program, Bob?"

"It's something you've participated in for almost four years; ever since you became a Marine. PFT stands for Physical Fitness Test, and as you know, every Marine has to pass the test every six months. Also, as you know, there are three events in the test; pull ups, abdominal crunches, and a three-mile run.

There are charts showing what is required for each Marine by age and gender, and I want you to administer the tests and keep charts on each Marine. This should be a cream puff job, and you can do it until your enlistment is up in about ten months. In the meantime, I've requested that you be promoted to Captain asap, and that should help considerably on your retirement.

"Thank you, Bob. This should work out just fine. I've been wondering how I would do certain things with this leg, but it looks as if you've solved the problem. Thanks again."

He went to work with the Physical Fitness Test and worked hard at it. He had lost a lot of his muscle when he was wounded, and that gave him a chance to recover some of it. Many times, there weren't any Marines in the gym, and Max was able to work out as he felt like it, and after a while, he could feel his muscle tone returning. He had always liked to work out and working in the gym was right up his alley.

Ten months was what was left on his enlistment when he began his work at PFT, and now, the ten months are about up. His promotion to Captain came through after eight months, and then, he began looking forward to getting out of the Marines and going home.

Finally, the day came. He was granted a discharge due to his enlistment being up, but more importantly, he was going to get a very nice lifetime pension because of his battle wounds. He called his parents and asked them to meet him at the airport.

His Mother met him the next day and took him home. It was a strange feeling for him because he had been gone for eight years except for visits; four years at Memphis State and four years in the Marine Corps. He had done quite a bit of thinking, especially during the last ten months, and he thought that he would like to get his own apartment or house. He was used to being on his own, and he knew that at his age, living with his parents was not a good idea, so apartment hunting was high on his priority list. He didn't have to be in any hurry because his parents were happy to have him home with them.

The first night he was at home, he and his parents were in the den, talking, when his Daddy asked, "Well Son, what are you going to do now? Have you thought about it?"

"I've thought a lot about it, and I don't know for sure, but I think that one of the first things I need to do is find an apartment or maybe a house."

"Son, you don't have to find an apartment. We're happy to have you here."

"I know, Daddy, but now that I've been on my own for eight years, I'm used to doing what I want, when I want, and besides, I'm twenty six years old now, and I think it's time I moved out."

"We'll go along with whatever you say, but don't you think it would be a good idea to have a job first?"

"You're right. I'll have to get a job."

"Back to my original question; have you thought about what you're going to do?"

"I think I told you one time that I might like to coach high school football, but then when I think about how little they get paid, I think I might try to get on with some company as a sales rep."

"Any thoughts about who that might be?"

"No, not really. Growing up, I saw a lot of the reps that sold supplies to your company, and how well they did, and I've thought a little about maybe trying to get on with somebody like that."

"I'll call some of our suppliers, tomorrow, and maybe one of them might be looking for somebody, if you want me to."

"I think that would be great."

Max said, "Another thing I've got to do is buy a car. I think I may have outgrown my Jeep."

"What do you think you'll get?" his Daddy asked.

"I don't know. I'm just going to shop. I think I want to be sure and get something that is made in America, if I can find something."

"You know just about all the cars, including Toyota and Nissan, are made in America now, and a lot of the American names are made overseas."

Max said, "You know, that being the case, I guess it doesn't matter what I get, as long as I like it."

Talking about cars with his Daddy the night before gave him the 'new car fever', and he went out early the next morning to shop around for a car he liked. He knew people that drove pickup trucks, and they all seemed to like them, so those were the first things he looked at. He looked at Chevrolets, GMC's, Ford F-150's, and Rams, and he really did like the F-150. He also looked at BMW's, Mustangs, and Audi's, but he kept going back to the Ford F-150 pickup. He didn't buy anything that day, but he talked money with the Ford and BMW dealers.

That night, Tony Solomon, from Middleton Ford called and made him a counteroffer. Max told him, "Tony, I appreciate you calling, but I told you this afternoon what I'd do, and I don't feel like I can go any higher. If you all decide you want to take my offer, I'll be happy to hear from you."

He went shopping again the next day without hearing from Tony Solomon again. He fell in love with a Corvette zr1 until he found out the price was one hundred and twenty thousand dollars, and then his love waned considerably. He looked at the BMW's again, but couldn't really get happy with anything he saw, so he went home, empty-handed again.

When he got home, his Mother told him that a fellow named Tony Solomon had called and wanted him to call him. Max didn't want to sound anxious, so he didn't call him back that afternoon. He thought he would give him a call the next morning, but he didn't have to wait. Tony called back that night and said, "Max, I took your offer to my sales manager, and he fought me on this, but finally he said that since you just got out of the Marines, he would accept your offer as a thank you for your service."

"Cut the crap, Tony. You all tell everybody basically the same thing. My being a Marine doesn't have anything to do with it. My wanting to pay cash for the truck is why you're thanking me. If I take the truck, when will it be ready?"

"We can have it ready by tomorrow afternoon."

"Okay, I'll be there tomorrow afternoon."

"Thank you, Max. If you can, get here early so you can sign some papers, okay?"

"Okay, I'll see you."

He hung up and went in and told his Mother and Daddy, "Well, I just bought a pickup truck."

His Daddy asked, "What did you get?"

"A Ford F-150."

"Oh boy. They're nice. I believe you'll like it."

"I think I will. I'm going to pick it up tomorrow afternoon."

"What color is it?"

"Ruby Red."

"Oh, I almost forgot, talking about buying a pickup, I talked to the Sales Director of Southern Yarns today, and he told me that they have a rep that is about to retire, and they're looking for someone to replace him. I told him that you were thinking about getting into sales, and I told him a little about you, and he said he'd like to talk to you."

"Where is he?"

"In High Point, North Carolina."

"Did he say where the territory is?"

"It's here. I think he said it was Tennessee, Alabama, Georgia, and the two Carolinas. I think most of their accounts in Tennessee, Alabama, and Georgia aren't too far from here, so if you're willing to do some extra driving, you probably wouldn't have to stay out overnight very much."

"That sounds pretty good. Yeah, I'd like to talk to him. Can you set up an appointment with him?"

"I can, but I think it would be better if you call him and set it up yourself. He's a really nice guy. You'll like him."

"Give me his name and number, and I'll call him in the morning."

"Okay, his name is Pete Morris, and his number is in my Rolodex. I'll have to call it to you when I get to my office in the morning."

"Good deal."

At eight fifteen the next morning, the phone rang, and Max answered it. It was his Daddy. "Here's Pete Morris's number. It's 336-555-1212."

"Got it. Do you think he'll be in now?"

"Probably, but why don't you wait 'til around ten o'clock to call him. Give him time to get his day started."

"Will do. I'll let you know what he says."

At ten o'clock, he called Pete Morris like his Daddy suggested, and when he answered, Max said, "Mr. Morris, this is Max Norwood, Jack's son. How are you this morning?"

"I'm good Max. I hope you are."

Max said, "My Dad said he talked to you, and you wanted to talk to me about maybe selling for you."

"That's right. I'd like to talk to you, but I want to talk to you in person. Do you think you could come to High Point?"

"Yes sir. I can come just about any time you want me to."

"Can you come Thursday of this week?"

"Absolutely. Just tell me a time."

"How about two in the afternoon?"

"That sounds perfect."

Pete said, "Your Dad said you just got out of the Marines. Did he tell you that I'm a Marine?"

"No sir, he didn't tell me."

"Well, it sounds as if we have something in common, doesn't it?"

"It does."

"Well, Max, I'll look forward to seeing you on Thursday. Do you know anything about High Point?"

"No sir. I've never been there."

"Let me give you directions. Have you got something to write with?"

"Yes sir. I'm ready," and Pete gave him detailed directions on how to find him, and he said, "I'll see you Thursday."

"I'll be there."

When he hung up, Max thought, *I don't know if I have anything to wear for a job interview. About all I've worn the last four years is fatigues. I'd better go find me some clothes because I feel sure those people dress nice and expect their people to dress nice. I'll look in the yellow pages to see if I can get an idea of where to go.* One name stood out; Clyde Brown Clothiers, 755 S. Main Street, Middleton.

He went to Clyde Brown's and decided he would look for a couple of nice sport coats and slacks instead of a suit. He knew some companies required their sales people to wear suits, but he didn't think Southern Yarns was that kind of company. He reasoned that if they hired him, and if they required their salesmen to wear suits that they would tell him.

Clyde Brown's had a very good selection of sport coats, slacks, shirts and ties, and anything else a well-dressed man would like. The guy who waited on him knew what he was doing, and he steered Max in a direction that he liked. He was around Max's age, and he knew what most guys like Max and himself liked, so that's where he took Max.

Max told him, "I just have left the Marine Corps, and I don't have very many clothes other than fatigues, but I'm going for a job interview Thursday, and if I get the job, I'll be back to get some other things. My problem is, I don't know what their dress requirements are, and if they require suits, I'll be back to get some suits, and if they think sport coats are okay, I'll come get some more sport coats. I think I'll just get one sport coat today, so help me pick out something that will bowl the sales manager over at the interview. Pick out something that shows good taste and is not too loud and let me have some good-looking pants and a tie that's not too gaudy.

The sales guy's name was Jim, and he and Max became buddies before Max left the store. Everything Max bought fit perfectly, and the only thing that had to be done was for the pants legs to be cuffed.

Max remembered that he had to pick up his new truck, so he left the clothing store and went to the Ford place. When he went in, he asked for Tony Solomon, and it wasn't but a minute until Tony came out. "Is my truck ready?" he asked.

"It should be," Tony said. He picked up a phone and called somebody and asked them, and they apparently said it was. Tony said, "Come in here and let's get the paperwork done, okay?"

"Okay," Max said, and they went into a small office and he signed what seemed like a hundred papers, and then he wrote a check for the truck. "Can I leave my Jeep here? I'll have to get my Daddy or somebody to bring me back to get it."

"Yeah. Leave it as long as you need to."

"Okay, we'll probably be back to get it tonight."

He got in his new truck and drove it home, and he felt as though he was in a Rolls Royce, it was so smooth. After supper, he and his Mother and Daddy went to the Ford store to pick up his Jeep, and his Daddy drove the truck, and Max drove the Jeep. When they got home, his Daddy said, "Boy, that's a fine ride. I may have to think about one of these for myself sometime."

Max had talked to some people that traveled to North Carolina on a regular basis, and he was told that it would take him around six hours from Middleton to High Point, and they gave him the best route. Based on what they told him, he left home at seven o'clock Thursday morning, hoping to get to High Point by one o'clock, and that would give him an hour, in case he ran into a traffic backup of some kind.

There were no problems of any kind, and his new F-150 ran like a dream. As he had hoped, he got to High Point at one o'clock, and just to be sure he would not be late, he read his directions and drove to Southern Yarns ahead of time, so he could be sure he knew where to go. He was hungry, and he passed a Mickey D's close to Southern Yarns, and he was tempted to go in and get something, and then he thought, *no I'm not going to do it. All I need to do is spill something on my shirt or coat before I go in for my interview.* He had thought to take a pack of nabs with him when he left that morning, and he opened them and ate some peanut butter crackers.

At ten 'til two, he went into Southern Yarns and told the receptionist why he was there, and she told him to have a seat. At five 'til, Pete Morris came out and said, "Max, I'm Pete. It's great to see you. Come on back."

They went down a long hall and into a very nice office. Pete went behind a desk where his chair was, and he told Max to have a seat. They did the required small talk before they got into why Max was there, and Pete wanted to know about Max's Marine experiences.

"How long were you in, Max?"

"Four years. I took NROTC in college and four years is a requirement when you do that. How long were you in," Max asked. "Did you see action?"

"No, I was a peacetime Marine. Your Dad told me that you were decorated. Where were you, and what kind of decorations did you get?"

Max said, "I was in Iraq twice. The first time, I got hit by a roadside bomb that nearly took my leg off, and I spent several months at Walter Reed. For that, they gave me a Purple Heart and a Bronze Star with a Combat V.

The second tour was more fun. I got shot in the neck, I was too close to an RPG that exploded in front of me, filling me with shrapnel, and it burned my face, and last but not least, I was shot in the face. I spent several more months at Walter Reed and for those experiences, they gave me three Oak Leaf Clusters, a Silver Star, and the Navy Cross. I got so banged up, I thought it best if I got out when my enlistment was up."

Pete said, "Man, you were decorated weren't you? I'm

talking to a sure enough war hero. I've got to say, Max; I'm impressed."

"Thank you."

"Now, let's talk about why you're here. Do you know anything at all about yarn?"

"Just that you make hosiery and things out of it. I used to work at the mill where my Daddy works, and I saw a lot of yarn there, but I really don't know anything more than that about it."

"Not many people do. Did you do good in college?"

"Yes sir, I did. I think I did extra good because I played football for four years, and that took a lot of my study time."

"You played football four years? Where did you go?"

"I went to Memphis State University."

"Did you start?"

"Yes sir. I started three years."

"What position did you play>:

"I played tight end."

"You look like a tight end."

"Is that good?"

"It's more than good. It's great. Max, let me say this. I knew before you came that you didn't know anything about yarn. I mainly wanted to see what you looked like and what kind of personality you have, and you have passed both tests.

"Now, we don't actually have an opening right now, but one of our old line sales reps is going to retire at the end of next month, and if you think you would like to replace him, you can have the job."

"Yes sir, I'd really like to have the job. Can I still live in Middleton, or will I need to move?"

"I think unless you just want to move, you can keep living in Middleton. Let me ask you this. Our current rep is named Les. Would you have any problem riding with him for a while to get used to how we do things here at Southern? You can learn a lot about yarn from Les, too."

"I would have no problem at all. Just let me know what I need to know. Where does Les live?"

"He lives in Atlanta, but he'll be working Tennessee for the next little while, and we'll put you two together. I'll have him call you with more information, and in the meantime, we'll set you up as the new rep, replacing Les, and you'll probably need to come back here before you start on your own. Okay?"

"Okay. Thank you so much, Pete. I won't let you down."

"I know you won't. I'll talk to you again in a day or two. Oh, Max, do you happen to have a cell phone?"

"No sir. I don't."

"Well, I suggest you get one. Cell phones are beginning to be an important part of doing business nowadays."

"Okay, I'll get one when I get home. Thank you."

He got in his new truck after he finished with Pete and took Highway 70 from High Point until he picked up I 40 at Statesville. The whole way, he thanked God for helping him, and he asked God to please continue to help him when he began covering his territory on his own. He was almost in a state of euphoria.

He stopped at a convenience store outside of High Point and bought a large Mountain Dew because it had so much caffeine, and he was planning to drive all the way home. He figured it would take him until ten o'clock to get there, and he didn't want to get sleepy.

Driving his new pickup was almost like floating. He could hardly feel any bumps in the road, and his estimate of the time was incredibly accurate. He pulled in his driveway at ten minutes until ten. It had been a long day, but a good day. When he went to bed, he slept like a baby until six o'clock the next morning, and then he went in and had coffee with his parents.

His Daddy asked, "How was your trip to High Point?"

"Good. I got the job."

"Really? That's great."

"Do you know one of their salesmen named Les?"

"Les Tomkins, yeah. He's the one that calls on us."

"Well, he's going to retire at the end of next month, and I'm going to take his place. He's going to call, and I'm going to ride with him for a while to learn something about yarn and to learn the territory."

Later that day, he went to AT&T and got a cell phone the way Pete suggested. He was intrigued by it, and on his way home, he called his Mother. When she answered, he said, "Hey, Mother. Guess where I am."

"I have no idea. Where are you?"

"I'm in downtown Middleton, in my pickup. Can you hear me okay?"

"I can hear you just fine. I can't believe you're calling from your truck."

"Well I am. I've got a couple of things to do before I come home, so I might not be there until after lunch. See you then. Bye."

When he hung up, he was almost to Clyde Brown's, and when he got there, he went in and looked up Jim Brown, the one who was so helpful the other day. He told Jim that he could wear sport coats to work in, and he wanted to pick up two or three with some pants, shirts, and ties.

Jim was just as helpful as he was the first time Max went in, and it didn't take long to get all that he wanted. He left the pants to be hemmed and cuffed and told Jim he would be back Saturday to pick them up. Then he went home.

He didn't eat lunch while he was out, so when he got home, he fixed himself a pimento cheese sandwich and ate it with some chips and a Coke. When he finished eating, he went into the den and called Duke on his new cell phone. There was no answer, and he figured Sissy was at work and Duke was at football practice. He left word on their answering machine that it was him, and he would call back when they had had time to get home.

Later, that afternoon, the phone rang, and when he answered, it was Les Tomkins. "Hi, is this Max?"

"Yes, it is. Who's this?"

"Max, this is Les Tomkins. I just got off the phone with Pete Morris, and he said he would like for me to take you around my territory for a while, and that you're going to take my place when I retire next month."

"Yes sir. I've been expecting to hear from you."

"Well, here's the deal. I'm going to be working Tennessee most of next week, but I've got to be in Fort Payne, Alabama on Monday. Now you can wait 'til Tuesday and go around Tennessee with me or if you want to, you can meet me in Fort Payne Monday and meet some of our key accounts down there. It's up to you."

"I'd like to meet you in Fort Payne."

"That'll be good," and he gave Max instructions on where and what time to meet him, and they hung up after talking for a couple more minutes.

After he picked up his clothes at Clyde Brown Clothiers, Saturday, he rode around, looking at apartments and condos. He didn't go in any of them. He was just trying to get an idea of what was out there.

He tried to call Duke again, and once again, he got the answering machine, and he thought that maybe the Falcons were away, and Sissy had gone to the game with some of the other wives. He thought he would try back Monday.

Chapter Seventeen

It had been several months since Neal died, and Amy was still living in their house. Karen was staying with her, some, but she had found herself a boyfriend, and she was thinking more about her boyfriend and courting than being a companion to Amy, and Amy was starting to get lonely.

Every time she talked to her mother, she was reminded that she could still come home instead of living by herself in a place where she didn't have any people except her in-laws. Her Mother kept telling her how lonely she must be, living by herself, and after months of hearing the same thing over and over, she began to think that maybe her Mother was right.

Then, one day three months later, her Mother called her while she was at work and said, "Honey, I hate to bother you at work, but I have something to tell you that you might be interested in."

"What's that Mother? I'm real busy right now."

"I know, and I won't take but a minute. This morning, I took Toby to Dr. Freeland's, and Dr. Freeland said he is getting ready to retire, and he would like to find some young veterinarian to take over his practice, and I thought that that would be perfect for you. If you're interested in talking to Dr. Freeland, you can call him. Honey, I think this would be perfect for you. I hope you'll call him."

"Mother, I don't have time to talk about it right now. I've got to go."

"Will you at least think about it?"

"I'll think about it. Bye, Mother."

That night, Karen had a date, and Amy was at home by herself, and loneliness began to seep into her mind. She pretty much dismissed the conversation she had with her Mother earlier, but when she felt such loneliness, she began to think about it a little more. The longer she sat there that night, the more depressed she got, so she changed into her night clothes and went to bed early.

She was still depressed the next day at work, and Dr. Brock asked her, "Is something wrong, Amy?"

"No, I just miss Neal so much."

"I miss him, too. It's been a year now. Maybe you need to get out and do some things."

"What would I do, Dad? There's not much a single woman can do by herself, other than go to bars and get picked up by men, and I'm not interested in either one of those options. My Mother wants me to come home."

"Do you want to go home?"

"I didn't think I did, but I'm so lonely, I'm beginning to think about it."

"Sweetie, I'd sure hate to see you leave, but you'll have my full support with whatever you decide to do."

She felt a little better after talking to her father-in-law, but the feeling only lasted until that evening when she was by herself again. Neal had been an avid reader, and he had many books, so she looked through many of them to try and find something that she might like. Finally, she found one that she thought might be good, and she began reading it, but she couldn't get her mind on it, and the loneliness persisted.

The Brocks loved her like she was their own, but it just wasn't the same as it would be if they were her blood relatives, no matter how hard they tried to make her feel like family.

Another month went by, and the loneliness got worse. She did her job satisfactorily, but it wasn't the same as it would have been had she been happy. She went to lunch by herself one day, and instead of going somewhere to eat, she went home and called Dr. Jack Freeland. Dr. Freeland was really happy that she called, and he did a pretty good job of trying to convince her that Middleton Animal Hospital was where she was supposed to be.

She agreed to go to Middleton in about a week, and she promised she would come see him when she got there. She was excited when she got back to the clinic, and before she left that afternoon, she told Dr. Brock that she wanted to go to Middleton the week after next, and he readily agreed to let her off.

She caught a plane on Sunday of the week after next, and her parents met her at the airport. Over the years, she had always had a hard time getting along with both her Mother and her Daddy, but when she walked into their house, she felt as if she was relaxed and at home again.

When she told her Mother that she had talked to Dr. Freeland and had told him that she would come see him, her Mother was elated. She asked if she could borrow her car to go see him, and of course, her Mother said yes.

On Monday morning, she called Dr. Freeland, and he asked her to come in that afternoon, if she could. They set a time of four o'clock, and she was there right on time. She went in and told the receptionist who she was and that she had an appointment with Dr. Freeland at four o'clock, and the lady called back and told the doctor that she was there. It wasn't but a couple of minutes until Dr. Freeland came out, himself, and got her and took her back to his office.

They sat in his office and talked quite a bit about everything from Amy's Mother's dog to her time at the University of Illinois School of Veterinary Medicine. She told him about how she married her roommates' brother, and how Neal died a little over a year ago. She told him about his family owning the Brock Animal Hospital in Decatur, and she told him how she worked at the clinic all four years while she was in school. She told him that she had wanted to be a veterinarian ever since she was a little girl and how lonely she was since Neal left.

Dr. Brock or Amy. Is it okay if I call you Amy?"

"Yes sir. That's what I prefer."

"Amy, I started this hospital nearly forty years ago, and it has been very good to me and my family. My wife and I talked it over, and we feel as if it's time to do something else, such as travel, maybe buy a place at the beach or whatever we want to do. We have made a good living here, and we won't have to worry about anything financial when we retire, but we would like to have someone younger take over.

"All our equipment is up to date and paid for. Our building is in good shape, so there shouldn't anything have to be done to it, such as a new roof or anything else. About two years ago, a young vet came to work with me, and I thought for sure he would be the one to take over the hospital, and then, all at once, he decided that he wanted to move to Nashville, where his girlfriend lived, and he left, so Amy, here's the deal.

"If I can't find someone to come in within the next couple or three months, I'll just close the hospital and go on with my life, but I've got to tell you. You or anybody else would be crazy not to take over this practice because this is what I'm prepared to do for you. First of all, we have a thriving, established business, and all you'd have to do would be to move in. Second, I'm prepared to finance it for you because I know that someone your age has not been in the business long enough to accumulate adequate funds to buy a business such as this that's already established. I know you're a hometown girl, and you have a lot of friends here, so when you add their pets to the ones we already have, you might have to have someone help you.

"Amy, I've given you my best sales pitch, so what do you think?"

"You're a good salesman." She smiled and asked, "Can I start in the morning?"

He laughed and said, "I wish, but seriously, what do you think?"

"Dr. Freeland, I'm very interested. Do you have any P & L Statements or other financial statements, along with your proposal for financing the business that I could show to my Daddy and my father-in-law. Especially my Father-in-law since he's been in this business for so long."

"Yeah, I can give you those things, but I need to be pretty sure that you're pretty sure before I do."

Amy said, "I'm pretty sure, but I've got a problem. I own a house in Decatur that I'll have to sell, and I don't know how long that will take."

"That shouldn't be a problem. You can put it on the market, come here to work, and when your house sells, you can go out there to finalize the deal. I'll even come work for you while you're gone."

Amy smiled and said, "Dr. Freeland, you should have been a salesman instead of a vet, did you know that?"

"Believe it or not, I almost was."

"Dr. Freeland, if I come in here, I would want to give my father-in-law plenty of notice. How much do you think would be fair?"

"Is a month enough?"

"It may be more than enough. When I tell him about coming here, he might just tell me to go ahead and leave. I don't know what he'll say. We're almost like father and daughter, and I know he'll tell me what's best for me to do. But still, I feel like I need to at least offer to work out a notice."

"I know you should, and whatever you decide, I can work around. Let me get you some papers to take with you. By the way, when are you going back to Decatur?"

"I'm going back at the end of this week. I'll be back at work next Monday."

"Amy, when do you think you'll know what you're going to do?"

"I want to talk to my father-in-law when I get back. Will sometime next week, be okay?"

"It'll be perfect."

"Well, I guess I had better go, and I'll call you next week.

I'll say this right now. I'm probably going to come in here if we can get everything worked out."

"When you all digest my proposal and the P & L statement, there won't be much to work out. Everything is here just waiting for you."

***

Max had been selling yarn for about a year or a little more, and he just loved it, and his customers loved him, too. When they found out that he was a bona fide war hero, they couldn't do enough for him. His sales figures were increasing with every report, and Pete Morris, his sales manager, couldn't be happier.

He lived at home with his parents for about three months after he got the Southern Yarns job, and finally, he found a house that he really liked. He chose a house over a condominium because of the HOA fees charged at nicer condos. He felt he would be better off getting a nice house and could afford to pay a little more payment rather than have to pay almost the same amount for condo payments and then have the HOA dues on top of that.

His territory was very large. It consisted of the states of Alabama, Georgia, Tennessee, and both Carolinas, but it wasn't as bad as it sounds. Many of his main accounts were in North Alabama, and when he worked them, he could make it home every night. The other main accounts were in central North Carolina, and while he couldn't work them and get home at night, he could work them all in two or three and sometimes four days, and he was only out two or three night a month.

Duke and Sissy had moved to Atlanta to be close to his team, the Atlanta Falcons, and that was perfect for Max. He didn't have many accounts in Georgia, and none south of Atlanta, so he could work the ones north and west of Atlanta, and most of the time have time to go by and see Sissy and Duke and then make it home that night. He always tried to make his trips to Georgia on Tuesday because that was the off day for the NFL teams. Occasionally, if they knew he was coming, they would have supper for him, or else they might go out to eat together. Theirs was a special friendship; Max and Duke from college, and Max and Sissy from childhood.

On a couple or three occasions, Duke would come through Middleton on his way to see his Mother or on his way back to Atlanta, and he would always stop to see Max.

Since Max moved out of his parent's house and into a house, he began going to a different church, because his house was on the other side of town from his parent's and the church he was raised in was close to where they lived. He had been noticing a pretty black-haired young lady sitting in the section next to where he usually sat, and she was always friendly if they had a chance to speak. Always at the morning service, they would have everybody that wanted to speak and shake hands with as many people as they could. Max made it a point, one Sunday, to walkway out of his way to speak to the pretty lady. He introduced himself and said, "Good morning. I'm Max Norwood", and she said, "Hi Max. I'm Lucy Wells."

Then, in November, on the Sunday, before the closest Sunday to Veterans Day, the pastor asked Max if he would speak to the congregation the next Sunday. Max asked him, "Are you sure? What do you want me to speak about?"

"Well, it's Veterans Day, and since you're a veteran I thought it would be interesting if you told about some of your experiences as a Marine, if they're not too uncomfortable for you to talk about. I think the people would like to hear how you felt that God was with you during some of the rough times. Are they too uncomfortable to talk about?"

"No, they're not too uncomfortable. It's just that I'm not a very good public speaker. I actually like to tell people about my experiences because, to me, it's a sure way to convince people that God is real, and that he will take care of you if you'll just let him."

"Then you'll speak Sunday?"

"Yes sir, I will."

"Oh, Max. Do you still have your dress blues?"

"Yes sir. In all their glory."

"Would you mind wearing them with any medals that you might have."

"Yes sir, I'll wear them."

When he got to church, the next Sunday and looked at the morning's program, he saw that the pastor had given him the full time that would normally be for the sermon. He thought, *man, this pastor surely doesn't know what he's doing. I can't speak that long. What am I going to talk about? My notes are only for about five or ten minutes. What will I do? Lord I hope you'll help me out on this. Thank you in advance.*

He hung around down in front of the sanctuary until the choir and the pastor came in, and the pastor shook his hand and led him up on the stage where the pulpit was located.

The service started, and Max stood up on the stage when the hymns were sung and at other times when everyone stood, and every time he looked down toward Lucy Wells, he noticed that she was staring at him. Once, he smiled at her, and she just beamed.

After the offering, the pastor read a scripture that lent itself to patriotism and the matters at hand that Sunday, and then, after he prayed, he got everyone's attention by talking a little about Max. He gave him a real nice introduction, and then he sat down. Max stood up and walked to the pulpit.

Since he hadn't been going to that church very long, he started out by introducing himself. He said, "I haven't been coming to this church very long, so most of you don't know me. I was born and raised here in Middleton, but we lived on the other side of town, and we went to the Concord Baptist Church. When I got out of high school, I went to Memphis

State University, where I played football four years and from Memphis State, I went into the United States Marine Corps and spent four years as a Marine, and that's why I'm up here this morning.

"Since Veterans Day is this week, Pastor Miller thought it would be good to have a veteran, such as myself, speak to you and maybe tell you about some of my experiences, and I'm happy to do it. I won't bore you talking about the training the Marines gave me. I'll just say it was rough and long.

"I was deployed twice to Iraq, and I've got to tell you, it was rough both times. Historically, Iraq is where many Biblical things happened, but with the radical Islamic insurgents trying to cause the problems they're causing, nobody had time to see or enjoy the history. In our case, we were just trying to stay alive. Much of the time, somebody was shooting at us, and we were happy to be able to lay down at night and know that God brought us through another day, and we hoped and prayed that He would bring us through the next day.

"One morning, my Platoon was getting ready to go out on a mission, and my Platoon Sergeant and I got in the back seat of our Humvee with two members of the Platoon up front. We had only gone a short way, when BOOM, we were blown up with an IED. In case you don't know what an IED is, it is an Improvised Explosive Device. IEDs are one of the insurgents' favorite ways to kill you. The two Platoon members in the front seat were killed instantly, and thanks to God, my Sergeant and I survived. Penny, short for Pendergrass, lost an eye and had other wounds, and I, fortunately, did not have my leg blown off. It was questionable for a while, but the doctors decided they could save it. I spent time in the hospital in Germany, and then they brought me back to the States and put me in Walter Reed Army Medical Center, where I spent the next several months. Fortunately, I got almost back to normal, and I requested that they let me go back.

"They did, and it was rougher than it was the first time."
He told about getting shot in the neck, almost getting blown
up with an RPG, and getting shot in the face. He made it a
definite point to let everybody know that God was the one who
brought him back. He finished by telling the audience that he
enjoyed telling them about some of his experiences, and he
stood there for what seemed like an hour to a standing ovation.
He then sat down, and Pastor Miller came up and said a few
words, and then he looked at Max and said, "Captain
Norwood, I'm sure everyone would like to know about your
medals. Would you mind telling us what each one is for?"

Max said, "I'd be happy to," and he stood back up and
began to point to each one. I guess some of these are not too
important, but these are the ones I'm the proudest of." He
pointed out the marksman ribbons, the infantry medal and then
said again, "These are the ones I'm the proudest of." He wore
the medals instead of the ribbons and pointed them out one by
one. "This is the Purple Heart, and these three are Oak Leaf
Clusters. You can only get one Purple Heart, and after that, if
you're wounded, you get an Oak Leaf Cluster I was wounded
four times, so I have the Purple Heart and three Oak Leaf
Clusters. This next one is the Bronze Star with the Combat V,
and this is the Silver Star, and last but certainly not least is the
Navy Cross."

Once again, the congregation stood and gave him a huge
round of applause. The whole time they were applauding, he
tried to keep his eyes on Lucy Wells, and when he looked at
her, she was staring straight into his eyes. He winked at her,
and her face turned red. After the ovation, Pastor Miller
announced the final hymn, which was the invitation. Everyone
remained standing and sang "Just as I Am," and three young
people went forward to the Altar and told the pastor that they
wanted to accept Jesus.

Max was probably more surprised than anyone to think
that maybe something he had said brought those young people

forward. Pastor Miller talked with each of them, and when he finished, Max wanted to say something to them. As he was standing there, waiting, he noticed that Lucy was leaving. He put his hands around his mouth and said in a pretty loud voice, "Lucy," and she turned around. He motioned for her to come to him, and she did. When she got to him, Pastor Miller finished talking to the three, and Max told Lucy, "Lucy, just a second, and he went over to talk to the three, and he told them that if they ever wanted to talk to him to call him. The church had his number.

He finished congratulating the young folks and turned to Lucy and said, "Thanks for waiting. How are you doing?"

"I'm doing fine. I really enjoyed your talk. I've got to tell you, that you look wonderful in your uniform."

"Thank you." Trying to be funny, he said, "It's just something I threw on."

She said, "I'm probably being too forward, but you look like a million dollars."

"Thank you again. The reason I asked you to come back is to ask you if you might like to go out to dinner with me sometime."

"I'd love to. When are you thinking about?"

"I'm thinking about Friday night. Is that good for you?"

"Yeah, or we don't have to wait until Friday, if you don't want to."

"Really? When would be good for you?"

"Actually, any night this week. How about Tuesday?"

"Tuesdays aren't good for me, but maybe Wednesday. What about Wednesday?"

"Wednesday's fine. Where are we going?"

"I don't know. I haven't had time to think about it yet. Give me your phone number, and I'll call you."

She gave him her number, and he put it in his billfold.

He had to work East Tennessee the next day, and he got home around four o'clock in the afternoon. After he had rested for a little while, he went out to grab a bite to eat, and when he got back, he tried to call Lucy, but she wasn't home.

A man answered, and Max asked, "May I speak to Lucy, please?"

"Lucy's not here. Can I take a message?"

"No, no message. My name is Max Norwood, and we met at church, and I was just trying to get in touch with her, but I'll try back later."

"Did you say Max Norwood?"

"Yeah."

"If you're the guy who spoke at church yesterday, I know she wants to talk to you because you're all she's talked about. I'm sorry, my name is Larry, and I'm Lucy's brother."

"Nice to talk to you, Larry. Tell Lucy I'll call her back."

"Please do. I know she'd want to talk to you."

"I will. Thank you."

He didn't call back that night because when he sat down, he went to sleep and slept 'til bedtime and was afraid it was too late to call when he woke up.

The next day, he went to North Georgia and stopped by Dukes when he finished working, but he didn't stay. Duke wanted him to, but he said he had to get home to call a girl he was supposed to go out with the next night.

Sissy perked up when she heard that and said, "You're going out with a girl?"

"Yeah. It's a girl I met at church. I really don't know her, but she's really pretty."

Duke smiled and said, "Well, that's all that matters, isn't it?"

Sissy came back with, "Shut up, Duke. You wouldn't know a pretty girl if you saw one."

Duke said, "I would, too. I married the prettiest girl I know."

"Yeah, right. I still love you even though you lie."

"Did you show Max our babies?"

"No, but I will right now. Come here, Max, and let me show you something."

They went to the back of the house where the laundry room was located, and just inside there was a fairly large box with Dolly, their Golden Retriever, and eight cute puppies. Max asked, "When did this happen?"

"About two weeks ago, and one of them is yours."

"Duke, I can't have a dog. What would I do with it while I'm gone, and that's a lot."

"You can take it with you. It will love riding in that big truck of yours, now, pick out the one you want. You can have the pick of the litter. Besides, you're alone and a man needs a companion."

"Alright. I'll pick one," and he examined each one carefully, noting the sex of each one.

Duke said, "If I were you, I'd get a female."

"Why?"

"Because a female will be closer to you than a male will. Whichever one you get will have to be fixed, so there should be no difference except for the emotions of the dog, and again, I'd get a female."

The litter consisted of four males and four females, and based on Duke's suggestion, Max concentrated on the females. Finally, he said, "I think this one looks like a Norwood. What do you think?"

"It's definitely a Norwood."

"Okay, I'll take this one. Are you selling them?"

"We are, but it just so happens, the one you picked out is free. That's because it's the pick of the litter."

"Are you sure?"

"I'm sure. She'll be ready for you in about four to six weeks, so be thinking of a good name for her."

"Look, I've got to go. I've got to try and call that girl I'm supposed to go out with tomorrow night."

Sissy said, "Good luck, Max. I hope you find a good

woman pretty soon. Since you're like my brother, I need for you to find me a sister-in-law."

"Okay, I'm trying."

"Maybe the one you're seeing tomorrow night will be the one."

"I doubt it, but we'll see."

They said goodbye, and Max headed home. When he got there, the first thing he did was call Lucy. She answered the phone and he said, "Lucy, Max. How're you doing?"

"I'm good. I was beginning to think you weren't going to call."

"I know. I'm sorry. Did your brother tell you I called last night?"

"He did, but you didn't call back."

"I'm sorry about that. After I hung up from your brother, I sat down to watch TV, and I went to sleep and didn't wake up until late, and I thought it was too late to call you. I've been in Georgia all day today, and I just got home. Are we still on tomorrow night?"

"Yeah. Where are we going?"

"Do you like the Depot?"

"I love the Depot."

"Okay, it's the Depot, then. Oh, do you work, Lucy?"

"Yeah, I work at Jordan Farms."

"What do you do there?"

"I'm their bookkeeper."

"Good. I was afraid you were going to say that you milked cows," and he laughed, but apparently Lucy didn't think it was funny because she didn't respond at all.

They talked for just a few more minutes and then Max got her address and told her what time he would pick her up and asked, "One more question. I drive a pickup truck. Do you mind riding in a pickup?"

"No. I drive one myself."

"Great. I'll see you tomorrow night."

He picked her up at six o'clock, and while he was at her house, she introduced him to her parents and her brother. He and Larry said they had already met on the phone, and her parents were very nice.

They left and went straight to the Depot. They both wanted to have some time to get better acquainted, so they ordered appetizers, and they knew that would give them a little more time before they had to order.

It turned out that they had a few things in common. He was twenty-eight; she was twenty-seven. He went to Memphis State; she went to Tennessee State. They both drove pickup trucks, and most importantly, they both liked the outdoors and pizza. Neither one drank, but both would take a drink if it was at the right time. They agreed that there weren't any movies playing that they were interested in seeing, and neither one had any interest in going to a club. Lucy suggested they go back to her house for a little while, and then Max could leave whenever he wanted to. The next day was a workday for both of them, so it needed to be an early night, anyway. For a first date, it turned out to be okay, and they both said they would like to go out with each other again, but no date was set. Max told her he would call her, and she thought, I hope he does, but I'm afraid *I'll never hear from him again.*

***

Amy returned to Decatur from Middleton and talked to her father-in-law, Dr. Mike Brock. When she showed him the P&L Statement from Dr. Freeland's Animal Hospital and the proposal for financing the business that he sent, all Dr. Brock could say was "WOW!!. Amy, if you don't grab this, I might. I suggest you get on the phone this minute and call Dr. Freeland and accept his offer. You'd be a fool not to."

"Well, I can't leave you so short-handed. With Neal gone, and if I leave, you'll be two people short."

"Don't worry about that. I may have that covered. Do you remember a fellow named Cory Arnold that graduated with you and Karen?"

"Yeah, I remember Cory."

"Well, he came to see me a couple of weeks ago wanting to come to work with us, and I told him we were full, but if you leave, I'll call him, and that'll take care of the situation, so don't worry. Everything is working out."

Amy said, "Dad, I'm truly filled with mixed emotions. I love you and Mom and Karen so much, I don't want to leave you, but at the same time, I'm only twenty eight, and I have a lot of life left, and the opportunity offered at home is just too good to pass up."

"We love you, too, Amy. Just as much as if you were our own, and we'll miss you terribly, but you need to take this deal. I think you need to call Bracky Robinson and have him list your house. Do you know what you want for it?"

"I don't have a clue."

"Well, it will need to be appraised, and that should give you some idea of what it's worth. Bracky can help you as well. When do you think you'll want to leave?"

"I'll have to leave before the house sells, but I can come back and close it out when it sells. As far as when I'll leave, I'm not sure. I have a lot of things to do before I go, so I'd say in about ten days to two weeks. What do you think?"

"I think two weeks would be about right. Now go in there and call Dr. Freeland and tell him you'll be there in two weeks"

She stood up and hugged Dr. Brock, and said, "I love you so much, Dad. I sure do hate to leave you."

"I hate for you to go, too, but we'll stay in touch and maybe visit a few times a year."

"I hope I can count on that."

"You can count on it. We may be there so much you'll have to run us off."

She didn't say anything to that. She gave him a really hard squeeze and then broke away and went into the office and picked up the phone.

She looked in her purse and found Dr. Freeland's phone number and dialed it. When the lady answered at Dr. Freeland's, Amy asked to speak to Dr. Freeland. The lady said, "I'm sorry, but Dr. Freeland is with a patient right now."

Amy said, "If you don't mind, would you just stick your head in the room and tell him that Amy Brock is on the phone. I'm pretty sure he won't mind."

"Hold on just a minute and let me see."

"Thank you."

Before the receptionist had time to get back to her phone, Dr. Freeland picked up. "Hi Amy. Are you coming?"

"I'm coming. My father-in-law said that if I didn't call you and accept your offer that he would call you and take it himself."

"He sounds like a very smart man."

"He is. Very smart."

"When are you coming?"

"Well, I've got quite a bit of stuff to do. I don't have to work out a notice, but I have to list my house, close bank accounts, and all the stuff that has to be done when someone is moving out of town, so we think I should be able to leave in two weeks. Does that sound alright?"

"It sounds better than alright. It sounds perfect."

They talked a few more times during the next few days, and then on Saturday, the day before two weeks was up, Amy loaded her car and left for Middleton, early. It would take her about seven and a half to eight hours to get to Middleton, and she tried to concentrate on what was ahead instead of what she left behind.

She pulled into her parents' driveway around three thirty, and she was pretty tired. She had Dr. Freeland's home phone number, and after she and her parents got her car unloaded, she called him. His wife answered, and Amy said, "Hi, Mrs. Freeland. This is Amy Brock. Is Dr. Freeland at home?"

"Hi Amy. I'm very anxious to meet you. Yes, Jack's here. Just a minute."

In a minute, he picked up and said, "Hi Amy, where are you?"

"I'm at my parents. I just wanted to let you know that I'm in Middleton. Am I to come in Monday morning?"

"Absolutely, everybody's anxious to meet you. We open at eight. Is that alright with you?"

"Yes, that's good. That's when we opened in Decatur."

She rested most of Sunday and thought about her future, and on Monday morning, she wasn't sure just how long it would take from her parents' to the clinic, so she left in plenty of time to get there without being late. She got to the clinic at seven forty-five, and there wasn't anybody there yet. She sat in her car, and at about seven fifty-five a couple of cars drove up, and then in another minute or two, a couple more arrived, and Dr. Freeland was the last one to get there. Everyone got out at the same time, but Amy waited until Dr. Freeland got out, and then she got out and walked in with him.

When they got inside, Dr. Freeland introduced everybody, and the whole staff seemed to be people that she could easily work with. Then, he took her back to the office and said, "I came down Saturday after you called and cleaned my stuff out so you'd have room for yours. What's the first thing you'd like to do, now that you're here."

She said, "You know, I think I'd like to order a sign with my name on it."

"That's a good idea. One of our clients is a sign man. Why don't I call him to come by, and then you can tell him just what you want."

"That will be good. When I was here before, you showed me everything, I think. But that's been a while, and I hope you'll go over everything with me again."

"I'll stay with you 'til you get your feet on the ground. It shouldn't take you very long, but ever how long it is, I'll be here with you."

In about an hour, Tom Berry with Berry Sign Service came and talked to Amy about what she wanted on her sign. She asked, "Did you make the sign outside now?"

He said, "Yes ma'am."

"Well, a sign like that is fine. I just want my name on it."

"Dr. Freeland asked, "How do you want it, Amy? Dr. Amy Brock?"

"No sir. I would like for it to say, 'Dr. A.H. Brock."

"Dr. A.H. Brock?"

"Yes sir."

"Okay, if that's what you want, but I can't help but wonder why."

"Well, here's why I want it that way. I found in Decatur that men accepted women vets after they got to know them or us, but if they had the choice between choosing a man or woman, a large percentage of the time they chose the male vet. If I just have my initials on the sign, they won't know if I'm a man or woman until they get here. They'll assume they're coming to see a man. Is that silly?"

Dr. Freeland said, "No, it's not silly at all. I've never thought of that," and Tom Berry said, "I don't think it's silly either. I think it's a great idea."

Chapter Eighteen

The transition from Dr. Freeland to Amy at the Middleton Animal Hospital couldn't have gone any smoother. Dr. Freeland stayed on for two weeks after Amy came in, and by the end of the first week, he and Amy could both see that it wasn't going to be necessary for him to stay the second week, but since he told Amy he would stay two weeks, he did.

Amy found out during her third week just how busy the clinic was, and without Dr. Freeland there to help her, she almost didn't have time to go to the bathroom. She began debating with herself about the pros and cons of possibly bringing in another Technician or Assistant or maybe even another veterinarian.

It didn't take her long to decide against bringing in another veterinarian, but she still felt that she may have to bring in a Technician or an Assistant, probably a Technician, since they're able to do more toward treating animals than Assistants are.

On Friday of her third week, the phone rang and her Assistant said, "Amy, there's a Bracky Robinson on line one for you. Should I take a message?"

"No, I'll take it," She went to the phone and picked up and said, "Hi Bracky, how are you doing?"

"I'm doing great, and I think you will be too. Some people have made an offer on your house, and based on the parameters you gave me, I accepted their offer. It looks as though their credit is really good, and the lender says they can have everything done on their end by the end of week after next, and they want to set Tuesday of the following week as the closing date. Do you think you can come then?"

"I can come anytime with two or three-day's notice. Do you think that will be a definite date?"

"I feel confident that if you are out here three weeks from next Monday, we can get everything done on Tuesday. Why don't you plan on that, and if there's any change, I'll call you in plenty of time."

"Would it be better if I came a week or so later?"

"No, I think that date will be good."

"Okay, but it's harder for me to plan on taking off than it used to be, so I hope you're right about this."

"I am. See you in three weeks."

There were still patients to be seen at the clinic, so she didn't call anyone when she talked to Bracky. She would have to wait until after they closed for the day.

As soon as the clinic closed and everyone had gone, Amy went into her office and called the Brock's home, thinking she would talk to whoever answered the phone.

Mrs. Brock answered, and Amy said, "Hey Mom. It's Amy. How are you doing?"

"Amy, I'm thrilled to hear your voice. I'm fine. How are you?"

"I'm fine, too. Look, the reason I'm calling is to tell you that the Realtor called me and said he sold my house, and I'll be coming to Decatur in three weeks to close it out. Do you think you might can find me a bed for a night or two?"

"I'll bet I can. When is it that you'll be here, Honey?"

"I'll be coming in on Monday, three weeks from this coming Monday."

"I can't wait to see you. How long can you stay here?"

"Well, I'm afraid not very long. We close on the house on Tuesday of that week, and I'll have to come back here on Wednesday."

"Do you have to leave that soon?"

"Yes ma'am, I'm afraid I do. We're really busy at the clinic, and I need to be here."

"Well, you know what you have to do. I'm just thankful that you'll be here for a couple of days."

"Me too. I'll see you in three weeks. Bye."

When she hung up from Mrs. Brock, she called Dr. Freeland. Mrs. Freeland answered. "Hi, Mrs. Freeland, this is Amy. Is your husband at home by chance?"

"He is. Hold on just a minute, Amy."

In a minute, he picked up. "Hi Amy. What's up?"

"The Realtor in Decatur called and said some people bought my house, and I need to go out there on Monday, three weeks from this coming Monday to close out the house on Tuesday. I'll be back on Wednesday, so I'm calling for your help, since you offered to fill in for me when I had to go back and close my house."

"I'll be more than happy to fill in while you're gone. Is that going to give you enough time?"

"I'm sure it will. I hate to be gone three days, since things are so busy around here. Maybe I can take some vacation and go out there next summer and spend a little time, if things slow down a little. I'll see you before I leave and thank you."

"You're quite welcome. Bye, Amy."

Yarn prices were getting ready to have a major price increase, and Max was trying to reach all his customers before they went up. The way customers had to work with yarn prices was to estimate how much of their product they would sell for the next several months and try to figure how much yarn it would take to make that much product.

They could book the yarn quantities ahead of the price increase and have it shipped to them as they need it. That way, they could beat any of their competitors who failed to book their yarn before the increase.

While Max travelled a lot, his normal travels didn't have to be done at break-neck speeds the way they were prior to price increases, and right then, he was staying really busy. It would take him a steady three or four weeks to cover all his customers, and he felt that he had to see them before prices went up.

He had already travelled two solid weeks, and he figured

it would take him another two weeks. On Friday of the fourth week, he finished up in Aiken, South Carolina, and after breathing a sigh of relief, he headed home by way of Atlanta. He never thought much about coincidences, but he had been thinking a lot lately about Duke and Sissy and getting his puppy. After he left Aiken, he thought that he would go get it next Tuesday, since Tuesdays were the best days to see Duke.

Actually, while he was thinking about going to get the puppy, his cell phone rang, and he answered it. "Hi Max. It's Sissy. What are you doing?"

"Would you believe that I'm almost to Atlanta on my way home?"

"Really, where have you been?"

"Around the world. No, we're getting ready to have a major price increase, and I've been travelling non-stop for the last four weeks to make sure my customers bought yarn at the old prices. I just finished up in Aiken, South Carolina, and I'm on my way home. What have you guys been doing?"

"Same old, same old. Duke wanted me to call you and tell you that your puppy is ready whenever you want to get it."

"Sissy, that's amazing. I was actually thinking about that when you called. Is that scary or what?"

"It is. When do you think you'll be down to get her?"

"Well, normally, I'm down there on Tuesdays, but since I'm only an hour or so away, why don't I run by and get her right now? Would that work?"

"It works for me. Duke should be here by the time you get here. I'll have her ready for you."

Sissy and Duke lived not too far off of I 75 on the north side of Atlanta. Max got off of I 20 onto I 75 and drove just a few miles and then got off onto the road leading to their house. He pulled in the driveway, and Duke was standing at the door, holding his puppy.

Max got out and walked up to the door and Duke handed him the puppy. It was beautiful. Sissy came out and they hugged. The dogs were registered, so they had to take a few minutes to do the paperwork, and then Max said he had to go. They found a big box for him to carry the puppy in until he got home, and he left.

Duke and Sissy highly recommended that he get the puppy spayed real soon, and he said he would; maybe next week. On his way home he wondered where he would take the puppy to have her fixed, and since he had never had a dog since he was a little boy, he didn't know. His next-door neighbor had a dog, so he would ask him the next morning. That night, he fixed up the box to be as comfortable as he could, and he put it in his bedroom next to his bed. The puppy cried when he turned off the lights. He heard somewhere that if you would put a shoe in the bed with a puppy, that it would help, so he got one of his flip-flops and put it in the box. When he turned the light on to get the flip-flop, the puppy stopped crying, and started crying again when he turned off the light, but that time, it didn't cry long. Apparently, the shoe helped.

The next morning, he took the puppy outside to play and to use the bathroom, and while he was out, his neighbor came out. "Hey Max. What you got there?"

Spontaneously, the words just came out, and he said, This is Molly." He hadn't thought too much about names up to that point, and Molly just sounded right. "Bill, I need to find a vet. Who do you use?"

"We take Jimmy to the Middleton Animal Hospital. We've used them for years, and they're very good. Do you know where they are?"

"No, but I'll find them."

"They're easy to find," and he gave Max the address. They talked a little more, and then Bill went back in the house, and in a few minutes, Max and Molly went in.

Before the morning got too late, Max put Molly in the box he brought her home in, and put the box in the laundry room and shut the door. He got in his truck and went to a strip mall he knew where they had a pet store. He went in and told the lady that he had a new, eight-week-old Golden Retriever, and asked her what he needed to get started.

She suggested a kennel, which could be used for double duty. It could serve as a bed as well as something to carry the dog in when in the car. She suggested getting one large enough for the dog when it grew up, and that way, it would be used to it from puppyhood. In addition to the kennel, she sold Max a pillow, a collar, a leash, some toys, and some treats. He was shocked when he got to the check out and found out how much he had spent.

The pet store sold him a pillow to go in the kennel, and Max did everything he could to make the puppy comfortable that night. Again, he put a flip-flop in the bed with her, and she cried for a while, and then she stopped for the rest of the night. He tried to wake up every two or three hours to take her outside, and he hoped it wouldn't take too long to housebreak her.

First thing, Monday morning, he called the Middleton Animal Hospital and told them he needed to have his puppy spayed, and he asked if they could do it that day. They told him that the regular vet was out of town, and she would have to see if the fill in vet could do it. In a minute, she came back and told Max that he could bring Molly in at ten thirty if he wanted to, so he took her then. When he got to the animal hospital, he saw the sign out front with the name Dr. A.H. Brock, and he thought, *A.H. Brock. That name sounds familiar.*

When he got inside, they told him that Molly would be ready to go home around three o'clock, and Max asked if they would keep her overnight, and they agreed to do it. He told them he would pick her up the next day, so on Tuesday afternoon he picked her up and took her home with him. She didn't act as if she felt very well, but she tried to love him when he got close to her, and he thought, *I guess if I had my music taken out, I wouldn't feel good either.*

In the meantime, Amy had arrived in Decatur on Monday, and she was scheduled to close on her house on Tuesday.

Even though she called ahead and told Mrs. Brock when she'd be there, Mrs. Brock failed to mention, nor did any of the other Brocks call to say they would meet her at the airport. In the absence of those offers, she decided that she would just rent a car because that would probably be the easiest. If she rented a car, then she could come and go as she pleased without having to depend on someone to take her, and she wouldn't disrupt anyone's schedule or routine.

The plane landed at one forty-five, and Amy was on her way to the baggage claim when a familiar voice said, "Hey, Mrs. Brock."

She turned and it was Karen. The two had a happy reunion and Amy said, "I sure am glad to see you, but you didn't have to come meet me. I was going to rent a car."

Karen said, "That would have been foolish. We have plenty of cars, and you can use mine while you're here."

Amy asked, "How will you get around if I have your car?"

"I'll use the clinic's van. That's no problem."

"Okay, if you say so. Thank you."

Karen asked, "Where do you want to go now?"

"To the house, I guess. I don't have to be at the closing until in the morning."

"Would you like to go by the clinic and see everybody?"

"Yeah, that would be great."

Karen took her to see everybody at the clinic, and then, Amy took Karen's car and went to the Brock's. She had time to rest after her trip, and it wasn't too long until Dr. Brock and Karen got home from work. Mrs. Brock had cooked a delicious meal in the slow cooker while she was at bridge club that afternoon, and it wasn't too long before dinner was served.

It was like old times around the dinner table, except it wasn't an old time. Dr. Brock wanted to know how Amy was doing with her new Animal Hospital, and she filled him in with all the details.

The next day, she met Bracky Robinson at the mortgage

lenders place, and they went in together. After the obligatory small talk was over, they began to hand out papers that Amy as well as the buyers had to sign. It seemed as if there were at least a hundred of them, but of course, there weren't. Finally, it came time to give Amy the money, and they asked her if she wanted a check or if she wanted them to wire transfer it to her bank account. Bracky suggested she have them wire transfer it because it would not be safe for her to carry a check around with her, especially a check in that amount, so she agreed to have it wired.

That ended the business with the house, and afterwards, Amy thanked the people for buying her house, she thanked Bracky for selling it, and she thanked the lenders. She gathered up all her papers and left to go back to the Brock's.

The house was empty when she got there, so she fixed herself a cup of tea and thought about her house. A question came to her when the lender mentioned how much money she was getting wired to her bank because he had no idea she was going to get that much. She did some figuring while she drank her tea. She knew what she and Neal paid for the house, and she knew how much she sold it for, but the proceeds were much more than she thought they would be. When she put it all on paper, she came out with twenty-five thousand dollars more than she expected. The only thing she could think of to come out with that much money was if Neal's Daddy had put it in when they financed the house when they bought it. She knew that she and Neal didn't have that much more to pay down, so Dr. Brock must have done it.

She will try and get him by himself ask him that night, and if he says he did, she'll thank him. She thought maybe she should offer to pay him back.

That evening, the whole Brock family was there for dinner, even Karen. That was two nights in a row that Karen was there, and when Amy asked her about it, she told her she didn't date those two nights because she was there, and she wanted to be with her. Amy never did get the chance to ask

Dr. Brock about the money, because there was always somebody around, but she wouldn't forget it. Maybe she would call him after she got home.

Dr. Brock and Karen were tired after a very busy day at the clinic, and pretty soon after dinner, Dr. Brock excused himself and went to bed, followed by his wife in a couple of minutes. Karen and Amy stayed up for a while, talking, and then, in a little while they turned it.

The next morning, Karen took Amy to the airport to catch the plane to Middleton. The two close friends said goodbye, and both of them cried and promised to stay in touch, and they hoped they could visit each other in the not too distant future.

On the plane, Amy did a lot of thinking. The first thing she thought about was where was she going to buy a place to move. She debated with herself about a condominium versus a house. She told herself that with the extra money she came out with on her house in Decatur, she could afford pretty much what she wanted. She would just have to find what she wanted. She had always wanted to live on the lake, and that would be where she would start looking.

She got to the clinic about fifteen minutes before they opened, and there were already people with their pets waiting on them to open. The rest of the staff got there about five minutes ahead of time, and Amy told them to go ahead and open the doors. They operated on a first come, first served basis, except for people who called ahead and made an appointment. Surgeries were always done by appointment, and that morning, no one had an appointment for anything, and that was the way the entire day went. Busy, busy, busy.

They told Max that Molly needed to have a series of shots from then until she was about sixteen weeks old, and since he didn't usually work on Fridays, he took her Friday morning to get her what they called a DHPP, which covered multiple illnesses as well as parvovirus. There were several people in the waiting room, waiting to have their pets treated, and when it was Max's turn, a technician came out and got Molly and took her to the back where she would get her shot. In a little while, he brought her back out and said she did good.

When Max went up to pay, he asked the lady at the desk if the vet ever saw the animals. All he had ever seen were who they called technicians. "Oh yes," she said. "In fact; she's probably the one who gave Molly her shot. She is so busy that she doesn't have time to come out to get the pets. That's why we have Technicians. Do you need to see her this morning?"

"No, it's just that I haven't seen a vet except for the guy who spayed her, and I was just wondering about it. No, I don't need to see her."

"Mr. Norwood, the shot this morning brings Molly up to date. Now, all she lacks is her rabies vaccination. Do you want to bring her next Friday for that?"

"I can. Next week, how about making my appointment late in the afternoon. I'm going to be out of town all week, and it will be hard to get here early."

"Would you rather come Saturday?"

"You're open on Saturday? Yeah, if you're open, that would be better for me."

"How about at noon on Saturday?"

"Sounds good. I'll see you next Saturday."

The next week was the week when Max had to stay out most of the week. He had to work North Carolina, and it took him until Thursday evening to finish up. The North Carolina week was always a tiresome week, and after getting home around nine o'clock Thursday night, he spent most of the day Friday resting.

He took Molly with him, and she did great. She loved her kennel and stayed in it most of the time while they were riding. Sometimes Max would call her to come up front with him, and she would lay her head on his leg as he drove. She stayed in her kennel while Max was inside with a customer, and if the weather was too hot or too cold, he would leave the motor running with the heat or air conditioning on. When riding, he would stop every two hours or so to let her out to use the bathroom, and it was surprising at how fast she learned not to use the bathroom in the pickup. It was the same at home. He would take her out every couple of hours, and she rarely used the bathroom in the house.

The appointment to get her rabies vaccination was at noon, so he left in plenty of time to get there without being late. He pulled into the parking lot a few minutes before twelve, and there were hardly any cars in the lot. He and Molly got out of the pickup and went in. He registered with the lady at the counter, and in a few minutes a male Technician came to get Molly. In about five minutes the door from the back opened and a lady was carrying Molly. Max only half-looked at her until she said, "I can't believe this. Hi Max."

Max looked into her face, and he saw a smiling Amy. "Amy, what are you doing here?"

She said, "This is my clinic."

"Are you serious? The sign outside say Dr. A.H. Brock. Who's that?"

"That's me. Amy Hatcher Brock."

"I thought you were living in Illinois."

"I was until my husband passed away, and then I moved back here."

"Your husband died?"

"Yeah. He had a heart attack."

"I'm sorry, Amy."

"Thank you. I thought you were in the Marines."

"I was until I got hurt, and they kicked me out. I'm living here now, and I'm selling yarn. I'm covering five states."

Appearing concerned, she asked, "You got hurt?"

"Yeah, several times."

"How?"

"I went to Iraq twice, and I got hurt over there both times. Sometime when we have time, I'll tell you about it, if you'd like to hear it."

"I definitely would like to hear it."

"Where are you living?"

"Right now, I'm living with my parents, but I'll be buying a place down here soon, and I'll move out on my own. Where are you living?"

"I bought a house," and he gave her the name of the section. "You'll have to come see it sometime."

"Maybe I will."

"I sure wish you would."

Amy said, "Look, I've got get back in there. Where are you going to be later today?"

"I'll just be hanging around the house."

She asked, "Would you like to go somewhere for dinner? My treat."

"Absolutely, I've been wanting to go to dinner with you for the last ten years." He reached in his pocket for a business card and handed it to her. "Call me."

"Okay, I'll call you around four or five o'clock. We're open here 'til then."

Max said, "You'll call me for sure, won't you?"

"I'll call for sure. It's wonderful to see you, and I can't wait 'til tonight."

Max went home and picked up and dusted everywhere just in case Amy would come over that night. He wanted to show her that he was a good housekeeper and not a sloppy somebody. He sat in the den and threw a ball for Molly until they both got tired, and then they both took a short nap.

At five o'clock, his phone rang. It was Amy. "Hi Amy."

"What are you doing?"

"Just waiting on your call. Are you through working?"

"Yeah. I've just locked the door. Do you still want to go get something to eat?"

"I definitely do. Is there anywhere special that you'd like to go to?"

"Not really. Somewhere where it's fairly quiet, and where we can talk."

"Do you like Ryan's?"

"I love Ryan's"

"Why don't we go there?"

"That sounds good. Do you want me to come by and pick you up?"

Surprised, Max hesitated for a minute, and then said, "Well, yeah, that will be great, or I can come get you."

"No, I'll pick you up. I want to see your house."

"Okay, I'll look for you. What time?"

"Well, it's after five now, and I'm still at the clinic, so why don't I just come on now. It'll be close to six when I get there. Is that too early?"

"It's not for me. Hurry, I'm anxious to see you."

"Okay, I'll see you in a few."

Max went into the bathroom and shaved real quick, brushed his teeth and hair and changed his shirt. No sooner had he done that than his doorbell rang. He went to the door, and there stood Amy, the most beautiful sight he had ever seen. He opened the storm door, and she came in and looked all around. She said, "Max, this is really nice," and the whole time she was standing there, Molly was nibbling on her shoe.

She acted as though she was comfortable, and Max became a little uneasy. He asked, "Do you want to go to Ryan's now or would you rather visit for a little while first?"

"We can go to Ryan's later. We haven't seen each other in forever, so why don't we just stay here and talk for a while?"

"That sounds great to me. Here, let me have your jacket."

He had a sofa and two recliners in his den, and she sat in one of the recliners and he sat in the other. She looked at Max and said, "Well, where do we start?"

Max said, "Why don't you start with when you left for U.T.?"

"Okay, I will. You know that from the time we were very young that I wanted to be a veterinarian, remember?"

"Yeah, I remember."

"Well, after high school, I went to Knoxville and finished my four years in three. Then, from Knoxville, I went to Champaign, Illinois where I enrolled in the University of Illinois School of Veterinary Medicine. I had a roommate there named Karen Brock, and we became very close. Her Daddy has a veterinary hospital down in Decatur, Illinois, and she would go down there every Friday and work in the clinic, and after the first week, I started going down there with her and worked with her. Her brother, Neal was also a student at U.I., and I was thrown with him all the time. He was two years ahead of Karen and me.

"After a couple of years, Neal and I began to have feelings for each other, and during the summer between my junior and senior year, we got married and moved to Monticello, Illinois which is midway between Decatur and Champaign. After I graduated, Neal and I bought a house in Decatur and moved down there. He was also a vet as is Karen. It was kind of funny. After Karen and I graduated with our Doctorates, there were four Dr. Brocks at the Brock Animal Hospital. A little over a year ago, Neal had a heart attack and died, and I lived alone in our house until about a month or so ago, when I had the chance to get the Middleton Animal Hospital, and I moved down here. I didn't dream I'd find you here. I thought you had vanished. Okay, it's your turn."

"Where do you want me to start?"

"Same place. When we got out of high school."

"Well, I was lucky enough to get a football scholarship to Memphis State University, and I played for Memphis State for four years. My first two years were awful because I was still mourning for you, and I didn't think I'd ever get over you, and I actually never did. You can't imagine how thrilled I am right now, sitting here with you."

Amy said, "Tell about after Memphis State."

"Okay. While I was at Memphis State, I enrolled in the NROTC, and being in the Navy ROTC, I had to commit to four years of service when I graduated. I chose the Marines, and as soon as I got out of college, I was inducted into the Marines as a Second Lieutenant."

Amy said, "Didn't you get engaged somewhere along the line?"

"Oh yeah, I forgot about that. She was a volleyball player for Memphis, and I thought I loved her, and I gave her a ring. She didn't want to get married with me going into the Marines, and while I was in basic training, she sent me a Dear John Letter, and you know what, Amy? It didn't even bother me, so I must not have loved her. Now, where was I?"

"You were talking about being inducted into the Marines."

"Oh yeah. After college, I was inducted, and I had to spend months in training. After I had been in for a few months, they sent me to Iraq, and you can't believe how Iraq is unless you're over there. You spend time with people you think want to be your friend, and then, if you turn your back, they'll try to kill you.

"One morning, our Platoon was going out on a mission, and my Platoon Sergeant, Penny Pendergrass and I got into the back seat of our Humvee with two other members of our Platoon in the front. We started to roll, and we hadn't gone hardly any distance until we ran over what they call an IED. It exploded, and the two guys in the front seat were killed instantly, and Penny and I were badly hurt.

"Penny lost one eye and had other wounds, and I had a broken arm and leg and different wounds with my leg being the worst. For several days, they kept talking about amputating it, and I told them that they were not going to cut my leg off. Finally, a different doctor came in and said he thought he could save it, and he did. I spent time in the hospital in Germany before being brought to Walter Reed Army Medical Center in Bethesda, Maryland. My leg kept improving, and I asked to go back to Iraq, and they finally let me.

"The second time was worse than the first time as far as

my health was concerned. That time, I got wounded three times, and I spent the better part of a year at Walter Reed. They wouldn't send me back, and I was not in good enough shape to be a regular Marine any longer, so they cut me loose, and here I am; back in good old Middleton, talking to my first love. Are you hungry yet?"

"Not yet. I had no idea that you were hurt. I wish you had gotten word to me."

"Why? What could you have done?"

"Nothing, I suppose. I guess I could have worried about you."

"Are you serious? Would you have worried about me, even though you were married?"

"I would have. I was married, but I never lost the feelings I had for you."

Amy stood up and walked over to a small display case that Max had set up to showcase his medals. "Are these what you got when you were in the Marines?"

"Yep, they are."

"Tell me what they're for."

Max went to the display and pointed them out, one by one. She said, "I guess that makes you a hero, doesn't it?"

"I don't know. Some people say I am, but I don't look at it that way. I just feel that I was a guy that did his job."

"You must have done it well," and she turned to him and gave him a quick kiss on the lips, and then said, "I'm getting hungry. Are you?"

"I was until you gave me that kiss, now I don't know what I am."

She said, "Come on, let's go to Ryan's."

"Wait just a minute. Let me take Molly out before we go," and she did just what she was supposed to do when he took her outside.

He offered to drive, but Amy said, "No, I'll drive. I told you that tonight is my treat, and that includes driving to the restaurant."

Max said, "I like your take charge attitude."

On the way to Ryan's, Amy asked, "Where did you get Molly?"

"Sissy and Duke gave her to me."

"Really? I haven't seen Sissy since she came to Decatur to be in my wedding. I need to call her, now that I'm back."

"You know they're living in Atlanta, don't you?"

"No, I didn't know that." The conversation slowed down as they neared the restaurant.

When they got to Ryan's and went inside, Max asked the Hostess, "Do you have a table in the back or in a corner where we can talk. We're playing catch up after ten years."

The hostess said, "I've got just the place. Follow me," and she led them to a spot in the restaurant that was just perfect.

When they were waiting on someone to wait on them, they talked. Amy said, "You said that sissy and Duke gave you Molly. Do you see them pretty often?"

"Yeah, pretty often. Duke is off on Tuesdays, and I try to plan my trips to where I can get by there on Tuesdays, and sometime, they'll have me over to eat or else, we'll go out, but I get to see them fairly often. While I was still at Walter Reed, the President of the United States gave me some medals, and I invited them to come to the ceremony, and they came up for that. They got to meet the President, and they loved that."

Amy asked, "Are you seeing anyone?"

"No. I think I've had one date since I got home over a year ago."

"Why? Don't you like girls?"

"Yeah, I like girls, but I haven't been able to find anybody like you, I guess. Did you say you're going to buy a house?"

"I think so. I closed on my house in Decatur earlier this week, and I liked living in a house. We lived in an apartment for a year before I graduated, and I like a house best."

"Do you know where you're going to buy?"

"Not at this point. I think I'd like to find a place on the

lake, but I may not be able to afford one. I really haven't had a chance to look yet, but now that I've sold my house in Decatur, I'm going to start looking in earnest. I don't want to have to keep living with Mother and Daddy."

Remembering his experiences with her parents, Max said, "I can understand that."

She said, "They're not too bad. They've changed for the better since you last saw them."

"I may go out to the lake tomorrow to see if there's anything for sale out there. Would you like to go with me?"

"Amy, I'd go around the world with you."

She smiled and said, "I can't go that far right now, but maybe we can plan a trip for later."

He looked at her as if he could eat her up, and said, "I hope we can."

The waitress came and asked if they would like to order something to drink, and Amy said she would like a glass of white wine, and of course, Max said he would like one, too."

"Amy, I know you have just taken over Middleton Animal Hospital, so what are your plans for it. Are you going to keep it as it is, or do you want it to get bigger, or what are you looking at?"

"I probably won't try to get any bigger, but I might have to bring in another vet to help. Dr. Freeland started the clinic about forty years ago, and he built a huge business, and now, with me going in and having a whole different set of friends with pets on top of what's already there, I may not be able to handle all the business myself without getting some help. Does that make sense?"

"It makes perfect sense. I know you're going to do very well."

She asked him, "Do you think you'll keep selling yarn forever?"

He laughed and said, "I don't know about forever, but for the foreseeable future, I probably will. Without getting too deep in finances, I make good money selling yarn, good money plus I get a nice pension from the government for the rest of my life. If I had to, I could live comfortably on my pension, but with my yarn income on top of that, I'm doing very well."

"Well, that's good. I won't have to worry about you, will I?"

"There you go talking about worrying about me again. Sweetie, you don't have to worry about me. I'm good."

They finished their food, which was delicious, and they talked a little longer, and then they left Ryan's and headed back toward Max's. Max figured Amy would let him out, and he would see her again, later, but that was not the way it unfolded.

Amy pulled in the driveway, and Max opened the door, intending to go around and tell her goodnight, but instead, she opened her door and got out and met him as he got to the front of the car. She took his hand and led him to the front door. They went in, and she sat down on the loveseat and patted the seat for him to sit down next to her.

He sat down beside her and she looked into his face and said, "Max, today has been a complete, wonderful surprise, and I'm so happy to be with you. I hope we can continue to see each other because I truly believe that we're sort of joined at the hip. It might be funny to say after being apart for so long, but Max, I love you, and I guess I always have."

Max went into shock when she said that. He told her, "I know I've always loved you, and I'm going to promise you and myself that I'll never lose you again. Now that we've found each other again, I hope we can start planning our future together."

She said, "I'd like that. I hope we can."

She got up and started to leave, but Max grabbed her and kissed her like he hadn't done in more than ten years. After the kiss, they remained embraced for a long time, and Amy said, "Did you say you'd like to go out to the lake and look for houses, tomorrow?"

He said, "Yeah, I'd like to go. Why don't you go to church with me in the morning, then we can grab some lunch and spend as much time at the lake as you want."

"Okay. Do you want me to pick you up?"

"You can, or I can pick you up."

"I'll come get you. What time?"

"Be here at ten forty. Church starts at eleven."

"Okay, I'll be here then. I've got to go. Give me a kiss."

They kissed again, and she left.

Chapter Nineteen

Amy was right on time Sunday morning, and she and Max went to church together. Not much was said on the way, and Max asked, "Are you okay, Amy?"

"Yeah, why?"

"Because you don't have much to say. I thought you might feel bad."

"No, I'm fine. I just didn't get very much sleep last night."

"Me neither. I bet I didn't sleep two hours."

"What was wrong?"

"Nothing. I was just excited about you and me, and if today goes like I hope it will, I probably won't sleep tonight either. Why didn't you sleep?"

"Same reason. You know, Max, my Mother and Daddy cost us about ten years of happiness just because I fell in love with you when I was seventeen and not eighteen. Do you think we can make that up?"

"I don't know, but we can sure try if you want to."

"Well, I want to. Max, am I being too forward?"

"Honey, you can't be forward to me. No, you're not being forward. We've always been able to say anything to each other without worrying about being forward or anything else. I like to hear your thoughts."

They went to church, and then came the decision on where to eat lunch. Both told the other it didn't matter to them where they went, and finally, Max asked, "Do you still like the Steak and Shake?"

"I love it. I haven't been there in forever. Let's go get a burger and shake."

They both ordered cheeseburgers, fries, and a chocolate milkshake and loved every bite. While they were eating, Max asked, "Did you tell your parents where you were last night?"

"I did."

"What did they say?"

"They didn't say anything, except, they did ask how you are doing. They know I'm grown, now, and I'm even a doctor, and they can't have anything to say about anything I do or anybody I want to see.

Finishing lunch, they headed to the lake with no destination in mind. All they knew was they wanted to see if there were any places for sale that they liked and felt like they could afford. The first section they went to was an older section, in fact, it was probably one of the first neighborhoods to be built on the lake. There was one house for sale, but they both agreed that it was too dated, and it would cost too much to get it to where they wanted it.

In the next section they went to, there was a huge, beautiful home with manicured grounds that had a for sale by owner sign out front. They stopped and looked at it and wrote down the phone number and address. Four doors up was another very nice home with a Realtor's sign with the Realtor's name and phone number. They wrote it down, also. For the whole afternoon, they took numbers for five homes, and decided to go back to Max's and call about them.

Then, it was decided that maybe they were moving too fast, and they should sit down and talk about what they were going to do before they went any further. When they got back to Max's, Max opened a couple of Cokes and brought out some peanuts, and they sat down at the table and began to talk about what they had seen that afternoon. Max said, "Amy, Honey, I think before we even think about buying a house, we need to decide when we're going to get married, where we're going to get married, and all those things. This only came up last night, so you probably haven't thought too much about it, but I think it needs to be thought about before we go too far with a house. What do you think?"

"I think you're right. Let's talk about getting married first.

What are your thoughts about that?"

"I just want to marry you. I doubt you will want to go to a Justice of the Peace, since we went that route before, however, that would probably work this time. Since you've been married before, do you want to go through a church wedding again?"

"No. I would just like to have your parents and mine and maybe Sissy and Duke, and of course, my brother, Stevie. Where would we do something like that?"

"You know, I've heard of couples getting married in the Pastor's study or in a little chapel in their church, if they have one. Maybe we could do something like that. What do you think?"

"I don't have a church. Do you think if we decide to do that that your church would let us have the wedding there, and do you think your Pastor will do it?"

"I feel sure we can, and I know our Pastor will perform the ceremony."

"Well, why don't we do that?"

"The next question is when."

"That could be a problem. I've only been at my clinic a little over a month, and I don't know if I can take off very long right now."

"Honey, why would you have to take off? We can take a honeymoon later. Let's look at the calendar and see if there are any long weekends, and maybe we can get married then."

"That's a good idea. Maybe we can do that. The first thing that comes to my mind is Easter. I think we're closed on Good Friday and Saturday before Easter."

"Okay, we'll figure out a date. Now the next important thing. When are we going to tell our parents?"

"We can do that whenever you want to. I'd like for you to be with me when I tell mine. Okay, I will, and I want you with me when I tell mine."

"Do you want to do it next week?"

"Any time you say."

Max said, "We can do it tonight, if you want to, at least, we can tell mine. Tell you what. Let's go get something to eat and then we'll go out and tell them. You want to?"

"Yeah. Let's do it."

They stopped at a neighborhood restaurant on the way to his parent's house and got some home cooked vegetables. While they were eating, Max said, "I hate to have to bring up this touchy subject, but if we're going to get married, and if we're going to buy a house, we need to know how much money we have, and how much we can count on each month. I have several thousand dollars put back from bonuses I got when I got wounded, and I get close to a hundred thousand dollars a year pension. My yarn commission is never the same, but I can pretty safely count on making at least a hundred and fifty thousand dollars a year, making my total annual income around two hundred and fifty thousand dollars. Do you care to tell me what you make?"

"I'm set up to earn three hundred thousand dollars a year, but in my contract with Dr. Freeland, I have to pay him a hundred thousand dollars a year for ten years, so actually, I'm only bringing in two hundred thousand, less taxes. Now, if I do more business, I'll make more, but we can count on two hundred grand."

"You know, Honey, with nearly a half million dollars a year, we should be able to buy any house we want."

She said, "You'd think. You know, getting married this time is a lot different than the first time, isn't it."

"In a way. The circumstances are a lot different, but the feelings are the same, aren't they?"

With that, they got up and paid the check and headed toward Max's parent's house. Max knocked and opened the door at the same time, and his parents acted really glad to see them, but they were surprised to see Amy. They hadn't seen her since she and Max broke up in high school. They always liked her and they were happy to see her. Max's Daddy said, "You all sit down. Amy, I'm glad to see you. It's been a long time. How've you been?"

"I've been good. I'm glad to see you all, too."

Max said, "Listen, you two, the reason we came by tonight is to tell you some news. Amy and I have decided to get married."

His Mother said, "WHAT?"

"We're going to get married."

His Daddy said, "Boy, this is a sudden thing, isn't it?"

Max said, actually, it's been over ten years coming."

His Mother said, "I don't understand."

Max said, "Let me tell you a story, and then you'll understand. You remember, of course, that Amy and I dated in high school, and we were pretty serious."

His Mother said, "Yes, I remember that. We always liked you, Amy."

Max said, "Let me finish my story. One week when we had an open date in football, Amy and I decided we wanted to get married, so we went to Ringgold and got a Justice of the Peace to marry us. We were going to keep it a secret 'til school was out and we had graduated, but her parents found out about it, and since she was only seventeen at the time, her Daddy had the marriage annulled and wouldn't let us see each other anymore.

"We both went off to college after graduation, and we haven't seen each other but a handful of times since then. Recently, circumstances brought her back to Middleton as they did me, and we found each other accidentally the other day, and we knew the old feelings were still there. We talked and decided that we would get married again, and this time, nobody could undo it, and we wanted you to be the first to know, and we hope you're happy about it."

His Daddy said, "We're definitely happy about it, right Mother?"

"Definitely."

His Daddy hugged Amy and shook Max's hand, and his Mother hugged them both. Max noticed they both hugged Amy first, and he took that as a good sign. They couldn't give any details because they didn't know themselves, but they promised to tell them as soon as they knew. They visited for a while longer and then said they had to leave. Amy said she had to get up early and needed to get home and get to bed. Max was going to upper east Tennessee the next day, and while he didn't have to get up that early, he said he needed to get home to let his dog out, and that was another surprise to his parents.

As they were leaving, his Daddy said, "We're sure glad you all came by, and we're tickled that you're going to get married, and Max, come back and bring your Mother and I up to date on what else is happening in your life. We didn't even know you had a dog."

"I will. I'll come back when we have details on our wedding."

On the way back to Max's, Amy said, "Max, I can easily get to love your parents. I forgot how nice they are."

"Good for you. You know, I'm scheduled to go up to east Tennessee tomorrow, but I don't think I'll go. I think I'll go, instead, to talk to the Pastor about marrying us."

"Well, you don't know when to tell him."

"I know, but I'd like to talk to him just the same, and whenever we get a chance, I want you to meet him. Now, the next question. When are we going to tell your parents?"

"Whenever you want to. I wish we didn't even have to tell them."

"I thought you said they've changed."

"They have, but they're still kind of hard to deal with, but you know what, Max? They sent me to school and saw that I always had what I needed, so they must love me."

"I'm sure they do. Let's you and I do what we have to do to make them happy."

"I love you. Do you know that?"

"I know you do. I love you too."

They arrived at Max's and Amy didn't get out. She said she needed to get home to go to bed because she had surgery early the next morning. They kissed goodnight and said they would talk to each other the next afternoon.

Max changed his mind about canceling his trip to upper east Tennessee and went up there as originally planned. He did call Pastor Miller to tell him about he and Amy wanting to get married and made an appointment for both of them to see him. The Pastor was always at the church on Wednesday night, so they made the appointment for eight o'clock Wednesday night, after Bible Study."

He got back to town around three thirty and sat down to rest. The phone rang at four thirty and it was Amy. "Hi, how long have you been home?"

"Oh, about an hour. Have you had a good day?"

"Yeah. It's been a busy day, but a good one. Do you want me to come over when I get off?"

"I'd love for you to. What are we going to do for dinner?"

"Anything you want to do. We can go out or I can pick up something on the way over."

"Let's go out. Is that okay?"

"That's fine. I should be there a little after six."

"I can't wait."

"Me neither."

"Listen, you haven't talked to Sissy have you?"

"No, I haven't talked to Sissy since I've been back from Decatur, why? Actually, I don't think I've talked to her since her wedding, and that's been over two years."

"Well, tomorrow's Tuesday, and Duke is off, and he's probably at home tonight. I thought we'd call him and Sissy, and if you agree, I'd like to invite them to the wedding."

"That would be great. I'm glad you thought about it."

"You won't believe how close the three of us have become

in the last couple of years. None of us do hardly anything without including the other."

"I had no idea. I think that's wonderful. I've got to go. I'll see you in a little bit. I love you."

"Love you too."

Amy pulled in Max's driveway and honked her horn. Max came out and got in the shotgun seat, and they headed to a restaurant to eat dinner. While they were at the restaurant. Max asked, "Have you thought any more about when we're going to get married?"

"I have, but I haven't come up with anything. Have you?"

"Yeah, I have, and I want to talk to you about that. I've gone over the calendar about half a dozen times, and there just aren't any long weekends that are suitable, and I got to thinking. You mentioned that Dr. Freeland said he would work for you if you need to be gone, and I think when we get married, you'll need to be gone. What do you think?"

"I really haven't thought about that. That's a great idea. When do you want to do it?"

"How about Memorial Day weekend. Most things are closed on Memorial Day, which is on Monday, and we could get married on the Saturday before. That way we could have Saturday through Monday off, and if you can ger Dr. Freeland to work for you the rest of that week, we can have almost ten days for a honeymoon."

"When is Memorial Day?"

"It's always the last weekend in May. What do you think?"

"I think that might work., except I think Memorial Day itself should be the day. The clinic is open on Saturday, and I feel that I should be there instead of having to ask Dr. Freeland to fill in for me too long. If you agree, I'll mention it to him tomorrow. And while we're talking about Dr. Freeland, I'd like to invite him and his wife to our wedding. Do you mind?"

"No, I don't mind." He grinned and said, "The more the merrier."

Her hand was on the table, and he grabbed it and said, "I can't wait to get you in bed," and she said, "Me too."

Max said, "Well, if we do it on Memorial Day weekend, we won't have that long to wait."

Amy said, "Well, I don't guess we have to wait 'til Memorial Day, do we?"

He said, "Yes, we definitely do."

"Why? Most men wouldn't want to wait. It's not like this would be the first time for us."

"I know, but we were married the first time, remember?"

"I've thought about that night for the last ten years. I'll always remember it, but why do you want to wait?"

"Remember me telling you how God brought me through the Iraq ordeals? I told Him that if He would just bring me back home safely, that I would do everything I could to honor Him and obey Him, and the Bible says we shouldn't commit adultery or fornication, and while I'm not sure what the difference is in the two, I know that God says they're both wrong, and I'm not going back on my word to Him. I hope you'll respect that."

Amy said, "Even in high school you had integrity, and I guess that's one of the reasons I've always loved you. Of course, I'll respect that, but you know what? I'll bet there will be a huge explosion wherever we are on Memorial Day night."

"I'll bet there will be too, and we need to decide where that will be. Any ideas?"

Max said, "If you're through, let's go to my house. I want to call Duke and Sissy."

"Oh yeah, I nearly forgot."

They went back, and Max picked up the phone and dialed Duke and Sissy's number. Sissy answered. Max didn't have to tell her who it was. She knew. He said, "What are you doing?"

"We just got in from eating out. What are you doing?"

"I wanted to tell you something. Remember a while back you told me that if I'm going to be like your brother, that I need to find you a sister-in-law?"

"Yeah, I remember that."

"Well, Baby, I've found you a sister-in-law."

She squealed and yelled at Duke and said, Max is getting married. Pick up the phone."

Duke picked up and joked, "Max, have you lost your mind? Who is this jewel? Do we know her?

Max said, "Hold on just a minute, and I'll let you speak to her."

He held the phone out and Amy took it and said, "Hey guys. What are you doing?"

Silence, then in a few seconds, Sissy said, "Amy, is that you? Where are you, in Decatur?"

"No, I'm in Middleton. I'm sorry I didn't call and tell you, but Neal died some over a year ago, and I came back home."

Sissy said, "I'm not believing this. Max you didn't say anything about this when you came after your puppy."

"I didn't know. I took the puppy to the vet for her shots and everything, and the vet turned out to be Amy. We didn't have to go through a courting process. Within a day or two, we knew we had to be together, and as it stands right now, we're going to get married Memorial Day, and we hope you guys will come."

Sissy said, "We wouldn't miss it."

Amy asked Sissy, "Sissy, will you be my Maid of Honor—again?"

"I'd love to."

Max said, "Duke, I'm going to get off of here and let these women talk, so I'll see you later."

"Okay. Buddy, and congratulations."

Amy stayed 'til almost ten o'clock, then she said she had to go and get to bed, because she had an early morning, but before she left, Max asked, "When are we going to tell your parents?"

She said, "Oh brother. I think I'll just let you tell them,

without me being there."

"Oh no, you won't. You said they've changed. We're going to see how much; now when are we going to tell them?"

"How about Thursday night? We have to meet with the preacher tomorrow night."

"Okay, Thursday night it is. You're not going to get drunk first, are you?"

"That's a good idea. I may do that. Kiss me goodnight and give me some courage."

They kissed goodnight and said they would talk the next day.

The next evening, they didn't do anything. Amy had had a hard day and didn't feel like doing anything. They ordered pizza in and after they ate it, Amy told Max that she just wanted to go home and go to bed, and he didn't try to talk her into staying, because he knew how it was to be tired after working hard.

Amy wasn't as exhausted the next day as she was the day before, and they were anxious to talk to Pastor Miller. They didn't get to the church in time for Bible study, and they waited in the outer hall of the sanctuary until Bible study was over, and then they went in and found the Pastor. Max spoke to a lot of the people when he got inside the sanctuary, and after everyone had left, Pastor Miller said, "Let's go back to my study where we can talk," and he led them back to his office where Max introduced him to Amy.

When they had sat down, the Pastor said, "Max, did you say you two want to get married here, and you want me to do the ceremony?"

"Yes sir. That's what we would like."

The Pastor asked them several questions, and when he was satisfied that Amy and Max were both believers, he consented to do the service. They discussed the dates and the location in the church, and before they left, Pastor Miller said, "Max, I hope you're going to wear your dress blues. Are you?"

Max answered and said, "You know, I haven't even thought about that. I don't know. I'm not in the Marines anymore, you know."

"Well, I've always heard that once you're a Marine, you're always a Marine. A lot of ex-servicemen wear their uniforms when they get married, and this might seem funny, coming from a man, but I thought you looked so spectacular the morning you spoke at the Veterans Day service, I would personally like to see you wear it again. Amy, have you seen him in his dress blues?"

"No sir, I haven't, but I'd like to."

"Well, see if you can talk him into it. You'll be happy you did."

"Okay, I may try to do that."

They settled everything at the church, and Max and Amy left and went to Max's. He asked, "What did you think?"

"I like the church, and I like the Pastor. I'm glad that's where we're going to get married. Now what about that uniform that he was talking about?"

"I spoke to the church on the Sunday nearest to Veterans Day, and I wore my dress uniform, and if you've never seen a Marine's dress uniform, you've missed something. They are really something."

"Well, why don't you wear it? I'd like to see you in it."

"I guess I can, if you're sure that's what you want me to do."

"I'm sure."

On the way to his house, he said, "Honey, I've thought of another couple I'd like to invite, if you don't care."

"Who is it?"

"My Boss, Pete Morris. He might not want to come this far, but I feel like I need to at least invite him and his wife."

"I think you should. I'd like to meet them, and oh, I forgot to tell you. Dr. Freeland said he would work for me the week we get married, and I invited him and Mrs. Freeland to the wedding."

"Well, the future Mrs. Norwood, I guess we have done everything except tell your parents, haven't we?"

She said, "Yeah, and that's going to be your job."

He said, "I don't think so."

It was nine thirty when they got to Max's, and as usual, Amy needed to leave around ten because of her need to sleep in order to work the way she does, and Max understood that. Once they got married, things would be different. They would probably still go to bed around ten or ten thirty, but they would get to see each other every morning, and that would be good.

Amy called Max Thursday afternoon and said, "Since we're going to talk to my parents tonight, why don't I go home after I get off and you come over later?"

"I can do that, but I was hoping we could go in together. If I ring the doorbell and your Daddy answers, he may slam the door in my face. I really do wish we could go in together."

"Okay, I'll come to your house when I get off, and we can go together."

"Do they know we're coming?"

"No, I guess they don't."

"Don't you think they need to know?"

"I guess. I'll call Mother before I leave the clinic. Are we going to eat before we go, or are we going to get something later?"

"It doesn't matter to me. How long do you think we'll be there?"

"I don't know. I guess it will depend on how they take our news."

"Why don't we eat before we go? That way, they'll have time to eat, too."

"Honey, can I make a suggestion?"

"Of course. What is it?"

"What would you think if I meet you at the restaurant and then follow you home when we finish. That way, you won't have to bring me all the way back home. If we decide we want to go somewhere, we can go, but you won't have to do so much driving."

"That's a good idea."

"Okay, tell me where were going to eat and what time, and I'll be there."

She told him, and they met before they went to her house to tell her parents.

As Max had suggested, when they finished eating, Max followed Amy to her parents' house, and they went in together.

When they got in, the atmosphere was very tense at first, and then Max broke the ice by showing his outgoing personality and shaking her Daddy's hand and telling them both how happy he was to see them again. Neither of them said anything when he told them that, and then Amy got into the conversation, and things began to relax a little.

Amy's Daddy wanted to know where Max had been all those years, and he was especially interested in his Iraq stories. They wanted to know if he had been married and several other things about him, and by the time he was through assuring them that he had been living the 'straight and narrow', they seemed to welcome him into their world. Then came the shocker.

Amy said, "Mother, Daddy, you know that Max and I have been in love ever since we were in high school, and now that we're both grown and have careers, we want to take it another step. We want to tell you that we're going to get married Memorial Day and we hope we'll have your blessings.

Neither parent said anything. Mother looked at Daddy, and Daddy looked at Mother, and then Daddy said, "Well Amy, we knew you would get married again and we're prepared for it. It's just that we're surprised it's Max, but it looks as though Max has paid his dues and is an okay man, now, and you have our blessings."

Her Mother still didn't say anything, so it was assumed

that she was going along with what her Daddy said.

Max shook her Daddy's hand and Amy hugged both of them, and said, "Whew. I wasn't sure how you were going to take this, and we're both thankful for your blessings."

They didn't stay long. A few minutes after they told her parents about the marriage, Amy looked at Max and asked. "Are you ready to go?"

"Yeah, I'm ready."

They told the Hatchers bye and left. When they got outside, Max asked Amy, "Where are we going? I was surprised that you wanted to leave. I thought it went pretty well, didn't you?"

"Yeah, and I was proud of you, the way you just opened up to Daddy and told him your war stories."

"I think it might have helped."

"I know it did. You had him spellbound."

Amy said, "Let's go get some ice cream, and then I'll bring you back to get your pickup."

While they were at the ice cream parlor, Max said, "There's only one more thing I have to do."

"What's that?"

"I have to call Pete. I'll do it in the morning, and then it will all be over but the shouting."

"Are you going to shout?"

"I may. I'm so happy to finally have you as mine."

Pete thanked him for inviting him and his wife to the wedding, and he said he would definitely try to be there.

Memorial Day weekend was finally there, and Amy and Max were both excited. Amy worked on Saturday, and she wrote instructions for Dr. Freeland since he would be filling in for her the next week. She told Max that Molly could stay at the clinic with the other dogs they were boarding, so he took her on Sunday.

The wedding was scheduled for eleven o'clock in the Chapel and then a small reception at Grady's Restaurant.

Counting Amy, Max, and the Pastor and his wife, there were only sixteen people, and Grady's had a private room large enough to handle that many.

Max and his parents arrived at ten thirty and the other guests got there shortly thereafter. Duke and Sissy came in early, and when Sissy saw Max in his uniform, she said, "Max, you're beautiful, and Duke said, "Men aren't beautiful; they're handsome."

"I know, but Max is beautiful."

"Thank you, Sissy. I appreciate that."

Duke said, "Max, those medals look good on your chest."

"Thanks, Padna."

In a few minutes, the rest of the guests arrived, and Pastor Miller asked Max if he was ready, and he said he was. Then, the Pastor sent his wife to the Brides Room to get Amy. Her Mother was with her, and Sissy had gone in there also, and when they all got in the Chapel, Max and Amy stood down front with Sissy, the Maid of Honor and Max's Daddy, and Best Man.

Before the Pastor began, Amy looked at Max and said, "Max, you're beautiful," and Sissy whispered to her and said, "That's what I told him."

Pastor Miller read the standard wedding vows, and when he finished, he said, "I now pronounce you husband and wife, and before he had a chance to tell Max he could kiss his bride, Max grabbed her and gave her a very passionate kiss.

When he finished with the kiss, he turned to the group sitting there, held up both arms and shouted, "Yea. We finally made it."

After the ceremony, everybody sort of milled around, and some of them told Max how good he looked in his uniform, including Pete Morris, his sales manager.

A little before twelve, Max announced that they were expected at Grady's for lunch, and they should leave then to go over there. He knew Pete wouldn't know where Grady's was, so he told him and his wife to follow him and Amy.

They had a fine lunch at Grady's and Amy and Max had a good chance to visit with everybody. Even Amy's parents acted as though they enjoyed it. After about an hour, Max said they needed to go, because they had a long drive ahead of them. Everyone came by to congratulate them again. All the men hugged Amy and all the women hugged Max except for Amy's Mother, and she shook his hand.

Everyone began leaving as Max went to the register and paid for lunch, and then he and Amy were alone. He said, "We're going home to change clothes, aren't we?"

"Yeah, that's what we said we'd do."

They both had their cars there, so they drove them both home to Max's house and changed out of their wedding clothes into something more suitable for travel. They decided to drive Max's pickup on their honeymoon because it was so much larger, and it rode so much smoother. When they got dressed, Max asked, "Well Mrs. Norwood, are you ready to go to Daytona Beach?"

She said, "I'm more than ready, but I thought we were just going to drive halfway today."

Max came back with, "Well, we might not drive that far, but we'll go at least part of the way. I've got a surprise for you."

"What is it?"

"I'm not going to tell you. You'll just have to wait and see."

They headed south on I-75, and in a couple of hours, Max pulled off at an exit in Atlanta. He seemed to know exactly where he was going, and in a minute, they came to a familiar motel. It was the one where they spent their first night, ten years ago. They went in, and Max told the desk clerk that they had reservations for room three nineteen, the same room they were in.

Amy looked at him and said, "I can't believe this. When

did you come up with this idea?"

"Ten years ago," he said.

"Well, this is just about the sweetest thing I've ever seen."

"I'm glad you're not disappointed. I thought it would be neat to start our new life where we tried to start it several years ago. Let's get the car unloaded."

As they were unloading the car and rolling their luggage in on a cart, Max said, smiling, "It would be nice if they had an elevator, wouldn't it?"

She said, "Dummy, they've got one. Don't you remember?"

"I do, but the first time, we unloaded everything and walked up three flights of stairs until the last day when we found it."

After everything was unloaded and in the room, they met in the middle of the room and put their arms around each other and embraced, and Max said, "You know, Honey, with what we have both been through, it seems as though God has given us a second chance, doesn't it?"

"It does, and I'm so thankful that He did."

They had a wonderful night, that night, followed by a glorious week. Returning home the next Saturday, they settled into what they were sure would be a very happy life because each one realized that they had been given a second chance.

*9 7 8 1 6 3 0 6 6 5 0 1 2 *